THE
FOOLS' CROWNS

Volume 3:
The Court of Knaves

Published by Alresford Publishing

Hugh Robertson has asserted his right
under the Copyright, Designs and Patents Act 1988
to be identified as the author of this work

ISBN 978-1-84396-568-8

Available also in paperback
ISBN 978-1-69708-312-5

Kindle ebook
ISBN 978-1-84396-570-1

A catalogue record for this
book is available from the British Library.
and the American Library of Congress

Cover design
coversbykaren@gmail.com

Typesetting and pre-press production
eBook Versions
127 Old Gloucester Street
London WC1N 3AX
www.ebookversions.com

Other books in
The Fools' Crowns series
by Hugh Robertson

Volume 1
King or Pawn

Volume 2
Traitors' Games

*My thanks as always to my
ever-patient editor Fiona Jennison and
the unflappable John Ransley
of ebookversions.com*

To my darling Janice and our true friends

THE
FOOLS' CROWNS

Volume 3:
The Court of Knaves

Hugh Robertson

Alresford Publishing

"A lie doesn't become truth, wrong doesn't become right and evil doesn't become good just because it's accepted by a majority."

Booker T. Washington

Prologue

'Fuck 'em! Fuck 'em ALL! The effing lot of them. Fucking bastards the whole shoddy bunch!'

The Duke was no longer pacing to and fro but now standing shaking, his purpling normally wan face contorted between rage and tears as he crumpled the letter in his hand. With a despairing gesture he threw it to the floor.

As ever he was dressed meticulously, a show of his extravagant nature in an artesia patterned cashmere pullover, fuchsia cravat, pink checked worsted trousers and two-toned light brogues.

Wallis sat straight backed with a set expression that was supposed to pass for sympathy, alert to the fact that her husband was on the brink of one of his childish explosions of frustration and anger.

'There, there darling man. Come to me my little fella' she drawled in a saccharine tone very different to her normal clipped style. 'Come sit with me and tell me just what is so very different? Now sit down and enjoy your G & T and let's talk.'

The Duke of Windsor waved away her offer and instead sat in his favourite wing chair, carefully adjusting his trousers to avoid any risk of bagging the immaculate creases. He took a cigarette from his gold case and with a shaking hand lit it, inhaled deeply and reached for his drink. After a few minutes, during which the Duchess merely watched him carefully, he visibly calmed and then spoke, his voice hardly wavering.

'You see, Wallis, my bloody brother Bertie and that podgy little wife of his...'

Wallis gave a malicious laugh and then snarled 'Darling don't you mean Mrs Cake?' The Duchess' smile was ice cold.

'Thank God' she thought as the Duke allowed a flicker of a smile to cross his face, dispelling at least some of his childlike petulant expression.

'Ha,' he continued. 'That woman cracks the whip over Bertie and is in total control I think. She is spiteful and determined to ruin our happiness... and as for those turncoats like Alexander Hardinge... what a motley crew eh?'

'They are what they are my love, and we are what we are, so let's drink to that and our happiness. Unlike us my love they are really so ordinary whilst we are worldwide stars. Unless we let them they cannot take that away can they? Remember my love they can only spoil that which we let them. We have our love. Come.' The Duchess rose, smoothed her skirt over her slim hips seductively, took his hand, drawing him out of his chair and leading him towards the door.

'I know what you need little fella!' she whispered into his ear. 'You know what happens to naughty boys... Now then undo your trousers and bend over that chair.'

'Yes Ma'am' replied the Duke as he dropped his trousers and Wallis gripped the waistband of his pink silk Sulka undershorts. A few minutes inflicting mildly sadistic punishment was a small price to pay for harmony. 'After all' she thought with a thin-lipped smile. 'I can really go to town with Helga tonight...'

Chapter 1

'My word Wallis, that was quite a welcome, what?'

'It sure was dearest… with the crowds chanting 'Sieg Edward' and 'Seig Windsor'. It kinda brought a lump to my throat, honest to God.'

'That welcome, my love, is what we have been cruelly denied in Britain but perhaps it is fitting that we should be treated as we deserve, as is our God given right, here in my spiritual home of Germany.'

'Let's not forget David that we are promised a return to Britain when the Greater Germany has control of the unified nations.'

The Duke smiled broadly and lit a cigarette. 'Yes, I must ask Ribbentrop about the crowns that the Fuhrer ordered made for us. They should be here in Germany now.'

'What will you do with the present British Imperial Crowns at our coronation in Westminster Abbey with the new ones bearing the Swastika?'

'Well, my dear, in the case of my mother's crown as Queen Consort of my late father, I have in mind that the Koh-i-Noor diamond be set in a brooch for you as it was worn by Queen Victoria. It should be magnificent.'

'Won't people be very critical of it being removed from what are known as the Crown Jewels?' asked Wallis.

'When will you get it into your pretty head my darling that as King I shall decide what happens in all such matters. The nonsensical system which allowed me to be forced to abdicate will be swept away. The New Order of government will no longer put power in the hands of little men elected to positions of great power. Government including the Monarch will be in the hands of men of vision and belief representing the best and strongest in our German British alliance.'

'David darling, I must change the subject. I am very tired after our overnight journey and, of course, the excitement of our arrival. Do you mind if I do not accompany you on this afternoon's visit?'

'No, not at all my love… I quite understand. You want to be rested for this evening's dinner at the home of Doctor Robert Ley. Many of the leading members of the Nazi Party will be there. According to the timetable I should be back here at about four thirty and perhaps we could go for a little walk with Johnny and Celia then?'

'That suits me just fine my love. Now please ask Doctor Ley to have the drivers take things more slowly. I was petrified this morning and I do not want to spend the afternoon fretting about you.'

'Very well, I shall' responded the Duke with an indulgent smile.

The Windsors' butler entered the sitting room of their suite announcing that the British Charge d'Affaires, Sir George Ogilvie-Forbes, wished to pay his respects and was asked to show him in.

Sir George struck an imposing figure as his name might suggest. The Duke was aware that unlike the British Ambassador Sir Neville Henderson who favoured appeasement of Hitler, Ogilvie Forbes – whist agreeing that the Treaty of Versailles was unnecessarily harsh – considered that Hitler and the Nazi Government sought world-wide domination just as Germany had sought in the Great War.

'Ah, Sir George. We last met when I was Prince of Wales as I recall.'

'That is correct Your Royal Highness.' Sir George turned towards Wallis and nodding in what was almost a bow simply said 'Your Grace.' A frown flashed across the Duke's face.

'We are expecting great things from this visit Sir George, indeed great things,' the now smiling Duke commented.

Sir George avoiding a direct response took the opportunity to make his position and that of the Embassy clear.

'Sir, in the absence of the Ambassador, who is on leave, it falls to me to explain that your brother His Majesty the King has made it clear that both this visit to Germany and your intended visit to America are entirely of a private nature. Accordingly neither Embassy nor its officers can be seen to play any part. That includes local consular officials.'

'Well that sounds rather petty to me not least considering the efforts being made by the German Government' riposted the Duke.

'Sir, I cannot possibly comment save to say that please rest assured that if I can be of any assistance in a personal capacity albeit unofficially you must not hesitate to ask.'

'Thank you for that Sir George. Now, if you will excuse me I am due to leave on a visit to a new model factory with Doctor Robert Ley in just a few minutes.'

'But of course, Your Royal Highness, Your Grace.'

After he had gone the Duke turned to Wallis, clearly angry.

'This, my dearest, is yet another slap in the face. I shall bloody well show them and I will not forget when the time comes. I will not forget.'

'Doctor Ley this is a most impressive vehicle. It is certainly comfortable and well suited to this magnificent autobahn.'

'It was designed by the Fuhrer himself and as you have seen it is equipped with a shower room, a bar, this sitting area, a bedroom, and the small office area with a desk for a secretary with typewriter and a radio telephone.'

'It is really most impressive – I am tempted to commission one for myself and the Duchess. The only thing is, there are no roads to match your wonderful autobahns anywhere else in Europe except possibly in Italy.'

'Sadly that is the case. Sophisticated communications are at the heart of our enlightened beliefs. The Fuhrer is determined that within the Reich all transport must be as fast and reliable as possible. Our trains run like clockwork and no excuses for delay or disruption are accepted.'

'Is such dedication achieved solely by the Fuhrer appealing to the national pride of his people?'

'To a great extent that is true as you will see when we reach our destination. Nevertheless there are inevitably some degenerate beings who whether due to their race or sickness do not share our vision and must be rooted out and dealt with.'

'That sounds eminently sensible. I suppose that it is no different to imprisoning criminals for the benefit of society at large.'

'Just so Your Royal Highness although we have introduced measures that do away with the need for costly trials, and instead of prisons we have embarked on a programme of building work camps so that these unfortunate misfits make some contribution to society.'

'Do they all work in these camps?'

Doctor Ley laughed and then continued in his strangely slurred voice 'Those who don't work have no place anywhere in our society.'

'Is all the work government sponsored?'

'That is a very interesting question. I have opened discussions with some of our largest manufacturing companies with a view to establishing factories focused on Germany's present and future strategic needs. There are great advantages to them in that the Reich will provide a guaranteed number of workers at a very low daily rate. Furthermore they will have no rights such as is the case with normal workers.'

'When you say 'strategic needs' what sort of things do you envisage?'

'Well, by way of example, I.G.Faben is developing synthetic rubber called 'Buna' after its chemical components. Siemens, Krupp and General Motors are also interested. We are looking for a suitable site where we can build the camps for the workers and the satellite manufacturing plants.'

'I am sure that Charles Bedaux approves of this approach' commented the Duke.

'But of course... Charles and I have worked on this together. In fact we see it as the perfect model for super-efficient manufacturing. The effective dehumanisation of the workforce achieves excellent results.'

'I assume that the workforce that you intend supplying from the camps will be largely unskilled?'

'That is so. It enables us to concentrate on providing the excellent working environment for our skilled workers as you will see when we reach the Stock machine tool factory... we shall be there soon. You will be impressed I am sure.'

Their arrival at the Nazi flag bedecked factory was marked by a large gathering of workers and Nazi officials including uniformed SS officers. The Duke decided to leave his hat in the coach but slipped on a light tweed overcoat.

As he stepped down he was greeted with cheers from the workers and Nazi salutes from the uniformed men, party officials and managers.

Doctor Ley introduced the Duke to Walter Hewel who was officially Ribbentrop's liaison with Hitler but spent much of his time collating information from his many connections and agents both in the Nazi party and Germany generally. The ever suspicious Hitler regarded him as extra eyes and ears.

As the party entered the office building that fronted the complex, Doctor Ley kept up a constant running commentary which his speech impediment made irritating to the Duke, however interesting he found the subject matter.

They walked through a large restaurant, gymnasium and then the factory itself. As they toured the immaculately clean factory the Duke commented 'I should like some of our British managers to see this. They begrudge any spending that they cannot see turned to quick profit. Many of the works that I have visited are relics of the last century or even before.'

Doctor Ley and Herr Hewel smiled at this remark and the factory manager responded 'We have a different view. Just as the Fuhrer has long admired Henry Ford's philosophy and referred to him in Mein Kampf so do we industrialists admire his vision and the way that he has turned that vision into reality. Quite apart from bringing the production line concept to the process of manufacturing there is the well-being of the workforce. Not only do our skilled workers enjoy a fine restaurant serving a nutritious and balanced diet but also a gymnasium where they are encouraged to keep fit during their rest periods.'

'We shall discuss that later Your Royal Highness. Now, may I introduce you to some of the workforce?' interposed Doctor Ley.

'Most certainly… please do,' responded the Duke, warmly.

A succession of workers was brought up to the Duke's party. He asked detailed questions about not only their particular work but also their conditions. The enthusiastic responses could not have been in greater contrast to those of the stoic but depressed men of South Wales. It was their plight that had moved him to blatantly break the protocol dictating that as a member of the Royal family, let alone Monarch, he was not permitted to make any political comment.

The response of these German workers who were enthusiastic, optimistic and well fed was depressing for him as he could not get the contrast out of his mind.

His mood did not lighten as the party then entered the Nazi banner lined recreation hall of the huge complex where over a thousand workers and managers rose as one as they entered. The Duke's overcoat had been taken by one of the office staff and he looked sombre as he and Doctor Ley led the party down the centre aisle.

On either side the audience cheered, gave the Nazi salute and cried out 'Sieg Heil.'

Before they sat down in the front row the Duke was presented with a bouquet by a worker's daughter.

Doctor Ley went onto the stage where the Berlin Labour Front Orchestra were seated beneath a huge portrait of the Fuhrer.

He tapped the microphone then began his speech of welcome to the Duke which rapidly turned into a eulogy extolling the working conditions and the benefits enjoyed by the workforce in this and other model factories which were the brainchild of the Fuhrer.

He ended his blatantly political speech calling for the audience to give three salutes to the Fuhrer. This they did with gusto. When he returned to his seat and sat down next to the Duke he smiled warmly as the Duke without irony thanked him for his kind welcome.

The conductor raised his baton and the orchestra began its hour long concert of Liszt and Wagner.

The Duke sat with his arms folded most of the time, his legs crossed and foot beating time. Occasionally he fidgeted and fiddled with his woven silk dogs-tooth patterned tie. His expression remained pensive throughout.

When the concert finally finished the audience noisily rose to its feet for the German national Anthem 'Deutschland Uber Alles'. They then lustily sang the 'Horst Wessel' Nazi marching song.

The orchestra concluded by playing 'God Save the King'.

The official party then filed out as the audience applauded enthusiastically then Nazi saluted and shouted 'Heil Hitler'.

Once the Duke and Doctor Ley were settled back in the coach their small cavalcade drove off from the works through its manicured grounds.

'Food for thought, Doctor, food for thought' mused the Duke.

Wallis had enjoyed a long bath, a relaxing massage from Helga and then a sleep. She now felt relaxed and refreshed.

Helga knocked on the bedroom door.

'Come in my dear' called Wallis.

'I have a visitor for you Ma'am… it is Lady Celia.'

'Wonderful! Do show her in please.'

'Wallis! How lovely to see you. How are you after your long journey?'

'Thank you my dear. I am well rested now… and you?'

'Johnny and I flew over this morning so it was nothing like your overnight train journey. It's jolly hard to sleep on a train in my experience.'

'It sure is' laughed Wallis. 'Now, when David's back, assuming that he is not too tired, I fancy having a look at the shops. How about you and Johnny come along too?'

'Delighted – will there be time before dinner?'

'Oh yes. David is due back at four thirty and you know just how punctual these Germans are. Tonight's dinner is at Doctor Robert Ley's house in the Grunewald – that's one of the forests around the city so it is not far to go. It is described as an informal dinner but a lot of the big wigs will be there.'

'Righto then Wallis. I shall go and get sorted out. Perhaps Helga could let me know when David returns. Our suite is just down the corridor. Number 3.'

'I shall do that.'

Celia left and walked along to the suite that she and Johnny were sharing.

'Darling, Wallis has suggested that we join them and have a stroll around the shops when David is back. Can you bear it?'

'I cannot imagine anything much worse frankly but it may give me a chance to pump him about his trip today. Count me in old thing.' Johnny rolled his eyes as he spoke.

'Of one thing I am greatly relieved – Wallis has Helga to look after her so no pressure on that front.'

'Excellent. I just hope that Wallis is not too daunted by the programme… it's pretty damn full and a heck of a lot of travelling.'

'I think that you will find that so long as she has plenty of adulation and fuss made she will be happy. By the way, I have a note here from Herr Strack who is the protocol thingy in the German Foreign Ministry. I have met him actually – he was at the reception here in Berlin when I met Hitler at the Berlin Olympics.'

'What is it?'

'Here, see for yourself – it's a crib sheet of who's going to be at tonight's dinner.'

Johnny took the note which was typed on heavily embossed thick cream paper. He looked at it quickly then commented:

'Well it may be rated as informal but some of the heaviest hitters in the Nazi Party or should I simply say, Germany, will be there.'

'Hair up or down darling?' asked Celia.

'Oh, up I think and wear your grandmother's diamond and sapphire necklace. We don't want to look like poor relations, do we?'

Chapter 2

Celia and Johnny were back in their suite in the Kaiserhof Hotel after the dinner.

'Well, that was quite an impressive array of Nazi top brass Celia, eh?'

'It certainly was darling. I rather liked Rudolf Hess and his wife. He is a thoughtful man.... deep might be more like it. She is awfully straightforward. They met just after the Great War when they were in the same lodging house. I didn't realise that he was imprisoned in the Landsberg fortress at the same time as Hitler after the beer hall thingy. He edited Mein Kampf as it was written.'

It had become apparent to Celia that the beetle-browed Hess was much less of the enforcer than his looks suggested but more a man of intellect and strong beliefs.

'Really, he seems a genuine sort of fellow' Johnny continued. 'So he and his wife have been together all the way through the rise of the Nazis. He's a close confidante of Hitler you know and they trust each other implicitly.'

'I suppose you know that from your Princess Stephanie' commented Celia with an edge to her voice.

'Now look old girl, for the last time, she is not 'my' Princess Stephanie and it is you that I love. Please don't make a difficult situation more of a problem than it really is. In answer to your question, yes it was she that explained Hitler's relationship with Hess. She has also provided some other very useful background information which I have passed on to Tar. You know, the sort of stuff that we could not pick up otherwise.'

Celia smiled as she spoke in almost a diffident tone.

'I'm sorry Johnny... I am in no position to be jealous... it's just that... oh well... you know... I realise that I have fallen in love with you... completely and utterly.'

'I understand darling girl and the feeling is mutual. Bed I think, busy day tomorrow. I am off with the Duke and your thuggish Doctor Ley. You know in spite of appearances he really did get a doctorate in chemistry.'

'That's as may be, he still looks like a thug and he didn't half pack away the wine at dinner. Anyhow, enough of that I have something else on my mind.'

Celia gave Johnny a knowing smile and leaving her chair she moved in front of him, reached forward with both hands and pulled on the ends of his bow-tie drawing him out of his seat as it unravelled.

'Steady old girl… you are going to strangle me' gasped Johnny as he awkwardly got to his feet.

'Don't worry' she laughed. 'That's not what I have in mind. You are no use to me strangled…'

Celia dropped the ends of the bow tie and taking Johnny's hand-led him towards the bedroom kicking off her shoes as she went.

Early the following morning Johnny was awoken early by his valet and drank a quick cup of tea before getting ready for the day's trip to Pomerania.

He and the Duke were immaculately dressed as they left the hotel and climbed aboard the same specially built observation bus the Duke had travelled in the previous day.

The Duke was almost proprietorial as he showed Johnny the facilities. Doctor Ley indulged the Duke's enthusiasm but then suggested that they should have some breakfast. The dining salon on the coach was not large but comfortable and very much in the style of aircraft accommodation.

The steward who sat next to the driver when his services were not required served a simple breakfast of ham, cheese, hard boiled eggs and black bread with a jug of piping hot coffee.

By the time that they had finished and made their way to the upper observation deck the coach was on the autobahn.

'This coach is designed to cruise at over 130 kilometres per hour on the autobahn – that is 80 miles per hour. Impressive eh?' commented Doctor Ley.

'It certainly is' responded the Duke, adding with a smile 'Just do not tell Wallis, she will have a fit. Now Johnny, as I told you we had a very interesting visit yesterday. The model factory should be a blueprint for all.'

Johnny interrupted the Prince 'I understand your point David but without in any way denigrating from it, the same model was adopted on a larger scale by for instance the Cadbury family when they built the model town, Bournville, south of Birmingham in the 1890's and when the Lever Brothers similarly built Port Sunlight up on the Wirral before the Great War.'

'Yes Johnny but as I said last night, the difference is that here in Germany the model factories and worker facilities are being developed hand in hand with the Government. Is that not so Doctor Ley?'

The Duke was clearly irritated by Johnny's remarks.

Doctor Ley's enthusiastically delivered response was chilling in its implications.

'Your Royal Highness, that is so. The German Government has far-sightedly embarked upon a policy of providing excellent conditions for its valued workers.'

The Duke nodded approvingly. Johnny showed no reaction.

'It is also getting rid of the trouble-making trade unions that are run by communists and Jews... a breeding ground for dissidents, malcontents and the work-shy. Those of the workforce who do not voluntarily exert all their energies in the interests of the Nation, the Reich, will be compelled to do so.'

'How will the German Government achieve that?' asked Johnny without a hint of irony.

'Where necessary such people as with all dissident elements in society will be housed in work camps and their labour contracted to industry at very economic rates.' Doctor Ley responded smugly.

The Duke had clearly regained his equanimity and added, 'So you see Johnny that this enlightened approach makes for a happy and well rewarded society which is not dragged down by the shirkers and malcontents nor by Soviet-inspired cant.'

Johnny decided that he had heard enough on this subject for the moment and changed the subject. 'Today we are visiting the elite Death's Head Regiment of the SS – the Totenkopf. They are the crème de la crème of the SS are they not?'

'That they most certainly are' replied an earnest Doctor Ley. 'The SS generally are very carefully selected and in themselves the unit that you will see in training is the very cream of the Aryan race in our forces. Their title is now the 'Liebstandarte SS Adolf Hitler' which distinguishes them from the regular army, the Wermacht, and all other units. As you will see today they are not a mere ceremonial bodyguard for the Fuhrer. That was the unit's origin. They are arguably the best and most dedicated fighting force in the world…in fact that the world has ever seen.'

Johnny could not help making a riposte. 'Well Doctor I am not sure that the British Sovereign's Household Brigade, the Guards Regiments, would agree with that assessment.'

'Johnny that was not called for…' riposted the Duke angrily. 'I must apologise Doctor. I am afraid that my companion, who was an officer in the Guards, as was I, is naturally imbued with his own *esprit de corps*,' commented the Duke giving Johnny a thin-lipped hard stare.

'So that's the way the land lies' thought Johnny. 'We are to play the naive admiring visitors and lap up all the propaganda that our hosts dish out.' He decided to say no more.

When they reached the border with Pomerania the coach picked up the Area Governor and introductions were made with great formality.

As they arrived at the training barracks at Crossensee the coach swept through a massive gated arch in the great tower that marked the entrance and stopped at the edge of a large parade ground.

A black uniformed SS band was drawn up next to a battalion strength guard of honour of young soldiers also in black. Their helmets bore the Totenkopf death's head symbol and shoulder flashes of a skeleton key.

As Doctor Ley and the Governor led the Duke and Johnny away from the coach, at a barked command the guard of honour presented arms with mechanical efficiency.

The Duke and Johnny stopped and came to attention each with a bowler hat in hand.

The Regimental band then played the German and British National Anthems.

As the music stopped the guard of honour was ordered to shoulder arms. The Commander of the guard and an older more senior officer, who was later introduced as Colonel Josef 'Sepp' Dietrich, the first commander of the regiment, marched up to the Duke and gave the Nazi salute which the Duke returned.

On the order of the guard commander the guard of honour bellowed a rousing 'Seig Heil'.

The Duke was then escorted by Colonel Dietrich, with drawn sword, along the ranks of the guard of honour, stopping occasionally to speak to individual soldiers. Whilst this review took place the band played a haunting slow melody. After the inspection the Duke showed interest in a large group of young, predominantly blonde-haired men undertaking gruelling physical training.

The Colonel explained that such training occupied five hours of every day in addition to parade drill, military training, German history, archaeology, politics and genetics throughout a four year course.

The barracks buildings were thatched which looked at odds with the harsh regime in Johnny's mind. After a tour of inspection it was suggested that it was time for lunch in the Officers' Mess. The lunch itself was substantial but plain, and only water was served with a choice of still or sparkling Apollonaris which both Johnny and the Duke chose.

'Ah' said the Duke. 'Apollonaris...' the Queen of table waters'... as my late father the King always used to say when it was served. Now then Colonel, can you explain the significance of the skeleton Key symbol? The Death's Head, I can understand well enough, but not that.'

Colonel Dietrich who was no longer the active commander of the Regiment but was its honorary commander explained that the skeleton key symbol marked his name.

The Duke laughed and said 'But of course Colonel, now I see... 'Dietrich' means a lock pick or skeleton key. Nice touch Johnny, eh?'

'Most certainly. I must congratulate you Colonel, your men must hold you in high regard.' Johnny responded not only out of politeness but also respect for the ramrod-straight, much older man who sported a duelling scar and close-cropped iron grey hair.

The Colonel smiled thinly in response to Johnny's compliment and responded 'Thank you. We have the privilege of picking our men from the finest young members of the Nazi movement – the Hitler Youth. It is our privilege to forge them into the perfect fighting force. They will be invincible.'

When lunch was over the small party went back onto the coach and left for a military aerodrome where they boarded the twelve-seater aircraft that was held at Doctor Ley's permanent disposal.

'Well, what did you think of that?' asked a beaming Doctor Ley. 'Impressive wasn't it?'

The Duke replied 'Excellent and most interesting. Those young men will go on to be the backbone of the army I imagine.'

'Well, strictly not the army but the SS forces that are planned, most certainly. We are building an elite fighting corps within the SS. The Totenkopf, the skull and crossed bones on the headgear, has its own meaning which has been summed up by Reichsfuhrer SS Heinrich Himmler. I quote 'The skull is the reminder that you shall always be willing to put your life at stake for the good of the whole community.' The unit that you saw in training is devoted to the Fuhrer and all members have vowed to give their lives in his protection.'

Doctor Ley smiled as the Duke nodded then continued. 'Shortly, as we fly up the Baltic coast I shall show you a site where we are creating one of many recreational facilities for our loyal party members and workers. It will also cater for the Hitler Youth. We believe that good healthy holidays are vital to the health of workers.'

On a hunch Johnny asked an apparently innocuous question. 'Doctor, you mentioned the work-shy and malcontents being put to work at very competitive cost. Are you able to use them on projects such as this?'

'But of course. They are supplied to the contractors at very low rates which in turn keeps the cost down for the government.'

'What sort of people are these workers?' asked Johnny even though he could sense that the Duke was becoming agitated.

'Oh, as I explained earlier, people who have no place in our society. They may hold extreme political or ideological views, such as communists, or are otherwise unacceptable – you know, Roma... I believe that you call them gypsies... homosexuals, Jewish usurers, mental defectives and such like. So long as their backs are strong they can have the privilege of working for the good of the Reich.'

Johnny could not resist adding quietly 'And if their backs are not strong.....?'

Chapter 3

The aircraft landed at Templehof Airport in the City of Berlin just after six in the evening.

As they taxied from the runway to the original terminal building Doctor Ley proudly pointed out the massive construction works which were to be the new terminal.

'It is designed by Ernst Sagebiel and will be one of the twenty largest buildings on earth when completed. It is a good example of the way in which the Reich is utilising all available labour resources economically.'

'By that do you mean using the camp occupants?' asked Johnny in a deceptively mild tone.

There was no hesitation as Doctor Ley mechanically replied. 'But of course… it would be foolish not to. At the moment we do not have camps within the City itself but it is still much cheaper to bring the workers in every day.'

'What is that building?' asked the Duke pointing at a large old building that looked totally out of place even in comparison with the original terminal let alone the new one under construction.

'Oh that is the Columbia Haus… it is a detention centre run by the SS for the Gestapo. Three times a day transport takes detainess to the Gestapo headquarters on Prinz-Albrecht-Strasse for interrogation whilst they are housed here.'

'What sort of people might they be?' asked Johnny.

'Oh, you know, political undesirables such as communists and social democrats and intellectuals who are openly hostile to and critical of the Reich. There is also a large number of homosexuals arrested since the passing of section 175 of The Penal Code in 1935 forbidding indecency between men. That was brought in after the Rohm affair and the purging of the corrupt SA organisation that he had headed.'

Neither Johnny nor the Duke chose to refer to that purge which had been dubbed 'The Night of the Long Knives' given the ruthless way in which the Gestapo and SS units had acted to get rid of the 'Brownshirts' who had been the original Nazi Storm Troopers.

'Do any of these detainees work on the new airport terminal construction?' asked Johnny.

'No. Those who are not sentenced to other punishments may be sent to camps elsewhere. Ah, we have stopped and the cars are here. I shall escort you back to your hotel now.'

'Thank you Doctor, that is most kind and I should like to give you my sincere thanks for a most interesting day. You must be very proud of all that you are achieving and well justified if I may say so' said the Duke.

After the Duke and Johnny climbed into yet another huge Mercedes Benz with Doctor Ley and settled down he turned to the Duke.

'Well Your Royal Highness, I am glad that you found your day of interest' commented Dr Ley.

'Most certainly… in fact I would say enlightening wouldn't you Johnny?'

'Yes, it was. The precision shown by the young soldiers both on the parade ground drilling and in physical training was as good as I have seen and I believe that I have seen the best.'

The Duke shot Johnny a warning look knowing full well that Johnny was referring to the Brigade of Guards whose maroon and dark blue striped tie both he and the Duke were wearing.

The Duke pre-empted Johnny from taking his point any further with the bumptious Doctor Ley saying 'I was also impressed with the degree in which the young men are schooled in not only history but the ideology of the Reich and its aims for the people of the Greater Germany.'

This statement clearly pleased Doctor Ley who nodded his head fervently several times in quick succession.

'It is essential that their education over the four year period of training is thorough. These young men will be leaders and are sworn in loyalty to the Fuhrer in life and death. The very insignia of the Death's Head signifies the world beyond death which they do not fear, neither will the men that they will lead in due course.'

The Duke and Johnny were escorted to the Duke's suite by two young SS officers who had been waiting in the hotel foyer. There were SS guards posted at each end of the corridor and by the lift doors. On entering the suite their bowler hats and umbrellas were taken by two footmen and they entered the sitting room where Wallis and Celia were sitting talking.

'Ah, here you are dearest' Wallis said getting to her feet and embracing her husband with a kiss on both of his cheeks. 'Prompt and on the dot… the itinerary for today said that you would return here at six thirty and you are bang on time.'

'Yes Wallis darling… they are damned efficient blighters are they not Johnny?'

'On that score I must agree' responded a smiling Johnny. 'There is something almost mechanical in their approach to so many things. I can see how the methods of Henry Ford and Charles Bedaux must appeal to the Nazis so much.'

'Now Johnny, enough of that… The Aga Khan is joining us for dinner tonight… splendid fellow and President of the League of Nations. Anyhow, he is not due here until eight o'clock so we have time to whet our whistles. Champagne for us and a perfect Manhattan for you Wallis?'

Celia and Johnny were back in their suite and had changed for dinner.

'Well now Johnny darling, tell me what you really thought about today.'

After a long pause Johnny bleakly replied.

'Chilling really. David is totally in thrall to the whole Nazi business so far as I can see. He loves it and, of course they make a grand fuss of him… he is almost role playing subconsciously… do you know what I mean?' Johnny asked with his face creased with concern.

Celia nodded. 'You know Johnny, being with Wallis today I felt the same. She is really behaving as if he were King and she was Queen. It is a cross between being embarrassing and funny. When we were out today we had our own little convoy with outriders and so forth. She loved it and she clearly enjoys being addressed as Your Royal Highness…'

Celia moved towards Johnny and sat on his lap. As she cuddled him she smoothed his hair, slowly massaging his head.

'Do you know that the latest thing is that she has instructed Helga to ensure that the maids iron the bank notes before they go into her pocket book although I have yet to witness her pay for anything.'

'You are right Celia' replied Johnny in a very low voice. 'David is playing along as if he were still King. He has yet to see the irony of the Germans playing the British National Anthem and his then giving the Nazi salute having just listened to something called 'God Save the King'… it is as bizarre as it is frightening.'

The two were quiet for a moment as they held on to each other whilst their minds whirred.

'But that is not as frightening as listening to the good Doctor Ley.'

'What do you mean?'

'He enthusiastically talks about the removal of communists, malcontents, delinquents, queers and frankly anyone who fails to toe the line into labour camps. Their forced labour will be then sold on to 'strategic' businesses at very cheap rates. I dread to think how they will be treated.'

'Well I witnessed a bit of that in Nuremburg' said Celia with a shudder. 'Callous extreme brutality is how I would describe it.'

Johnny hugged Celia even tighter.

'Add into that the racial purity thing so the Jews and gypsies will be rounded up, and bearing in mind that most of the leading intellectuals are Jews… it is awful.'

'But they are hardly going to be people equipped for hard labour are they?'

'Of course not but you know the young SS soldiers we saw being trained today are being brainwashed. They will do whatever they are ordered down the line … you mark my words. I don't think that they will have a moral or human qualm to prevent them doing absolutely anything.'

Celia cradled Johnny's head into her neck.

'That's bad but then you have to look at the leaders Johnny. Wallis had just run through her impressions of the bigwigs we met last night when you and David returned.'

'Tell me.'

Celia gently disentangled and getting to her feet began to pace the room.

'Well, she thought Rudolf Hess to be, and I quote all of these, 'charming of manner and good looking'… Goebbels was 'like a wispy gnome with an enormous abnormal skull but obviously clever'… oh and his wife clearly 'had class.'…'

'What did she think about the decidedly unsavoury Heinrich Himmler the terror chief?'

'Oh that he was 'like a clerk caught up in politics and has a bespectacled meekness.'

Celia laughed bitterly, eyes rolling.

'I really cannot believe that she could get that so wrong… the man is a monster, evil through and through. You can bet your bottom dollar that history will show him to be as evil as anyone in this bunch.'

Johnny stood and placed both his hands on Celia's shoulders.

'Going back to today, Ley flew us in his personal twelve-seater aircraft to see a seaside recreational resort that is being built for the young party faithful. 'Strength through Joy' is the slogan apparently. Ironically though, it is being built with what I believe will become known to be slave labour.'

'What happens to those who are unfit to work or become ill?'

'I dread to think but I cannot imagine any holiday camps will be built for them to rest and recuperate. I fear that only God will help them' said Johnny as he kissed Celia's head.

'Johnny, this is so depressing and it is only our second day.'

'This evening should be better' said Johnny, playfully slapping Celia's bottom. The Aga Khan is a splendid fellow and I doubt whether he will want to talk politics. Have you met him?'

'Yes, a few times' replied Celia, gently pushing Johnny's hands away. 'He and Papa share a love of horses and the turf he and his wife the Begum have stayed with my parents a few times. He is rather imposing but very jolly…I remember that he was like a great big happy puppy when his horse won the Derby in 1935.'

Johnny chuckled. 'Hard to picture but he used to be very dashing and slim but over the years the good living has taken its toll though he keeps pretty fit. His visit is organised by the Office of Von Ribbentrop so there will be something that the Nazis are after… presumably in his capacity as President of the League of Nations. His wife Andree will be with him.'

Celia smiled softly as she continued. 'Papa said that she was once a saleswoman in a sweet shop and then became a partner in a hat shop. She is apparently very pretty. His first marriage was one of those arranged jobs… to his cousin I think… anyway it was apparently very unhappy. He then married a ballet dancer and was very happy but sadly she died after an operation. She was French as is the present Princess. Or Begum – I am never quite sure what to describe her as!'

'I would stick with Princess… anyhow, this evening is informal. He's a remarkable man. Quite apart from being a man of the turf and something of a ladies man in his time, he is an acclaimed Islamic scholar and has stressed Islam's compassionate nature. He caused a bit of a rumpus when he ordered that women should not be veiled in his presence. It was explained to me that his belief is that the Islamic religion gives guidance but does not impose rules. He believes that everyone should follow their own moral conscience.'

'A bit different to the Nazi view I would say – chalk and cheese.'

Celia's hands were on Johnny's chest as she gently but firmly pushed him into an upright occasional chair. Ignoring his puzzled expression she reached down and unbuttoned his fly then hoisting her skirt over her hips straddled him. He grunted involuntarily as she pulled her French knickers to one side and guided him into her.

It was some time before they hurriedly prepared themselves for dinner.

Since the Aga Khan had only arrived in Berlin that day the Duke had decided that dinner should be a black tie affair and not full evening dress.

Celia was stunning in an elegantly tailored formfitting silk sheath dress and was wearing more of her grandmother's jewellery. Johnny was looking as dashing as ever as they entered the Duke and Duchess' suite.

'Well then. I guess that we should carry on where we left off, what?' asked the Duke with a raised eyebrow. 'Our guests will be here in a few minutes.'

The Butler entered the sitting room and announced that His Serene Highness the Right Honourable Sir Sultan Aga Khan and his Begum had arrived.

The Duke rose to his feet and strode across the large room with his hand outstretched and a broad smile.

'Sunny, my dear fellow, and you sweet Andree darling.'

The Aga Khan was not particularly tall but he was a large man who exuded an aura of serenity, good humour and above all power. He was clearly a man at ease with himself and the world.

After the Duke had shaken his hand and kissed the Begum on both cheeks he introduced Wallis simply as his wife. The rotund and twinkly-eyed Aga Khan whilst bowing kissed her hand.

'Your Royal Highness it is an honour and a privilege to at last meet the lady who married the elusive fish that is David. May I present my dear wife Andree.'

The Begum was a trim and very attractive woman. Her figure was only a little fuller than that of Wallis and she was supremely elegant.

Johnny and Celia were then presented by the Duke.

'But of course I know you two! Celia I recall when you were something of a smudge nosed tom boy always in jodhpurs and in a hurry to be back in the stables! My word you have turned into a rare beauty. Johnny you are a very lucky man. And at the risk of my wife's wrath, I speak as a connoisseur.'

'I trust only on the sidelines my dear' said the smiling Begum.

'But of course,' responded the Aga Khan with a great rumbling and infectious belly laugh.

The Duke coughed loudly to politely attract the attention of his guests.

'Now this is an informal evening amongst friends… we have quite enough formal obligations – so please let us all relax.'

The dinner was a convivial affair with plenty of laughter much of it generated by the stories and anecdotes of the Aga Khan.

'You know David, my size has been of direct benefit to my people of the Ishmaili faith. Last year to celebrate my Golden Jubilee I was weighed in gold in Bombay, in Hasenbad actually… and that gold was then distributed to good causes in Africa and India. This year the same thing was done in Nairobi. I don't think that you would achieve quite so much for the people David!' he laughed.

The Duke looked nonplussed for a moment and then apparently realised that the joke was really about relative sizes and not a comparison to the Aga Khan's position as leader of his people and that of the Duke as a former monarch and emperor.

Later Johnny was to comment to Celia that at that moment he sensed the fragility of the Duke's state of mind.

Inevitably the subject turned to politics and the problems that beset the world.

It was the Duke that brought up the subject.

'Sunny, you are the President of the League of Nations… elected by a landslide I believe.'

The Aga Khan made a deprecating gesture but smiled as the Duke continued. 'Is the League really strong enough to hold onto peace through negotiation and international co-operation as was envisaged in its original principles in 1919?'

'That is not an easy question David, not at all. One of the tenets of faith of the League was and remains that the limitation of rearmament is a necessary element in keeping peace. The League has no armed forces of its own but relies upon its members to perform under its terms.'

Johnny joined in the conversation. 'But that must be difficult to achieve with countries such as Germany, Italy, Spain and even Japan withdrawing from the League?'

'Precisely the point my boy. They withdrew because they are determined to re-arm. It is most dangerous and when I visit Herr Hitler later this week I shall be telling him that I pray for the day when Germany re-joins the League.'

Meaningful looks were exchanged.

'I fear that I may be praying for a long time.'

The Duke and Wallis were not looking at all comfortable as Johnny continued.

'I cannot quote the whole piece but just before Christmas last year Herman Goering addressed a group of senior German industrialists on the question of the need to re-arm at any cost and he ended with 'We live in a time when the final battle is in sight. We are already on the threshold of mobilisation and we are already at war. All that is lacking is the shooting.' Those were the exact words… That certainly does not sound like a government that would contemplate any measure of disarmament to me.'

There was an awkward pause after which the Aga Khan spoke.

'I recall the speech, and even allowing for the somewhat rumbustious style of Herr Goering I believe that he was honestly stating the thoughts of the masters of the Reich.'

The Aga Khan clearly was not eager to prolong this line of conversation. 'Now, we have had a long day today, as have you and I think that prudence dictates that after this most delicious dinner and delightful evening we should take our leave.'

After the guests had left and Celia and Johnny had retired to their suite the Duke and Duchess sat quietly whilst he enjoyed a smoke and a cognac.

'Delightful couple don't you think my love?'

'Yes, they certainly are. Of course you know that she is a fan of Suzanne Belperron's jewellery too… anyhow… that's why I chose to wear this necklace and bangle bracelets that you commissioned for me tonight. She did not comment but I could see that she recognised the style.'

'I love it Wallis… it is so modern and yet it has a timeless air' said the Duke, gazing admiringly at his lover's adorned neck and arms. He swilled his cognac in his glass whilst watching it thoughtfully.

'Changing the subject, I think that Johnny is getting a bit uppity about the Fuhrer and the German Government. I was rather irritated by him today… almost vexed… and tonight he went too far in my book.'

'I cannot comment on today, my love, but this evening I think that he was merely playing what you call a 'customer's game' with the Aga Khan.'

The Duke drew The Duchess towards him and gently caressed her back. Then he whispered, 'Maybe you are right dearest but, you know, like a lot of people I just don't think he realises what a wonderful vision the Fuhrer and his Nazi Party have for the peoples of the Greater Germany and even further afield than that. And they have the determination to make it happen. What the German Nation is doing will ultimately be seen as a wonderful thing for mankind. Now what can I do for my exquisite woman?'

Chapter 4

The following morning turned out to be too stormy for the Duke to be flown to Brunswick as had been planned. He conferred with his private secretary and occasional confidante Dudley Forward.

'Dudders with this awful weather we find ourselves at a loose end. We are due to visit the Goerings this afternoon but that leaves the whole morning to fill. Hardly a day for sightseeing… far too wet and blustery, what?'

'No, Sir, that it is not!' laughed the fussy Dudley. 'In London when at a loose end one tends to end up in one's club or a museum.'

'Well, I cannot sit around doing nothing… too damned claustrophobic… please have a word with the protocol chap who sorts out these things and see what ideas he comes up with and make arrangements accordingly. Wallis my dearest, how about you?'

'No my love, a museum is not for me. This morning I shall have a quiet session with Helga catching up with my correspondence. After that I think that a long leisurely bath and massage before the hairdresser comes at one thirty.'

'Capital idea… Dudders fix me up for a Turkish bath and a massage after the museum eh? That should set me up.'

'Certainly Sir, and if that is all I shall take my leave and make arrangements. Oh, and a light luncheon in the suite?'

'Absolutely, do you agree Wallis? Goering's idea of a light snack with them will probably be on a pretty grand scale.'

Wallis laughed. 'Yes, Dudley ask for something like steamed sole fillets with just a green salad.'

Johnny and Celia were relaxing having a lazy start to the day and after leisurely making love were entwined in their crumpled bed sharing a cigarette.

'Well Johnny, at least we have a day off whilst David and Wallis go off to meet the Goerings.'

'Yes, I would have loved to have been a fly on that wall but the invitation was very much for the golden couple alone… apart from Dudley 'Fuss Pot' Forward. Anyway we have lunch with Neville Henderson the British Ambassador here. He is on what can best be described as 'diplomatic leave' you know to avoid embarrassment over the Windsors' visit.'

'Where are we meeting him?' asked Celia 'I need to know what to wear.'

'Well, because he cannot risk being seen in the City we are going to a restaurant in the Grunewald Forest… you know, near Doctor Ley's place where we were the first night. It is in the forest… not super smart, but on the telephone he said that it was good solid traditional German fare. The speciality is roast goose which is apparently delicious. So, to answer your question my pretty sweet I would say 'town and country smart'. You have not met Henderson Celia. He is always the quintessential English diplomat abroad and, as Chips Channon put it, probably in his typical waspish style, 'always faultlessly dressed.'

'Helpful as ever, darling. You men have it so easy you know. Actually, you are wrong. I met Henderson when he stayed at my parents' place in Scotland three or four years ago. He came up for some stalking. Papa said that he was one of the best shots he had ever seen. He seemed a decent sort of man… that's really all I can remember. Right O, tailored tweed suit, cream silk shirt, a trilby and my favourite brogues.'

'Spot on old girl and a Burberry, looking at the weather. Now, if you would be good enough to untangle yourself from me we can start getting ready… no Celia, stop that… we don't really have time you insatiable little monkey… if you don't behave I shall tickle you!'

'Not that!' she cried in mock terror as she leapt from the bed and dashed to her bathroom. Johnny admired her long almost coltish legs and delectable bottom, smiled to himself and stretching enjoyed a few moments of pure relaxation. What a lucky fellow he was to have Celia.

His good humoured mood lessened as unbidden thoughts of Princess Stephanie came to mind. He tried to banish memories of her – she belonged in his shadowy other life – but failed as his professional mind took over and he was reminded that Henderson was yet another member of the Clivedon Set that favoured appeasement with Germany as was Stephanie. He would have to be careful.

He climbed out of bed in a less relaxed frame of mind and padded through to his bathroom but he smiled broadly and instinctively as he heard Celia in her bathroom belting out one of her favourite songs.

Celia and Johnny travelled into the forest by taxi at the suggestion of Sir Neville. Their arrival in an official car could draw unwelcome attention.

As they walked towards the restaurant, which was nestled in the dense forest, Celia commented 'It isn't quite the style of architecture perhaps but I can imagine Hansel and Gretel in this bosky spot, can't you?'

'Well I suppose so in a remote sort of way but it certainly looks inviting in this weather. Come on slow coach let's get inside and wrapped around a decent drink. I doubt that it harbours a wicked witch... only one way to find out darling.'

After their coats and hats had been taken by a heavily moustached elderly but ramrod straight and unsmiling man they were ushered into the restaurant itself.

'Ah there he is... look over there near the fire place.' As they approached the table where Sir Neville was rising from his seat Celia noted the beautifully cut light tweed checked suit, crisply starched white collared shirt and dark tie that he was wearing.

'Henderson my dear fellow, how good to see you... you know Celia I believe?'

'Johnny... please stick to Christian names today old chap' he swivelled his eyes around the dining room meaningfully. Johnny realising his gaffe made to apologise which Henderson waved aside.

'No, no, no need for that and Celia my dear it is so good to see you. I remember you well as a something of a tomboy and, my word, just look at you now! I am forgetting myself. How are your dear parents?'

'Splendid Neville... Papa still reminisces over your ability to invariably shoot a deer through the heart with your first shot.'

'Well, you know, it is the hunter's duty to kill as cleanly and humanely as possible. Now then, something to drink?'

The pre-lunch conversation was light and social; mostly London gossip and talk of mutual friends as a crisp hock was served.

The menus were brought and the little party accepted the recommendation of a hearty vegetable soup to be followed by the famous roast goose. As the plump young waitress in traditional costume left their table Sir Neville smiled reassuringly and said 'You will not be disappointed in the goose I can assure you. So, what are your plans for the rest of the trip?'

Johnny responded 'Well they are pretty hectic Neville… today is really our rest day. The Duke and Duchess are off to the Goerings' home, Carinhall, for the afternoon and there is nothing in the plan for this evening. Just an informal supper with the Windsors.'

'Well they will have a very entertaining time with Goering – he is a munificent host to put it mildly. His unbounded enthusiasm can be exhausting just as a light meal is out of the question. In my book he is by far the most sympathetic of all the Nazi leaders but make no mistake in any crisis as in war I believe that he would be utterly ruthless.'

Johnny chuckled as he responded 'Well both the Windsors eat like sparrows… they are both obsessed with staying slim.'

Sir Neville smiled. 'Well I wish them luck. Mind you Frau Goering, Emmy, is an absolute delight. She is charming company and can contain his enthusiasm when it becomes overbearing for guests.'

'That will be a relief' commented Celia. 'He always appears rather a comic figure with his great size, white uniforms and masses of medals and gongs and scrambled eggs and stuff.'

'Don't believe what you see – nor the popular view – which is a misconception, Celia. Let me put it this way, he may love the pomp and circumstance and has the instinct of a natural showman but he never forgets that he is his master's man heart and soul. He is quite without braggadocio – you know, quite boastful – over his greatest achievements. There is a saying going the rounds which translates roughly as 'Hitler's brain may have conceived the impossible but Goering did it'. There is hardly a part of the Government where Goering does not have great influence if not control. He is not to be underestimated. Or to put it another way, those who do so do so at their peril.'

'You sound very impressed with him Neville?' commented Johnny in an enquiring tone.

'I most certainly am. My task as ambassador is in part to become close to the true rulers of the state where I am posted. That task is simpler when one can identify a person with whom there is an empathy. I make no bones about it, the love of hunting is a strong bond between us.'

'Is it true that he has set up a massive steelworks in Lower Saxony with the help of the Brassert Company of Chicago?'

Henderson gave a dry laugh. 'That's an astute choice of example Johnny may I say that you are uncommonly well briefed for an international art dealer… I hope that we are not boring you Celia?'

'Not in the slightest… do please carry on it really is fascinating.'

'Well the steel men of the Ruhr, who have always regarded themselves as all powerful, rejected German mined iron ore as rubbish… too acidic for economic smelting they said. They insisted on importing from Sweden and elsewhere. Goering considered this to be a serious strategic vulnerability and went to Brassert – incidently his distant cousins – and commissioned the building of furnaces that could handle the German ore. Red faces and utter fury in the Ruhr when he calmly announced that he was going to build the largest integrated steelworks in the world. It is sited right on top of the largest German iron ore source. That's the shrewd part. The ego part is that the works will bear his name. Now Johnny, how did you pick up on that?'

Johnny knew that he must be very careful in his reply and not give away that he had been thoroughly briefed before leaving London.

'Oh I must have heard it somewhere along the way – possibly from Doctor Robert Ley. I have had to spend quite a bit of time with him including most of yesterday. Not an attractive fellow in my book.'

Sir Neville laughed. 'I am more than inclined to agree but vastly powerful all the same. Ah, time for the goose I see.'

A waiter wearing kitchen whites and a tall toque wheeled a silver domed trolley to their table. With a theatrical flourish he swung back the dome revealing a huge golden roasted goose.

'Magnificent!' cried Celia. 'It looks as big as a swan!'

'It's a goose for sure' laughed Henderson as the waiter started to carve thick slices from the bird.

Johnny commented 'But for the different surroundings, definite echoes of Simpson's in the Strand or a London club. There is something rather magnificent at having the carving at one's table. What's the form here?'

'Oh, same as Simpson's, one gives the carver a tip – I shall do that as host. I quite agree about the ceremony… now you must have some of the gravy it is delicious and unsurprisingly a secret recipe known only to the family owners.'

Conversation faltered and became almost desultry as they concentrated on their food.

Johnny wiped his mouth with his napkin and leaning back in his chair patted his flat stomach and with a satisfied smile said 'Wonderful, I am at peace with the world.' He exchanged a discreet smile with Celia.

'It was truly memorable. Thank you Neville' added a smiling Celia.

'Quite the ticket' commented Henderson. 'Perhaps we should get all the world leaders here and serve them goose until they agree to disarm and accept non-aggression, eh?'

Conversation ranged over many topics relating to world politics but inevitably came back to Germany.

'Neville, do you think that a European conflict in which Britain and Germany will be pitted against each other is inevitable?'

'Johnny, I made a speech at the Nuremburg Rally... not the rally itself, obviously... but to the Deutsche Englische Gessellschaft and I stressed the many things that our nations have in common. I was hauled over the coals by my Foreign Office Masters because I was openly critical of the Treaty of Versailles but, frankly, after working in Paris after the Great War I am deeply suspicious of French so-called diplomacy. France may be a republic but its establishment is as tight or tighter knit than any other I have encountered. The men of real influence share a common schooling and ethos. They energetically profess to have broad vision and philosophy but as we witnessed in their vindictive and short sighted approach in the negotiation of the Treaty of Versailles they are blinded to anything beyond their own conception of events and issues.'

'I recognise your drift Neville' commented Johnny. 'Just look at their self-proclaimed Maginot Line. Pals of mine at the War Office see it as a monumental folly merely translating the fixed trench lines of the Great War into concrete. They believe that the French have blinkered themselves into denying that mechanised mobility will be a key factor in any future land conflict.'

'Quite so... that's a good example... but don't waste your breath trying to tell them. But, going back to the legacy of the Treaty of Versailles, I see a strong case for the return of what is actually the German populated Sudetenland from Czechoslovakia to Germany. If that does not happen by agreement I fear Germany will take it by force.'

'But that is not the only goal so far as the Nazis are concerned is it?' asked Johnny.

'Absolutely not. There is pressure for Austria to be taken into the greater

Germany. And mark my words no one believes this more strongly than Goering. If handled skilfully that should not cause conflict. I doubt whether Italy will march on that one, nor anyone else for that matter. However, Poland might fall victim to a German Russian agreement and that could be the final straw. If that were to happen then I fear that Britain and France would be compelled to take action. I hope and pray that reason will prevail.'

The cavalcade bearing the Windsors swept up the long driveway to the Goering's home, Carinhall.

'I say David, it is rather magnificent isn't it... positively baronial... it is huge.'

'I suppose that it is dearest and, I say, look at that statue of a resting stag... I assume a reflection of his love of hunting.'

Wallis mock-shivered in exaggerated discomfort. 'I do so hope the walls are not hung with loads of hunting trophies.' Wallis grimaced and gave another theatrical shiver before continuing 'I find all those glass eyes and teeth really unpleasant.'

'I know you do my sweet but I am sure not.' responded the Duke smiling reassuringly and taking her hand affectionately.

The white uniformed and much-be-medalled Herman Goering and his wife Emmy were standing by the open doors to the house.

Beaming broadly Goering greeted his guests warmly and then introduced his wife who gave a welcoming smile. The little group including Dudley Forward, entered a vast hall hung with magnificent tapestries.

To the Windsors' eyes everything seemed to be larger than life. The dining room could comfortably accommodate at least a hundred guests, there were vast halls and the genial host enthusiastically pointed out the man-made ornamental lake by which he had just had a magnificent new boathouse built.

The inescapable impression was that Carinhall reflected massive self-indulgent expenditure; the indulgence of an insatiable ego. The Duke was not critical of this, as were others, but instead saw it as a symbol of Nazi success. Something not to be envied or decried but admired.

Goering's enthusiasm was infectious and even the controlled Wallis laughed until her sides ached as their grossly fat host leapt around in his gymnasium demonstrating the machines and equipment. The incongruity of this huge man doing so in his elaborate uniform with highly polished riding boots complete with spurs was total.

After his efforts in the gymnasium Goering insisted on taking his guests up to the attic where he had a huge and complex model railway set up. He gleefully demonstrated his wire controlled model aircraft that dropped small wooden bombs.

The final port of call on the tour was Goering's office where the Duke and Duchess could not help but notice a large map in marquetry on the wall behind his desk.

The Duke commented with a smile when he noticed that Austria was coloured the same as Germany. 'Isn't this a little premature, perhaps presumptuous?"

Goering replied smiling broadly. 'Well there is no point in having to re make the map is there?' his smile then faded as he added in a very different tone 'It must be. Austria is part of Germany.'

In that moment the Windsors recognised the steel core of this apparently jovial and jolly pantomime figure of fun. They glimpsed the man of ruthless resolve residing within. As the Duke had previously informed Wallis, Goering was one of the few surviving fighter pilot aces from the Great War. That visceral ruthless instinct would never leave him.

After enjoying pudding and coffee Johnny and Celia thanked Sir Neville and bid him goodbye. Johnny pressed him with a firm invitation to come and shoot on his family estate in Sussex.

They decided to take a stroll in the forest as the rain had stopped and the sun was glittering through the trees.

'Thank goodness the weather has cleared Johnny... I really need a little exercise to settle that super lunch. Gosh, the portions were gargantuan weren't they?'

'They certainly were... it beggars belief that the locals tuck into something that heavy every day... and so rich. I'm surprised they are not all like Goering... I wonder how the visit is going?'

'Well darling I am sure that we shall hear all about it tonight.'

Johnny responded 'I expect so over dinner. By the way, there are two visitors before dinner. David asked whether we would be joining them. He was a little half-hearted but I thought it best to accept if that's acceptable to you?'

'Of course it is... you can brief me when we get back to the hotel. Johnny, are we being followed? I am sure that the man further back on the path was hanging around near the restaurant when we left?'

'You are right… well spotted. I noticed him too and, yes, I think that he probably is tailing us.' Johnny tried to make light of it. 'Nothing to worry about so long as he didn't recognise our host, the truant ambassador, and word gets to the Duke!'

Celia looked at Johnny quizzically 'Oh come on Johnny, pull the other one. It's more than that or you wouldn't have your hand on your pistol… I have eyes you know. Anyhow, shall we turn back and flush him out? Its rather spooky being followed in this place…'

'Yes, I think so. Right my girl. About turn and a brisk walk back to the restaurant where our taxi should have arrived assuming that they booked it as I asked. If my guess is right our friend will make himself scarce.'

'Righto…anyway… so who would be bothering to have us followed?'

'Celia, we are in a police state. Nobody trusts anyone… there is national paranoia. It could be any one of a number of agencies but my money is on the Gestapo. Himmler knows that we have contact with Ribbentrop whom he despises.'

'I wonder how people sleep at night.'

'The short answer is many do not and that includes those high up the Nazi ladder. Their lives will always be spent looking over their shoulder and fearing a knock on the door and arrest in the night.'

Celia undid the clasp on the top of her baby crocodile handbag and slipping her hand inside felt for the comfort of her Beretta pistol. Instinctively she moved away from Johnny as they walked back along the wide path. She knew that they must not present too easy a target.

The suspicious character had also turned and was maintaining the distance between them.

'Christ' muttered Johnny as another man appeared out of the forest and started to walk alongside the man they had seen following them. 'Celia, I am sure that they will have orders merely to watch and do no harm to us but, if I shout 'break' dive into the trees and get on the ground as fast as you can. OK?'

'Yup.'

As they approached the restaurant the two men climbed into a black saloon that roared off scattering gravel.

'That's a relief' said Johnny. 'And that should be the taxi that I asked the restaurant to book for us. Not a word when we are in it… the chances are that the driver is one of their stooges.'

'Mum's the word' replied Celia nervously, more shaken by the sinister encounter than she had anticipated. 'That's horrible… we'll never know who was behind our being watched.'

'Welcome to the joys of a police state my dear.'

Chapter 5

'I am grateful to you for making the journey to see me in Washington… and I should say… welcome to the Cosmos Club.' Cordell Hull, the Secretary of State of the United States of America welcomed his guest and gestured for him to take a seat after warmly shaking hands.

The guest settled into the deep club chair and ordered a dry Martini from the club servant who had appeared at his side as he did so. He noted that his host was smoking and, raising his eyebrows in query, took his pipe and tobacco pouch in its Princeton University colours from his jacket pocket.

Secretary Hull smiled and nodded and the guest slowly filled his pipe. After putting the pouch back in his pocket he produced a silver Vesta box and selecting a red tipped match, struck it and proceeded to light his pipe. As he drew on it his cheeks puffed, the flame leapt in time and a cloud of fragrant smoke surrounded the two men.

This little pantomime may only have taken a minute or two but it sufficed to show that the guest was not awed by his host and would play by his own rules. He was in no doubt that Secretary Hull would be requesting a favour and the choice of venue implied that he would not be doing so on an attributable basis.

His experience had taught the guest that the higher up the ladder of power, politics, diplomacy or finance one climbed, the thinner the line became between apparent sincerity, belief and honesty and the world of shadowy deception, half-truths and even ruthless betrayals.

They were meeting in the prestigious and ultra-exclusive Cosmos Club in Lafayette Square, Washington DC. The Club's reputation was as a sepulchre of excellence and discretion for the great achievers and men of note in the United

States. Members including former Presidents and Nobel Prize winners.

However, whilst the ideals of the club were set high and jealously guarded by its members, whatever might be declared or avowed about the Cosmos Club, Washington DC was the 'company town' of the United States of America. In Washington, including in this club, a quiet word could change the course of history. These were two men who were comfortable with that power.

The suave guest, Allen Dulles, was no stranger to such places or indeed holders of high office. Nevertheless he was intrigued by the invitation, and that the subject for discussion should justify the venue for their luncheon appointment.

'Mr Secretary, I am delighted to be here. The train journey from New York is just the right length of time to allow for some reading and reflection. I have to say that I am a little surprised that we are lunching here rather than your dining room in the State Department building, but none the less I am looking forward to it.'

'Well, for a start, please call me Cordell as I shall call you Allen. As for this venue, rather akin to you train journey I find this place something of a haven away from the pressure house of the State Department. You know, somewhere in the World there is an event of potential significance to the interests of Uncle Sam every minute of every day. As Secretary of State I am supposed to be aware and evaluate them all… every darn one of them.'

'I can well imagine that the Department staff all vie for your attention.'

'That is for sure. Now, before we go into lunch I should let you have an inkling of why I wanted to have this opportunity to talk to you without the dubious benefit of others being present. Naturally, ours will be a totally deniable discussion...'

Dulles interrupted with a wave of his hand 'Cordell, you may rest assured that such is my natural assumption and let us agree on our mutual understanding and undertaking.'

'Thank you Allen. Right, to set a little of the scene at the risk of being pedantic – but, that is how I like to conduct meetings and discussions – I shall start now if I may.

'You have served in the diplomatic service, qualified as an attorney and then joined possibly the largest and most influential law firm in the USA and therefore, possibly the World, Sullivan & Cromwell on Wall Street, where your brother John Foster Dulles is also a partner. Now, you have become very involved in the affairs of the Bank for International Settlements I understand.'

'Yes, that is correct… I met Hjalmar Schacht, the man described as 'the saviour of Germany's currency' and a prime mover in establishing the bank some years ago. He was based in the United States at the time.'

Cordell Hunt nodded and continued 'Quite, it has been said that Schacht manipulated the leading financial powers in the world into agreeing to establish the bank in order to resolve the chaos surrounding Germany's obligations to pay the reparations established by the Treaty of Versailles. I must be frank, Allen, it has also been asserted that in the midst of financial chaos in Europe you and your brother were instrumental in brokering deals to refinance Germany that nobody outside of your offices could fathom, let alone understand.'

Allen Dulles gave a deprecatory laugh. 'I hardly think that that is fair comment… you know what the affairs of continental Europe are like… particularly post the Versailles Treaty… utter chaos. Hang it, even Sir Montagu Norman, Governor of the Bank of England, was in on trying to resolve matters. It was he who hatched the idea for the 'Bank of Banks' with its independence enshrined in its constitution and protected by international agreement… actually, I would go further, protected by international covenant.'

'Yes, Allen, I am fully aware of the… well, shall I call it the 'sanctity' of the Bank for International Settlements. May we simply agree that it is protected to the extent that no nation or group of nations or conflict, even total war can deflect the Bank from fulfilling its objectives?'

'Very well, Cordell, for the purpose of our discussion let us proceed on that basis.'

It clearly riled Cordell Hull that his guest had somehow weakened his position without in any way challenging him – and that was even before he had started. No wonder FDR, as he thought of his good friend President Roosevelt, had warned him that there was nothing to choose between the Dulles brothers when it came to playing high stakes poker. As a diversion and in an attempt to re-establish the upper hand he asked 'Would you care for another Martini or shall we move on to our luncheon?'

'Well Cordell, if it's all the same with you, having made the long dry trip from New York I would just love another. It will give you an opportunity to continue setting the scene for whatever it is you are looking for from me.'

Allen Dulles was smiling apparently amiably as he spoke through a cloud of pipe smoke but Cordell Hunt again felt that he had missed a point. He was becoming irritated but he knew that to let it show would serve his purpose ill.

'Allen, my dear fellow, delighted to join you in another drink. Ah here comes our steward... and I can assure you that I shall be seeking no favours, merely sounding you out.'

'In that case Cordell, I shall continue to relax and enjoy what promises to be an excellent and relaxed luncheon. Now, do please assuage my still youthful curiosity. Do you think that the Duke of Windsor and his Duchess will be visiting the President when they visit us soon?'

Allen Dulles was smiling pleasantly as he asked this question in a light conversational style. He had settled back in his chair, stretching out elegantly clad legs and crossing his ankles.

Now Cordell Hull was even angrier. His infernally charming guest had gone straight to the heart of the very matter which he had wished to approach delicately. There was little point in playing a diplomatic hand now. 'Allen, I shall put my cards on the table. It is that visit and matters connected with it that prompted me to arrange this luncheon. I did so in the belief that you are admirably placed to perform a significant service.'

Allen Dulles showed no change of expression as he responded 'Very well, I am happy with that. At this moment I am not certain just how I may be of assistance to you or anyone else for that matter but my mind is open to what you may say Cordell.'

'Very well. Charles Bedaux has amassed a fortune internationally... it all stems from the business he started here when he arrived from Paris. You know of him of course?'

'Not only 'of him'... I have met him on a number of occasions Cordell. I am afraid that I must declare what might be called an interest, or perhaps, more aptly, a distinct negative prejudice. I did not like him. Not one little bit. Nor would I trust him even with a plugged nickel! My apologies for being so blunt but I think that it is better you know where I stand before you go any further.'

'Thank you Allen. That will make my task considerably easier... there are so many who honestly believe that the man is a genius. In truth, in my opinion, he has only shown genius in creating his vast and obscenely profitable empire. As you know then, he has formed very close relationships with many of the most influential industrialists and bankers both here in the United States, Europe and elsewhere around the world but especially Germany.'

Allen Dulles nodded again. 'Yes, and from my work in New York I can say, and with some considerable authority, that he has done everything he can to engineer that he is at the centre of the so called 'New World Order' that is being talked about behind closed doors. I do not need to tell you that the whole concept is predicated on a financial supra power modelled and centred on Nazi Germany.'

As the Secretary of State pondered his response Allen Dulles popped the olive from his martini into his mouth.

'Allen, it is a terrifying prospect for anyone who believes in democracy let alone the sanctity and integrity of statedom.'

'In my view Cordell the raison d'etre for his hosting the Windsors' wedding at his Chateau Cande in France was to put on a show for Herr Hitler and his cronies.'

Cordell Hull laughed wryly commenting 'Damned small show but it sure got the international coverage sought after and Charles Bedaux was bang on centre stage.'

'Cordell, Hjalmar Schacht… now he is a big player in this whole 'New World Order' concept… far more than might be realised. He is the weirdest of men. Have you met him?'

Cordell Hull shook his head and Allen Dulles continued 'When he was brought in to save the German currency and appointed Currency Commissioner in 1923 he set up his office in an old cleaning cupboard. It reputedly smelt of old polishing rags and his cigarettes. He set the printing presses rolling and within weeks he had convinced, or some would say bluffed, the entire financial world that Germany's disastrous inflation was cured. An absolute sleight of hand but it took him straight from his cupboard to being appointed President of the Reichsbank and getting a seat in the Cabinet.'

'What are you saying Allen?'

'I have had many dealings with him. He is a caricature of the prudent banker. With his centre parted hair and pince-nez he stalks rather than walks. He appears to be the essence of propriety; the embodiment of probity. I can tell you, don't be fooled. He is the arch con man – almost a magician. He is not to be trusted.'

'That is a very serious accusation Allen…'

Before Cordell Hunt could finish his comment Allen Dulles leant forward and in a quiet voice said 'Cordell, I would not have said what I have without the strongest of conviction based on my first hand observation of the man in his dealings.'

'Well, Allen I believe that I must bow to your experience in that you have worked directly with the man. Anyhow, the point towards which you are working is?'

'The Bank for International Settlements was the brainchild of Sir Monatgu Norman, Governor of the Bank of England then and now. Montagu Norman is as weird as Schacht. Whilst Schacht looks like a caricature of a prudent banker, Montagu Norman looks like an actor or an artist. The very last thing he resembles is the Governor of one of the World's most powerful central banks. Schacht was brought in by him, and like the 'sorcerer's apprentice' has effectively taken over. The essence of the Bank is that, and I quote from its charter *'The bank, its property and assets and all deposits and other funds entrusted to it shall be immune in time of peace and in time of war from any measure such as expropriation, requisition, seizure, confiscation, prohibition or restriction of gold or currency export or import, and any other similar measures."*

'So what you are saying Allen, if I get your drift, is that this 'bank of banks' will continue to trade with whomsoever it pleases at any time regardless of war, sanctions or any other impediment.'

'In a nutshell, yes, and that is precisely the way in which the self-styled 'Fraternity' intends to operate also.'

'Allen, what you are telling me is deeply disturbing. Effectively, these powerful organisations are operating at a level above the influence or control of elected governments… indeed, any governments?'

'Yes.'

'Very well, luncheon beckons… we can continue our discussions at table.'

Allen Dulles unfolded himself from his deep chair and knocked out his pipe in the ashtray before returning it to the side pocket of his elegantly cut light grey tweed checked suit. He gave his shoulders a little shake to settle his jacket and checked the maroon silk handkerchief in his breast pocket.

Cordell Hull noted the little ritual with amusement as Allen Dulles shot his shirt cuffs and then alternately adjusted his lapis lazuli cufflinks.

'I can quite see that he is a ladies man as reputed' thought Cordell Hull 'and he's damn shrewd into the bargain.'

Their lunch was quickly ordered when they had been guided to their table. Allen Dulles noted that they were comfortably out of earshot of any other. Cordell Hunt was not slow to revert to their serious conversation.

'So Allen you and your firm act for this Bank of Banks but you have no truck with its, let me call him its architect, Herr Schacht. So what about the other significant players... you must have dealings with them?'

'Of course I do. New York is not that big a place once you get to a certain level. I am not talking about the Social Register of course. Some of the most powerful players are way below the salt when it comes to the elite social order.'

Cordell Hunt permitted himself one of his rare laughs – it was more of a rasp than a laugh as Allen Dulles heard it but the accompanying expression convinced him that this was an attempt at humour, laboured as it might be.

'Ha Allen – so you perforce sup with the Devil?'

Allen Dulles could not resist the temptation to riposte 'Not today Cordell, eh?'

As Cordell Hunt's smile faded Allen Dulles leant forward and in a quiet voice carried on 'Cordell, my brother is on the board of the International Nickel Company. That company is a joint venture with the US arm of I G Farben, General Aniline and Film, on whose board Walter Teagle, President of Standard Oil sits as does Edsel Ford – need I go on?'

Cordell Hull looked at Allen Dulles rather blankly as he responded 'So what are you telling me?'

'Cordell, these men and the others with whom they are in close liaison are all powerful in the US economy. They or their counterparts are in the same position in Germany. Personally I abhor Herr Hitler and his Nazi policies and ambitions. However, I am a pragmatist. To be blunt, I do not bite the hand that feeds me. At least, not yet.'

Allen Dulles was staring at Cordell Hull intently as he said all of this and his meaning was clear. Nevertheless Cordell Hull wanted it spelt out. 'Allen, just let me get this straight. You and your brother are playing along with these men and their activities so long as it suits but you have no conviction that supports what they are doing?'

'That is correct. The moment that we believe that anything being done is contrary to the interests of the United States we shall cease to be involved. However, we will then know precisely what has been engineered... its strengths and its weaknesses. Now, what do you wish me to do?'

'Well Allen, after all that, it is really rather a simple request. Could you use your position and that of your brother to put the man Bedaux out of the picture in the United States?'

'I see no reason why not.'

'Do you wish to know why it is wished, and if I may say so, this comes from the top?'

'No. That will not be necessary. We know that to have his German business licence reinstated he made very substantial payments to Nazi Party funds and to Herr Schacht. The latter not only engineered the payments but also that Doctor Robert Ley should be his business partner for all activities Bedaux might undertake in Germany.'

'The partnership with Ley will be the last straw with our unions here in the United States.' Cordell Hull indulged in another of his rasping laughs, satisfied that Charles Bedaux would soon be a totally discredited and broken man in the United States of America.

The beauty was that this could be achieved without a complex trial for alleged criminal tax evasion let alone having to touch the evidence that J Edgar Hoover's FBI had gathered.

That evidence of suspected espionage would be kept on file for another day.

Both had ordered consommé to start their lunch which was served from a large silver tureen. As the trolley was wheeled away Cordell Hunt wished Allen Dulles 'Bon Appetit' as he tucked his starched white napkin into the top of his tight-fitting waistcoat.

'Oh David my love, this schedule is killing me!' exclaimed Wallis, puffing out her cheeks and blowing out theatrically.

The Duke was shocked that the resolute facade that Wallis normally presented not only to the world at large but even to him in private appeared to be cracking. He felt helpless – after all he had so much wanted her to enjoy the whole experience of being the absolute centre of attraction during a tour that in in every sense was designed to replicate a royal state visit. He caught Helga's eye and she responded with a sympathetic moue.

'David, you know that I am not a good or happy traveller. Day after day we are whisked from pillar to post… it is all becoming a blur… Dresden, Stuttgart, Munich… and everywhere we go more uniformed men, parades of soldiers, bouquets and bands.' Wallis paused dramatically and then continued with more than a hint of exasperation in her voice. 'And then, to cap it all we are saddled with the thuggish lout Doctor Ley. I swear to God he is drunk half the time and he plonks himself between us at every opportunity. I am at my wits end....'

'Now then Wallis, we always knew that it would be a very hectic schedule...'
The Duke stood up and taking Wallis's hands drew her to him and gently kissed
her on the forehead.

'Remember that part of the idea is that you are seen by as many of the
people as possible. You will be their Queen one day and it is important that as
many as possible see you and they must all know you have visited. I agree about
Doctor Ley but I am not sure that there is anything we can do about that. Let
me think about it.'

Helga had every sympathy with what Wallis had said and as soon as the
Duke left the room to deal with some administrative matters with Dudley
Forward she laid her hand on Wallis' shoulder and asked 'Wallis... I can have a
quiet word with von Ribbentrop about Doctor Ley... the last thing that anyone
wants is for you to be in any way distressed I am sure.' Wallis turned to Helga
and placing her hand over hers responded 'You are an angel Helga. I am afraid
that nothing can be done about today's trip... a coal mine in Essen... but that
would be marvellous. Thank you.'

The journey to Essen had seemed interminable but was much improved by
Celia very pointedly placing herself between Doctor Ley and Wallis then
turning her back on him as she engaged Wallis in conversation. Meanwhile, the
Duke, Johnny and Dudley Forward kept Doctor Ley occupied with a barrage
of detailed questions.

Their usual cavalcade with SS outriders and cars packed with armed guards
and uniformed officers arrived at the mine. Predictably there was a guard of
honour drawn up and a military band.

As their staff car rolled to a halt by the red carpet, at a barked command,
the guard of honour slammed into presenting arms and the band struck up the
British National Anthem.

The Duke had been the first to step out of the car and immediately came to
attention and gave the Nazi salute. The incongruity of his doing so whilst the
band played 'God Save the King' was far from lost on his British companions
who exchanged glances. In the case of Dudley Forward, his look was one of
acute discomfort.

The German National Anthem then followed with more salutes. The Duke
joined in with raised arm. After that the rest of the visitors joined the Duke and

he and the Duchess were formally introduced to the mine director and local dignitories.

The mine director's wife then took Wallis and Celia to meet a group of ladies who were waiting near the doors to the offices whilst the Duke and his companions were led towards the entrance to the mine workings.

In a clear voice the Duke turned to the mine director and said 'We should very much like to inspect the mine itself... would that be possible?'

'Your Royal Highness, it is almost 500 metres deep, I do not....'

The Duke interrupted him with an almost imperious hand gesture 'My dear fellow, we are no strangers to mine shafts. If you would be so kind as to organise some suitable clothing... overalls or suchlike... that would be appreciated.'

Clearly there was to be no argument and the party went into the mine buildings. Overalls and helmets were quickly found and the little group set about changing. 'Big buggers these miners, eh Johnny?' laughed the Duke as he rolled up first the sleeves then the legs of the one piece white overalls that he had been given.

When they were all kitted out they were escorted to the head of the mine shaft. 'I am afraid that the cage is at the bottom of the shaft at this time unloading some new machinery so we must wait for a few minutes' explained the mine director.

'No, no, that will not be necessary... we can go down on the ladders here and the cage can bring us up. That would be acceptable, eh?'

Again, the Duke's tone was one of command Johnny noted. The mine director looked very uncomfortable as he responded 'As you wish Your Royal Highness, I shall lead the way.'

Johnny was not keen on heights but fortunately the shaft was only dimly lit and he focused on the wall in front of him as they slowly climbed down using the iron rungs set into the sides of the shaft. Water was running down the shaft walls and the rungs felt slippery. 'This is a bugger' thought Johnny as the descent seemed interminable. 'The blasted Duke is making a point – that is for sure.'

After what seemed like an age the party reached the working level of the mine. Johnny could taste the gritty dust that hung in the air and blurred the light from the lamps on their helmets onto the walls of the chamber.

'Right, let's be off' said the Duke and the mine managers led them into one of the tunnels.

After the trip down the mine and the return to the surface in the cage lift the party changed out of their now filthy overalls and were led to the office block where the ladies awaited them.

The Duke was in good humour and immediately spoke enthusiastically to Wallis. 'Most interesting, most interesting my dear… the tunnels are made higher and wider than in Britain. They are so much less claustrophobic and there is much more working room for the miners. A point that I have noted.'

'That is very interesting. Frau Deutz has been telling me about the miners' hospital attached to the works and has suggested that we visit. Shall we?'

'Most surely – shall we go now?' The Duke quickly asked the mine director who agreed to take the visitors immediately.

The hospital was housed in a separate block where they were met by a formidable matron who bobbed a small bow to the Duke and Duchess before leading them around the small wards. The rather stern matron was clearly most displeased when Wallis stopped and perching on the side of their beds endeavoured to talk to some of the patients.

The Duke was still displaying an almost childlike excitement as he said 'This is fascinating Wallis! I say Johnny, Dudley, what a capital notion… not only can they look after injured chaps from the mine but there is a maternity section and even a children's ward. That jolly well shows the miners and their families that they are valued and cared for eh?'

'Yes, it certainly does' interjected Johnny. 'It is rather like our cottage hospitals….'

The Duke turned his head sharply and gave Johnny a withering look. 'It most certainly is not! This hospital is dedicated to the miners and their families… why, in Wales they are lucky even to be on the panel. You have read the novels of A J Cronin haven't you? He practised as a doctor in the Welsh Valleys and lifted the lid on what went on there and in Harley Street. If you have not read 'The Citadel', you should before you choose to comment' the Duke ended angrily, his affable mood apparently lost.

Johnny could see that nothing was to be gained by saying any more. He knew from experience that once the Duke had fixated on an idea there would be no room for logical argument let alone contradiction.

When the Duke had insisted on climbing down into the mine it gave every indication that he was a man of the people and not hidebound by his privilege. Johnny had seen it as no more than a cynical theatrical gesture on the Duke's part. Now, he was not quite so sure. Could it be that the Duke was genuinely interested in the miners' working conditions? Or was he putting on a cynical performance for the ever present reporters, photographers and newsreel makers?

Of one thing he could be sure, the Duke remained an enigma.

Helga had telephoned Von Ribbentrop at the first opportunity and relayed as much as she could of Wallis' reactions to the visit so far, the people she had met and in particular the distaste for the presence and behaviour of Doctor Ley that both she and the Duke shared.

'Worry not' responded Von Ribbentrop. 'I shall speak to Fritz Wiedemann immediately… Ley will be sent off to do something well out of the way. Please tell the Duchess that the problem is as good as solved. Now then, we must meet. I am missing you my dear. This evening the Duke and Duchess are guests of honour at a dinner given by his cousin Carl-Eduard Duke of Saxe-Coburg and Gotha so you will be free. They are to stay in Nuremburg where it is to be held so I suggest that I arrange a suite in your hotel and you join me for dinner. We can spend the night together, liebchen. Also, you can bring me up to date properly.'

'That would be wonderful Joachim. Just let me know the details later on.'

'Wallis my love, you look exquisite tonight.'

The Duke was resplendent in white tie and tails adorned with various jewelled orders. He was also wearing the pale blue silk sash and star of the ultimate Order of British Imperial Chivalry, the Order of the Garter. The Order had been bestowed upon him by his father King George V in 1910 when his parents had given him the exquisite mother of pearl, rose diamond and enamel oval cufflinks that he was also wearing. The Duke smiled warmly as Wallis walked towards him.

She was wearing a severely tailored and fitted Schiaperelli gown with a square-cut neck in an almost iridescent dark blue silk. The Late Queen Alexandra's sumptuous diamond and sapphire necklace, earrings and tiara all perfectly complemented her alabaster skin and glossy black tightly drawn hair. Wallis smiled and then turned as Helga slipped a white mink stole over her shoulders. 'I know that this is a very important evening for you David …'

The Duke responded 'Dearest Heart, you are a beautiful picture, a masterpiece… I am so proud.' Concerned for her make-up the Duke leant forward and touched Wallis's cheek gently with his own.

The Duke and Duchess were at the head of the long receiving line as the uniformed Major Domo formally announced each of the one hundred guests. The guests' sometimes lengthy and cumbersome titles rolled off his tongue like a recital of the Almanac de Gotha as the Duke's kith and kin were formally presented not only to him, but in his eyes, more importantly to Wallis. He felt a prickle of emotion as he noted that each of these members of the former royal ruling families of the German and Central European states paid due deference to Wallis, his consort. The men bowed and the ladies all curtsied deeply and formally, addressing Wallis as 'Your Royal Highness.' As the chamber orchestra played in the background the Duke found himself swallowing a lump in his throat, feeling rather overwhelmed. Wallis acknowledged these gestures of the guests bestowing warm smiles and as she did so she thought to herself 'If only those bitches at the snobbish Oldfields school in Glencoe County, Maryland could see me now.' Her smile broadened at the sweet thought.

Doctor Joseph Goebbels was sitting with the Fuhrer in the vast room that served as his Berlin office. 'Well Joseph, you visited the Duke and Duchess of Windsor last night… tell me, what do you make of them? Frankly I am puzzled… there seem to be conflicting opinions. Some describe him as an empty headed immature hedonist, others as an intelligent, perceptive and caring man. All seem to agree that he is deeply hurt and angry at the manner in which he feels that he and his wife have been treated.'

'It is always dangerous to jump to conclusions Mein Fuhrer but I found him to be progressive and attuned to the plight of the under privileged. He is undoubtedly very pro-German and absolutely set against any conflict between Britain and the Fatherland. Perhaps because of the way in which he feels he has been ill-treated by his family and the British government he identifies very strongly with his German ancestry.'

'So you believe that he is sincere?' asked Hitler reflectively.

'Yes, I do' nodded Goebbels. 'I shall go further. His view of life and his role and, indeed that of all rulers, is very akin to mine. You will recall my words when I became a Minister – *I have not become a Minister to be above the people but, rather, I am now more than ever the servant of the people.*'

'Yes Joseph, I recall you saying that. Now then, what about the Duchess?'

'That is more difficult' replied Goebbels, scratching his chin. 'I believe that she is clever and manipulative and that she has a strongly developed political sense to match her ambition. She will certainly channel his thoughts and efforts, of that I am certain.'

'So, then, in conclusion?'

'I believe that they will suit our purposes admirably in all respects.'

'Excellent. Now then, the propaganda benefits of this not inexpensive visit are…?'

'Hello Billy… is that you my friend?'

Billy Brownlow knew that the voice was very familiar… as was the almost reedy American accent… but it was out of context somehow.

The caller sensed Billy hesitate. 'Billy, how about 'a hair of the dog my friend?'…'

'My God! How are you? And a hair of the dog to you too Bill! I haven't seen you since we last met in the Cafe Louvre in Vienna. Is it still your lair and the haunt of the foreign Press Corps?'

'But of course… nothing changes on that front.'

Recovering his composure Billy asked 'What news have you?'

'Well Billy it's been a rather dramatic time for me… quite a change but in some ways, no change.'

'Stop being so bloody enigmatic, what do you mean? Is your finger still 'on the pulse' of European affairs?'

'I guess so. You remember my old poor joke that when I joined William Randolph Hearst's wire service in 1934 I went from 'bad to Hearst'?'

'How can I forget the worst pun I have ever heard!'

'Yup… you are right there! Anyhow that service folded earlier this year and I was under notice of termination from Hearst's other service when Edward R. Murrow approached me to become the Columbia Broadcasting System Continental correspondent. And so I am and, guess what, I am based in Vienna.'

'I must listen out for your dulcet tones then…'

Shirer interrupted. 'You are spared that. CBS in their wisdom do not allow us correspondents to broadcast – we have to employ reporters to do that. I am not pleased but then I've never printed and sold newspapers on street corners either.'

'Hardly the same Bill! I hope to be in Vienna soon so we can chew the fat then.'

'That would be good Billy. Now, apart from the utter delight… ahem… in speaking to you, I am calling to do you a little favour. Now, do not protest too much but just hear out a newshound who has scented something of interest.'

'I shall do as you command' responded Billy who was now listening attentively. Bill Shirer had never called him like this before and he sensed that there must be a very good reason for him to do so now.

'Very well. A reliable and very uptight member of the Washington 'establishment' who, surprisingly you may think, is a close friend of mine, happened to mention a piece of gossip. Apparently the august Secretary of State, Cordell Hull, lunched Allen Dulles, who with his brother is lawyer to the great and the…er… not always so good… in the stuffy Cosmos Club in Washington.'

'Yeeees – but, if I may say so, is that newsworthy?'

'Oh yes, oh yes. Hull rarely ventures outside of the State Department except to hob nob with his pal FDR in the White House. Allen Dulles is a rare fish and by no means typical of Hull's friends and acquaintances. Take it from me there is something afoot. Putting two and two together it could well involve Europe… hence my interest. Dulles acts for some very powerful interests who have a foot in Germany as well as the USA.'

Billy instantly responded. 'If I can find out what they were discussing, might it be useful to both of our interests?'

'My friend, you have never told me what your 'interests' are but I guess that my answer is a big 'Yes'. Allen Dulles has the reputation of being a ladies' man… that may help.'

'Right Bill, I shall have a few words… it may take a week or so to put something in place but, rest assured, I shall share whatever I find out with you.'

'Good. Now, how is your romance with the international lady of mystery that you were so taken with when we last met?'

Chapter 6

'My God Celia! Talk about rising to the occasion! Our Wallis was unbelievable!'

Celia was laughing so much that she was holding her sides and doubled forward as she and Johnny crossed the living room of their suite after the dinner in the Grand Hotel in Nuremburg.

'To think that she had the crème de la crème of Central European Royalty and aristocracy bowing and scraping to her... and she accepted it as of right.' continued Johnny.

Celia had just about regained her composure. 'Oh come on Johnny, it was priceless, but really rather sad at the same time. How many of those people whose grand families are recorded in the Almanach De Gotha really want to bend a knee to an upstart adventuress like Wallis?'

'Hey... 'Steady the Buffs' old girl! That's not like you at all! I always thought you believed in a meritocracy.'

Celia laughed again then replied 'Oh but I do darling but, well, there are limits. OK, before you say it... 'the Prince and the showgirl'.... or in my family's case... newly minted American dollars as a dowry buying into one of England's oldest families.'

Johnny responded in a slightly subdued and more thoughtful tone 'It's just that the European 'royal' families are now virtually all dispossessed... particularly so when you looked at tonight's gathering.'

'Oh well Johnny, please give me a little champagne and let's relax. Tomorrow is another long day... back to Berlin then off in the special train to visit Herr Hitler in his mountain lair.' Celia giggled and playfully put her finger under her nose parodying the Fuhrer.

'Tomorrow will be an odd one I think. Apparently Dudley Forward has been told that David is to have an audience with Hitler alone so we will not be privy to what is discussed.'

'I expect that you will find it all out by hook, crook or whoever my dear' countered Celia, taking a seat suddenly, and speaking in a slightly waspish tone.

'Hey old girl, no need for that. Yes, I shall have to ask Princess Stephanie to grill dear Adolf but, with respect, that's my job just as you will no doubt be squeezing Von Ribbentrop.'

Celia realised that she had gone too far and crossed the undrawn but clearly established line between their private lives and their intelligence service activities. 'Oh darling Johnny, I am so sorry... that was below the belt and unforgiveable. Take me to bed before I put my other foot in my mouth.'

'Nothing to forgive....'

Johnny reached over and took Celia's glass from her hand and placed it on the side table. He then swept her up into his arms and carried her towards the bedroom.

'Oh yes... quite the cave man' she said with a mocking laugh as she swung her legs and kicked off her shoes.

Allen Dulles was with his brother, John Foster Dulles. They were in a panelled boardroom in the offices of their Wall Street law firm. Allen had outlined his conversation with Secretary of State Cordell Hull. His older brother appeared to be deep in thought for a minute and then smiled broadly.

'Allen, this is perfect. It suits you and me to a tee. We can get Bedaux railroaded out of business in the United States and still leave him in place in Germany and elsewhere. Personally I think that he is a busted flush but he may be useful in the future and he seems to have an ongoing relationship with the ex-King of England.'

Allen Dulles did not share his brother's good humour and voiced his concern. 'The question is, how best to do it without any dirt sticking to us?'

His brother's reply was instant.

'As Sherlock Holmes would have put it, "Elementary my dear Watson." Is not the man hated by the Unions and their members? Am I correct?'

'Yes.'

'Good, he is not really trusted by the big players here and in Germany. Correct?'

Allen Dulles out of habit fiddled with his tie and cufflinks then responded.

'In part that is correct but he does have significant support in Germany. However, I would accept that such is in direct relation to his perceived usefulness.'

'Fair enough Allen. Now, let's work this out. First step for us is the unions. Once we have them fired up… a few words in the right ears… then we can lean on the bankers and industrialists and they will pressure the board members of Bedaux's company here. I reckon he will be out very quickly indeed.'

Allen Dulles took a deep breath and massaged his forehead briefly. 'I am a director of the Bank for International Settlements of course. I can drip some poison there as required. I think that a quiet word with Baron Von Schroder would not come amiss.'

John Foster Dulles pondered this response and then spoke very slowly as if thinking aloud. 'We must be careful not to startle anyone Allen. It will have to be a slow burn operation. You should not speak to Schroder or anyone in the Bank yet… rather, leave the door open at the right time for them to come to you. Remember that you and I are very closely linked to all these international operations and a word in the wrong place could put us in an untenable position both professionally and personally.'

'Yes, I accept that but, hang it, FDR, the President I remind you, is wholeheartedly in favour of our involvement in order to monitor just what is going on.'

John Foster Dulles gave a hollow laugh. 'That my dear younger brother is true but, I fear that if things became unpleasant you would find that we would be out on a limb. But then that's the excitement!'

'Well, I am glad you think so. Now, to change the subject slightly, a little bird tells me that our esteemed Ambassador in France is becoming rather close if not intimate with the… er… shall we say… delectable… and I use the word advisedly… Duchess of Windsor. Have you heard that?'

'But, of course. Bill Bullitt is a strange fellow. Rumour has it that he has a little trouble… shall we say…'down below'. But he loves the ladies. Never forget though that he is a close friend of the President and they speak on the telephone every day. Clever chap… talented author and all that, but from our point of view, possibly not to be trusted. He has become very close to some of the French politicians. I know that some at the State Department question his objectivity.'

'The Duchess? Well, I would think that they make an ideal couple for a little Parisian fling! What say you younger brother?'

Allen Dulles quickly responded 'It's an unhealthy situation in my book. Before you say anything, I am not taking any moral line here... merely that her political sympathies, and actual allegiances are very suspect. He could be a very weak link in the President's intelligence armoury.'

Sir Vernon Kell, Head of the British Secret Service, had been summoned to 10 Downing Street for a meeting with the Prime Minister, Neville Chamberlain, and the Foreign Secretary, Anthony Eden.

'Ah, Sir Vernon do please take a seat. Would you care for a cup of tea?'

'No thank you, Prime Minister.'

The panelled room was depressingly dark with the only light being the green shaded reading lamp on the Prime Minister's clear leather topped writing table that served as his desk. Its austerity matched the sombre almost doleful expressions of the humourless Prime Minister, thought Vernon.

'Very well. Anthony Eden will be joining us shortly. There will be no note of this meeting... it is to be strictly off the record. I trust that you are comfortable with that?'

Sir Vernon paused before replying. He had served under enough Prime Ministers since starting the Secret Service in 1909 to be well aware of the perils of 'off the record briefings'.

'Prime Minister, I shall be frank. In so far as this is a discussion only meeting, I am happy for there to be no record. However if there is any action agreed to be taken, whether covert or overt I shall insist upon a written memorandum of record.'

'Very well Sir Vernon' said the Prime Minister, looking slightly irritated. There was a knock on the door that swiftly dispelled the awkwardness in the air.

'Ah, Anthony, thank you for joining us.' Said the Prime Minister, clearing his throat and gesturing for the Foreign Secretary to take the button backed leather covered Gainsborough chair facing Sir Vernon.

The suavely elegant Anthony Eden shook Sir Vernon's hand before sitting down after carefully adjusting his trousers over his knees. His appearance was bordering on fastidious perfection. Sir Vernon thought to himself that he had the look of an exhibit in Madame Tussaud's waxworks.

The Prime Minister opened the meeting.

'Gentlemen. I sought this meeting because I have concerns about the way in which international financiers appear to be manipulating matters political and, from your perspective Anthony as Foreign Secretary, diplomatic.'

Eden hardly moved a muscle as he responded 'That is just so Prime Minister. The worrying reports that I am receiving indicate that very substantial finance is being invested in Germany both from Britain and the United States... the greater part from the latter. The payments are parcelled up and made through some apparently legitimate channels and others that are best described as secret. The Foreign Office is anxious to monitor and if appropriate put a stop to both.'

The Prime Minister looked pained. 'Anthony my dear fellow, we all are aware that in order to circumvent some of the more inequitable restrictions imposed by the Treaty of Versailles there has been much clandestine financial activity to enable Germany to get on its feet again.'

'Yes, Prime Minister, of course, and that is one thing and generally agreed by all but the French to be essential. However, what I am talking about is the creation of a supranational commercial undertaking outwith all governmental controls. That organisation – and I believe that it already exists – is not helping a defeated Germany to get back on its feet but is intended to fully re-arm and equip that nation for total war.'

'I cannot believe that Herr Hitler wants any such thing Anthony... he has repeatedly made it clear that the extent of his ambition is to re-create the Greater Germany that existed before it was arbitrarily carved up in Versailles at the instigation of the vindictive French. Our best interest is for Germany to be a bulwark against the growing Bolshevik threat.'

Sir Vernon cleared his throat and as the others turned to him spoke very carefully.

'Prime Minister, Foreign Secretary, you must forgive me for expressing a somewhat different view. Reviewing our intelligence reports, it does seem to me that Hitler is working to a plan that is significantly different to that which he and his cronies publically avow. Deceit Gentlemen is the name of the game and mark my words, he who believes the utterances of that man will rue the day.'

The Prime Minister was clearly annoyed by Sir Vernon's remarks.

'Sir Vernon I find it most distasteful that you should seek to cast aspersions upon an elected Head of State. I have no reason to doubt the bona fides of Herr Hitler. Anthony, what say you?'

'Neville, I must resonate with Sir Vernon's remarks. The banking and industrial grouping and activity which we are meeting to discuss today is in my view and that of my advisers a clear signal that these powerful, let us call them 'interests' are hedging their bets. They sniff the smoke of conflict on the air and they are now, and for some considerable time have been, establishing structures that will protect their interests whatever may be the outcome.'

Still looking most uncomfortable the Prime Minister bridled. 'I think that such unsubstantiated talk is utterly dangerous and, Anthony, if I may say so, unworthy of you.'

Sir Vernon spoke again 'Gentlemen. There is substantiated evidence of such activity.'

The by now agitated Prime Minister responded 'Well, in that case I require to see full evidence before I shall accept what is being said here either about Herr Hitler or this spectral organisation that you both hint at. I think that there is nothing further to discuss today gentlemen. I thank you for your time.'

As Sir Vernon climbed into the back seat of his official Humber motor car he indulged in an uncharacteristic bout of criticism of the present holder of the great office of Prime Minister.

'Bloody pompous fool. His naievity is going to land us all in the soup.'

Helga spent the afternoon preparing herself for her evening with Joachim Von Ribbentrop.

A bell boy delivered a note with details of the suite that he had taken and the time that she should be there.

Careful as ever she followed her usual instinct and calling the Concierge asked him to come and see her. With his help, which she was confidant of buying, she would know the layout of her lover's suite.

Once back in her own suite she felt unaccountably nervous.

'Why this you silly woman,' she thought to herself. After all, she and Von Ribbentrop were lovers and he craved the special attention that she was pleased to give him. She had no difficulty fulfilling her other role as his liaison with Wallis Simpson with whom she also enjoyed an occasionally intense and at times painfully unwelcome physical relationship. So why was she nervous?

Helga decided that a steam bath, massage and short sleep would restore her normal confidence and telephoned to make the appropriate booking. She then selected her outfit and gave some thought to the toys that she would have in her handbag.

Helga was not alone in anticipating the evening to come. Von Ribbbentrop was finding it hard to concentrate on the dreary issues that were being discussed in the foreign policy meeting he was chairing.

His mind wandered to the heady days of his time in London as Ambassador. Now, promoted to Foreign Minister, he was hemmed in within the Foreign Office. He enjoyed the power and prestige but was stultified by the endless protocol and meetings.

So much of his time was being wasted in overseeing what he regarded as petty issues. He had inherited the post from Von Neurath a career diplomat of great skill and experience who had unfortunately revelled in detail.

By contrast Von Ribbentrop thought to himself that he saw his role in terms of broad brushstrokes on the great canvas of history. 'That sounds rather grand' he thought to himself and smiled. 'I must use that.'

A flicker of a smile still played around his mouth before he turned to his secretary seated on his left and raised his hand to stop the civil servant who was currently droning on about crop rotation in the Sudetenland. In a commanding voice he announced 'Gentlemen. May I commend you upon your zeal and enthusiasm which does not go un-noticed. I have to leave for a meeting that… let me say… cannot be postponed….'

He paused theatrically and looked around the table meaningfully. 'I would ask that you all submit your reports in writing to Herr Schlagel my Secretary, indeed, this regular meeting will not be necessary in future so kindly clear it from your diaries. Thank you gentlemen. Heil Hitler!'

As he walked down the steps of the Foreign Office towards his gleaming staff car he thought to himself 'Now that's what I call delegation.'

'Helga my dear, you look positively ravishing.' For once the usually glib charmer really meant the compliment.

Helga's afternoon had been well spent and she had decided upon her tactics.

Von Ribbentrop was as elegant as ever in a midnight blue velvet smoking jacket with elaborate silk cord frogging that he had had made in London's Savile Row, a cream woven silk shirt and a toning dark blue cravat. 'Now then Helga, some champagne, yes?' he asked smiling broadly.

She did not speak but simply stalked up to him and reaching into his shirt front grasped the ends of his cravat and firmly drew him after her to the bedroom. 'Not so stupid' she thought as she recalled her earlier visit to this suite that had cost her 50 Reichmarks with the Concierge.

She turned and pushed Von Ribbentrop onto the bed and then leapt onto him straddling his chest as she reached into her hand bag and produced a set of what appeared to be police issue handcuffs. In a moment he was handcuffed to the bedpost. She then spun around and knelt forward as she attached more cuffs to each of his ankles.

He groaned as her skirt rode up and he could see that she wore no underwear and was already glistening with excitement. His erection felt as if it would burst as she climbed off the bed and then slowly peeled off the few clothes that she was wearing leaving only a black velvet collar.

He was still fully dressed and straining at the restraints as she lowered herself onto his face and started to grind against him. He felt her hands undoing his trousers and then their being pulled down a little with his silk undershorts. He gave a muffled yelp as she raked him with her nails then in dramatic contrast he felt a light tickling sensation.

It was then that he remembered telling Helga of the two horrors in his life – spiders and being tickled. Helga was smiling wickedly as she started to caress Von Ribbentrop's straining erection with the goose feather that she had taken from her handbag. Her smile broadened as his writhing and muffled groans became more frenzied. She ground down on his face and felt her first convulsions beginning to build. 'Oh yes,' she thought. 'Oh yes.'

Over an hour later Von Ribbentrop and Helga were ready for their champagne which they drank still naked on the dishevelled bed, redolent of sex.

'Well my little temptress… that was quite something eh?'

Helga responded by simply giving him a long and languorous smile and a smouldering look. She had yet to speak.

'Very well you little hell cat, stay silent if you will. Now then, to business. Please inform the Duchess that the matter of Doctor Ley is resolved and he will not be actually accompanying them on any further visits although he may well be present at the actual events. Now, you mentioned that she is finding the whole exercise somewhat taxing. Is that so?'

Helga decided that the time had come to break her silence.

'Yes, that is so. The Duke has explained the necessity of their having as much exposure to the German people as possible but I am not sure that she is totally convinced. Actually, that is not quite right… it is hard to hit the nail on the head… but she does not seem wholly comfortable with the notion that she will be Queen.'

'I thought as much. Very well, I shall arrange something to convince her. Please advise her that in the course of the next few days I shall arrange something a little special for her and, of course, the Duke. Now, I think I owe you something ….'

Von Ribbentrop put his glass onto the bedside table and reaching across took Helga's glass out of her hand. He rose onto his knees and drew her up from the bed and then laid her face down. She was limp and un-responding which excited him even more. He roughly pushed her legs apart.

As he gave a grunt of pure lust Helga stifled a cry and bit on her knuckle.

Chapter 7

The Duke and Duchess of Windsor, Celia, Johnny and Dudley Forward were travelling with the Deputy Fuhrer Rudolf Hess in the comfortable salon on the Fuhrer's special train. It was taking them from Berlin to his mountain retreat at Berchtesgaden.

The Duke was on good form which was a relief to all.

Hess had just asked the Duke why he had refused to meet Herr Julius Streicher, the Nuremburg Nazi Party Chief.

'It is very simple Rudolf. Herr Streicher owns the newspaper 'Der Sturmer' and some months ago now it carried an article saying that my Duchess is Jewish. As I see it, in German eyes that is an insult and therefore something which I shall not tolerate.'

Hess looked uncomfortable and there was a pause before he responded.

'Streicher is a good man… he has been with the Party since its beginning. I really cannot think that he could have known about such an allegation let alone sanctioned it. However on his behalf and the Party I must apologise for any unintended offence.'

'Thank you Rudolf but I have to tell you that I fully intend to take up the matter with Doctor Goebbels. I do not understand the reasoning but it seems to me that in Germany today it is something of an insult to call somebody Jewish. I personally have nothing against Jews… we have some good Jewish chums don't we Johnny?'

Johnny was stunned by the Duke's apparent naivety. Could he really be blind to the brutal pursuit of its ideals by the ruthless Nazi regime?

Surely the Duke could not be unaware of the Nuremburg Decrees of 1935 and their implementation in taking away the rights of citizenship of Jews, more recently confiscating their businesses and even banning them from their professions. These things were bad enough without the ugly rumours that were circulating of even worse ill treatment and abuse.

'Well David, of course… after all, your hosts in Austria the Rothschilds are a case in point.'

Johnny could recognize that Hess was extremely uncomfortable with this conversation but saw it as an opportunity to find out more without the interference of the Nazi propaganda machine.

'Rudolf, how do you reconcile the ideals of National Socialism in relation to race with the future of the large Jewish community in Germany?'

Hess hesitated before responding.

'Well Johnny, as you can imagine, it is not an easy matter. I am in favour of the Jews being given the opportunity… or indeed be encouraged… to leave the Greater Germany.'

'What and leave their homes and wealth behind?' persisted Johnny.

'In a sense, yes' responded a now visibly shaken Hess.

The Duke intervened fixing Johnny with a hard eyed glare despite maintaining an easy going style of speaking.

'I say Johnny old chap… I think you are rather overstepping the mark… you know we are guests here…'

'Quite David… no offence meant Rudolf but I was keen to have things clear in my mind. One last question, do others share your view about the Jews emigrating or do they have other ideas… a different solution in mind?'

The Duke was clearly furious and now his tone was biting.

'Enough Johnny! No more of this. I will not have it. You are distressing Wallis and I think Celia too. Now, Rudolf, should we not be arriving soon?'

In fact neither Wallis nor Celia looked the slightest bit discomforted by Johnny's exchange with Hess. The discomfort was apparently limited to Hess and the Duke. Johnny wondered whether the Duke knew the answer that Hess was clearly unhappy to give.

The train pulled into the station and the Duke's party were led to their cars.

There was a small crowd that cheered the Duke and Duchess. Both the Duke and Hess stopped and gave Nazi salutes to cries of Heil Hitler and Heil Windsor from the onlookers.

Celia had of course been there before but Wallis was enchanted by the colourful gingerbread style houses as their open topped black Mercedes limousine led by its escort of SS motorcyclists and vehicles packed with uniformed officers swept through the little town.

As they headed into open country Rudolf Hess had the embarrassing task of explaining that their train had arrived early and as a consequence they would be going on a sightseeing tour.

'We shall go and see Lake Konigssee first,' he announced.

When pressed he had to admit that the delay was occasioned by the Fuhrer having not yet completed his afternoon sleep.

The Duke received this information impassively but out of sight of Hess Wallis raised an expressive eyebrow.

The mountain scenery was magnificent but the party was soon bored. After their long journey the last thing that any of them wanted was to sit in the car killing time.

The Duke leant forward and said to Hess whilst pointedly tapping the face of his wristwatch

'Rudolf my friend I think that we have had enough of this… and in any event the Duchess has a fear of heights and these mountain roads are upsetting her… so may we now proceed with our visit?'

'But of course Your Royal Highness. I am sure that the Fuhrer will now be ready to receive you when we arrive.'

Sir Vernon Kell was with Tar Robertson and Maxwell Knight, his two most senior operational officers in the rather scruffy offices of the Secret Service. It was a rare trip to the offices for Maxwell Knight who worked from home surrounded by his weird collection of animals in eccentric isolation much of the time.

'Now look chaps, I have carefully reviewed your reports and those of your officers and I think that we must set out our plans for the imminent if not immediate future. I make that qualification because Johnny and Celia are with the Duke and Duchess at Berchstesgaden with Herr Hitler as we speak. Now, dispositions.'

The others drew their notebooks closer and watched Sir Vernon intently.

'First, Vera Schalberg – or Von Wedel – as you wish, is now in London ostensibly at the behest of her new Abwehr masters endeavouring to work her way into London Society. Billy Brownlow is aiding her and pointing her towards those whose loyalties we regard as… let me say… less than assured. She is now a double agent but, we must accept that she is a very nimble young lady and adept at changing sides and allegiances as suits her.'

'Yes Sir Vernon, accepted, but only up to a point. I am genuinely of the belief that she and Billy have a very special bond' interjected Tar.

'What do you mean?' asked Sir Vernon.

'In confidence gentlemen she is carrying Billy's child. Apparently after what she suffered at the hands of her pervert husband Ignatieff she was told that childbearing was almost certainly out of the question. So you see…'

'Ah, yes… well, that puts a different complexion on things' Sir Vernon responded.

'The pregnancy isn't showing yet so she is off to Germany to put in a report on progress to date in setting up her little 'salon' of Hitler's British admirers and appeasers' Tar continued. 'Billy has been carefully introducing her to what I would call 'do nothing windbags'. There are a lot of them around who are openly admiring of the Nazi Germany portrayed in Doctor Goebbels propaganda. In some circles it is quite fashionable to do so but, deep down they will not actually do anything in our opinion.'

Sir Vernon was fiddling with his pipe but nodded for Tar to continue.

'Anyhow, Vera will see her husband. Of course he is now promoted General Von Wedel. He may be very … let's say understanding… but she believes that pregnancy might be a bit of a strain even for him to accept.'

She will then come back here and Billy is making arrangements for the child to be looked after – identity and so forth. The tricky thing is that Billy has no heir and has really fallen for the girl.'

'Yes, but what about the title?' asked Maxwell.

'There's the rub' responded Tar. 'He wants to acknowledge the child and for her to obtain a divorce and marry him as soon as possible.'

Sir Vernon harrumphed 'Well he might, but the immediate answer is no, absolutely not.'

Tar responded 'If I may Sir Vernon, the outline plan that I have agreed with Billy is that all will be kept 'sub rosa' for now. In due course a new identity can be arranged for Vera and Billy can marry her. To get around any other problems there may be an interim sham marriage on Billy's part – poste-haste – so that the child can apparently be born in wedlock. When he and Vera marry they will adopt the child.'

'Tar as ever you chaps seem to have come up with a solution but, I have to say, a damn convoluted one eh?' laughed Sir Vernon.

'I am afraid so but she is just too good a source to waste and Billy is a fine agent Sir Vernon.'

'Yes, yes… I have agreed. Right then, next. The beautiful Princess Stephanie von Hohenloe – another damned dangerous woman in my book. Maxwell… your view?'

'Sir Vernon, she is that and of course ferociously intelligent. Unlike Vera and Billy, her liaison with Johnny is one of convenient attraction. She knows her value and is another survivor. She is hedging her bets. Hers is a much trickier game and I will not be surprised if she drops out of the frame fairly soon. However, in the meantime she is exceptionally useful… after all she has the ear of the Fuhrer who treats her as a close confidante.'

Sir Vernon raised his hand to interject.

'She must find out what he and the Duke of Windsor discuss and anything of use that comes out of that tea party. Johnny will presumably deal with all that on his return?'

'Correct Sir Vernon.'

'Now we have this meeting in Washington between Cordell Hull the Secretary of State and Allen Dulles. They are clever blighters those Dulles men, so I have heard.' In Sir Vernon's terms, 'clever' in such a context was rarely a compliment and could be deeply derogatory.

Tar Robertson dealt with this. 'I have had a quiet word with the Legal Attache here in London, my old friend Chester Harris. I have mentioned him before, and I hardly need tell you that per tradition, his true role is head of American Intelligence Services here. He has put it to me that with Ambassador Bingham in failing health and with Joseph Kennedy tipped as the next incumbent we can expect greatly reduced 'under the counter' help from him and his colleagues. Kennedy is rabidly anti-British and FDR would dearly love to avoid posting him but apparently the immensely wealthy rogue – Chester's words, not mine – has the President and his party in hock and to be Ambassador in London is the deal.'

Sir Vernon interrupted 'Disgraceful that such a man – little short of a gangster – should be appointed to the Court of St James. It is not just the Democratic Party that is tied into him. President Roosevelt himself is personally. Even Roosevelt's son James is in business with him – they are sole importers of

Gordon's Gin and Dewar's whisky into the USA. Anyhow, I digress Tar, point taken though. Do carry on.'

'We have another card to play. Celia has a grand home in New York and is wonderfully well connected there. She will go straight over and stalk Allen Dulles. His reputation is as an inveterate womaniser and Celia will be sure to find out what is going on.' Tar informed the group.

'You sound very sure Tar?' questioned Sir Vernon.

'Oh yes, I most certainly am. We must not underestimate that young lady's abilities' continued Tar. 'On another subject, Charles Harvey tells me that the Duke has been in touch with his wife. She was of course – as Mrs Beauchamp – the King's housekeeper and at times confidante at Fort Belvedere. The Duke advises that he and the Duchess are looking for a permanent home in Paris and would like the Harveys to work for them.'

'Well, that could be convenient, but what does Charles think about it?' asked Sir Vernon.

'I have to say, he is less than keen. It is one thing to play the part of Johnny's 'man' every so often to pick up below stairs gossip – that has been darn useful on occasions – but quite another thing to enter into full time service. Elizabeth, his wife, feels a great obligation to the Duke as he was her benefactor, but Charles is set on retiring from the Service in two years when he is eligible. He wants a place in the country.'

Sir Vernon had listened to Tar carefully. After a pause he said

'Charles Harvey is a serving officer and my orders are that the post should be accepted. At the end of the two years they can resign. Understood?'

Tar and Maxwell Knight nodded .They well knew that Sir Vernon had made up his mind and that was the end of the matter.

'Ah, here we are – our Fuhrer's Berghof' announced Hess as the outriders pulled into the sides of the road in front of a narrow causeway that led to a modest gatehouse.

It was an unprepossessing single storey construction with a heavy stone pillared arch and an integral timber guardhouse to one side. The gates themselves were only waist high and looked lightly constructed.

Hess continued 'Normally there are many tourists, but today, as you will see, in honour of your visit only twenty have been permitted.'

'I have to say that it does not look a very formidable protection for the

Fuhrer's house' commented the Duke voicing the thoughts of all the guests.

Hess laughed. 'All you see is the public face of the entrance. Shortly you will see the true entrance to the Berghof.'

The car swept through the arch saluted by only two black-uniformed soldiers from the SS Regiment of Hitler's personal bodyguard.

As they swung around a corner they faced a massive stone wall pierced with weapon slits and behind a protective wall, twin-barrelled, rapid firing anti-aircraft gun manned by more black-uniformed and steel-helmeted SS soldiers who faced them menacingly.

The massively thick gates in the wall seemed to be made of steel and as the cavalcade of cars slowed down they opened slowly and were clearly mechanically operated.

As the gates opened wider they revealed a series of concrete and steel defensive firing positions bristling with machine guns served by yet more SS soldiers. Finally at each side of the road manned 88mm anti-tank guns faced the road.

'Ha!' laughed the Duke. 'I should have guessed that there would be some pretty heavy protection.'

'Actually there is much more that you cannot see' Hess confided. 'You have just driven along three kilometres of mined road controlled from the command room in the Berghof and monitored by camera – and that is just one thing. I can assure you that nothing is left to chance here. Now you will see the real Berghof.'

Their car swung into a large courtyard. On the steps in front of the tall open double doors stood the Fuhrer. He was wearing the plain brown double breasted jacket of a senior Nazi official, highly pressed black trousers and, rather incongruously, black patent leather shoes.

He was flanked by Doctor Robert Ley and another man who transpired to be Doctor Paul Schmidt the official German Foreign Office interpreter.

Wallis leant towards the Duke and muttered under her breath 'God, that awful man Ley is here.'

The Duke patted her hand and muttered back with a smile. 'Every organ grinder has a monkey.'

Wallis gave a throaty laugh. Hess looked on in puzzlement.

As their car drew to a halt the Fuhrer stepped forward. Despite his almost drab clothing and strikingly strange hair and moustache he emanated an immense sense of power and notwithstanding a smile, an air of menace.

Doctor Schmidt was behind Hitler but almost at his shoulder.

The Duke climbed out of the car first and then handed out Wallis. The Duke and Duchess and the Fuhrer bobbed their heads to each other, then in German the Fuhrer spoke as he stepped forward to shake his guests by the hand.

'It is a great pleasure for me to welcome you to my home in these beautiful mountains.'

Doctor Schmidt started to translate into English but the Duke interrupted him in his perfect German, raising his right hand with a smile.

'That will not be necessary, thank you… we understand perfectly well.'

Doctor Schmidt looked perplexed but since the Fuhrer had apparently chosen to ignore the Duke's remark he did not respond even though his strict orders were to translate all conversation in full.

Johnny, Celia and Dudley Forward had now also left the car and Hess stepped forward and after exchanging salutes with Hitler he formally introduced them to the Fuhrer.

Hitler smiled broadly for the first time as he was introduced to Celia.

'How could I forget such a beauty as you Lady Celia… in your case it is welcome back to the Berghof. I am sorry that Eva is not here… she would have been delighted to see you again.'

'Thank you for the welcome, and indeed the kind invitation Herr Fuhrer. I am sorry that I shall not be seeing Eva – she is such a sweet woman – please convey my very best wishes to her.'

'But of course, I shall be delighted to do that' responded the smiling Hitler ignoring the fact that he had expressly overruled Eva's repeated requests to be present.

'Now everybody, please follow me.'

Hitler turned and led the way up the steps and through the doorway into the hallway which was dominated by a display of cactus plants in large antique majolica vases.

He led them to an ante room where well-muscled young SS men took their coats, hats and the ladies' gloves.

As this was happening Hitler broke the silence.

'You will be interested to know that last year a re-modelling of the whole Berghof was completed to my design under the supervision of the architect

Alois Degano. My wish was to marry the need for technology – for this is after all a seat of Government – with our teutonic ideal and heritage and the beauty and majesty of our mountains.'

'Ah, quite,' responded the Duke, a little puzzled by Hitler's statement which almost sounded like a quotation from a guidebook.

The group was then led by the Fuhrer into the Great Hall, a vast room dominated by a picture window that was in effect a wall of glass framing a stunning view of the mountains.

'Oh my!' exclaimed Wallis. 'What a view Herr Hitler… it is breath-taking.'

She had clearly reacted just as Hitler had hoped.

'Your Royal Highness I am so pleased that you and I appreciate the finer things… what could be purer than such an unsullied view?'

Doctor Schmidt started to translate but was irritably interrupted by the Duke.

'Really, I have already told you, no translation please… in any event what you have just said is inaccurate.'

This time Hitler clearly took note and turning to the hapless translator instructed him, 'I shall inform you as and when any translation is required.' He turned towards the Duke and Duchess and continued. 'These are the mountains of Austria that you see in all their glory. This window can be screened by an armoured shield in seconds.'

The Duke could not resist asking Johnny in his capacity as an international art dealer for his opinion of the huge painting adorning one of the walls of the Great Hall.

'Well Sir, if I am not much mistaken that is 'Venus and Amor' by Paris… quite a contrast to the mountain view.' Johnny kept a straight face as he said this to the Duke whilst both of them looked at the voluptuous naked reclining woman who dominated the picture.

Hitler continued as he led them into his commodious study which was panelled in rare cembra pine.

'This place is mine… I built it with the money I earned from Mein Kampf.'

The Duke caught Johnny's eye but did not give the slightest hint that he would regard such a statement as being in poor taste.

Hitler then took the covers off some bird cages in each of which there was a small rather insignificant looking bird. As one they started to sing. At first the sound was strangely mechanical but then became loudly tuneful.

'And these are...?' The Duke asked with a smile.

'Ah, they are my Hartz Roller canaries bred in the Hartz Mountains of Germany, not for their beauty but their singing. See, their beaks do not move as they sing.'

'Fascinating, eh Wallis?'

Wallis smiled and replied.

'Wonderful my dear... Herr Hitler you are a man of many surprises I think.'

'My Dear Duchess, are we not all a paradox to a degree?'

He smiled almost wistfully to Wallis as he spoke and then after a pause, repeated

'Yes, a paradox.'

Chapter 8

Billy and Vera were relaxing in his exclusive London apartment, known as a 'set', in The Albany, just off London's Piccadilly.

He had not brought her home before as previously he had always visited her in her apartment. However things had now changed dramatically and they had serious plans to make not only for themselves but also their unborn child.

Vera was intrigued by the apartment and its surroundings.

'Billy, before we talk about anything else, tell me about this place… it seems so strange right in the centre of the City… almost like an oasis.'

'Well, it is quite simple really but, in a way, a typically English sort of thing I suppose. The original building was known as Melbourne House and in 1791 Prince Frederick the Duke of York and Albany took up residence. In 1802 the architect Henry Holland converted it into over sixty bachelor apartments. They were known as 'sets' simply because they were 'sets of rooms'. No women were allowed, no children, dogs or pets, in fact noise of any sort was forbidden. In common with the nearby Burlington Arcade, which was built rather later, whistling and running were expressly forbidden. I'm not sure how many whistling runners there would have been here but… there you are… banning them was obviously considered important.'

Billy laughed at Vera's puzzled expression and continued 'Anyhow, women have been permitted since 1880 so you will not be thrown out!'

'That's a relief!' laughed Vera. 'But if the 'no children' rule still applies I shall not be able to stay here once our child is born.'

'I'm afraid so but we'll have to box clever on that whole issue. I am working on a plan that will keep you safe and enable our child to inherit my titles, properties and so on. Obviously we cannot marry at the moment.'

'That's for sure' replied Vera somberly. 'I must keep up the facade of my marriage to Von Wedel and of course my role as an Abwehr agent here in London. I do not plan to be in Germany for more than a week or so when I return. I shall make my reports, play the dutiful General's wife for a few days and then return to you.'

'Well one thing's for sure, the Gestapo will not dare to touch an Abwehr General's wife who is on the active list.'

'I wouldn't be so sure… frankly I am still very nervous but there is really no alternative. I must report as ordered, whatever the risks.'

Billy looked very thoughtful as he commented 'You know darling I would give anything for you not to go but, if you do not, there will be an immediate suspicion that you have been turned and become a British agent. Then you would lose the protection that you now have. There is no doubt that Himmler's SD are prepared to do his dirty work abroad.'

Billy stroked her hair, playing with it and curling it around all of his fingers as he did so.

'Ah, there… do you hear that? Those are the clock chimes of St James' Church… that's the other thing living here, you don't need a clock' laughed Billy. 'Right then, we are due to be at Daisy Fellowes' place in an hour and I expect that you will want to get ready?'

'Most certainly I do. Just one thing before that Billy. I would like a guarantee that both my child and I will be safe so far as the British authorities are concerned even if I have to apparently act against British interests in my role as an Abwehr agent.'

'I totally understand, Vera. I know that both Tar Robertson and Maxwell Knight have stressed to Sir Vernon that double agents like you must be protected and immune from risk of prosecution or hostile action. Please leave this to me. I shall ensure that your position is secure and safe before your trip back to Germany and that you have satisfactory proof of immunity.'

'Thank you Billy… that would be a big weight off my mind. Now come with me… I am going to have a bath and I need you to scrub my back… unless that too is forbidden by the Albany rules?'

The Duke of Windsor was enjoying the Fuhrer's company and for his part Hitler was going out of his way to be charming to his guests.

Wallis was finding him more interesting than she had expected. She was inevitably attracted by men who exuded power and this strange and unnaturally pale man certainly fulfilled that expectation. His eyes fascinated her with a staring quality that she found almost hypnotic. His voice was a warm baritone and surprisingly soft compared with the almost screeching tones and straining vocal chords of the recorded speeches that she had heard. His delicate hands were also a surprise; more those of a pianist than a soldier.

Hitler had instructed Paul Schmidt to translate for the benefit of Wallis since the Duke and he were conversing in German. Wallis could follow some of the conversation but was largely excluded by the Duke's constant interruptions of the translator who was clearly annoying him.

In the perfect high German of his family upbringing the Duke repeatedly complained 'No, that is incorrect… that is not an accurate translation.'

Ultimately the exasperated translator gave up. This afforded Wallis an opportunity to look around the enormous room with its bright red carpet, wall hanging tapestries depicting mythical teutonic scenes, oak panelling and a grand piano on which stood a bust of the Fuhrer's beloved composer Wagner. Again Wallis was surprised to note that in so overtly masculine surroundings the room was filled with flowers.

'This man really is a paradox' she thought to herself. 'He mixes the pomp and militaristic spectacle of his immense power with this softer sensitive side.'

Tea was ordered by the Fuhrer. The conversation was superficial and almost banal. In spite of the presence of the Fuhrer's official photographer, Deputy Fuhrer Rudolf Hess, Hitler's 'special adviser', Walter Hewel, Doctor Robert Ley, who was mercifully subdued in Wallis' opinion, and the Duke's party it reminded Johnny of a polite English tea party akin to when his parents invited the vicar and his wife for a duty visit.

Tea was being served when the Fuhrer suddenly stood and fixing the Duke with his compelling stare spoke in a firm tone 'Your Royal Highness. Come with me to my Teehaus. It is only a short walk across the Obersalzberg Valley, less than a kilometre, and we may converse in private.'

'Most certainly' responded the Duke smiling broadly. 'After so much travelling I welcome an opportunity to stretch my legs. Wallis darling you will excuse me?'

'But naturally dearest' Wallis replied bestowing a warm smile on both the Duke and the Fuhrer.

As the Duke and the Fuhrer left the Berghof they were joined by two black

Scottie terriers who scampered around and sniffed at their trouser legs as they set off at a fast pace.

'Ah these are Eva's dogs. I am afraid that she could not join us today but her dogs have. I prefer my German Shepherds but they are not allowed to roam around like these two.'

The Duke stopped and squatting down on his heals made a fuss of the dogs. He looked up at the Fuhrer and said with a smile 'Actually I am something of a terrier man myself… the Duchess and I have a pair… all terriers have great personalities I find.'

Hitler ignored the Duke's comment and abruptly changed the subject. 'You know that Lord Halifax the British politician visited me here just three days ago?'

'Yes, I had heard but, since we have been so busy travelling I have no detail.' The Duke had been told of the visit by his cousin Charles, Duke of Saxe-Coburg Gotha at the dinner hosted by the cousin for the visitors in Nuremburg. 'The visit was organised by Princess Stephanie von Hohenloe… I believe that you know her… she lives in London now.'

'Yes, I do. She is a long standing friend of Her Royal Highness, the Duchess… they were close neighbours at one time as I recall.'

'A remarkable woman' the Fuhrer enthused. 'She shows true wisdom and a deft diplomatic hand. I greatly value her advice. The purpose of Lord Halifax visiting was to assure me of the stance that Britain would take in relation to German intentions in mainland Europe and, possibly, to the East. He told me that both Prime Minister Chamberlain and the King were fully supportive of his visiting me and, indeed, encouraged him to do so.'

'That is interesting' commented the Duke. 'I got into very hot water when I poked my nose into political matters when I was King, as you may know.'

Hitler nodded. 'Yes, so I gathered, but apparently your brother has been doing so.'

'I am surprised. In my opinion the King is weak and is totally under the thumb of his anti-German advisers Sir Alexander Hardinge and Sir Robert Vansittart. They are an evil influence. I digress… what precisely did Lord Halifax ask of you?'

'It was rather a case of his telling me of the British position rather than making any request. I was left with the firm impression that Britain would support Germany in opposing any Japanese and Russian accord and would not provide any active support to the French in any arrangement that they might have with Russia.'

'That must have given you considerable comfort Herr Hitler?'

'It most certainly did and I stressed to him that neither I, the German people nor their Government have any wish to find ourselves in conflict with Great Britain or its Colonies and Empire.'

'That is admirable and I have to say that speaking for myself I can see no reason why Britain should have any interest in the lands to the East of Germany which I believe to be of, let's say, interest, to you.'

The path narrowed and it was a minute before the two could walk side by side again and continue their conversation.

'Your Royal Highness, we have previously canvassed the idea of your becoming the King Emperor of a united Germany and Britain. You were willing to accept our offer of that role?'

'Most certainly, with Wallis at my side naturally.'

'But of course. Her Royal Highness will be your Queen.'

'Herr Hitler, I cannot put it plainer than this… the German and British races are one, they should always be one.'

'Are you saying that both races are of Hun origin?'

'I most certainly am… look at me. I am German and yet I was King of England.'

They had now reached the Teehaus and sat down on a rustic wooden bench in front of the small wooden building. There was a commanding view of the whole valley. A traditionally dressed maid brought a large tray and from a side table served tea and the Fuhrer's beloved torte.

The Duke declined the rich and cream filled cake. Remembering Celia's vivid description of the Fuhrer's eating habits he was not surprised at the gluttonous way in which Hitler demolished a large slice of the cake.

'Hmm… that was excellent' beamed the Fuhrer as he wiped cream and crumbs from his moustache. The terriers were jumping up excitedly. If they had been the Duke's dogs he or Wallis would have given them some cake as a treat.

Hitler appeared to read his mind as he said 'My German Shepherd, Blondi, is too well trained to beg at table like this. To do so shows weakness in the owner as much as the dog don't you think?'

Without hesitation the Duke responded hypocritically. 'But of course it does.' The Duke was not minded to contradict his host.

The Fuhrer was not to be diverted from the subject that was uppermost in his mind and then continued almost fervently.

'I believe that you and I and the British Government recognise that the greatest threat to peace, stability and prosperity in Europe lies with Bolshevik Russia. I also believe that as indicated by Lord Halifax and now your visit it is implicit that Britain recognises that a strong Germany must stand against and challenge the threat of communism, if necessary by force of arms. That is so?'

The Duke was still avoiding any disagreement with his host and responded enthusiastically. 'But, of course. I totally understand the Bolshevik threat. I only have to think of my family members who were vilely butchered.'

'It is good that we have no misunderstanding' responded a now smiling Fuhrer. 'And now I think that we should return.'

The Duke did not realise that he had inadvertently encouraged Hitler's vision that Britain, whose intervention he feared more than any other nation, would not challenge Germany as its armies fulfilled his dream of overwhelming the countries to the East and then the greatest prize of all, Russia. The Duke and the Fuhrer spoke little as they walked back briskly and rejoined the remainder of the group.

'Ah Mein Fuhrer. I trust that you and the Duke enjoyed some wonderful fresh air and exercise with your tea?' asked a smiling Rudolf Hess.

'Most certainly Rudolf. We had a most helpful and productive conversation did we not Your Royal Highness?' responded a smiling Hitler turning to the Duke.

'Rather. Most enlightening,' the Duke replied, returning the smiles.

It was clear that the visit was drawing to an end and the Duke thanked the Fuhrer for his hospitality. After coats and hats were collected the visitors were escorted back to their cars. The Duke beamed as the Fuhrer took both of Wallis' hands and held them as if this were the parting of old friends. She too was clearly delighted as was recorded in an official photograph which was released to the World's Press.

As the cavalcade drew away Hitler turned to Paul Schmidt and said 'She would have, or correctly I should say, she will make a good Queen.'

The motorcycle outriders cleared the roads ahead of the cavalcade which returned the Windsors and their party to the station. The special train was waiting and prepared in readiness to take them to Munich where Rudolf Hess and his wife were to host a dinner party in honour of the Duke and Duchess.

Once settled in their luxurious carriage the small British party could relax. Rudolf Hess and Doctor Ley were to follow later.

'Well that sure was an interesting visit' drawled Wallis. 'Herr Hitler is a fascinating man… even without those magnetic eyes… but they really are the icing on the cake.'

The Duke roared with laughter. 'Only Celia and I can truly see the funniest side of what you have said… 'icing on the cake'. It is positively hazardous to be in the vicinity of the man when he sets about his beloved torte. What say you Celia?'

'I have to agree. I wasn't sure that you all believed me but now you know. He's very impressive though don't you think?'

'I agree with much of what he says you know' responded the Duke. 'But I am uncomfortable with some of his notions. He seems to say that the Jews and other "unacceptable minority groups", as he describes them, must be removed from the Greater Germany. When I asked whether he meant enforced emigration he did not answer me directly.'

Wallis smiled. 'Whilst you were away with Hitler Celia and I asked Rudolf Hess about this and he said that he believes that these people should be found homes away from Germany. He did not hint at any other solution.'

'Now then, dinner tonight Chez Hess' interrupted the Duke, clearly signalling a change of subject. 'We have an interesting fellow there… he will act as interpreter Wallis… he was born in Bradford and then taken to South Africa as an infant. He eventually studied in German Universities and is now an SS Lieutenant General. He works with Hess. Interesting fellow.'

Wallis poured herself a drink as she listened.

'I feel a certain affinity with him you know. He too is caught between the two nations. The one of his birth and the other of his blood and heritage. Of one thing I am certain after what we have seen around Germany and, of course today's meeting, as I said when I addressed one of Doctor Ley's Labour Front meetings, what I have seen in Germany is nothing short of a miracle… and can only be understood when one realises that behind it all there is but one man and one will.'

After his guests had departed the Fuhrer allowed himself a broad smile of satisfaction and striding through his sprawling house hummed the tune that unbidden so often came into his mind 'Who's afraid of the big bad wolf?'

* * *

Prime Minister Neville Chamberlain was in a meeting with Anthony Eden, the Foreign Secretary, Lord Halifax, Sir Robert Vansittart of the Foreign Office, Sir Alexander Hardinge, the King's Private Secretary, and Sir Vernon Kell of the Security Service. The Prime Minister was clearly annoyed.

'Like it or not the Duke of Windsor is doing immense harm with this infernal gallivanting around Germany as if he is a puppet of the Nazi regime. We have done all that we can to keep the lid on the British press and newsreels but the story, albeit toned down, is still headline news.'

'At least they are not showing him giving his Nazi salutes' commented the suave and elegant Anthony Eden. 'There is no doubt that he has been throwing them up at every opportunity and the idea that he is merely waving to acknowledge the crowds is preposterous.'

'My concern is precisely what message he has given to Herr Hitler either deliberately or, with his penchant for gaffes, inadvertently' responded Antony Eden. The immensely tall slightly cadaverous Lord Halifax commented.

'When I met Herr Hitler just a few days ago I was extremely careful in what I said but I am not convinced that he fully appreciated the finer nuances of my remarks. That is always the problem when there is an interpreter involved.'

Sir Vernon cleared his throat. 'Prime Minister, as you are aware there are two of my agents in the Duke's party and arrangements are in place to ascertain precisely what passed between the Duke and Herr Hitler. I would also add that Mr Hoover the head of the American FBI is sending his Assistant Director and head of Counter Espionage, Percy Foxworth, to London and he will be meeting my people in company with their head of station here.'

Prime Minister Chamberlain visibly stiffened as this was said and appeared about to speak but Sir Vernon held the stage.

'Their specific concern is the security threat posed by the Duchess of Windsor. I am at liberty to tell you that the FBI is of the view that if the United States were not constrained by other considerations... diplomatic and political... the Duchess would be arrested and charged with treason.'

'That is somewhat dramatic stuff Sir Vernon!' commented the Prime Minister acerbically.

He was instantly corrected by Sir Robert Vansittart. 'It is no surprise to me. My own investigations are entirely consistent. Sir Vernon, have the Americans given any hint of what they have unearthed?'

'Unofficially they corroborate our suspicions and concerns. However they are also focusing on the man Charles Bedaux… you will recall that he hosted the Windsors' wedding in France. They believe that he is an active Nazi agent and acting in conspiracy with some very powerful people in the United States and Europe.' The look of distaste on the Prime Minister's face was even more pronounced as he tried to conclude the meeting there and then, saying 'Gentlemen, Sir Anthony and I must return to the House shortly… do we have any conclusion?'

Sir Vernon was not to be put off by so hackneyed a line and spoke again. 'Prime Minister my department will be assisting the Americans in the… let us call it… removal of the man Bedaux from their shores. It is in our interest to do so because however much damage the Windsors' German tour may cause, it is as nothing to the harm that will be wreaked if their planned American visit goes ahead. We intend to manipulate matters with their co-operation, rid America of Bedaux and stymie the Windsors' plans.'

'Excellent. Are we agreed gentlemen?' As they all nodded assent the Prime Minister closed the meeting.

Back in his office Sir Vernon had summoned Tar Robertson and Maxwell Knight. 'Well chaps, a little white lie did the trick… I could not risk our squeamish PM letting things slip through his fingers again. Tar, please get onto your friend in the US Embassy, Chester Harris and make sure that you persuade him to get this. Percy Foxworth fellow over here as a matter of the utmost urgency.'

Almost as an after-thought again Sir Vernon added 'Oh by the way…rather reluctantly the PM has agreed to immunity for our double agents and the Attorney General has been instructed to prepare documentation immediately. Please inform Billy and he can tell Vera that she need have no concern pending the formal documentation since I hold the signed private minutes of my conversation with the Prime Minister.'

Chapter 9

Frau Hess was nervous. She and husband Rudolf were to entertain the Duke and Duchess of Windsor and their two intimate friends, Celia and Johnny, that evening. An informal supper party was to be held at their home in Munich. Her husband the Deputy Fuhrer and, contrary to popular belief, a man of great influence over Adolf Hitler, tried to reassure her. 'Ilse my love, do stop fretting – it will be perfect, you will see.'

'But the Duke and Duchess are royalty and the other two are aristocrats – I feel so humble and I am sure that I shall say or do the wrong thing.'

'Now, listen to me. I have spent considerable time with them all including most of today and I can assure you that they are charming. The Duke speaks perfect German and the Duchess a little. Anyhow, our friend Wilhelm Bohle will be here and has agreed to act as her interpreter, also for the other two English guests. So please, no more worrying. This is to be a totally informal evening at the Duke's request – he felt that everyone had had enough of dressing up and should be able to totally relax and that includes you.'

Ilse Hess smiled. 'Oh, I know but compared with the Duchess and Lady Celia I feel so dowdy – let's face it, whatever the hairdresser does I still look as though I have just been walking in the wind.'

'That is precisely why I wished to have this supper at home. You are the epitome of ideal German motherhood in every sense and that includes your hair. Hanna Reitsch is a good friend and another guest. She is more interested in her flying than clothes and make-up. She will get on well with the Duke. He loves flying and as our only woman test pilot I am sure that he will find her fascinating.'

* * *

'Interesting evening ahead I believe – what do you think Johnny?' asked the Duke of Windsor who was enjoying a quick drink with Johnny before leaving for the supper party at the Hess home.

Johnny looked again at the guest list and short profiles provided by the ever efficient protocol office of Herr Strack and replied 'Well the guest list is, that's for sure. Wilhelm Bohle seems a decent enough fellow and Hanna Reitsch is fascinating. She's not only an outstanding pilot but also a pin up girl for the Nazi government. Celia met Elly Beinhorn the other German woman flying ace and her husband Bernd Rosemeyer when she was over for the Nuremburg Rally. There is also Sefton Delmer, Beaverbrook's Daily Express Berlin correspondent. Another interesting one. Born in Germany but then came to England and went to St Paul's School in London and then up to Oxford. I've met him a few times, he certainly still has a bit of a German accent.'

The Duke commented 'I have rather taken to Herr Hess. At first he seemed to be brooding but actually I think that is the impression given by his saturnine looks, you know what I mean, his dark eyes under those great black bushy eyebrows. Anyhow, he is a very powerful and thoughtful man in my assessment.

'Ah, here are the ladies looking splendid as ever,' said the smiling Duke as he and Johnny leapt to their feet.

'Now David' drawled Wallis. 'Don't use up all your charm before we meet our hostess and the other guests.' Wallis was wearing a closely tailored dark blue silk Schiaperrelli dress that accentuated her slim figure. Against the dark material her flamingo brooch of diamonds, emeralds, rubies and sapphires sparkled and flashed, as did the Jarretiere bracelet that the Duke had commissioned whilst they were forced to be apart at the time of her divorce. He had given it to her on their wedding day.

The King and Queen received Prime Minister Neville Chamberlain at Buckingham Palace.

After the formal greetings the King suggested that Sir Alexander Hardinge his Private Secretary should be invited to join them. The Prime Minister readily agreed. After everyone was settled Chamberlain tackled the issue that was on all their minds.

'Your Majesties, it behoves me to appraise you of the views of your Government and in particular the Cabinet in connection with the current and planned activities of the Duke and Duchess of Windsor. I must preface such with the sincere qualification that such views give no comfort and are communicated with regret.'

Chamberlain carried with him the air of a straitlaced and humourless schoolmaster.

'I shall not generally refer to the Duchess but, rather the Duke as a Prince of the Blood and a senior member of the Royal Family. The Duchess is relevant however and casts a shadow over the matters concerning the Duke to which I shall refer.'

Sir Alexander Hardinge felt a stirring of impatience. Chamberlain's approach was as ever pedantic and didactic, and he found it deeply irritating. 'I believe that your position is well understood Prime Minister and I suggest that you provide us with your views.' Both the King and Queen nodded their agreement.

Chamberlain either did not notice or chose to ignore the impatience of his audience and continued 'Very well, if I may I shall comment on the Duke's present visit to Germany.

'It is feared that not only the visit in itself but also the way in which it has been stage managed by Herr Hitler's lieutenants has given the impression that the British Government and Monarchy supports the Nazi Government of Germany. On the contrary, there are elements of German Government policy with which the British Government takes issue, in particular, the treatment of minority elements of their society.'

The King interrupted at that point 'Are y y you s s s sure tha aat these st st stories are t t true?'

'Sir, we have it on good authority that the Nazi government is pursuing Herr Hitler's philosophy as spelt out in the two volumes of his at times impenetrable political treatise 'Mein Kampf' Your Government has received detailed reports of actions against the Jewish and Roma communities and political opponents of the regime that are at best oppressive and at worst, unacceptable by our, or indeed any, civilised standards.'

The King and Queen nodded.

'The activities of the German Government are skilfully portrayed and stage managed by the very powerful Ministry of Propaganda run by Minister Doctor Joseph Goebbels. It is that Ministry that has masterminded the set pieces of the Duke's visit – everything from the military bands, cheering crowds at every station when they arrive chanting 'Seig Windsor' and 'We want the Duchess' amongst other things.'

The Queen looked at her husband knowingly and her voice dripping acid declared 'That woman must be wallowing in such attention!'

Chamberlain continued in his monotonous style. 'The Duke has acknowledged Nazi salutes in kind and although we have censored their publication in the United Kingdom, they have been widely seen abroad. This leads me to the next point of concern, namely the Duke's planned visit to the United States of America.'

The King spluttered as he drew deeply on his cigarette and gestured wildly that he wished to speak. When his coughing fit was over, in a weak voice he said 'I I I I d don't c c care h ho how bbut t t that mm must n n not h h happen.'

Alexander Hardinge noting not only the King's distress but also that the Queen was looking both angry and at the same time concerned as she laid a hand on the King's sleeve added 'Prime Minister, I understand from Sir Robert Vansittart that the Foreign Office has made it plain to the American State Department that any such visit is by nature an entirely private affair. The Duke has apparently indicated already that having been entertained by Herr Hitler he expects the President to extend the same courtesy. Our Ambassador has been instructed to indicate that the visit to Herr Hitler created no precedent and it would be preferred that the President does not issue an invitation.'

Chamberlain quickly responded 'Your Majesties it is my experience that our American friends do not take kindly to what they regard as imperialistic interference. My recommendation is that another means be employed.'

Hardinge was looking as puzzled as the King and it was the Queen who asked 'Precisely what do you have in mind Prime Minister? Surely this is a matter to be addressed through the normal diplomatic channels?'

Smiling thinly Chamberlain replied 'With respect, Ma'am, I believe not. I understand that our intelligence services have identified an indirect and un-attributable course of action which is intended to cause the whole visit to be cancelled. I would ask that for the time being nothing is done on the diplomatic front. There is another issue that must be borne in mind. The Duchess is an American and to many of her compatriots something of a heroine. That too will weigh in the President's mind as will the reaction of many albeit ill-informed working people if he declines to meet a former King who professes to be their champion. I do not normally agree with Herbert Morrison MP, the leader of the London County Council Your Majesties. However he has said in effect that the choice before ex Kings is either to fade away or become a nuisance and that the Duke would be wise to fade however hard that might be for him…'

'W www would that h h he w w w will' muttered the King. 'I I I a g agree w with your somewhat mysterious proposal' continued the King. The Queen nodded in agreement.

Chamberlain summed up. 'Very well, I believe that it is agreed that in the first instance we allow an opportunity for arrangements for the proposed visit to founder. May I take that as a decision?'

Everybody concurred and with the usual formalities the Prime Minister left. As soon as he had gone Alexander Hardinge who had established himself as a close confidante of both the King and Queen could not suppress a broad smile. 'It is surely evidence that our Prime Minister is a politician at heart that he, as a man who abhors intelligence operations on principle and will not take account of information gleaned from clandestine sources, is now proposing to employ the 'dark arts' himself!'

'Phwah!' exclaimed the Queen who then laughed and riposted 'I really do not mind what means are employed to scupper that ghastly woman's ambitions.'

Ilse Hess soon realised that her fears had been unfounded. The Duke and Duchess were charming and relaxed as were the two guests who accompanied them.

Over the initial drinks Wilhelm Bohle not only acted as interpreter but was affable in himself joking about his English birth and wondering whether he had a regional accent having been born in and spent his early years in Bradford. Sefton Delmer was suave and behaved more like a diplomat than a journalist. He too bridged the language gap effortlessly but as Johnny had earlier observed definitely had a trace of a German accent. 'Delmer responded to Bohle saying 'My dear fellow you have no Yorkshire accent and that is fact. However I was educated and brought up in England and yet I have German accent for which I cannot account.' His response prompted a gust of laughter in the already relaxed atmosphere.

The conversation faltered when the diminutive Hanna Reitsch entered the reception room. She was strikingly pretty with sparkling blue eyes, blonde hair and an infectious smile that was almost a grin. Even beside the Duke and Duchess she was tiny.

'I say' said the smiling Duke after they had been formally introduced. 'I expected a much more robust lady as Germany's leading test pilot.'

'Oh, I manage Your Royal Highness… actually it is an advantage being small and light particularly if the aircraft struggles to keep in the air.' As her response was translated everybody joined in the laughter. Any ice was broken and Rudolf Hess remarked with the hint of a smile 'Do not be misled, this young lady has wrists and nerves of steel.'

As the small group circulated Celia and Sefton Delmer found themselves talking to Hanna Reitsch. He was asking about the aircraft she had recently been testing and in particular the revolutionary helicopter the un-glamourously named Focke-Achgelis Fa 61.

'It is extraordinary,' she commented with her famous ready smile. 'To be able to take off and land without an airstrip and even to hover over one place. It is better than being a bird I think.'

'And I believe that you are the only woman to have flown the aircraft?' asked Sefton Delmer.

'Yes, that is so… in fact very few people have flown it. I have been asked to demonstrate its capabilities actually inside the Deutschlandhalle at the next Berlin Motor Show which will be quite a challenge I think.'

Celia commented. 'That sounds jolly dangerous to me. Changing the subject, you must know Elly Beinhorn – I met her when I attended the Nuremburg Rally. She was with her husband the racing driver.'

'But of course I know her very well .She has generally concentrated on long distance flying challenges. She is very frustrated at the moment. She is due to have her first child in November and has not been allowed to fly for some time.'

Celia decided to take the risk of testing the water a little and commented 'When I met him he said that he would be unlikely to wear his official uniform as a grand prix driver let alone that of the SS of which Herr Himmler made him a member,' commented Celia earning a sharp look from Sefton Delmer who recognised just how dangerous such a comment could be in the ever suspicious Nazi regime.

Hanna laughed as she replied 'Lady Celia, if you are a national hero of the stature of Bernd Rosemeyer you do not need to wear a uniform if you choose not to. On the other hand, I am proud to wear my uniform as a Flight Captain of the Reich.'

At that moment they were called in to supper.

Wallis was seated on the right of Rudolf Hess with Wilhelm Bohle on her other side. Bohle had already proved himself to be a charming and amusing companion and whereas the Deputy Fuhrer's natural diffidence in such social circumstances translated into an apparent awkwardness Bohle revelled in the company of this fascinating and well-travelled woman.

The Duke was sitting on the right side of Ilse Hess. She proved to be an excellent dinner companion and as her confidence grew it became clear that she was no mere housewife but actually played an important role in her husband's thinking and political philosophy. The more time that he spent talking with her the more the Duke was impressed. She was no conventional beauty but her direct and forthright manner reflected her intelligent eyes and firm jaw.

'Your husband is Deputy Fuhrer. Does that mean that he deputes for the Fuhrer or, does he act on his own initiative?' asked the Duke.

Ilse Hess paused before she spoke 'Your Royal Highness my answer is that he fulfils both roles. He has played a very influential part in forming the cult of the Fuhrer that is so pivotal now in the Third Reich. Rudolf considered that without a true figurehead leader the nation could drift back into the disastrous doldrums as happened in the Weimar Republic. It was Rudolf who first addressed the Fuhrer as 'Mein Fuhrer' and it was he who created the universal salutation 'Heil Hitler' and the populist slogan 'Adolf Hitler is Germany and Germany is Adolf Hitler.' It is he who has organised the Nuremburg Rallies which both galvanise and cement the will of the people. However, he is also prepared to subjugate his earlier role when the Fuhrer was to an extent his protégé and is now content to act fully and sincerely in his support. I am sorry, that was rather a speech… I do apologise.'

'Not at all, that was most interesting Frau Hess. I note that your husband does not drink alcohol and appears to be a vegetarian… is that so?'

Ilse Hess gave a chuckle 'Even great men have their weaknesses and in Rudolf's case it is a sort of hypochondria – he is always complaining about his digestion. He became so obsessed that he took his own food with him when he visited the Fuhrer. Adolf was so incensed that he refused to eat with Rudolf so now they dine in separate rooms.'

As they both laughed the Duke responded, 'That certainly is extraordinary. Clearly they are two most singular fellows. Now then, you met as students when you lodged in the same house I believe?'

* * *

Admiral Canaris the head of Geman military intelligence, the Abwehr, had just finished a staff meeting with his most senior officers. He had asked the recently promoted General Von Wedel to remain and they were now alone.

'Hans-Friedrich I asked you to stay because I must broach a delicate matter with you. Your wife Vera is now London based and due here for debriefing very shortly. Her brief was and remains to assist in compiling a list of British people of influence who are either supportive of German interests generally or admire the achievements of the Third Reich. She is also to identify those who for other reasons would seek an accommodation, even a unification between Germany and Great Britain.'

'That is correct Herr Admiral.'

'I am further informed that at the request of Joachim Von Ribbentrop when you were in Vianna she was instructed to find out what a particular British agent's brief was. Is that correct?'

'It is. We were in the Hotel Bristol and von Ribbentrop approached me shortly before I had to return to Germany.'

'I anticipate that von Ribbentrop applied some, let us call it 'pressure' to ensure that you complied with his request?'

'He did. He alluded to his having had a relationship with Vera in Paris when she was a very young dancer there, before she married the appalling Count Ignatieff. He also hinted that her bloodline was less than pure.'

'In other words, he threatened you?'

'He indicated that he could cause me embarrassment. I took it as a threat and in any event, Vera and I have an understanding. Let us say that I was prepared to turn a blind eye. She is after all a very young, spirited and attractive woman and thirty years younger than me.'

The Admiral felt great sympathy for his old friend and colleague and said. 'Von Ribbentrop is over reaching himself in trying to curry favour with the Fuhrer. He has done very well so far but he has some implacable enemies in the upper reaches of the Nazi Party, not least Himmler and Heydrich. Goebbels is no fan either.'

Von Wedel nodded in acknowledgment.

'I should like your wife to continue with her mission. The British agent with whom she is involved is a highly regarded member of Sir Vernon Kell's organisation. They will seek to turn her as you can guess. Are you prepared to act as if nothing is happening? I ask you because she is potentially of greater value to us if the British believe that they have turned her without our knowledge.'

'For two reasons I shall do so. First because I truly care for her and, to be blunt, she is safer in England than here under the nose of the Gestapo. Perhaps I care for her more akin to a father than a husband. Secondly, it is my duty.'

'This looks as though it will be great fun,' laughed the Duke as their small party was led to their table in the Hofbrauhaus am Platzl in the heart of Munich by the innkeeper Hans Bacherl. Ernst Wilhelm Bohle with whom both the Duke and Duchess had struck up an instant friendship accompanied the couple as did Celia, Johnny and Sefton Delmer.

The huge room with its high painted vaulted ceiling was packed and the band broke from the tune that they were playing to welcome these special guests with a stirring fanfare. For a moment there was a hush amongst the hundreds of drinkers, then there was a mighty cheer as they all stood and raised their stone beer mugs and toasted these special guests.

'I should have worn my shorts,' joked the Duke to Wallis as they sat down. Wallis and Celia were presented with small tankards of beer whilst the Duke and Johnny received large ones like the rest of the men. They were served by a pretty girl in traditional costume.

Johnny leant over the table almost shouting to make himself heard over the roar of voices and the band. 'How on earth do these waitresses manage to carry so many large mugs of beer at the same time?'

Bohle responded with a laugh. 'These Munich girls are very tough however pretty they may be. They have a long tradition and such girls have worked here since it opened as the Royal alehouse in 1589. It was only in 1828 that it became a public beer-house – that's the origin of the toast that you will hear here regularly. Now you must all try the famous Weisswurst and some dumplings.' He was aware from the previous evening's dinner that both the Duke and Duchess ate very sparingly and with a broad smile said 'You cannot leave Bavaria without tasting this marvellous Bavarian food and that will include also delicious suckling pig with the most wonderful crackling you will ever taste.'

'Faced with that charming persuasion General we shall oblige' replied the broadly smiling Duke who then raised his beer stein to Bohle and nodding shouted 'I propose a toast!' As they rose to their feet drinkers on neighbouring tables did so and soon nobody was left sitting in the vast room.

The Duke seized the moment and climbed onto his chair to a great cheer from the crowd. With his beer mug raised in his right hand he paused for a few moments and silence fell.

'Good people of Bavaria I wish you to know that Her Royal Highness the Duchess and I love your beautiful city and wish you every good fortune in the future. A toast – to Munich and its fine people!'

The throng responded with a roar, repeated the toast and then cheered enthusiastically some banging their stone beer mugs on the tables. With a final wave the broadly smiling Duke jumped down from his chair and as he and his party all sat down and the cheering faded he shouted to his companions. 'Dashed fine place this and by Jove I have an appetite and a great thirst.'

'Spoken like a Bavarian!' responded Bohle. 'Now, some food and more beer I think.'

The mood was light hearted and the food as delicious as Bohle had promised. The Duke had insisted that both Bohle and Sefton Delmer dispense with formality and Christian names be used.

The lively drinkers on a nearby table who were all wearing traditional costume sent a waitress to the Duke's table with another round of beer. Accompanying her was another waitress who presented the Duke with a side plate on which there was a false toothbrush moustache.

Laughing the Duke slipped the elastic over his head and with the moustache in place raised his beer mug in salute to the other table where the drinkers immediately stood and raised their mugs to the Duke returning his salute.

Once again across the whole room the drinkers rose from their seats. With false moustache in place the Duke climbed back onto his chair and he called out loudly. 'My friends, a toast – to the most famous beer hall in the World the Hofbrauhaus, the people of Munich and the Gemultlichkeit of Bavaria!'

If anything the cheers and noise of the banging beer mugs was even louder and the Duke stayed on his chair smiling broadly and waving to the crowd. Eventually he jumped down again. As he and his party sat down the cheering died away and the band stuck up again.

'By Jove Wallis, that was quite something eh?'

'It sure was my darling.' Responded the smiling Duchess patting him on the arm as he pulled off the moustache.

Later that night Sefton Delmer filed his story with the London Daily Express. He did not mention the false moustache but he commented that the

Duchess took away fond memories of the little white sausages. Of the Duke he reported that the cheers and applause he received were of the kind that only the old kings of Bavaria could have expected.

Chapter 10

When Tar Robertson first met Percy Foxworth an Assistant Director of the American Federal Bureau of Investigation and Head of Counter Espionage he was immediately impressed with the younger man's demeanour. Foxworth was dark skinned and haired, and Tar guessed that he was only in his early thirties. Presumably to hold so critical a position he must have a very wise head on such young shoulders, thought Tar when they met in the American Embassy.

'Assistant Director, it is a pleasure to meet you and indeed I must convey the sincere thanks of our Service to you for making the journey to London.'

'On the contrary Colonel Robertson… when my old mentor Chester outlined the concerns of your Service of course I recognised that they resonated with ours so it was the natural thing to do.'

'Perhaps a little less of the 'old' Young Percy' laughed the jovial Chester Harris. 'Tar and I share many confidences and I have to say suspicions and concerns. In Tar's presence I can tell you that he was closely involved with the intelligence aspects of the abdication of King Edward and views the now Duchess of Windsor in the same light as do we do.'

'That is as I believed.' commented Foxworth. 'Now, how can we effectively work together on this "potentially explosive problem"… and I should add that those are the very words of our Director, J Edgar Hoover.'

Tar responded 'The common ground is that the Duke through naivite or cunning has allowed his forthcoming trip to the United States to be portrayed as being both prompted by social concern for the conditions of the working man and yet at the same time he has allowed the man Bedaux and his cronies in big business and international banking to organise it. By so doing he is aligning himself and his wife with the "New Order" that has funded the rise of Nazi

Germany and seeks supranational power.'

'That is about the strength of it, don't you think Percy?' asked Chester Harris.

'Yes it is. It is the view of the FBI and the President's office that the visit will actually be stage managed to demonstrate the unreliability of the working people in comparison with the steady hand of the New Order. Or as they like to think of themselves 'The Fraternity'. An unofficial view held by the President's office of course.'

Tar decided to reveal his hand a little. 'One of our agents is a most attractive young woman who is both an English aristocrat and an American heiress. She will be travelling to New York on the RMS Queen Mary later this week. Her brief is to talk to Allen Dulles and convince him that His Majesty's Government will not permit the so called Fraternity to enlist the aid of the Duke. To put it bluntly, their worldwide interests will be unofficially the target of painful sanctions. Dulles will be told that to avoid such an unfortunate outcome Bedaux must be taken out of circulation in the USA and consequently abandon the plans for the Windsors' visit.'

Foxworth thought for a few moments and then posed a question. 'And why should the patrician Allen Dulles co-operate in this way?'

Tar laughed as he replied 'Oh there is a little matter that he would rather forget and most certainly would not want to see the light of day. I hasten to add, it is not a security matter nor does it involve dishonesty but, we believe that it is enough. However we believe that our very attractive agent Ladia Celia Ffrench-Hardy will succeed in her mission using her charms alone.'

'Very well. The Bureau has excellent relations with the trade unions, sub rosa of course, and naturally we profess to hate each other. I am sure that they will play ball and let it be known that there will be strike action if the visit goes ahead.'

Foxworth paused and then continued almost as if thinking aloud. 'As to your plan Colonel, we will be pleased to be rid of Bedaux. He has been suspect for a number of years and keeps company with... let's just call them 'friends of the Nazi regime.' This is a delicate matter with so strong a German lobby in the States but we are satisfied that he has accumulated a huge amount of data concerning our strategic production capabilities, even down to blueprints of factory layouts and production figures for those companies where his consultancy has been retained.'

'Oh and not just in America I might add' commented Chester Harris. 'A thoroughly dangerous man. We would be delighted to see him leave the United States. Now Tar, I recall that you promised us lunch ...'

'Yes Chester I most certainly did and before you utter another word the Reform Club it is.'

'Splendid' replied a beaming Chester. 'Percy you will just love the place – it has the most stunning architecture and ambience. What's more it might be dignified and terribly British but it sure ain't stuffy. Fair comment Tar?'

'I could not disagree with you.'

'Well Wallis what say you now that our trip is over?' asked the Duke as he, Wallis, Celia and Johnny relaxed in the lounge section of the special carriage that was taking them back to Paris. They had been escorted to the border and there had been even more cheering flag waving crowds.

'My dears I can honestly say that it was exhausting but my God so interesting and just so much to remember. I think that it will take me a year to marshall my thoughts.'

Celia laughed commenting 'Wallis I know exactly what you mean… it is almost overwhelming. I think that it is the combination of the spectacle, the uniforms, the settings, the music and then the people that one meets from the Fuhrer to even the ordinary people in the street and at the stations. It felt to me as if one were transported into the cast of a giant cinema film.'

'I say old girl you're waxing rather lyrical today' commented Johnny wryly.

The Duke was smiling as he said 'No Johnny, I think that what both Celia and Wallis said is just so true. It echoes some of my experiences when I was on tour as Prince of Wales, but really this has been so much more impressive. I leave Germany full of admiration for the achievements of a nation that is truly great again and so much thanks to the vision and spirit of one brilliant man.'

'It was Rudolf Hess who opened my eyes the other night at supper' commented Wallis pensively. 'He explained that the whole concept of the Fuhrer is that the people see the symbol and the man as one… in other words, the Swastika and Hitler as one… which is more powerful than either in isolation.'

Johnny interrupted 'Yes, but Wallis surely that is the same as the symbolism of the Crown and the Monarch in Britain and its Empire?'

The Duke joined the exchange. 'No Johnny, it is different I can assure you. For instance, except way back in history when the Monarch led his army into battle… you know, think Henry the Fifth… the Monarch has not set out to become a cult figure in himself. Contrast the Fuhrer with that. He courts the people with his rhetoric, his personality and his powerful beliefs. At the same time the swastika, the symbol is everywhere.'

'I can tell you something' continued Wallis. 'The other night Hess told me that Hitler practices his speeches word by word with him and it is he who not only writes much of the content but almost stage manages the style of rhetoric and the timing of the changes of tone.'

'That does not surprise me' continued the Duke. 'Changing the subject slightly, another thing that impressed me was their amazing attention to detail. I had a fascinating discussion with Frau Hess about marriage. She is a woman of principle and doughty I would say to ask me for my views on that institution' laughed the Duke. 'She explained that Himmler established the Reichsbrauteschulen… Brides' Schools. Once potential brides of SS officers have passed all the tests to establish that they are true Aryans they enrol in the residential school where they learn not only the essentials of housekeeping but also even the correct political inferences that are to be included in the stories that they will tell their children. Over a million brides and mothers to be have so far been through these courses and the compulsory ones for mothers to be. Nothing is left to chance.'

'Golly' laughed Celia. 'A bit different to my finishing school. There it was assumed that nannies and governesses would be reading any stories to one's offspring!'

Unsmiling the Duke appeared to correct Celia. 'That is not the point Celia. The purpose is to elevate marriage and motherhood to a level that enhances and enriches the Reich.'

'Well David, at the risk of disagreeing with you, I think that sounds a bit much' persisted Celia.

Wallis clearly noted that the Duke's previously euphoric mood was rapidly turning to one of anger which could lead to one of his tiresome tantrums. She had learnt to avert his mood swings. 'David, let's change the subject darling… didn't you have a grand time in the beer hall in Munich last night?'

'I certainly did, and what a wonderful crowd eh? They cheered me to the rafters!'

'Disaster diverted' thought Wallis as she continued. 'I just loved those little white sausages. Just thinking about them makes me peckish. Let's have a bite to eat shall we? David, please ring for the steward.'

Princess Stephanie Von Hohenloe was shown into the Fuhrer's Berlin Office in the Reich Chancellery.

The Fuhrer who was in military uniform having just returned from a formal review of a newly formed SS battalion came from behind the large Empire style table that served as his desk and placing a hand on each of her shoulders kissed the Princess on each cheek. He then held her at arms' length and stared at her intently. He did not smile as he said 'My beautiful and clever Princess... I trust that you are well and happy?'

The Princess did not flinch at being greeted so strangely and simply replied with a smile 'I am pleased to report Mein Fuhrer that I am both well and happy. May I be so bold as to repeat the same question to you?'

'Oh yes, of course. I am content and wish to thank you for your efforts and advice concerning the visit of the Duke and Duchess of Windsor. I have been reviewing the reports and they are most satisfactory. Importantly both the Duke and Duchess appear to have been suitably impressed by all that they saw and of course the welcome they received. Your advice that the Duchess must be addressed as 'Your Royal Highness' was invaluable.'

The Princess smiled almost coquettishly. 'I am pleased to have been of service Mein Fuhrer. Did the Duke clarify or enlarge upon his position vis a vis Germany, its aspirations and the future generally?'

'Most interestingly he did on a number of occasions. It is the opinion of Ley, Goebbels, Goering, Ribbentrop and indeed me that the Duke is a strong supporter of what we are doing in Germany.'

'Did he express any criticism of the 'Labour Camp' that he was taken to or the principles of Aryan supremacy and the means adopted to achieve it?' she asked.

'On the contrary, he gave every impression of enthusiastic endorsement. The only person who detected any reservations was Rudolf Hess but then he can be rather negative.'

'What prompted Rudolf's concern?'

'As you know, Hess favours mass deportation of the Jews over any other solution. He is a good soldier but when it comes to such matters as this he can be squeamish. I have taken the precaution of investing full authority in Himmler to resolve the Jewish issue. He will do so efficiently.'

'Is the Duke still happy to wear the crown of a united Germany and Britain even if Britain is a partner as a consequence of defeat?'

'Most certainly he is' replied Hitler. 'I believe that he has no moral qualms in that regard. As with so many other monarchs in history including some English he feels that he was deposed and forced into exile. When he and I talked in private he was very bitter and complained that he was the victim of a regicide with all but the killing.'

Princess Stephanie sensed that any further direct questions might annoy Hitler and decided to change tack. 'He is our man. Of that I am sure. If I may change the subject Mein Fuhrer. The British Press is carrying the story of a 'pogrom' in Danzig. If I may read an extract from the 'Daily Herald'?'

In an instant Hitler's expression visibly changed from the affability with which he had greeted the Princess to a stony faced almost fixated blank look. He nodded imperceptibly.

The Princess pressed on undeterred. 'I shall read parts of the report credited to their Danzig correspondent.'

'*The World Jewish Congress at Geneva has notified The League of Nations that the Nazi Government and the Police have organised anti-Jewish outrages and has requested the restoration of law, order and due process. Refugess are streaming across the frontier to escape the almost indescribable bestialities which are a prelude to the totalitarianisation of the Free City where Polish Nationalists are the only neo-Nazi party left. The Polish community denies the Government organs' allegations that they are responsible for the excesses. Storm Troopers in fact led Hitler Youth in attacks against Jewish merchants in Danzig, Langfurt and Zoppot (all in the Danzig Territory) and destroyed goods bought at Jewish shops, which were picketed preparatory to the launching of a street pogrom, in which armed and semi-uniformed bands attacked Jews and painted extracts from Herr Forster's speech on Jewish shop windows. Storm Troopers the next night smashed windows and shop signs, destroyed merchandise and thrashed Jews, one of whom was killed by a Storm Trooper in Langfurt, his skull being fractured with a poker.*'

The Princess then commented 'Mein Fuhrer, this article and those in other British newspapers, including 'The Times' have reported the events in Danzig and the remarks of Herr Forster the Danzig Nazi leader in detail. The attacks are portrayed as German Government inspired atrocities. This is doing great harm to your cause and that of Germany as are newsreel reports that the Spanish Civil War is being utilised by Germany and Italy as a proving ground for their weaponry and latest tactics which will then be deployed and applied in war.'

Hitler's face had not moved whilst the Princess read the newspaper extract and made her comments. His eyes appeared not to have flickered even. He then spoke in a mechanical measured monotone. 'Princess it is inevitable that young men enthused with an ideal and a vision of a future without the Jews become frustrated, even impatient, and take matters into their own hands.'

The Princess then did something that few of Hitler's closest advisers and old friends would ever risk. She argued with him. 'I am sorry to disagree Mein Fuhrer but, please try to see this through the eyes of the rest of the world. Nazi Germany portrays itself as a disciplined and law abiding Nation whose efforts led by you and the Nazi Government are to be admired and aspired to. How can that disciplined society be reconciled with the behaviour displayed in Danzig?'

Hitler broke into a smile. 'But my dear Princess, you and the British Press are missing the point. The Storm Troopers were dealing with the Jewish menace that threatens us all… don't you see?'

'But Mein Fuhrer …'

'No Princess, there are no 'buts' in this argument. Now, to change the subject. In anticipation of the Duke and Duchess of Windsor's visit to America I wish you and Fritz Wiedemann to go to New York and visit branches of the German-American Bund and ensure that they accord the same sort of welcome as you and Fritz organised here in Germany.'

The Princess maintained her smile as Hitler continued.

'You will sail to New York and from there go to Washington where you will stay with the Ambassador. This is an important mission for which you are both admirably suited.'

'Very well Mein Fuhrer I shall do as you wish.'

The Princess had recognised that nothing would be gained by prolonging the discussion of the Danzig situation and she had best placate the Fuhrer and avoid compromising his trust in her. A minute later she realised that she need not have worried.

'Now my very dear Princess Stephanie, I have a present for you.'

Hitler opened a drawer in his desk and drew out a heavy official-looking document.

'This is a lease of Schloss Leopoldskron which was owned by the theatre director Max Reinhart. You will see that it is at a purely notional rent. Please think of it as a gift from your grateful Fuhrer. It is both a worthy home but also somewhere in keeping with your standing where you can entertain in style.'

'Mein Fuhrer I am overwhelmed by your kindness! May I embrace you?'

For a moment Hitler looked flustered by the request from the striking titian-haired woman that he so much admired but then with an almost child-like smile he put both hands flat on his desk, pushed himself up from his chair then held out his arms. The Princess embraced him resting her head on his shoulder. He buried his face in her hair and closed his eyes.

Chapter 11

Johnny and Celia did not break their journey in Paris as Wallis had suggested but pressed on, arriving in London utterly exhausted.

'I don't know about you Johnny but I think it is a case of bath and bed for me… I feel bone-weary.'

'Me too and I have an important meeting in the morning. I shall call Tar and tell him that we will go in at say four pm and give a verbal report on the Duke and Duchess' German trip?'

'That would be perfect. Just let me know where and when. Very well darling I shall look forward to seeing you tomorrow. I shall try and make some notes as you suggested.'

After Johnny had dropped Celia at her house he was driven by Charles Harvey to his home.

'Well Charles, are you and Elizabeth ready to join the Windsor household in Paris?'

'As much as I ever shall be. Elizabeth is entirely relaxed about it but for me it will be quite a stressful time, at least until I learn the ropes. She has been putting me through an intense training programme and, thank goodness, Wallis has done the dirty on Charles Bedaux and pinched his butler from the Chateau Cande.'

'No! For heaven's sake, the woman has no shame!' laughed Johnny. 'Surely she knows the rules? Sleep with who you like but never ever cheat at cards or pinch your host's servants.'

'Apparently not it would seem. The latest message from Dudley Forward came this afternoon. The Duke and Duchess will not stay in their suite at the Hotel le Meurice. The house they have leased in Versailles has been made ready.

Elizabeth and I are to go to Paris in three days' time.'

'Fine, I shall give you an up to date briefing on the German trip and I assume that Tar and Maxwell will be spelling out the specific intelligence targets that they have in mind for you. Celia and I will be seeing Tar tomorrow afternoon to give our initial verbal report.'

Charles dropped Johnny at his house and then took the Hispano-Suiza to park it in the mews garage at the rear where for the sake of appearances he had the apartment above the garage.

Johnny had just stretched out in an armchair with a whisky and water in hand when the telephone rang. His butler appeared and informed him that Princess Stephanie de Hohenloe was calling. Johnny leapt up and went to his study where he closed the door and sitting down at his desk picked up the receiver. As he did so his butler formally announced Stephanie then with a click put down his extension.

'Stephanie, my dear, how are you? It is so long since we have spoken let alone seen each other?'

'Oh my dearest man, I am well but, more to the point, how are you? You must be tired after the German visit I think.'

'Weary at the moment but nothing that a good night's sleep will not cure. I cannot wait to see you. Are you in London now?'

'No, I am in Berlin returning to London tomorrow evening so perhaps we could meet the next day? Will you join me for a light lunch at the Dorchester?"

'That sounds excellent. Unless I hear to the contrary I shall be with you at twelve forty five if that suits.'

'Perfect. And now a kiss goodbye my dashing friend.'

A few weeks before their visit to Germany the Duke and Duchess had been in the sitting room of their suite in the Hotel Meurice having an early evening drink.

'Now David, there is no point in us arguing about where we live. As Walter Monckton has advised, America is out of the question because of our tax position whereas the French Government have graciously offered us a tax free special status. Anyhow, France suits us well.' Wallis sipped her drink and continued. 'You know that I love living in the heart of Paris where everything is to hand but I know that you desperately hanker after a garden in which you can work in privacy just as you loved to do at the Fort. Remember I have found just the place – the Chateau de la Maye in Versailles… we both liked it. It is owned by the widow of a politician and Dudley Forward has had discussions with her lawyers. We can have the house fully furnished on an initial lease of six months.'

'Wallis my love, I only want you to be happy and if that means living in or near the City I shall be content.'

'Oh David don't be a chump. The chateau sounds perfect and remember it has a swimming pool, tennis courts…'

'And a nine hole golf course!' interrupted the Duke. 'It will be capital fun… the Metcalfes can join us. You and she can have a good time together whilst Fruity and I play a little golf.'

Wallis smiled thinly as she replied 'I am afraid that Fruity's wife and I do not really hit it off David… remember just how frosty she was at our wedding.'

'Don't be put off by Ba Ba's rather aloof manner… she's a good egg really otherwise she wouldn't be married to Fruity. She inherited her regal manner from her father Lord Curzon who regarded himself as close to God when he was Viceroy of India. Anyhow, Fruity can always come on his own. Be like old times, what!" responded the smiling Duke.

The Duchess replied with a wry look. 'Yes it will my love, just like old times.' Wallis was satisfied that on their return from the visit to Germany Armand Gregoire her lawyer would have seen to the legal formalities and they could move to the Chateau de la Maye.

Wallis had retired for a rest, still complaining of tiredness after the gruelling trip to Germany and journey back to Paris. After slipping into a negligee she asked her maid to send Helga to her. Within a minute Helga appeared notebook in hand as Wallis reclined on the bed.

'Close and lock the door for me Helga and then come here. We shall have to be very quiet. Now then, perhaps you would like to make yourself comfortable and slip out of your suit? I have a little surprise for you' chortled Wallis as the statuesque Austrian girl began to undress. 'Now Helga, help me out of my negligee and then I want you to close your eyes and lie very still. Now then, no peeping…'

Wallis slid open the drawer in her Louis Quatorze side table and drew out a Y shaped black silk ribbon with a clamp at each of the three ends. Helga bit her lip, flinched and jerked as Wallis fixed two clamps to her nipples but did not utter a sound as she felt a hand holding the third clamp and trailing the silk ribbon down her body.

The only sound apart from the distant noise of the City was Wallis who was quietly humming then as the third clamp closed whispered 'Now relax...'

Johnny Johnstone was taken to Princess Stephanie's suite by a uniformed bell boy who stood aside as the Princess threw the door open and cried out 'Johnny, how delightful to see you.' She caught the eye of the bell boy as she drew Johnny inside and mouthed the words 'thank you.'

The exotic Princess was a firm favourite of all the staff at the Dorchester in London and the Adlon in Berlin. She was always a polite and generous guest. The bell boy knew that he could expect a handsome tip when next he encountered the captivating woman. She may have been older than their mothers but all the bell boys thought that Princess Stephanie exuded more sex appeal than any of the Hollywood actresses who stayed at the grand hotel.

Johnny and Stephanie enjoyed a long embrace. 'God it's so good to see you again!' Johnny exclaimed.

'Oh yes, you handsome devil. Now, before we have lunch, a drink and I shall tell you what I found out directly from the mouth of the Fuhrer.'

Over the next fifteen minutes the Princess repeated her conversation with Hitler almost verbatim. It was very much as Johnny anticipated but he made careful notes after asking Stephanie's permission to do so. He had assured her that his note would be burned later that afternoon.

'Now Johnny, there is something else I must tell you. Fritz Wiedemann, the Fuhrer's Adjutant, old comrade and friend and I have been instructed to go to America immediately to ensure that the German American Bund and other similar organisations give the Duke and Duchess of Windsor the same sort of welcome as they enjoyed in Germany. He doesn't trust Charles Bedaux to achieve that without our help.'

'When do you leave?' asked Johnny.

'We are sailing on the Bremen at the end of the week, on Saturday. We shall board at Cherbourg... that is as also planned for the Duke and Duchess when they go later.'

The light lunch was elegant in its simplicity. A tartare of salmon with a horseradish reloute followed by poached breast of chicken in rosemary with a green salad, and finishing with mango sorbet. Lunch was washed down with a flint dry Sancerre. Both the Princess and Johnny declined coffee and after the waiter had left Stephanie dabbed her mouth and stood. As Johnny placed his napkin on the table and also stood the Princess reached out and took his hand.

'Well Johnny… it's been a little while I think…' she murmured coquettishly and drew him towards her.

Johnny hesitated for a moment and then took her in his arms and kissed her deeply.

'Come' she said, talking his hand and drawing him towards her bedroom. 'I need this' she laughed as she drew him closer.

Chapter 12

Having sent Charles Harvey and Stephanie's lady's maid ahead with their luggage, Johnny and Princess Stephanie drove to Clivedon in Johnny's powerful two-door Rolls Royce Phantom drophead coupe. He had chosen it over the Hispano-Suiza as not only was the weather good but he associated the Hispano with Celia.

After the heavy traffic of Central London and the arterial Great West road it was a relief to drive into an almost traffic free world of beech woods and picturesque country villages and cottages as they drove towards the great Cliveden Estate, home of the fabulously wealthy and politically minded Astor family.

'Johnny I hope that my arranging for you to be invited for this weekend does not cause you any… shall I say… personal problems.'

'My dear Stephanie I can assure you that if it did I would have politely declined' he laughed.

'You must know that I am referring to Celia… it is common knowledge that you are very close!' Johnny chuckled and continued. 'However there is a convention that applies to touring English sporting teams whether it be cricket or rugby football and also to weekend house parties. In the case of the sporting tour it is put very simply as 'what happens on tour stays on tour'. In the same vein, what happens in a house party stays in that party.'

Stephanie laughed. 'I guess that is pretty much the same in the aristocratic and Royal families of continental Europe. Musical beds eh?'

'I'm sure that it is' responded Johnny flashing a sardonic smile as he swung the great car through the ornate gates of the Cliveden Estate. 'After all old girl don't we all operate on the basis that once a wife has produced "an heir and a spare" it is perfectly acceptable for there to be a little… shall I say… relaxation with the opposite sex?'

As the drive wound through the beautiful gardens Stephanie stretched her arms forward towards the windscreen arching her back against the seat back.

'Johnny when we reach the turn into the formal drive please stop for a minute or two. I just love the way the house looks from next to the fountain.'

'Delighted my dear… anything to oblige Your Royal Highness' replied Johnny in a facetious tone and bowing his head. Stephanie playfully delivered a light smack to his left arm thinking to herself 'this weekend is going to be rather fun.'

'Oh Johnny… please stop here for just a moment. I so love this fountain… it is called 'The Fountain of Love' you know… It was sculpted by a man called Thomas Waldo Story in 1897 from Sienna marble.'

'For heaven's sake Stephanie! You sound just like one of those awful tour guides! I have been here before you know… I have had dealings with Lord Astor. Right old girl, we must press on.'

At that he released the hand brake and the car moved forward almost silently approaching the elaborate fountain set in a large shell within a round pond. As they reached the fountain the vista of the broad Grand Avenue leading arrow straight to the imposing Italianate front of Cliveden House opened before them. Johnny stopped the car.

'It is just so beautiful… it is so, oh how can I say, so light in spite of its size. I'm sorry Johnny' laughed Stephanie. 'My English has let me down but you know exactly what I mean, yes?'

'Well that was Sir Charles Barry's intention when he designed the house in the Italianate style. His placing the tower to the right of the house is a trick on the eye and a jolly clever way to disguise a water tower in my book.'

Johnny drove slowly forward again and swinging round in front of the great house stopped in front of the pillared portico. A morning-suited middle aged man with heavily oiled almost black hair stood flanked by two liveried footmen.

The footmen quickly moved to open the car doors as the older man stopped a few feet away. As Johnny and Stephanie joined each other on the gravel he bowed and then in a clear and cultured voice greeted them with a smile.

'Your Royal Highness, my Lord, welcome to Cliveden. I trust that you have had a pleasant journey.'

Johnny replied 'Thank you and yes, a quiet drive. And you are?'

'Cresswell my Lord, the Under Butler. Now if I may I shall escort you to your suites. Her Ladyship thought that you would enjoy the view as they are on the upper level.'

Johnny took Stephanie's arm and they followed Cresswell into the huge dark panelled Great Hall with its hanging antique Belgian tapestries.

Cresswell led the couple up the stairs to the second floor and then to a door at which Stephanie's maid waited. Charles Harvey who was posing as Johnny's manservant was standing by the door of what was obviously the adjoining suite.

Cresswell stopped next to Stephanie's maid and turning informed them formally, 'Her Ladyship and her other guests have just returned from exploring the Maze. Tea will be served in the Great Hall in half an hour, the dressing gong will sound at seven o'clock with drinks in the Library half an hour later. Dinner will be at eight fifteen and served in the French Dining Room.'

'If I can be of any further assistance ..?'

'Thank you Cresswell that will be all.'

After he had left Stephanie turned to Johnny. 'I shall freshen up after our little journey and then perhaps you would be gallant enough to escort me to tea… although I must say that I would prefer champagne.'

'Oh there will be plenty of that later even though Nancy Astor is vociferously opposed to drinking alcohol… say ten minutes?'

'Perfect' smiled Stephanie turning and entering her suite as her maid Emily held the door open.

As soon as he was in his suite and the door closed Johnny shook hands with Charles and patted him on the back.

'So Charles, have you picked up anything interesting below stairs yet?'

'Not yet but I am getting along with the other valets well and I am sure that later on there will be some tale swopping. It's a pity that we could not have one of our people instead of Emily. But she's a bright and chatty girl and I will do my best to see what gossip she picks up too.'

'Good man. Right I am going to wash after the drive then it's time for tea and to meet the other guests and of course our hosts.'

'The Viscount is unlikely to be here this weekend… he is attending some meetings in London as I am given to understand.'

'Thank you for that snippet. Just lay my things out for this evening and I will see you after dinner.'

Shortly afterwards Johnny and Stephanie walked across the Great Hall and joined the group standing around the huge 16th-century fireplace that dominated the far end wall.

After formal greetings and an introduction to Geoffrey Dawson, Editor of 'The Times', Nancy Astor whose aura of grandeur overcame her stark almost harsh features stiffly asked Johnny how Celia was.

'Top notch Nancy. She's on her way to New York on the Queen Mary with Daisy Fellowes. To take a short holiday after our German trip.'

Nancy Astor laughed. 'Really? Daisy and I have but two things in common… we are both American born and both had our portraits painted by John Singer Sargent. One difference is that she was so shocked by her appearance that she had her nose reduced surgically and without anaesthetic.'

Johnny looked shocked and blurted 'But that is barbaric!'

'Her choice, Johnny. She told me that the operation was to be her rebirth so great pain was appropriate. From then on she got hooked on haute couture and became a culture vulture. And now look at her...' As she allowed her comments to sink in, Nancy raised her eyebrows quizzically. Philip Kerr, the Marquis of Lothian laughed and said 'But Nancy all you well off American ladies who come over here do so to find husbands, don't you?'

Nancy responded briskly. 'Certainly not Philip. As I once responded to that comment 'If you knew the trouble I had getting rid of mine........' Anyhow, dear Daisy prefers other people's husbands.' She appeared to laugh but her eyes were hard.

'Now, time for tea.' Nancy Astor reached and pulled a long embroidered silk bell pull. Almost immediately white gloved footmen appeared with tea, dainty sandwiches and cakes which were deftly laid on a side table.

'I gather that you have all been into the maze today…. was it a challenge?' Johnny enquired.

'Actually it was' replied Lord Lothian. 'Waldorf's father designed it. I say Nancy, you still have his original drawing don't you?' Nancy nodded and he continued. 'It is very complex. I think that I would prefer to tire myself on the golf course. Johnny do you fancy a round?'

Nancy Astor quickly interposed. 'That may be difficult to fit in. Tomorrow I have arranged a picnic on the river. We will take the Suzy Ann which is a restored Royal Navy launch from 1911 I believe, and I shall follow in my electric canoe. I shall have a man with me so that whilst we are moored up for luncheon any of you can go for a spin in her.'

Geoffrey Dawson appeared quite animated as he exclaimed 'Oh capital Nancy… it is an absolute must for any of you who have not been in the canoe to do so. It is an amazing experience as she slips through the water without any engine noise and, I would add, she is amazingly fast.'

'Somewhat like Daisy' muttered Nancy.

Conversation was light-hearted as old friends and new relaxed in congenial company. Nancy Astor had explained that her husband hoped to join the party the following evening but was presently detained in London.

Lord Lothian and Johnny decided to take the air on the grand terrace that ran across the back of the house before the Dressing Gong was sounded.

'Wonderful view Philip… the parterre in full bloom is quite something. Anyhow, I am curious and will come straight to the point. That mischievous and politically far left journalist Claud Cockburn has given the group who regularly meet here the soubriquet 'The Cliveden Set'. Is there such a group?'

'You are right about him being mischievous. To digress for a moment, it may be an apocryphal story, but when he was a young sub-editor on 'The Times' he is reputed to have won a competition amongst the staff to invent the most accurate yet boring headline. He claimed to have won with 'Small Earthquake in Chile, Not Many Dead.'

'Anyhow, your question. First, Cockburn himself. Mark that he is a dangerous man. Under the pseudonym 'Frank Pitcairn' he used to contribute firebrand copy to the communist 'Daily Worker'. Now he publishes 'The Week' which, on good authority, is believed to be funded by the Soviet Government. It is strongly critical of Prime Minister Neville Chamberlain's policy of appeasement of Hitler's Germany, as it now is, and equally of course his predecessor Stanley Baldwin's policy of 'masterful inactivity'.'

'Well the present situation certainly throws together some unlikely bedfellows Philip, that puts him alongside Winston.'

Lord Lothian chuckled. 'Yes, chalk and cheese but, of course they arrive at the same conclusion from opposite ends of the spectrum. But, you see, some of us, and that includes Lord Halifax who has of course secretly met with Hitler, believe that there is another way and a war can be averted.'

'With respect Robin, is that not a naive view given the Nazis' published goals and intentions? I am recently back from the Duke and Duchess of Windsor's trip to Germany and I can assure you that we saw a nation gearing for war both by patriotic fervour and rearmament on an unprecedented scale. In my assessment the horse has bolted from the stable and it is too late to close the door. You cannot reason with a bolting horse can you?'

After a moment's hesitation Lord Lothian replied 'Johnny, I fear you may be right but we as a generation owe it to the millions who perished in the Great War and to our next generation of young men to do our damnedest to prevent the same thing happening again.'

Looking grave, Johnny responded, 'But Robin we must take note and remember that whatever one believes or disbelieves about the Spanish Civil War both Germany and Italy have been using the conflict as a testing ground for their tactics… just look at the bombing of Guernica in the Basque country. We can be sure that in any future conflict the civilian population will be subjected to sustained terror bombing. Yes, there will be strategic bombing of legitimate targets but also, as in Spain, sustained attacks to break the morale of the civilian people at home and consequently the fighting soldiers themselves.'

Johnny paused then in a subdued and pensive voice asked 'So what precisely is your argument in favour of appeasement if I may put it like that?'

'Very well. The revision of the provisions of the Treaty of Versailles should be undertaken with the agreement of Germany'.

Lord Lothian raised his hand in a typical politician's gesture to deflect interruption.

'Such revision is not only morally correct but also in the interests of Britain, Europe and indeed, the World as a whole. There are two raisons d'etre. Firstly, like it or not a strong and rearmed Germany is a bulwark against the threat of Bolshevism.'

He looked Johnny hard in the eyes as he spoke.

'Secondly without an agreement for such a revision Germany will almost certainly move unilaterally to annexe those territories and bring back into Germany its people who were forced into becoming citizens of other nations. If that takes place Britain may be compelled to take up arms over matters that are, frankly, of only marginal interest or concern.'

At that moment the Dressing Gong could be heard.

'Thank you Robin… we will have to continue another time. As I recall, Nancy is a stickler for punctuality.'

* * *

Drinks and dinner afterwards in the magnificent gilded rococo French Dining Room were pleasant and elegant. Whilst both Nancy Astor and Lord Lothian had become Christian Scientists, he after a crisis of faith as a staunch Catholic, and in consequence did not touch alcohol, the wines were a superb complement to the food.

The convention that neither religion nor politics had a seat at the dining table was scrupulously observed by all.

After the ladies had withdrawn and the men settled to their port and cigars Dawson of the London Times commented 'I fear that Nancy's picnic on the river may not take place looking at the weather. I am sure that I heard a rumble of thunder and it is deuced humid.'

Bill Montagu, the Duke of Manchester, laughed. 'Ah but like the Red Sea parting Nancy will expect the weather to bend to her will and the sun to break through. Johnny you are just back from Germany where you were accompanying our erstwhile King and his wife. I know that the reports here in the press and newsreels were heavily censored so how did he actually behave?'

Johnny decided that there was no point in dissembling. He was sure that it was a loaded question and Dawson who despised the former King would have discreetly briefed his friends using his inside knowledge. 'The whole visit was staged to mimic a royal progress whether it be the organised welcoming crowds, the military pomp, glittering occasions with the Nazi elite... even down to a stage managed farewell in a Munich beer hall. The Duke and Duchess loved it, they lapped it up and, of course the grand finale was the visit to Hitler in his mountain stronghold.'

Geoffrey Dawson then asked a question, the answer to which he was well aware both he and Johnny knew. 'Did the Duke and indeed the Duchess openly signify support for Herr Hitler and the Nazis?'

Johnny was annoyed by the simplistic question. 'Dawson, you well know that the Duke gave the Nazi salute on many occasions, some where the crowds were chanting 'Heil Windsor'. It could be argued that in doing so he was returning a courtesy.'

Dawson cracked back 'Or that he has become a Nazi.'

'I find that remark bordering on the offensive' replied Johnny icily. 'I believe that he has an admiration for what Hitler and his Nazi cronies... and they are a disparate bunch... have achieved in Germany. I am of the opinion that he fervently hopes that a future war can be averted.' Johnny paused. 'There can be no doubt that he is deeply wounded by what he now sees as his almost ritual humiliation by the British Government and his own family, the manipulation by Baldwin and the poor advice that he was given. A Nazi? I do not think so. However you can only push a man so far. He is near that limit.'

Dawson was too old a hand to let the matter drop although the others at the table were looking increasingly uncomfortable. 'But what of that woman of his... I understand that she happily basked, indeed almost wallowed in being addressed as 'Your Royal Highness' a title from which she was most expressly excluded by the King. I also understand that she toadied up to her Nazi spymasters.'

Johnny decided that the time had come to close the matter and fixing Dawson with a gimlet stare. 'There is legal debate about her style of address. As for her allegiances I cannot comment from knowledge and will not speculate. That I believe is the purlieu of you gentlemen of the Fourth Estate... the press. Now I for one intend to join the ladies.'

Johnny pushed back his chair and stood as did all of the others except for Geoffrey Dawson who sat glowering down at his port.

Johnny and Stephanie were in his suite having pulled two armchairs up to the French doors that led onto a small Juliet balcony. They were each nursing an Armagnac that Johnny had poured at the sideboard where there was a selection of spirits and other drinks.

Lit by flashes of lightning accompanied by the rumble of distant thunder the couple were sitting companiably.

'Johnny darling, how far away is the storm? I usually count between seeing the lightning and hearing the thunder but the whole sky is ablaze like one great panoramic picture that is constantly changing.'

'I'm not sure. We are very high here and obviously looking out for miles. I am sure that the storm is moving fast and will be quite something when it gets here.'

'How long Johnny?'

'Probably an hour... that's only a guess.'

Stephanie's response was to reach forward and place her glass on the small table and then take Johnny's hand. 'Come' was all she said.

Stepanie drew Johnny towards the bedroom and kicking off her shoes turned him to face her and then pushed him back onto the bed.

She raised her skirt and revealed that she was wearing no knickers.

Johnny could sense that he was hardening at the sight as she reached forward and started to undo his trousers. He frantically reached down and helped her then after wriggling out of his braces raised his hips when she pulled down his trousers and undershorts.

The Princess wasted no time and quickly straddled him taking his whole length inside as she began to rock to and fro at an ever increasing pace.

Johnny could feel her using her strong and controlled muscles to send ripples of pleasure through his whole body.

He reached a fabulously strong orgasm very quickly.

'Oh my God… Stephanie that was awesome!' gasped Johnny. 'How the heck do you do that?'

'A little secret Johnny' she giggled and moving off him reached into the top drawer in her bedside table pulled out a velvet bag from which she took out two highly polished jade eggs. 'I carry these inside of me and keep them in place with my muscle control which builds strength. It's a Chinese trick that funnily enough Wallis told me about when we first met in Bryanston Court.'

Some time later as Johnny lay blowing smoke rings Stephanie jumped when there was a particularly loud clap of thunder. 'Quick Johnny we must watch!' She leapt off the bed and ran to the window where her naked form was silhouetted by the now almost continuous lightning flashes.

Johnny joined her and standing close behind her put his arms around her slender waist. As she wriggled back comfortable against him he felt a familiar stirring as clearly did she. She turned her head and whispered 'Later darling… now the storm.'

Then the rain came. First single large spots which smacked down onto the small balcony like large coins. In what seemed like seconds it became a drum roll. The downpour was gusting through the doors and soon they were both drenched. Stephanie turned in Johnny's arms and turning her face to his briefly kissed him then raising her voice over the increasing roar and crashing of the storm shouted in his ear 'Isn't this wonderful?'

At that moment the torrential rain turned to hail and they were pelted with a barrage of freezing hailstones. As Stephanie squealed Johnny pulled her back into the room. In an animal frenzy they kissed and fell onto the Persian rug which was soaking wet. Stephanie's nails dug hard into Johnny's buttocks as she pulled him deep into her with a grunt of pleasure.

* * *

The following morning when they awoke entwined in Johnny's bed the sun was blazing.

They went back into the sitting room which was now flooded with light. Johnny opened the French windows which he had closed before they staggered to bed in the early hours. 'A few hours of this sun will soon dry things out. Now, we had better get ready… it will soon be time to be on parade for breakfast.'

Stephanie responded by turning Johnny so that his back was to her. 'Oh My God Johnny what have I done?'

'Don't worry it was a truly amazing experience. Even if I am never invited again after flooding the place I shall always have wonderful memories of Cliveden and 'The Night of the Great Storm'. Now then, boating attire… which means rubber soled flat shoes. But first let's relax a little longer… come on, back to bed…'

Johnny and the Princess were lying in a tangle of sheets and legs after making love leisurely.

'That Johnny really 'hit the spot 'as the Americans would put it…'

'Yes but without your wonderful accent. I swear that you purr like a kitten when I caress you.'

'Oh but I do… just move your hand a little now my love and I will soon be purring you again, you beautiful man.'

'Never let it be said that I did not do as asked particularly by a beautiful Princess…'

'Oh Dahling…' she gasped as his fingers knowingly began to caress her again 'Yes, yes… oh yes!' she groaned.

Chapter 13

Tar Robertson was ensconced with Maxwell Knight, his brilliant but eccentric colleague in the British Secret Service and close friend.

Knight had always insisted that he could not work in the offices of the Secret Service which were cramped in any event and he worked from his maisonette at 38, Sloane Street in London's fashionable Knightsbridge. From an early age he had been obsessed with all animal life and his home was filled with fish tanks and roaming animals ranging from tortoises to dogs and insects, even a bush baby and a mimicking parrot. Tar was a regular visitor and was resigned to having serious discussion interrupted by Knight's menagerie.

'Well Max it seems that it is time for us to put our feet up whilst the younger ones are scattered to the four winds. Actually I have a stack of outwardly tedious intercept and rumour reports from various of our embassies to sift through on the off chance that there may be a little gold dust there. How about you?'

'Vera Schalberg should be back from Germany tonight and with Billy on the high seas on his way to New York I am taking her out to dinner for a gentle debrief. I am hoping to receive her call any minute telling me that she is back on British soil. It will be a relief to know that she is safe. If anything happened to her I dread to think how Billy might react.'

Tar nodded in agreement. Maxwell continued 'After the weekend we need to sit down with Princess Stephanie and Johnny and see what they picked up at Cliveden. Viscount Astor was not there last night... I happen to know because I saw him in Boodles yesterday evening.'

'Has he gone the way of his wife and foresworn the demon drink and become a Member of the Church of Christ the Scientist?' asked Tar with a twinkle in his eye. He was well known to be a highly sceptical agnostic; a rebellion against his austere Presbyterian upbringing in Scotland.

'He had a couple of Scotches last night but you know… he was never a great drinker. If I were saddled with Nancy I certainly would be. She can be utterly poisonous and cannot help putting her foot in it. She is totally insensitive. You know that she is rabidly anti-Semitic and now almost as strongly anti-Catholic?'

Tar smiled mirthlessly and commented 'I loved the David Low cartoon of 'The Shiver Sisters' with the short-skirted high-kicking chorus line including Nancy Astor, Dawson of 'The Times' and Lord Lothian conducted by Goebbels with his leg raised in the goose step. I know that the so called 'Cliveden Set' mean well and their intentions are patriotic but considering that they are supposedly skilled communicators they have done a pathetic job of getting their message across.'

'The problem is that all of these sincere people… and I include the Prime Minister… are giving Hitler and by proxy Mussolini the wrong message' added Maxwell.

Tar nodded. 'Perhaps we should prime Princess Stephanie to have a word in Hitler's ear and remind him that by nature the British people are made of stern stuff… as he admires… and they will not stand by idly whilst he rampages around Europe.'

Tar was interrupted when Knight's iridescent blue-fronted parrot imitated the squeak of a corkscrew drawing the cork from a wine bottle, its pop and then the sound of wine being poured. He raised his eyebrows expressively then continued 'Actually Max, I would go further… if the chips are down Neville Chamberlain will be put out to grass at a rate of knots. He does not have the stomach or the ruthlessness or drive to be a war leader.' Knight vigorously nodded agreement and Tar continued 'But back to Hitler. I have read a private memorandum prepared by Lord Halifax after his visit to Hitler just a couple of days before that of the Duke and Duchess of Windsor. Utterly disastrous in my humble opinion. He genuinely believes that Nazi Germany will leave Western Europe alone provided that there is no interference with their expansion to the East, and neither will they interfere in our Empire or World trade. I learnt enough at Sandhurst to know that Hitler will not commit to his plans to attack Russia unless he feels that he has subdued the French with their huge army and of course Britain. He cannot risk fighting on two fronts.'

'Did Halifax indicate to Hitler that he thought that Britain would not intervene if Germany were to annexe its former lands… you know the territories effectively confiscated under the Versailles terms?' asked Maxwell.

'I am afraid that he did.' Tar raised his eyebrows and continued. 'What he told Hitler was almost chapter and verse of what we believe to be the avowed reasoning of the Cliveden set of which he is of course a member…the trouble is that the mutterings of Chamberlain appear to support that line and he in turn keeps Anthony Eden on a short rein.'

Knight responded 'I am amazed that Eden has not resigned. He has specific responsibility for our relationship with and the maintenance of The League of Nations. Sir Vernon who is good friends with Eden tells how Chamberlain insisted that he go and put it to Mussolini that the manufactured dispute with Ethiopia should be submitted to the League of Nations.'

Tar's expression was stony as he said 'Mussolini laughed in his face and later commented that Eden is 'the best dressed fool in Europe'. Eden then refused Chamberlain's offer to personally negotiate further with Mussolini not least because Italy was flaunting the non-intervention agreement and sending troops and munitions to Spain. Chamberlain circumvented him and approached Mussolini directly. Disgraceful.'

Maxwell commented wryly 'I imagine that made all the difference?'

'Mussolini simply said that there was nothing to discuss' continued Tar 'and to put the whole sorry mess in context Hitler refers to Chamberlain as "that pompous arsehole", according to our man in the German London Embassy, Goose Pulitz. Hardly inspires confidence that there will be any tough and effective negotiating with the fascist leaders, or should I say dictators.'

'Actually Tar we must not lose sight of the fact that the way things are going we shall also have a third Fascist leader to contend with… General Franco in Spain. His loyalty will surely be to Germany and Italy who have given direct assistance to his campaigns. They see him as forming a triumvirate and we would critically almost certainly lose Gibraltar.'

Tar laughed bitterly. 'If they can form a close knit mutual military alliance, France will be in a sandwich and from our point of view the fascists will control the Mediterranean which will block our use of the Suez Canal. Apparently the Duke of Alba, who is representing the Spanish Fascists in London and who is Winston's cousin, has given 'off the record' assurances that the Spanish Fascists will not ally themselves with the Germans because they suspect Nazi intentions with regard to Catholics generally. Franco is staunchly catholic and his personal confessor never leaves his side. Whilst they are happy to have Italy's help

Franco does not consider the Italians to have sufficient military capability and effectively lack backbone in spite of their fine equipment.'

Maxwell commented 'Our intelligence is that General Franco is a very shrewd operator. Mind you with the atrocities attributed to his North African Moorish troops who are sworn to him utterly and march to chants of glorious death his confessor must have a full time task! Also, of course, it was an unofficial British operation that picked him up from the Canary Islands and flew him to North Africa where his army was totally and fanatically loyal to him. The Foreign Office view is that his sole focus is Spain and he will steer clear of becoming involved in any conflict outside of its territory.'

Tar riposted 'That may well be the correct analysis but if we have a confrontation with Nazi Germany, Spain could be a major player that we must keep off the pitch. Even without Italy, Spain with her Morrocan lands could potentially effectively blockade the Straits of Gibraltar and close off the Mediterranean to us.'

Tar paused then added 'Naturally Princess Stephanie knows Alba well… he operates from a suite in the Dorchester and she lives there. Once again she is going to be an important asset.'

Maxwell picked up the thread.

'We still have two more assets within the Spanish right-wing group represented by Jimmy Alba. The soldier of fortune Hugh Pollard is one of ours and has infiltrated not only the Spanish right-wing catholic group but also British based Fascist groups. It was after all he who organised the Dragon Rapide flown by Captain Begg from Croydon to the Canary Isles to collect Franco.'

Tar laughed and added 'With the added twist that he had his nineteen year old debutante daughter Diana and her friend as the passengers and they had the operational orders for Franco hidden in a copy of Vogue. One really could not make it up.'

'I agree… quite extraordinary. Anyway, apart from Pollard in the Franco camp in London we have Alan Hillgarth in Majorca. Whilst British Vice-Consul he is not only very well connected on the island but also on the mainland. His friendship with the millionaire tobacco-smuggling arms-dealer and close friend and funder of Franco will be very useful.'

Tar interrupted. 'I am making a mental note to keep tabs on both Pollard and Hillgarth. I know that the Foreign Office will regard Hillgarth as one of their intelligence assets but experience dictates that we shall find out much more ourselves than they will divulge.'

'Now, I have a suggestion with regard to the actual "running" of Vera Schalberg' continued Maxwell, raising his hand to prevent Tar intervening. 'I know that Billy is first rate but I also think that he is a little too involved emotionally now that she is to have his child. Also in the longer term we shall want her to go back to Germany and work her cover as an Abwehr agent. He will find that very hard to bear.'

'Fair enough Maxwell... so you have already made up your mind... so spit it out.'

'Well I do have a serious suggestion. Jona von Ustinov or Baron von Ustinov otherwise known as 'Klop' to his friends should become her confidante here.'

'I can see a synergy' responded Tar thoughtfully. 'They have both led peripatetic lives moving from country to country and Ustinov had to get out of Germany when he refused to prove that he was not of Jewish descent. I had him in mind with regard to Princess Stephanie as well but, perhaps that can wait for now. We had better have him in for a chat. Will you fix that and I will let Sir Vernon know how we intend to use him. At least with Vera pregnant Ustinov will not be bent on seducing her.'

'I trust not Tar but his nickname 'Klop' translates as bedbug which not only describes his physical appearance but his extraordinary success as a seducer!'

The Duke and Duchess had been discussing the Chateau de la Maye outside of Paris that they had rented. Quite apart from the proximity to Paris which the Duchess so craved it had a nine hole golf course for the Duke. The move from their Paris hotel suite was imminent. The Duke eased back his shirt cuff and looked at the slim gold Chopard watch that he was wearing that afternoon and clearly in a greatly improved mood smiled broadly and asked brightly 'Well Wallis drinkies time?'
'Perfect darling, my usual please.'

The Duke went to the drinks trolley that was brought into the drawing room of the suite every evening at six pm and busied himself mixing a Perfect Manhattan for Wallis and a stiff pink gin for himself.

'Well, bottoms up old girl,' toasted the Duke raising his glass towards Wallis. 'Here's to our new home where we can have a little freedom. Shall we drink to that dearest?'

'Oh yes darling, most certainly. Our toast is freedom.'

'Freedom' responded the Duke enthusiastically.

The freedom that Wallis had in mind was rather different to the thoughts of the Duke. With the Duke ensconced outside of Paris in Versailles she would be free to pursue what would be one of her most daring affairs. Her target was none other than the American Ambassador to Paris the socialite, author, diplomat, intellectual and intimate friend of President Franklin D. Roosevelt, William Christian Bullitt Junior.

The Queen Mary's crossing was smooth and so far as Celia and Daisy were concerned very enjoyable. Celia had stayed on the sidelines as Daisy behaved in her usual outrageous fashion and made not a fair few conquests. Celia pulled her leg about her insatiable appetite to which Daisy replied in an exaggerated laconic drawl, 'Darling if you've got it, for God's sake use it.' Celia was content to flirt and dance but made it clear that so far as she was concerned there was no opportunity for shipboard romance or dalliance. On the first evening at sea shortly after the Queen Mary had left British waters Celia's maid and steward revealed that they were Secret Service agents and on board to protect her. Celia's immediate reaction was anger at what she saw as an invasion of privacy but then she reflected that it was a comfort to know that she was in safe hands and there was a real concern for her welfare.

There was only one discordant occasion when on the first evening she and Daisy were dining at the Captain's table. The other selected guests were very much older than Daisy and certainly old enough to be Celia's parents with the exception of one handsome couple. The urbane and avuncular Captain had invited his guests for drinks before going to dine.

'Ah, Lady Celia and Mrs Fellowes... delighted that you are sailing with us again and gracing the Queen with your elegance and charm.' Daisy almost simpered as she shook hands with the twinkle-eyed captain. 'You really are just too too kind' she responded. Celia took a different tack. 'Thank you Captain, or I believe it is now Commodore, which means that congratulations are due.' He nodded his thanks with a warm smile for this breathtakingly beautiful young woman. Regret that he was not thirty years younger flashed through his mind. Celia continued, as always unaware of the effect that she had on men of all ages. 'How could we travel on any other than the finest ship in the world!'

'Bravo!' added Daisy. The Captain then turned and introduced Daisy and

Celia to the handsome younger couple. The husband was revealed to be a member of the immensely rich German manufacturing family Krupp.

When the party was seated for dinner Celia was delighted to be sitting on the right side of the Captain with Daisy to his left. He clearly enjoyed the company of attractive and lively women. Celia thought that she could hardly blame him glancing at the liver-spotted hands and scrawny bejewelled necks of the others at the table, with the exception of the Krupps.

Herr Krupp was very interested in technical aspects of the ship which Celia found tedious and inappropriate for dinner table talk. She tried to divert the conversation commenting on the many facilities that were available on board. As she finished she remembered one other innovation. 'And there is even a Jewish prayer room to complement the Chapel.'

Herr Krupp visibly bristled and coldly commented 'You would not find such an abomination on a German vessel.'

Before Celia could respond the Captain stepped in. 'Well, you see Herr Krupp, British shipping lines are determined to show that they have a totally tolerant policy with regard to race, creed and colour. Indeed, that is and always has been the policy and belief of our nation and people.'

'A naive belief Captain.' Herr Krupp rudely responded. The Captain smiled and simply said 'That is as it may be Herr Krupp.' For the rest of the voyage Celia and Daisy avoided any conversation with Herr Krupp. Celia made a mental note to report the brief exchange.

Wallis was on the telephone at the desk in the sitting room of the suite in the Hotel Meurice. The Duke was off playing golf.

'Bill… hello, it's Wallis here… how are you my dear man?'

'I am well thank you Wallis… and you?'

'I couldn't be better. We have agreed to take a lease on a chateau at Versailles. I shall have my own driver so that I can come into Paris whenever I want whilst David is gardening there or playing golf.'

'So my girl you are a free agent?'

'I sure am and dying to see you. The move out of the Meurice is tomorrow and I will be tied up at the Chateau as we settle in but then I will be free. So as of Thursday I am in the clear.'

'It will be best if we meet in private in Paris, Wallis. If we are seen to be dining together people will gossip. I have a town house as you know, but that might cause difficulty...'

'Don't worry we can meet at Elsa Schiaperelli's salon and use the entrance at the rear.'

'Excellent. I know it. I had reason to meet Von Ribbentrop on a delicate matter. Our mutual lawyer, who is of course also yours and Elsa's, Armand Gregoire, made the arrangements.'

'Lawyer or not Bill I do not want him involved – I will fix it with Elsa now and call you back. Thursday at two OK for you? I can stay then for three hours or so.'

"Oh well, no problem. I love Louis MacNiece´s little ditty about Shiap... hold on... I have it.

Give me a new muse with stockings and suspenders
And a smile like a cat
With false eyelashes and fingernails of carmine
Dressed by Shiaparelli in a pill box hat.

I digress... That's fine. I am eagerly anticipating seeing you.'

'Me too... me too.'

'Wallis, you never cease to amaze me' laughed William Bullitt as he lay back on the pillow with Wallis snuggled up against him.

They were both naked in the dramatically decorated rococo style room that Elsa Schiaparelli had hastily had decorated with swathes of exotic fabric and an elaborate gilded bed with black silk sheets.

'Honey you were just fine yourself' smiled Wallis turning her head and kissing and nuzzling his neck.

'Only you Wallis. You know I worked with Sigmund Freud back in the 1920's after he psychoanalysed me. We wrote an analysis… a psycho-biographical study of Woodrow Wilson. I had worked with President Wilson but we fell out and I resigned when it became apparent that his aim in the Versailles peace talks, as with the French, was to destroy Germany. I realised that he was as naive as a coot. Anyhow, I digress… now is hardly the time or place, let alone occasion!' Bullitt laughed and his left hand slid down Wallis' back and cupped a small buttock.

'I am always interested Bill, everything you say fascinates me… it always has. I am just so glad that you have no problem having sex with me… boy I really enjoyed and needed that.'

'Oh well, my problem goes back a ways to when I was married to Louise. Crazy really, I divorced her when I found out she was having a lesbian affair… I had thought that I had become impotent when I could not make love to her. It was then that I experimented with homosexuality and I had no problem. I have had a male lover ever since. You are the first woman since then that I have been able to make love to.'

Wallis snuggled closer and softly said 'I have no problem with that. I like girls and I like men. David likes men as well as women and I am the first woman that he has really been able to sleep with. Now let me give you a little more pleasure eh?'

Chapter 14

Vera had a few hours to spend before meeting her husband for lunch. She found his apartment dark and stifling. It was no surprise that as a professional soldier who had been enrolled in a Prussian military school as a thirteen year old, seen distinguished service in the Great War and was still a serving officer at an age when most men would have been retired, General Von Wedel's home was Spartan in the extreme. She marvelled that he still had a five minute cold shower every morning, even in the depth of teeth chattering winter, refused to use the central heating system that served the apartment building and relied upon a small guttering gas fire to heat the large and gloomy drawing room. The apartment was large and impressive and furnished in austere good taste, with heavy gilt-framed portraits of the General's unsmiling uniformed ancestors and their severe, unsmiling wives in most cases. Vera accepted that this was entirely in keeping so far as the General was concerned but for her it was a cold cage of a place.

Vera had bathed and dressed quickly and whilst still feeling some warmth from her bath was enjoying a brisk walk down the Unter den Linden ignoring the enticing aroma of coffee and cinnamon that pervaded the bright morning. She very quickly reached her destination the Cafe Kranzler with its gleaming brass and scrumptious cakes displayed on tiered stands. Vera was recognised by a moustached waiter who bowed and showed her to a table with a good view of the whole cafe. She ordered a Baumkuchen butter cake which was at once a rich delight and a guilty pleasure. As was customary Vera lingered over two coffees and read the morning newspaper in its wooden holder. Looking at her watch she realized that she was due to meet her husband in little over an hour. Not surprisingly he was a stickler for punctuality and she wanted to do a little window shopping before meeting him. As she walked out of the cafe she nodded politely to the predominantly elderly women who were the other patrons noting their elegant formal clothes and their straight backs which conveyed an indefinable air of dignified hauteur. These were the 'Damen-Konditorei' where it was said that good ladies kept their hairdos and hats upright as they turned the pages of their magazines whilst studying the clientele minutely and critically.

As she came onto the pavement she noticed a large black saloon car by the kerbside directly opposite the entrance. She started as a youngish man in a leather coat raised his hat and addressed her formally. 'Frau Von Wedel please come with me. I am adjutant to Reichsfuhrer SS Himmler who wishes to talk with you. Karl Wollf at your service Ma'am.'

Whilst Vera felt a lurch in her stomach the smiling young man gave no major cause for concern although being aware of the antagonism between the Gestapo and the Abwehr she was surprised to be summoned to see Himmler. Nevertheless she felt confident that her husband's close relationship with Admiral Canaris, the Fuhrer himself and the inner circle of his military colleagues ensured her protection.

Wollf closed the car door and then sat in the front with the driver as the car sped the short distance to the imposing building in Prinz-Albrecht- Strasse. Vera had to suppress a shudder as Wollf opened the door for her at the porticoed main entrance to the most feared building in the Reich; Gestapo Headquarters.

Immaculate in their black uniforms SS Guards slammed to attention and saluted as Vera and Wollf entered a lofty entrance hall which could grace any grand hotel in its style. Vera felt a little bemused at the thought that this grand entrance was to a building which housed the many headed security apparatus of the ruthless German police state and the ultimate master whom she was about to meet, and reputedly the cells and rooms where enemies of the Reich breathed their last with relief. Another SS soldier stood to attention by the lifts and indicated the one which they should take.

A severe looking receptionist in a crisply starched demure white blouse with a black tie indicated that they should wait. After a brief murmured telephone call she gestured that they should follow her and escorted them across the marble floored vestibule and opening a tall mahogany door announced them both by name.

Vera had never met Heinrich Himmler the second most powerful man in the Third Reich and probably the most feared. He stood but did not offer his hand as without a smile he greeted them with a Nazi salute.

'Heil Hitler! Frau Von Wedel I am pleased to make your acquaintance. Good morning Karl. Kindly sit.' Himmler's voice was soft and somehow devoid of any feeling.

He continued in the same tone with no noticeable inflexion. 'As a loyal member of the Abwehr whose activities are always of interest it was considered that you might find it enlightening to have a little tour of parts of this building. It will of course be a short tour on this occasion as we must not delay your luncheon with your husband. That would never do. My adjutant Colonel Wolff will be your escort.'

Vera was shocked by the words 'on this occasion' and the threat that they implied; also that so powerful a man should have known of her private luncheon arrangement with her husband. She managed to respond formally. 'That is most kind of you Herr Reichsmarshall... Heil Hitler.' Himmler acknowledged her salute and then pointedly turned his attention to some papers on his desk. As they walked back to the lift two more men in the uniform of SS officers fell in behind them and the sound of the men's boot heels on the marble floor rang like a bell in Vera's head. She was now very afraid.

The lift had a half circle floor indicator which showed just one floor beneath ground level. Vera felt a sense of dread as she realised that the indicator was no longer moving with the arrow at basement level and yet they were still going down. She instinctively looked at Colonel Wolff with eyebrows raised questioningly. Both he and the other two officers laughed and as the lift finally came to a stop he said 'This is a building of many surprises as you shall see dear lady.' The doors slid open and immediately Vera's nostrils were assailed by foetid air carrying a mixture of obnoxious smells. Vera's hand flew to cover her nose. She almost immediately recognised the smells of burnt flesh, hair, blood and excrement overlaid with a stench of bleach. She gagged and stumbled as if punched. The Colonel stopped and apparently concerned asked in a polite tone 'Are you alright Madam von Wedel?' Through her discomfort Vera was surprised at his politely concerned tone as it registered that the vile smell was the stench of appalling human suffering.

Vera gritted her teeth and with a small but determined shake of her head then looked the Colonel in the eye and in a firm voice responded in a polite but clipped tone 'I am perfectly well Herr Colonel. Please carry on.' The Colonel nodded almost respectfully and they approached the first door in the pale green painted brick corridor. The Colonel slid open a small observation panel and called his name. Bolts could be heard and the thick steel door opened noiselessly. The stench was even stronger but Vera was determined not to show any weakness and swallowed the bile that had rushed into her mouth. Most of the windowless chamber was in deep shadow but in stark contrast what appeared to be an operating theatre light blazed down onto a sturdy wooden table which had heavy leather straps hanging from each corner. There was a large enamel bucket at one end of the table.

A shaven headed brute of a man in rubber boots and with a leather apron stretching over his vest and down to almost ground level was wiping down the table. Another man similarly dressed was fiddling with a blow torch. Both gave almost perfunctory nods acknowledging the Colonel and Vera's presence. As her eyes adjusted Vera saw that there was a galvanised steel sided gurney in the shadows. Colonel Wollf simply pointed to the gurney and the man with the blow torch pushed it into the light. The Colonel gestured for Vera to follow him as he approached it. Smiling he motioned for Vera to look into it with a sweeping gesture as if he were displaying a fine picture.

Vera did and once again her hand flew to her mouth as she realised that the mangled and burnt contents of the gurney had been a human being. Vera turned away and as they walked back to the door the Colonel spoke to the two men 'Well done, please carry on. Heil Hitler!' Their response was perfunctory.

Back in the corridor the foetid air was almost a relief. Onwards the little group marched further along the narrow brick lined corridor lit by fixed overhead metal industrial lights until they stopped at another door. This time the Colonel simply opened it. In contrast the walls were stark white and the whole long chamber was brightly lit. Along the side walls there were rails about seven feet from the floor and what looked like loops of piano wire every two or so metres. Along the centre there was a stout steel rail from which there hung butchers' meat hooks. Again the Colonel spoke to Vera with a slight almost playful smile. 'As you can see madam, this is an execution chamber for those enemies of the Reich who do not deserve a quick despatch at the hands of the merciful hangman.' Vera nodded and turned back towards the door simply saying 'Thank you Colonel.'

'There is just one more room for you to see before you leave for your luncheon.'

The final room was a high ceilinged chamber containing a blood stained guillotine.

'This Madam is reserved for those whose departure from this earth is considered to be appropriate or who have survived other procedures for longer than is consistent with efficiency. The mode of death is of course determined by the sentencing Court with the Reichsfuhrer having the ultimate authority and discretion. Now, we must leave.'

When they reached the doors onto the street the Colonel bowed stiffly and said 'Madam, it has been a great pleasure to make your acquaintance and I look forward to our next meeting. I must bid you good bye and do please convey the good wishes of the Reichsfuhrer our staff and of course myself to the General and assure him that we continue to take a close interest in his career as with all senior officers in the Abwehr. Heil Hitler.'

As she turned and walked away Vera realised that her hands were shaking uncontrollably. The message had been delivered bluntly and had left no room for doubt.

General von Wedel was shocked when he met his wife in their favourite restaurant. She was white as a sheet and did not greet him with her usual warm smile that he so treasured. 'Are you alright my dear? You look as though you have seen a ghost?' he asked in an affectionate tone.

'No darling I am not…most certainly not.'

As was his habit the General had specified the table that he wished to have and they were out of earshot of the other patrons. 'Tell me' he demanded in a firm but caring tone. He sat as though at attention and Vera leaned in to him as in a soft voice she recounted her experience and precisely what she had been told and seen. She had a great skill for remembering conversations literally word for word. His expression did not change as he responded 'My dear girl it is not safe for you to be here in Germany at this time. I shall see the Admiral this afternoon on my return and obtain an order for your immediate return to London.'

'But why?' asked Vera. 'What is the danger from which you wish to shield me?'

'I am afraid that we are pawns in a high stakes game being played between Himmler and the Admiral. At present The Admiral and hence the whole Abwehr has the ear and protection of the Fuhrer – notwithstanding that he likes to play one off against the other. The Fuhrer believes that all men perform best when they have a foresworn rival to beat. In this instance it is very uncomfortable not least because the Admiral believes in gathering intelligence whereas Himmler uses his various networks not only to gather information but also to take extreme measures against any person or group whom he considers to be a risk of any sort. That is a risk to the Fuhrer and the Reich but also his own ever growing power base. He is possibly one of the most powerful man in the Reich and in many ways the most dangerous. It is London for you my dear as quickly as possible.'

'Please take me home darling. I really do not have any appetite.'

'Of course.'

Chapter 15

Celia settled into the soft leather rear seat of the now venerable Springfield bodied Rolls Royce Silver Ghost that her dear grandmother had left her. She accepted that the motor was an anachronism in frenetic New York which as a city had more motor cars than the whole German nation. Modern America's love affair with the motor car had created a nightmare scenario in a City where everybody was in a hurry and yet more often than not the traffic was grid locked. New York's intensive music was a cacophony of motor horns.

One of Celia's grandmother's wishes, which she had stressed to her favourite granddaughter and chosen heir when they met for what they both knew to be the final time, was that Celia should so far as possible retain all of her faithful staff both in the central New York house and the shoreline mansion in the Hamptons. Celia had readily agreed having known many of them since she was a mere toddler when first brought over to New York on the grand old transatlantic liner the Mauretania. James the Negro chauffer was a case in point. He had started work for grandmother Evangeline, known as 'Evan' amongst family and friends, when he was a young man of 30. He went into her service in 1904 when she acquired her first motor car and soon proved himself to have an instinctive flair as both a mechanic and a safe driver.

As motoring progressed from being an amusing and fashionable diversion into a practical and then essential means of transport James adapted with enthusiasm. Evan was an emancipated woman and her much older husband benevolently indulged her. In 1914 even he was a little taken aback when she announced that she wanted a Stutz 'Bearcat', a road going version of the factory 'White Squadron' racing cars. He capitulated but with a condition. On public roads it should only be driven by James. Evan had countered by insisting that the car be painted yellow and James was to have a new uniform in dark blue rather than the pale grey that he normally wore. She also wished there to be a proper windscreen protecting the passenger as well as the driver. Evan could never bring herself to sell the car which she raced under a false name entering and posing as a man with James in attendance. Few were fooled but nobody gave away her secret and that included James who was in the car with her as her mechanic when racing.

America's entry into the Great War put an end to Evan's racing and she threw herself into voluntary work exhausting herself to the point where she hardly had the energy to worry about her two sons and her son in law who were fighting in far away Europe.

Both of her sons were killed. The eldest, Henry, named after her husband, died with awful irony only days before the end of the conflict. Neither had married.

Her son in law, the Marquis, Celia's father, survived the Great War and Evan's reaction to her grief was to dote on Celia, in whom she saw so much of herself as a young girl and later a young woman. Her husband Henry had died shortly after the end of the Great War, a man in despair having worked so hard to amass a great fortune and create an empire that his sons would take over. That they would not do so was a blow from which he never recovered. His dream had been shattered.

On Henry's death Evan, who had always shown an interest in the business, unlike most women of her age and class in America, decided to use her knowledge to bring together her late husband's many interests into a single powerful entity. She would then engineer a realisation of the business retaining sufficient of an interest to ensure that as well as great capital wealth there would always be a substantial and secure income for her and her heirs. Her daughter was well provided for in a very happy marriage to another hugely wealthy man, the Marquis, and agreed wholeheartedly that Evan should leave everything to Celia.

Her skill and prudence was rewarded in 1929 when the Great Crash wiped out many wealthy families almost at a stroke. She was only marginally affected and quickly recouped her minimal losses by the shrewd purchase of assets at bargain prices.

Her adoration of Celia never wavered and she died a happy woman knowing that not only would the young woman she so loved become one of the richest people in America but that Celia had grown up to be a delightful human being. She knew full well that Celia moved in a 'fast' set in London but believed that her protégé would soon grow out of what would prove to be nothing more than a passing phase.

Celia was remarkably unaffected by the knowledge of her inherited independent wealth. She had been brought up in a totally privileged environment, almost a cocoon of great wealth, and had never had to give a thought to money. Her father was always keen to save money and often commented that by his efforts he saved the cost of extra garden staff. To Celia this seemed no more than a poor excuse for him to enjoy one of his favourite pastimes, pottering in the gardens of whichever of his estates he was staying in at the time.

She was shrewd enough to comment to her mother that 'Papa does not seem so keen on gardening when we are in Scotland and he has his stalking, shooting and fishing nor in Leicestershire when he has his hunting.' Celia missed her grandmother terribly but as the Rolls Royce Phantom smoothed to a stop outside the house on the Upper East Side she felt not only that this was a homecoming but also that in the house, just as she had in the car with James, she would sense her grandmother's loving presence. 'Snap out of it girl… you are here to do a job of work… not wallow in nostalgia!' she rebuked herself.

James, resplendent in his pale grey uniform with mirror polished knee high black boots, breeches, high necked tunic and cap with the black badged cockade signifying that he was a Rolls Royce trained driver, held open the door and saluted crisply as Celia stepped out.

The only thing that surprised and rather shocked an elderly lady walking slowly past with a reluctant snuffling Pekinese on a lead was the broad smile the chauffer was bestowing on the beautiful young woman. She tutted to herself, muttering 'Most unseemly… quite inappropriate.' Celia was oblivious as she strode across the sidewalk towards the gleaming black painted double doors that were swinging open to reveal the 'family' butler as she thought of him also standing ready to greet his mistress to whom he too was devoted. Before he could speak Celia smiling broadly said 'Home Smithers, I'm home!'

'Yes Milady and we are all delighted to welcome you. There are messages on your escritoire when you have an opportunity.'

'Thank you Smithers.' Celia cast an eye along the line of staff in the hallway and smiled as she said loudly 'Good morning everybody. I am delighted to be home even if sadly it will only be for a few days.'

The staff who were mostly elderly were also smiling to have this young woman whom they had seen grow up with their late mistress return to the old house that was not only her home but theirs too. Some of the half bows and bobbed curtseys were a little shaky reflecting the effects of age but there could be no doubting their sincerity as Celia walked slowly along the line greeting each by name.

After that Celia strode off to her small sitting room where she had her writing desk, telephone and new-fangled American invention a rotary card index system with contact details of her friends and contacts worldwide. It was quite bulky and stood on a tall Chinese side-table next to her desk chair.

'You know Smithers… quite remarkable… I'm not sure whether I have mentioned this before, but on the Queen… you know, the Queen Mary… in every cabin and stateroom there is a telephone and you can call anywhere in the world. Isn't that extraordinary…'

'Yes Milady, that probably accounts for the number of messages that you have received.'

'Oh dear, I trust that they were not an inconvenience?'

'Certainly not Milady. After your journey would you wish for some coffee?'

'Oh that is most thoughtful and would be very welcome. Please advise cook that I shall take a very light luncheon… a tray here would be ideal. Also, I shall be dining out tonight. Mrs Fellowes who sailed over with me will be coming for drinks at seven o'clock. I shall receive her in the French drawing room. She will be in her motor so James will not be required this evening.'

'Very well Milady. I shall take my leave and send up some coffee.'

Celia started to rifle through the stack of messages and sort them by priority. Her focus was on those who might be able to facilitate a meeting with Allen Dulles.

As it turned out she would not have to look for long or indeed wait for an opportunity to present itself.

After drinks in Celia's house she and Daisy were driven to Sardi's. They had both agreed to turn down an invitation to attend an opening night after theatre party at the legendary Sardi's restaurant preferring instead to go there earlier and have a quiet dinner together.

Before taking their table, which was in a prime position reflecting Daisy's prominence in New York society, they had decided to have a drink in the Little

Bar at the front of the restaurant.

'You know Celia, we Americans are so darn desperate to create our history in double-quick time. Just look at this place with its hundreds of caricatures on the walls… you know, Vincent Sardi copied the idea from a Parisian restaurant cum jazz club Joe Zelli's.'

'Daisy, don't be such a grump… I think that it is a wonderful idea for a theatre restaurant like this although some of the pictures are… let's just say, less than flattering. You know we British have a tradition of caricatures of the famous and infamous going back to the penny papers which lampooned everyone from the Royal family to politicians. Then, of course, the famous 'Spy' cartoons by Leslie Ward in Vanity Fair for thirty odd years over the turn of the century.'

'My dear girl, I rest my case. What the British were doing two hundred years ago we are doing now.'

'And often rather better' laughed Celia. 'I meant to ask, have you come across a couple of brothers… lawyers… John Foster and Allen Dulles?'

'Oh I know Allen' replied Daisy with a knowing look that turned into a broad smile. 'He is a lot of fun. Would you like me to introduce you?'

'Would you? That would be so kind.'

'Of course I shall be delighted… but tell me why him if I may ask?' Celia had wracked her brains anticipating that someone was bound to ask this question when she evinced an interest in meeting him but she had failed to come up with anything that did not sound banal to her ears.

'Oh, his name was mentioned as one of the up and coming men in New York and I am intrigued.'

'Ha! He's that alright!' laughed Daisy wolfishly and winked. 'Ok… shall we eat?'

Billy Brownlow arrived in New York on the French liner Normandie the following morning after a relaxing voyage where he had caught up with some long overdue reading and had worked hard at brushing up his German. He also had plenty of time to think about Vera. That he was totally smitten with her was not in question. However that did not get over the problems involving their child that she was going to have. He had consulted his family's lawyers and had had a very helpful session with the senior partner, Sir Harry Rider. They had thrashed out a complicated plan that would enable Billy to make provision for

Vera and for their son to inherit Billy's titles and take over the family property on his death.

They were in Sir Harry Rider's rather gloomy book lined office in London's Lincoln's Inn Fields at the heart of what is known as 'Legal London', with various old and modern trust documents spread out on the large leather topped table at which they were sitting. The documents clearly set out the limits of Billy's discretion and that of the trustees.

Sir Harry was a tall man and although in his late sixties invariably sat ramrod straight, his back never touching his chair. At first glance he was a forbidding figure with his greying and rather sparse hair oiled and parted in the centre, round framed spectacles and starched wing collar. However his appearance was deceptive and hid a warm and deeply caring man. He was an astute student of human nature and a creature of habit. It was well known that on weekday evenings when he left his Club, Boodles in St James's, and walked briskly back to Eaton Terrace wearing his customary Homburg hat he would drop a handful of stamped postcards addressed to himself into the post box in The Ritz. His secretary would present them to him first thing in the morning as self-reminders of random thoughts he had had the previous evening.

His London house was very close to that of Sir Vernon Kell and he had a pretty good idea of what Billy's real occupation was. Certainly he did not believe for a moment that he had a tedious desk job in the Ministry of Defence as Billy had told him.

'Billy, I know you well enough to pose a very personal question. As you know your father and I were chums at Harrow, later when we went up to Oxford, then in the army. We remained very close until his untimely demise.'

'It was untimely Sir Harry but, you know that he had been diagnosed with an incurable progressive condition that would soon have paralysed him. Dying instantly on the hunting field whilst taking a fall would have been his choice, I know. I apologise, I digress. Please ask your question.'

'You have stayed single until now and you are almost forty. You could have had and still could have the pick of English Society and yet you have fallen for a lady with a mysterious past, who is married to a German General.'

Billy went to interrupt but Sir Harry was not to be diverted. 'By your own admission she has something of... let us call it a history... I would go so far as to say that she sounds like a bit of a femme fatale or even a Mata Hari. Are you absolutely sure my boy that you are not temporarily blinded by passion?'

'Absolutely not Sir Harry. I have never been more certain of anything in my life. I love her.'

'Very well, nothing more will ever be said.'

Shortly after arriving in New York Billy telephoned Celia.

'Billy… what a super surprise… but what brings you to New York?'

'I would rather not say on the telephone Celia. Would it be convenient if I were to call on you? I can explain then.'

'Come for lunch… it will be light because I am dining out tonight. You have not been here before… I'm on the Upper East Side, number eighteen East 67th Street – would one forty five suit you?'

'That's perfect. I have a couple of people to see urgently and then I shall come on to you.'

'Super Billy… until later.'

After a session with her hairdresser and beautician Celia spent the rest of the morning following up old friends generally explaining that this was only a flying visit and it might not be possible to meet. Nevertheless she kept her options open as far as possible with those who might be able to assist her in her task.

Billy arrived promptly and after a seemingly ancient liveried footman had taken his hat, coat and gloves, Smithers the butler led him to an elegant sitting room where Celia was waiting. She dashed up to Billy and gave him an enthusiastic hug. Smithers poured drinks for them both and after Celia said that she would ring when they were ready for luncheon, withdrew and closed the tall double doors.

'So Billy why are you here? I know that it is not a spur of the moment holiday.'

'Simple Celia. Since the wedding of the Duke and Duchess of Windsor and your accompanying them on the German visit both you and of course Johnny are of great interest to German intelligence. I am afraid that it is not so much interest on the part of the Abwehr but Himmler's SD… the international arm of the dreaded Gestapo. You recall the bodged attacks in France?'

'Don't I just… do go on.'

'We have it on good authority that the SD are liaising with the German American Bund here in New York… that's from the FBI. However we picked up a whisper that Himmler sees you as an asset of Admiral Canaris, the head of military intelligence, the Abwehr… whom he detests. Himmler would not flinch from letting the American Nazi sympathisers, who are a rough bunch from all accounts, know that if you were to have an accident it would be regarded as very favourable. The German American Bund is funded by the German Nazi Party by the way. We also believe that Himmler is aware of your relationship with von Ribbentrop – another of his enemies.'

'So it's a kind of double jeopardy for little old me eh?'

'Well, I hope not but we cannot be too careful. I had a meeting with the FBI this morning and they are now keeping you under light protective surveillance. They have also given the green light for me to run close protection with the couple who were with you on the Queen Mary and a couple of others that I have brought up from the Washington Embassy.'

'Would it be a good idea for you to stay here? Michael the steward on the crossing could come here as your 'man'?'

'That would be splendid' replied a smiling Billy as Celia stood and took their glasses to the drinks table.

'Well my news is that Daisy Fellowes has organised a little dinner party at Keens Chophouse tonight with Allen Dulles.'

'Who will be there?' asked Billy with an appreciative smile as Celia handed him his replenished glass.

'Just Daisy, Allen and me. Daisy is going to feign a headache and slide off early and leave me with him. She thinks that my interest is purely carnal.'

'She would from what one hears' laughed Billy. 'If I move in here later this afternoon, perhaps you could give me a lift and I will bail out before you reach the restaurant. Michael will already be there. Do you have the address? Just give it to me before I go so that I can instruct him.'

Celia could not quite make out Allen Dulles. He flirted with Daisy who shamelessly hinted at a previous intimate relationship and was, as she would put it, 'giving him the full treatment.'

In spite of this distraction he also managed to pay close attention to Celia and soon revealed himself to be a cultured almost scholarly man. That he had great charm was without doubt but Celia could not detect outward signs of the rake that he was reputed to be other than in very obviously playing up to Daisy.

As if on cue Daisy complained that she had the beginning of a migraine and must return home and lie down. After saying her goodbyes in the course of which she contrived to squeeze Celia's arm twice in quick succession whilst winking lasciviously she was gone.

'Well Celia, now we can get acquainted a little more. How do you like Keens?'

'It's very pleasant. Now, why is this named the Lily Langtry Room?'

'The story is that in 1905 Jersey Lily, as I believe she was known affectionately, was playing in a New York theatre and at the end of an evening performance was ravenous. She had heard of Keens which was founded on the lines of an English chophouse. However, unfortunately, ladies were not permitted.'

The dark panelled interior brought to mind Gow's Restaurant in the City of London where Celia's personal stock broker the debonair James Crawford normally entertained her.

'Lily was of course the mistress of King Edward VII, so to an extent infamous, as well as being a famous actress. She boldly marched straight into Keens. The staff stood with crossed arms ignoring her. She stared them out and eventually Keen himself came to her and showed her to an empty table and she was served. The rule was scrapped.'

Celia laughed 'A truly modern woman!'

'This is the only room in the place which does not have clay pipes lining the walls. There are over 90,000 of them stored here for members of the Keens' Pipe Club.' Dulles paused and took a sip of water before continuing. 'Now then Celia, tell me about Germany and your impressions of not only the place but the people from top to bottom.'

Celia was careful to take a neutral line as she spoke of the contrasts she had witnessed and the great shows of military strength and enthusiasm for Hitler's Reich. 'Allen, believe me that enthusiasm goes beyond patriotism. There are huge, and I mean huge, crowds at the rallies and parades. There is a feeling which can best be described as bordering on hysteria. But, you know, I just wonder how many Germans really want to be led into another massive conflict when they are still suffering from the repercussions of the last War.'

'Here is the waiter to take our orders. Celia, have you chosen?' Allen asked the question in a rather strange almost ambiguous way.

Celia decided to play him at his own game. 'I do so love a menu that is traditional but tests your loyalties, don't you Allen?' Celia asked with her head slightly lowered and looking up into his eyes through her thick lashes. 'I really fancy a change. I think I will have one of Mr Keen's famous double chops. You know Allen, in England they are called Barnsley chops.'

'I am glad that you fancy trying something different tonight Celia' responded Allen with an almost smug smile. 'I hope that you really enjoy it.' Celia managed to control the urge to wipe the self-satisfied look from Allen's face and made no reply merely smiling coyly.

Chapter 16

'Wallis my dear – did you have a satisfactory afternoon?'

'Why yes, my darling – Elsa was as welcoming as ever and the fitting was a great success. How was your golf?'

'I think that the move out of Paris has done both me and my golf the world of good – I was playing with the pro again and he was as delighted as I was that I have won back my form. I feel as though I am a free man!'

'That is wonderful darling. Also, now that we have our own place I feel much more inclined to entertain again properly. It will be fun.'

'Have you anyone in mind?'

'Well I did think that it might be an idea to have William Bullitt the American Ambassador – he reputedly speaks to President Roosevelt every day – Armand Gregoire, you know, the society lawyer that we share, actually it is he who apparently says that Ambassador Bullitt 'has the President's ear' and is his private mouthpiece here in Paris.'

'That is a good thought my darling. Bullitt is reputedly inseparable from his private secretary, Carmel Offie who has followed him from posting to posting and shares his home.'

Wallis gave a mirthless laugh and commented in a waspish tone

'The fact that he is homosexual is none of our business David, is it? We shall have to invite both of them and, I suggest that as our staff are familiarising themselves with this house we keep the evening intimate. Perhaps only Armand Gregoire and his wife. He is as the centre of everything here in Paris and very interesting company. He represents Von Ribbentrop as well, you know... almost a foot in both camps for us my darling.'

'That sounds very satisfactory Wallis… the idea of such an intimate evening appeals greatly.'

'It sure does honey,' replied a smiling Wallis relishing the thought of dining with her husband, a current lover and a link to another lover.

'What fun' she thought and aroused at the prospect turned to the Duke and said 'David do please excuse me for an hour or so, I am going to lie down and then dictate some letters to Helga including these invitations.'

'Of course darling – you just carry on. I am in the mood for some knitting.'

The Duke smiled at the thought of relaxing at one of his favourite hobbies. Unlikely that it might be, he had found knitting therapeutic on the long ocean voyages when he had toured the world as Prince of Wales.

'That's better… my God I needed that Helga' murmured Wallis as she nuzzled Helga. 'I didn't hurt you too much did I my sweet?'

Stifling a sob Helga turned her tear stained and flushed face towards Wallis. 'If I am honest Wallis, you did. If you had not gagged me first I think I would have screamed the house down. Your so-called "little present" from Coco Chanel is just vicious. Please never use it again.'

Wallis felt strangely aroused by what the younger woman had just said and reaching out caressed the polished ebony curved wand that was now lying on the bedspread. With a glint in her eye she replied in a cold monotone. 'We shall see Helga… after all you are mine… never forget my darling girl it is I who possess you, body and soul.'

Helga did not reply but hatred for her mistress was fast crystallising into a burning desire for revenge. *She would have her day* she thought, as she disentangled herself from Wallis and eased herself off the bed. She did so very gently in an attempt to avoid increasing the intense pain at her core.

Princess Stephanie and Johnny had strolled down through the gardens of Cliveden following the path that they had been told would lead them to Spring Cottage on the banks of the River Thames far below the great house.

'Johnny, be honest with me. I know that we are attracted to each other and we have enjoyed our intimacy… I am sorry to put this so formally but remember please that English is not my first language… but I do not feel that you are really letting yourself go with me. Is that so?'

'I have no choice but to be honest' replied Johnny, then after a pause, he took Stephanie's hand and continued, 'I am deeply attracted to you and you fascinate me in so many ways ... we go so well together ... emotionally and physically but...' Stephanie raised her right hand stopping Johnny in midsentence, then laid her palm flat against his cheek, almost a caress.

'I sensed that there was a 'but' Johnny. That is why I asked you. Now please do not say anything and let me speak for a minute. What I am going to say is important to you and us both personally and professionally. It must stay strictly between us.' Johnny was intrigued – Stephanie's eyes were burning with intensity as he nodded and then she carried on. 'I know that you are in love with Celia Ffrench-Hardy and she with you... you are the envy of every man in London and a few more I'll wager. That is what is holding you back... that is your "but"...'

'Yes Stephanie it is and...'

'Johnny, just listen to me please. I have the same problem. I am in love with someone who is just as much in love with me. I too have my "but"...' At this point they both fell into an embrace and laughed together then kissed softly as dear friends but not true lovers. After a minute they drew apart and Johnny asked 'Do I know him?'

'This is why I asked for discretion. You have met him. It is Fritz Wiedemann the Fuhrer's Adjutant.'

'Christ!' exclaimed Johnny. 'That's bloody dangerous for both of you – if Hitler found out there would be hell to pay.'

'Possibly for Fritz but I think not. Remember he was the Fuhrer's superior officer in the Great War and it was Fritz who campaigned for the Fuhrer's Iron Cross. He would be angry of course because it is me who is involved. The bigger danger comes from those jackals that surround the Fuhrer.'

'You mean Himmler and Heydrich?'

'For sure, but do not underestimate Goebbels and of course Goering who is possibly the most ruthless and clever of them all behind that buffoon exterior.'

'So, what shall we do dear Stephanie?'

'Oh you silly man, enjoy ourselves, here in this wonderful place but as free spirits knowing exactly where we stand.'

'Very well, a picnic on the river is the order of the day, so what are we waiting for?'

The path came to a clearing surrounded by beech trees and fronting the river. On the bank stood an elderly but ramrod straight boatman and his much younger assistant. There was a small landing stage to which the vintage "Suzy

Ann" was moored.

'Good morning… are we the first?' asked Johnny of the older bearded man who replied in his deep rumbling voice thick with a West Country burr. 'That you be My Lord.' He then turned towards Stephanie and bowed as did his assistant. 'Welcome Your Royal Highness. I am the Boatswain and will be in charge of the vessel today assisted by young Rawlings here.' Johnny replied. 'And your name is?'

'I answer to 'Boatswain' My Lord – that was my rank for many a year in the Andrew and I am content with it.'

'Quite so – Stephanie, the Boatswain here represents the backbone of a fighting ship and in case you are unfamiliar with the term, "The Andrew" is the services' nickname for the Royal Navy.'

'Would you wish to come on board now Your Royal Highness, My Lord?' Stephanie was sensibly wearing wide-legged cruising style trousers and flat heeled rubber soled shoes and had no difficulty in stepping down onto the highly varnished seat in the stern of the vessel. She did not need the helping hand that Johnny proffered before he followed her.

The bevelled glass in the doors leading into the spacious day cabin was intricately etched. Inside a white-jacketed steward stood by the centre table, on which stood large silver ice buckets beaded with condensation containing magnums of champagne.

'I say, Stephanie, just what the good doctor ordered, eh? Steward two glasses of champagne please, or rather should I say goblets?' laughed Johnny as the steward took silver goblets out of another large ice bucket, then after pouring the champagne with great care handed them to the couple with small linen napkins.

'Ah the American way' commented Johnny. He continued when Stephanie looked puzzled. 'Our cousins on the other side of the Atlantic load their drinks with ice and you need a napkin to deal with the condensation. We have the same problem here as our American born hostess clearly anticipated. Your Very Good Health my dear.' Johnny and Stephanie toasted each other just as a Rolls Royce shooting brake drove slowly into the clearing.

'I always think that putting a wooden body like that on a Rolls Royce chassis is sacrilege' commented Johnny.

'Oh you men and motors' laughed Stephanie. 'Don't forget that Lenin rushed around in a Rolls Royce armoured car during the Russian Revolution!'

The remainder of the boating party were helped into the Suzy Ann with the exception of Nancy Astor who was assisted into her electric canoe by another smartly turned out young man who it turned out was to be her crewman. Both vessels flew the Red Ensign of British merchant vessels and Lady Astor's canoe also an embroidered standard bearing the coat of arms of the Astor family.

The Boatswain went to the wheel which was to one side of the open cockpit seating area. The starter motor whirred for what seemed like an age prompting an exchange of slightly concerned looks between the guests. Then with a cough, a splutter, a cloud of smoke and gush of water from the exhaust the engine burst into life noisily. As it settled into a steady beat the Boatswain nodded to his assistant on the river bank who released the mooring ropes and nimbly hopped aboard as the Suzy Ann swung away from the bank into the fast flowing river. Lady Astor's canoe followed silently.

Allen Dulles was proving to be a fascinating host and in the ornate setting of the cream painted Lily Langtry Room set out to charm his much younger companion. He had soon realised that Celia was no mere spoilt little empty headed rich girl. It was apparent that his companion had inherited clever and insightful genes from both sides of her family. He had quickly decided that he wanted to seduce her and almost as quickly that she could be a challenge. First, he wanted to find out just what it was that she wanted from him. He was far too astute to believe that this privileged and clever young woman would have sought his company without a serious motive. He could not give credence to Daisy Fellowes' confidential explanation that word of his sexual prowess had brought Celia across the Atlantic, on a whim.

'Do you expect to accompany the Duke and Duchess of Windsor on their planned trip to America, Celia?'

'I have not been asked but of course I would be happy to. I am privileged to be counted a close friend of them both and sadly they are lacking friends at the moment.'

'You would of course have met Charles Bedaux at the time of their wedding in his chateau. What did you make of him?'

'He was perfectly pleasant but rather full of himself, as one might say. Nevertheless he was without doubt a most considerate and generous host.'

'Did he talk about politics?' Allen enquired.

Celia wanted to keep Allen's interest but did not want to give much away in response to this blatant fishing expedition.

'Oh Allen! Even in these enlightened times we mere ladies are kept in the dark and not included in such discussions.'

'Yes, but did he talk to your companion, Lord John?'

'Oh, he might have done. We were there for such a short time and the wedding took up most of it. Anyhow, why are you so interested?' Celia had decided that it was time to give Mr Allen Dulles some of his own medicine.

'Well, I have come across him in a peripheral way... he has advised some of my larger clients, indeed, is good friends with them, so naturally I am intrigued.'

'It was mentioned in London... oh I cannot remember by whom – no matter – that Bedaux was organising the Duke and Duchess' visit to America.'

'Well he does have some very good connections here.'

'Is he a very popular man to have so much influence?'

Allen permitted himself a smile. 'Well it would be fairer to say that whilst bosses and shareholders may be his admirers most unions and workers are not.'

'They are hostile?'

'You could put it like that.'

'Will the Duke and Duchess meet the President. They met Herr Hitler in private.'

'It is possible – now, that's enough. How did you enjoy indulging yourself with a change – would you consider doing it again?' Allen had again adopted the rather strange expression that Celia had noticed earlier. She could not put her finger on it. It was a look almost of diffident enquiry but at the same time there was an arrogance. Celia decided in a split second that the only way she would find out what was likely to happen to Bedaux and the plans for the Windsor visit to America was to play along with Allen's game wherever that might take her.

'Thank you Allen. The double saddle cutlet, as I think it was billed, was utterly delicious and I could neither eat nor drink another thing in this wonderful restaurant tonight.'

'A change of scene perhaps Celia?'

'That might be rather fun,' replied Celia coquettishly.

Billy Brownlow was sitting having dinner with Donald MacLaren in New York's fashionable '21' restaurant close to the Rockefeller Center. They were seated at MacLaren's usual table number 24 which gave him a good view of the other diners in this most popular restaurant without being too ostentatious. As well as being chief of his Scottish clan, MacClaren, a qualified accountant, was the eyes and ears of the Scottish Secret Service in New York. His covert task was to investigate the complex transactions through which America's big business and banks were financing Germany's epic growth.

'You must have eaten here before Billy?'

'Years ago actually Donald… it was when there was prohibition and this restaurant was the ultimate swanky speakeasy.'

Donald laughed. 'That it certainly was. I never saw the disappearing bar in operation. You know, the fabulous wine cellar was in the cellar of number 19 next door so staff could swear on oath that no wine was stored in number 21.

'The place was designed by the architect Frank Buchanan. Expense was no object to the wealthy backers including the old bootlegger Joseph Kennedy. There were false walls, secret doors and passages – you name it – to deceive the authorities.'

Billy nodded and then MacLaren continued.

'Now, to business. What brings you to New York out of the blue? All I know is that Tar Robertson asked me to meet up with you as a matter of urgency.'

'It's a long story Donald I'm afraid.'

'Worry not, I am a patient man. I am comfortably ensconced in my favourite restaurant with a magnificent wine cellar and I am blessed with a more than generous expense account. Before you start, permit me to order us some wine.' In response to the subtlest of gestures the sommelier appeared at MacLaren's side.

'Paolo, I trust that you are well. Now we shall have a bottle of my usual Montagny and if you would decant some Chateau Lafite-Rothschild I should be most pleased. Right, important business done, Billy, you now have the stage.'

Two hours later after an excellent dinner accompanied by exquisite wine Billy had finished the briefing. After a little ritual choosing cognac and cigars MacLaren spoke softly.

'Billy, the trouble here is that we have a very strong pro German Lobby in the USA. Furthermore, particularly here in New York and on this Eastern seaboard there is strong anti-British feeling. In addition to those interests directly related to the German American Bund there are the business and banking alliances.'

'By that do you mean 'The Fraternity' as Charles Bedaux described it?' asked Billy.

'I choose not to grace those greedy scoundrels with a title but, broadly, you are correct. Germany's remarkable phoenix like rise from the ashes of defeat, reflected in the disastrous and totally bankrupt Weimar Republic, has been largely funded through American channels.

'The Rockefellers' Standard Oil is entangled with Germany's largest conglomerate, I G Farben. The oldest private bank in the USA, Brown Brothers Harriman is in bed with Fritz Thyssen the steel magnate who unashamedly has been funding Hitler. Union Banking Corporation is the conduit for Thyssen's New York based US operation. Home grown American industrialist Henry Ford is an avid supporter of the Nazis and has even had an anti-Semitic pamphlet published titled "The International Jew" and that was before Hitler's "Mein Kampf" of course.'

Billy had been nodding at this recital.

'Accepted Donald, but where does that leave my mission?'

'On the question of Lady Celia's safety, leave it with me and I shall call you in the morning or before if I turn up something of interest. Are you chaps receiving real support from the FBI and American intelligence sources despite the efforts of the new ambassador to London the fiercely anti British Joseph Kennedy?'

'Actually, we are' responded Billy. 'He is not a well-liked man in London and makes no attempt to hide his loathing of the British and admiration for Hitler. Unlike posturing politicos, as you know first-hand, the international intelligence community knows full well that we are all dependent upon each other.'

'Good, I am glad to hear that. He is a loathsome man who has inveigled his way into a position of immense power. In that old definition of an entrepreneur, he truly lives between the wood and the bark… he is a louse in a rotten tree.'

'Strong words, Donald.'

'Not as strong as they could be.'

'Now, let me tell you a funny little story about this restaurant. Now, you know that my actual office is in the Rockefeller Centre?'

Billy nodded recalling that Maclaren had a strangely tangential way of carrying on a discussion.

'Before moving here and opening in 1930, the present owners Jack Kriendler and Charlie Berns had opened a club called The Puncheon amongst other names to confuse the federal tax men. Soon after opening they received notice to quit because their club was bang in the middle of what was to become the Rockefeller Centre. When they did open here on the first of January in 1930 with the help of some regular patrons they unhinged the iron gate from their former premises and moved it here. '21' was officially opened.'

Billy smiled at the image of the iron gate being moved on foot through the centre of New York.

'So, now you see, wherever I venture in this great City of New York I always come up against the name Rockefeller. Well, Billy, I should be away now and start a few enquiries before everyone has turned in for the night.'

'Thank you Donald for an excellent dinner. One of my London clubs has a reciprocal arrangement with the Metropolitan Club which I understand to be the refuge of the great and the good of this fine City. I should wish to return your hospitality there.'

'In view of what I am engaged in that is an ironic choice – it was J P Morgan, William Vanderbilt and William C Whitney who wished to have a club where financiers were not looked down upon as parvenus. It was they who started the Metropolitan in the late 19th century. Nevertheless, I shall be delighted to join you whilst you are in New York.' Switching again to a serious tone MacLaren added 'I shall telephone you as soon as possible. In the meantime I advise utmost vigilance with regard to Lady Celia's safety.'

'Allen, this is a much more modern apartment than I imagined you to have. I thought that your tastes would be very traditional… frankly, more English country house.'

'Now why Celia should you think that?' laughed Allen Dulles as he put his hands on Celia's shoulders.

'Allen, do you not think that you are rushing your fences a little?' countered Celia.

Whilst her gentle rebuke was tempered with a smile she did reach up and remove his hands. She then turned her back on him and walked over to an armchair and perched on its arm. Gesturing with her right arm she said, 'Now Allen come, sit and talk with me.' Allen was perplexed. This young woman was playing the sort of games of which he thought he was the grand master. She had outplayed him he realised. She now had the initiative and he was no longer the seducer, the predator. He suddenly felt awkward and no longer in control. In an attempt to regain what he saw as the upper hand he asked 'Would you like some music Celia?' He started to move towards the gramophone on a sideboard but stopped when Celia answered.

'Oh Allen, just do whatever you normally do when a young lady graces your chambers for the first time. In the restaurant you suggested that I should try something different tonight and I did. If you want to take me to bed you will have to prove that you are as skilled a seducer as I think you believe yourself to be.'

Now that the tables were firmly turned Allen felt frustrated and angry that he had been put in the ludicrous position of not knowing what to do next.

'Do you want to leave now Celia?' he asked in as gracious tone as he could muster.

'But why when you have worked so hard all evening Allen. Now, come here and answer me a question or two and then we may have a little fun n'est pas?' He turned back and switched off the gramophone then walked slowly towards Celia slipping out of his jacket as he did so.

'Now, sit here and make yourself comfortable' invited Celia with a smile again, indicating that he should sit in the chair on which she was balanced. 'Let's play a little game Allen. I will ask you a question and if I believe that you have answered honestly we shall each remove an item of clothing. Accept?'

'But Celia...'

Celia ran a fingernail down his cheek. 'No 'buts' Allen...yes or no?'

'Very well I agree but I cannot breach any client confidentiality.'

'Fair enough. Now, let's get rid of our shoes shall we. They do not count.'

After they had done so Celia wriggled her bottom on the armrest so that she was gently pressing against Allen's upper arm. 'Now Allen, your first question. Why are you interested in the Duke and Duchess of Windsor?'

'Because everybody is, Celia. Their proposed visit to America is big news.'

'Fair answer. I shall remove my jacket and you can get rid of your waistcoat.'

'Second question. Why did you ask for my opinion of Charles Bedaux? Your rich and powerful friends in American business and industry must have a much better idea than a young woman like me?'

'He is an enigma Celia. He undoubtedly has great talent but there is something almost sinister about him.'

'That's a good enough answer. I shall remove my skirt.' Now Celia decided to ramp up the pressure. She stood and with her back to Allen undid the side fastenings of her Dior skirt and then slowly wriggled out of it. She could not see him but knew that he would be transfixed. Her silk petticoat was so sheer that it was almost transparent and under it he would see the outline of her daringly cut Parisian briefs. She had rolled her stockings to avoid wearing a suspender belt this evening.

'You naughty man – take off your trousers, now...' She could see that her game was arousing him as he sat back in the chair in his pale blue silk undershorts from Sulka. Celia pointedly studied his shorts, then said 'They look nice Allen. Now question number three. Do you in fact think that the Windsor visit to America will take place?'

'How could I possibly say?' replied Allen.

'You naughty man' responded Celia giving his arm a mock smack. 'That's not true so now I must put my skirt back on.' Celia quickly stood and then instead of gracefully dipping with bent knees to pick up her skirt slowly bent forward from the waist to pick it up.' Shall I ask you again?' Celia was by now looking over her shoulder archly and was gratified to see that Allen was clearly in a state of straining full arousal.

'Yes,' he replied in an almost strangled voice. 'No need to ask the question again. I do not think that it will be allowed to take place.'

'Thank you Allen... so now I shall remove my blouse.' Celia again made a performance of slowly undoing the pearl buttons on her silk blouse. She could sense Allen's increasing agitation. *Poor man* she thought, suppressing a smile.

'Allen, whilst you take off those ridiculous suspenders and socks I shall pose my next question. Who will not allow it? Who wants to stop it?'

'I think that many interests are opposed to it, ranging from the Unions who hate Bedaux who is said to be organising the trip, to big business that is unsettled by the Duke's interest in working conditions.'

'That makes sense. Here goes my petticoat and your shirt I think Allen.'

Allen gave an involuntary groan when Celia stood before him in just her stockings, racily-cut knickers and brassiere. Celia went for the kill. As she asked the question Celia slid her thumbs into the waist band of her knickers and staring at Allen asked 'How are you involved Allen? Is that what Cordell Hunt wanted you to do? Is your task to derail Bedaux?' Allen was beyond reason now; all he could think off was the gorgeous young woman poised in front of him.

'Yes' he croaked.

'Good boy' said Celia as she slid her knickers down.

'Oh God!' exclaimed Allen as he leapt to his feet and swept Celia into an embrace.

Celia afterwards thought that she would never know whether his exclamation was an expression of passionate excitement or of guilt at what he had given away. She was not over impressed with his performance as she would delight in telling Daisy Fellowes. Daisy's inevitable gossiping and indiscretion would do little for the smug self-satisfaction of Allen Dulles thought Celia, with a wicked smile.

Chapter 17

'I have just heard from William Bullitt and he and his 'Personal Assistant' Carmel Offie will be delighted to join us for an informal dinner party next Thursday. I am yet to hear from him so I shall call Armand Gregoire to see whether he can join us.' Wallis announced.

'Very well dearest that is fine with me, but remember that I am off golfing with Fruity that afternoon… well all day in fact as there is a competition at St Cloud and the way that I am playing now, I rather fancy my chances.'

'That's no problem. I saw from your diary that you were away playing but no matter as I shall be going into the City for a fitting at Elsa Schiaperelli's salon in the afternoon. I am going to take Helga. I have been working the poor girl so hard of late I intend making a gift to her of one of Elsa's creations. Nothing too fancy or expensive darling so no need to worry on that score.' assured Wallis who was as ever conscious of the Duke's constant fretting over money.

'No, no… I trust and rely upon your judgement totally dearest.'

'Very well David I shall now go and see whether Armand can join us that evening. I shall probably be half an hour or so and then I think that it is drinks time, eh?'

'Rather, my love' replied the smiling Duke.

As soon as Wallis was back in her study, adjacent to her boudoir and dressing room, she sat at the desk and telephoned William Bullitt on his private line in the Embassy. He had warned her that there was no such thing as true privacy inside an embassy even for the Ambassador and that discretion was essential.

'Bullitt here, to whom am I speaking?'

'Bill it's me. Next Thursday afternoon same time and same place, OK?'

'But isn't that a little... er... difficult?'

'Not in the slightest and I shall be bringing a little surprise for you.'

'Very well, I shall look forward to that. Good bye for now.'

'And to you.'

Wallis pressed the bell which would summon Helga as she thought through her plan for William Bullitt. She quickly shrugged off a slight sense of unease, reminding herself that she was really rather fond of him and that essentially he was a very decent man. She had known him for many years and he was a most interesting individual even though his sexual performance was less than thrilling. Nevertheless, and, importantly, she knew that he had President Roosevelt's ear and that was a rare prize.

'Ah Helga. Next Thursday afternoon we are going to Elsa Schiaperelli's Salon where I shall commission an outfit for you... no, do not protest... you deserve it.'

Helga smiled as she was genuinely pleased.

'There we shall also be meeting a good friend of mine and we shall be having some... oh let me call it 'fun' with him. You will like him. He is a handsome and witty man. He has suffered from some sexual problems and our task is to help him. Do you understand what I am saying?'

'Perfectly Wallis. I shall do my best to help you with his... er... treatment.'

'I am sure that you will. Now come, give me a little kiss.' Wallis turned her cheek to receive a kiss that would not disturb her impeccable make up and reaching out gently stroked Helga's bottom.

'Hmmm. I think we are due a little dalliance Helga my dear' said a lustful Wallis as she looked up at Helga. Helga did not feel that a reply was necessary and merely gave a small and a non-committal nod of acknowledgement. She was still in pain from Wallis' last ministrations and the last thing she wanted or indeed could tolerate would be a repeat performance. Wallis, perceptive as ever, seemed to read Helga's mind and continued in almost honeyed tones 'My dear we can be very gentle.' The look in her eyes belied her words. Wallis did not notice the momentary flicker of apprehension in Helga's expression.

'First, my dear, I must telephone Armand Gregoire to see if they will be joining us for dinner.'

Billy returned to Celia's house after his enjoyable dinner with Donald Maclaren feeling relaxed but at the same time concerned. Michael Phillips and his fellow agent Sarah Mountford who were the two agents on the Queen Mary posing as Celia's servants, were settled in Keen's restaurant and positioned so that they had Celia and her fellow diners in clear sight. Michael and Billy had arranged with their FBI liaison that if Celia left the restaurant with Allen Dulles the Americans would provide cover and protection. If Celia were to return home, Michael Phillips and his companion would follow in an FBI vehicle and once she was in her house enter by the rear staff entrance. The FBI were keeping the house under what they classified as 'light surveillance'.

Billy asked Smithers the Butler if it would be possible to have a small glass of beer in the library and also that when Phillips his manservant returned he must be sent straight to him.

Earlier than expected Michael Phillips returned and after knocking entered the library carefully closing the heavy mahogany door behind him. He came straight to the point. 'Billy I think that we may have a problem to sort out tonight. After Daisy Fellowes left on her own Celia and Dulles had a serious looking conversation and it became pretty certain that they were going to leave together. I took the precaution of going out and alerting the FBI boys that they would need to take me back here but that I would be leaving in just a few minutes with a lady companion. I gambled that the Germans would know that it was an FBI vehicle and that it was on station to protect Celia.'

'Right' said Billy slowly and thoughtfully with furrowed brow looking troubled. 'Do carry on.'

'I went back into the restaurant, signed the bill and then told Sarah to come with me and collect her coat, hat and scarf from the cloakroom and wrap up well. I guessed that with the FBI bang outside the restaurant the Germans would have to keep well back. Sarah is of course about the same height and build as Celia.'

'That made sense' commented Billy 'Well done.'

'As soon as we appeared at the entrance to the restaurant one of the FBI chaps hopped out of the car and opened the rear door. We dashed across the pavement and jumped in as did he after he had slammed the door. The driver raced off. My hope was that if the Germans were after Lady Celia they would think she had left with the FBI.'

'But what about Celia?' asked Billy with a worried frown.

'The FBI chaps had called in their backup car to tail her and Dulles when they left. Interestingly the back-up chaps spotted what appeared to be the German agents gunning their car down the street in pursuit of us. They radioed that it was a black Studebaker sedan with four men in it. Sure enough our driver spotted it a few blocks later. Damned amateur effort if you ask me.'

'We are only supposing that they are Germans Michael… although I grant you that they may well be. On the other hand they might well be Americans. You and Sarah are both armed?'

'Yes Billy, and, like Celia, Sarah is a damned good shot… excellent in fact. The FBI have done us proud so far… they have loaned me not only a 0.45 Colt that would blow a hole in a battleship but also a drum magazine Thompson sub machine gun.'

'Good. I also have a short barrel M 62 carbine and a semi-automatic Browning '45' pistol. I intend to bring Smithers the Butler in on this. I will ring for him now.'

When Smithers entered the Library in response to the bell Billy got straight to the point.

'Smithers. I know that I can rely upon your absolute discretion. Michael Phillips here is not my manservant neither is Miss Mountford who is downstairs a lady's maid. As am I they are officers in His Majesty's Secret Service sent here to protect Lady Celia who is believed to be under threat.' If Smithers was shocked he did not show it and merely replied. 'I understand My Lord.'

'Right, this is what you must do. The staff quarters are all on the top floor. Which of the staff are still up and about the house?'

'Only me, My Lord. Lady Celia gave instructions that upon her return she would not require her maid and would only wish me to secure the house as usual. She also told me that if she had not returned by midnight she would be staying at the house of Mrs Fellowes. Normally, knowing that I worry, she telephones to say that she will not be returning and I imagine that tonight will be no exception. She knows that I never retire before one in the morning.'

Billy and Michael exchanged glances and then both mens' eyes sought the ormolu Parisian mantel clock. It was now five minutes to midnight.

'Please remain with us until midnight then close up the house but leave some low lighting on in Lady Celia's bedroom as if she were reading in bed. Then please retire to your quarters and warn all staff that whatever they hear they must on no account venture onto the stairs. They must stay in their rooms. Is that understood?'

'Perfectly, save that James the chauffer has quarters in the motor house behind the main house. I can bring him into the house now… there is a spare bedroom upstairs where one of the footmen used to sleep.'

'Please do that. Do not lock the motor house and also provide me with keys for all outside doors. All internal doors are to be locked. That includes the door from the servants' day quarters and kitchen into the main house. I shall require a duplicate key for that.'

'I shall attend to matters immediately Milord' replied Smithers as he nodded and left the room silently.

Billy couldn't help but be amused. 'Just like PG Wodehouse's Jeeves… he glides and seems to pour himself under doors… and of course never ruffled. Anyhow to business. I want you in the motor house… sorry I have to learn to call it the garage… with your Tommy gun. I believe that they will come into the house from the back. Just let them pass but then be ready. Any intruder who survives the ambush I am setting in the house will make a break for it to the rear. Use your discretion but ensure that at least one of them escapes if possible. We want a live one for interrogation. Apart from that, shoot to kill.'

Michael Phillips nodded and confirmed. 'Righto Billy, understood and I have agreed with the FBI that they will let them through to enter the house but they will capture any who later escape.'

'Excellent… and by the way very well done. Now, please fetch Sarah so that I can brief her. In the meantime I am calling my FBI Liason to give final confirmation.'

Celia stretched and leant over placing a light kiss on the tip of Allen Dulles' nose. 'Allen that was delicious. May I be a bore and use your telephone to inform my household that I shall not be returning tonight?'

'Of course… the instrument is on the bureau in the living room.'

Allen felt a tightening in his pelvic muscles as Celia's beautiful figure was momentarily silhouetted in the doorway. He could not help but subconsciously compare her with the many women he had seduced. She was near if not top of the list. Drained as he felt, he knew that he could not resist making love to her again.

'All done' she said as she came back into the bedroom and sitting on the edge of the bed began to idly fiddle with Allen. She did so lightly, playfully but also erotically. He groaned with pleasure as his pelvic muscles contracted and he felt himself hardening. Smiling to herself in the dark Celia then asked him in a gentle and quiet almost honey toned voice.

'What I cannot understand Allen is why these powerful men should want to sink Charles Bedaux when he can be so influential in Germany where they have major financial interests?'

Celia could sense Allen tense but his breathing was quickening and he was making small involuntary movements with his hips. She reached over with her other hand and cupping him began a gentle massage. His voice was shaking a little and he sounded short of breath.

'He has outlived his usefulness to them. Their interests are secure and potentially he is an embarrassment. Oh my God Celia, don't stop......the visit that he has planned for the Windsors will cause widespread disruption in the workforces and that means loss. The view now is to let him slink back to Germany and France and make a nuisance of himself there.' Now gasping with pleasure Allan was jerking spasmodically as Celia asked in a gentle voice, pausing her caresses.

'And when will you organise his downfall here Allen?'

'I have done it... Oh my God' he gasped 'Celia for God's sake...'

Celia smiled to herself as she increased the tempo. 'A task well done' she thought as Allen reached his climax.

The trap was now set.

The FBI had men stationed out of sight at either end of the service road that ran behind Celia's house and its neighbours. Their instructions had been agreed with Billy and as soon as intruders entered the rear entrance to the property they would move closer and seal off the road. The units at the front would also move in close to the house. It was expressly agreed that in no circumstances would they enter the property whilst any fire-fight was in progress. It was accepted that if anything went wrong this had to be an entirely unauthorised British operation and the FBI could deny any knowledge or involvement.

'Are you OK Sarah?' whispered Billy.

'I am fine but I wish they would make their move.'

'I know what you mean. Keep your safety catch off... it will be fast and furious when the fire fight starts. Remember do not give your position away or fire until they have taken up firing positions. They will assume that I am alone. When you open fire concentrate on the one who presents the best target and stay undercover… do not break cover under any circumstances. Right, silence now.'

Sarah could feel her heart beating hard and fast. She was dry mouthed as the adrenalin coursed through her veins. She was hidden behind the heavy mahogany sideboard which was against the side wall of the servants' parlour. Billy was behind a large butcher's block near the centre of the kitchen which was on the other side of a wide corridor.

The corridor led from the rear tradesmen's entrance to the green baize covered door that marked the boundary between the servants' domain and that of those they served in the main house. That door was closed and locked.

Billy heard a scratching noise at the rear door and then a click as the lock was successfully picked. He sensed the door being opened slowly. It was half glazed and some light had been coming through its frosted glass into the corridor and that now increased. Then there were shadows moving slowly. Billy could not tell how many intruders there were but guessed probably three with one left in the car.

Billy realised in an instant that the intruders were either poorly trained, totally without discipline or supremely overconfident. There were indeed three and they were moving forward in a tight group. As they drew level Billy took a deep breath and then fired three shots in rapid succession. From the screams he believed that he had hit two of them. He heard a scuffling noise as one took up a firing position using the side of the kitchen entrance as cover. In doing so he had his back to Sarah.

Billy fired again and the architrave surrounding the kitchen doorway splintered as the heavy round hit just above the intruder's position. The intruder snapped off a shot in Billy's direction but as he quickly regained his cover Sarah calmly shot him in the back. He appeared to stand and then take a step forward with his pistol pointing in the direction of Billy's position. Sarah leapt towards him and fired twice. Once more into his back and then, as she closed the gap, his head. He crashed to the floor.

'Get back Sarah!' Billy shouted but his warning was too late.

One of the wounded intruders had managed to fire at Sarah and in spite of his injury he simply could not miss. His bullet smashed into the young woman throwing her back across the servants' parlour. She fell like a broken doll.

Billy knew where the intruder was from the muzzle flash and pumped five rounds into the shadowy form on the floor. He could sense the body jerk with each one of them. He threw on the lights and could immediately see that two of the attackers were dead. The third was apparently still breathing but looked as though he would not last for long. He was lying in a spreading pool of blood and the gaping exit wounds were testimony to the havoc Billy's heavy calibre bullets had wreaked to his body. Billy kicked the dying man's pistol out of reach. He stood stock still for a few moments, his ears ringing from the noise of the shots and his eyes stinging from the cordite fumes. Just then FBI agents stormed into the house with Michael Phillips at their head. Michael shouted to the FBI 'It's Ok! It's my boss!' Billy dashed over to Sarah. 'Doctors and ambulance NOW!' he bellowed as he stared in horror at her wound.

'It's my fault' she whispered through white lips that were turning blue.

'Sssh. Don't talk. Save your energy. You did very well.'

Michael Phillips left the FBI men to deal with the bodies of the three intruders and kneeling beside Sarah took her hand as he cradled her head. Her eyes fluttered open when he spoke. 'Sarah, it's me Michael. Save your energy and do not speak. The medics will be here any minute.'

'She closed her eyes for a moment and there was the hint of a smile on her now bloodless lips as she whispered thinly 'Michael...'

'Oh God!' exclaimed Michael a few moments later. 'The fucking bastards... she's gone!' Just then the medical team rushed into the house as, with heaving shoulders, Michael cradled the young woman's body. Billy held up his hand and shook his head making it clear to the medics that Sarah was beyond help and they should wait.

Billy unlocked the green baize covered door and slowly walked into the grand house. He felt the all too familiar sensation of anti-climax that always followed being in action but there was another emotion building within him.

This was personal. He would find out who was responsible for killing one of his team and destroy them. He cursed fluently at the thought that judging from Sarah's monstrous exit wound the intruders had been using hollow point ammunition banned by international convention and commonly referred to as dum-dum bullets.

Sir Vernon Kell was in his dressing gown when Tar Robertson was shown into the study of his home in Eaton Terrace. His hair dishevelled, his grey stubble and lack of immaculate attire was a stark reminder of just how old Sir Vernon was despite his vigour and sharp mind.

'Sit down Tar. Right what's happened? I do not normally expect to see you at five in the morning.'

'Bad business in New York I am afraid. One of Billy's team Sarah Mountford was killed in a shoot-out in Lady Celia's house. Celia was not there. The actual intruders were all killed but the FBI have their driver. They have allowed Billy to be in on the interrogation.'

'Any early indication of who they were?' asked Sir Vernon.

'Too early to say. The FBI suspect German American Bund involvement but apparently J Edgar Hoover thinks that there is someone else or, to be precise a group of 'interested parties' involved. It will not be an easy investigation.'

'I would like to get my hands on the people responsible' muttered a clearly angry Sir Vernon. 'I hope that the FBI will not pussy foot around with their prisoner ....'

'I am assured that they will not. Apparently he resisted arrest and had to be forcibly restrained. He tried to go for his gun so he had to be immobilised. His injuries are very painful but not life threatening. One comment was that he might not be siring any children, ever.'

'First priority is to get Celia out of New York Tar. Please see to that. Check with the Admiralty if they have a vessel that she can be brought home on. Keep me posted any time, day or night. Billy must accompany her with the other back up agent young Phillips.'

'Now then, the poor girl's family. Presumably there is a cover story?'

'Yes, and the American end is being set up as we speak. Her death will be the result of a tragic traffic accident. There will be eye witness accounts, police technical reports and a supporting autopsy finding. Assuming her family wish her body repatriated it will of course be a closed coffin and the reports will be such that the British Coroner will not require a second autopsy. Her Family are London based and the Westminster Coroner will deal with the matter in an inquest without Jury.'

'Do you need me to intervene on that?' asked Sir Vernon.

'That will not be necessary Sir Vernon. I shall now return to the office.'

Celia had returned home by taxi and was surprised to see an unmarked black saloon car with two men in it parked outside her house. As she ran up the steps the doors opened and Smithers stood to one side and inclined his head in acknowledgement of her cheerful greeting. It was then that she saw Billy in the hallway.

'Celia, please come with me.'

'Oh Billy, I must just go and change and then I will join you.'

'No Celia, I should be obliged if you would come now.' His tone and manner were firm and she followed him down the corridor to the Library pausing only to ask Smithers to have some coffee and cookies sent in.

Once they were in the library they sat down. Celia who had been feeling rather pleased with herself for wheedling the requested information out of the normally wily Allen Dulles was annoyed at being effectively ordered about in her own house asked 'Well Billy' she asked in a steely tone. 'What the hell's all this about?'

Billy who was feeling bone weary after a sleepless night that had culminated in the prisoner telling all that he knew snapped in reply 'Sarah Mountford was killed last night when we had a shoot-out with three thugs who had come here with the intention of killing you. So kindly get off your high horse.'

Celia blanched at Billy's words and her hand shot to her mouth.

'Billy that's just too awful...' Billy cut across her.

'We are getting you out of here this morning. We are flying up to Canada, Halifax, Nova Scotia where we are joining a Royal Navy vessel that will take us back to England. It is not safe for you to be here.'

'The FBI have let it slip that there was a shooting here last night and a young woman was killed. She has not been named. The story is that the FBI became involved because a group of men were seen entering the rear of your house which was in darkness with the exception of a light in your upstairs bedroom.'

Billy paused for a moment.

'They are saying that they were already concerned for your safety. There was a shoot-out but not before the unnamed young woman was shot. The inference is that you were the victim. The press are on to it, but, obviously it has missed the morning editions and a press conference has been called for four pm when we shall be at sea. Anyhow, the cover story will suffice for long enough for you to be spirited away. Now go and get ready and grab some practical clothing. A Royal Navy destroyer is somewhat different to the Queen Mary.'

As Celia packed essential clothes for the Atlantic crossing she realised that her hands were shaking. It came as a shock for her to realise that for the first time since becoming involved with the British Secret Service she was afraid, and upset that the attractive young fellow agent had been mercilessly cut down. She faced the chilling realisation that this was not a game.

Chapter 18

'Wallis, I am delighted to say that Fruity Metcalfe has written to accept my invitation to visit and they will be arriving in time for our little dinner party. Rather jolly, because he can partner me at golf in the competition at St Cloud that day, and of course he knows Armand Gregoire pretty well.'

Wallis smiled somewhat thinly as she replied. 'Oh, that will be very nice for you to have his company David. You are quite right about Armand Gregoire and Fruity – such a silly name – knowing each other well. Actually as I understand that it, Armand organises the transfer of German funds to The January Club which is allied to Tom Mosley's British Union of Fascists.'

'Yes, I believe that is so, and of course Fruity is a member of the Club. He also confirmed that Paul Munster, who lent us Schloss Wasserleonburg for our honeymoon, will also be around. Paul's also in the January Club – of course he has British and German citizenship. Have you invited him and his wife as we discussed?'

'I had hesitated my sweet because I feared that our intimate little dinner was growing somewhat. However if you so wish I would be more than happy to do so. Actually, assuming that Peggy comes with Paul I can discreetly ask her whether she and Sybil Colefax will help us as and when we settle on a permanent home. They are just so, so talented and everything I read praises their interpretation of English Country House style to the nines. Also they would probably do a deal on price given the publicity it will attract.'

'Excellent – even better – I shall leave it all to you. Dudders has all the up to date contact details I am certain. Now, I am off to play a quick nine holes – just to keep me eye in you know.'

Wallis smiled thinly, inwardly furious that Fruity Metcalfe and his 'Oh so superior' wife would be attending her dinner party. 'Well you have a lovely game my darling. I am going to run through a few things with Helga and probably have a little nap.'

'A little session with Helga might restore my good humour' thought Wallis as she set off for her boudoir.

Billy was sitting with Celia in the Wardroom of HMS Faulknor as she made her way back to England after the mad dash to leave New York before whoever had planned the attack on Celia realised that the wrong young woman was dead.

Celia and Billy had been smuggled out of the rear of the house into an FBI saloon which then left at speed with other FBI cars ahead and behind. They left the City and were soon at Newark where an aircraft was waiting for them with its engines running. It had taken off immediately and Billy had made it clear that there would be no discussion of what had transpired in New York until they were aboard ship and could ensure total privacy.

The time to talk had now come. Billy had a foolscap notebook in front of him, a number of pencils and an eraser.

'You go first Celia please.'

'Daisy Fellowes, who is hardly romantic but loves juicy tit bits of gossip, engineered leaving Allen Dulles alone with me in Keen's Chophouse as you know. After she left there was some playful banter and I took the opportunity to wrong foot Allen.' Celia paused and laughed lightly then continued. 'Not as hard as you might think Billy. He is massively clever but that is matched by his ego. He really thinks he walks on water and all women are putty in his hands. I led him along by his – well, let me be polite and say, his nose.' Billy glanced up from the pad as he took a verbatim note and smiled.

'He swallowed the bait that I was desperate for him to seduce me and we soon went back to his rather Spartan apartment. Given that he affects the dress style of an English 'Country Gentleman' – New England version of course – so not quite spot on, if you know what I mean… I expected something more 'clubby' you know but it's stark. Rather weird in my view. Anyway, I teased him to the point where he was almost out of his mind – I had usurped his customary role and he hated not being in control. As a result, he spilt the beans and he told me just what Cordell Hunt had asked of him. He didn't even deny that it was the Secretary of State who had asked him.'

'I say, well done. I do not wish to know any details of the means by which you extracted the information, just precisely what he told you' laughed Billy. Celia repeated the conversation verbatim as Billy scribbled it down.

'And the final thing. I wheedled it out of him in the morning that he had already performed his allotted task and alerted the major players to oust Bedaux. Something for your confidential report Billy. Allen Dulles may be clever and shrewd but he is very vulnerable sexually and I do not think that his loyalty to anyone or any ideal runs very deep. Frankly I would not trust him to play straight with anything.' Billy raised a quizzical eyebrow.

'Billy – just look at the way he and his brother are snuggled up to these pro Nazi and pro 'New World Order' powerful men and organisations – their clients no less – and yet Allen implies that they are strongly anti Nazi and will abandon them when the time is right. Sorry to bang on Billy but it really concerns me.'

'Absolutely no problem Celia. I shall most certainly make your points in my report and verbally. I imagine that Tar will have a quiet word with his American opposite number.'

'Strewth!' exclaimed Billy. 'Bloody difficult writing with this damned ship pitching and rolling about!' as a particularly violent lurch sent his pencil flying over the page.

'You are right, the Queen Mary never feels like this,' commented Celia. As Billy rubbed out the offending line he commented 'The Queen Mary is God knows how much bigger than a destroyer, and bear in mind we are probably running in high seas at around 35 knots- that's bloody fast.'

Billy then continued. 'Of one thing I am sure, the people who were after you were not connected to your meeting Dulles. The driver says, and given the way he was interrogated I am damn sure that he wasn't lying, that they were briefed two days before – in other words whilst you were at sea.'

'Who were 'they'?' asked Celia.

'The driver is a New Yorker, a low-life petty criminal who apparently upset one of the 'families' – you know, gangsters who are referred to as The Mob. His only protection was to work with the Germans and the German Bund, for which read a Nazi supporting organisation. There is a truce or understanding between them and the gangs. He worked for the enforcement arm of the German American Bund taking direct orders from its leader – or *Bundesfuhrer* – Fritz Julius Kuhn. Kuhn was a soldier in the Great War and member of the Bavarian street fighting early days of the Nazi movement – he is what is known in the Nazi party as an '*Alter Kampfer*' – an 'old Soldier'.

Celia interrupted Billy.

'Why on earth can't the American authorities just kick him out as an undesirable?'

Billy raised his eyebrows and shrugged saying 'The FBI accept that Kuhn should never have been allowed to take American citizenship which he did in 1934. They have him and his cronies under permanent surveillance. However they freely admit that the Bund and other similar organisations are hugely complex with many sympathisers and, most importantly, rich and powerful members with immense influence in high places. Unlike Mosley's crew, who are open in what they are up to, the Bund has a lot of public profile with its marches and training camps but like an iceberg there is far more under the surface. The FBI believe that the operation against you was one of Himmler's efforts. Effectively as their Nazi paymaster he was calling in a favour.'

'But why Billy? He is aware that I am on good terms with the Windsors and have met the Fuhrer more than once.'

'Celia, nothing in this game we play is as it might seem on the surface. I still think that Von Ribbentrop is part of the problem for you. Apparently he is becoming more and more disliked within the top echelons of the Nazis. You are seen as a part of his operation, his 'sphere of influence'. His relationship with the Fuhrer is in turn greatly enhanced by his relationship with the Windsors. You are considered to be an integral part of that and, I am afraid, Himmler and his cronies almost certainly know that you have had a very close personal relationship with Ribbentrop.'

Billy looked at his watch. 'Well Celia, the skipper has invited us for a pre-dinner drink. Shall we join him now?'

It was only a short distance along the pitching corridor but even then Celia was glad that she had heeded Billy's advice and foresworn her high heels and elegant clothes suited for travelling on the Queen Mary for practical flat shoes, a jersey and slacks. She still succeeded in looking stunning, with a brightly coloured silk scarf knotted at her neck.

The Marine guard stationed outside the entrance to the Captain's quarters stiffened to attention then turning smartly knocked sharply on the bulkhead door.

A muffled almost dismembered voice called the single word 'Come' and the marine who incongruously held a Sten Gun as well as having a pistol holstered on his belt opened the door and then stood aside for Celia and Billy to enter.

Celia still found negotiating the threshold of bulkhead doors a challenge and was determined not to trip as she had on a number of occasions after first joining the vessel.

She was surprised that the Captain seemed so young on first impression, with fair curly hair cut short, weathered skin and twinkling green eyes. It was as he smiled warmly in greeting that she realised he was older than she had first thought when she noted the pronounced laughter lines around his eyes.

'Lady Celia, I am Commander Baird and I am delighted to welcome you formally to HMS Faulknor. I am afraid that when you joined us I was fully engaged in getting us away as quickly as possible as ordered.'

'I quite understand and I hope that you were not put too much inconvenience on our account.'

'Absolutely not. Destroyers are the work horses of the Navy, or so we like to think, and the crew are over the moon. We were due to spend the next three months stooging around out of Halifax and apart from it being a bloody cold spot – I apologise – we shall be back in Blighty early and they are due leave. So, you have done us all a favour.'

'Well that's a relief' replied Celia with a smile.

After their drinks had been served by a steward, Commander Baird thanked and dismissed him and invited his guests to sit.

'Now, Lady Celia, Billy. My orders are to get you back to the UK as quickly as possible. Hence the bumpy ride I am afraid. I am also instructed that your mission is Top Secret but I am not required to know more than that and, of course I would not dream of asking. So far as the other officers are concerned you are returning to the UK as close friends of mine and our speed of passage is a workout for the ship and her Company. They won't believe it – they are far too sharp – but they will know to keep their mouths shut.

'That being the case, may I call you Celia? And you must call me Mac – it's short for my middle name and I have been stuck with it since Dartmouth.'

'I was going to ask you to anyway Mac. So how long do you think we shall be at sea?'

'I reckon that if all goes well we shall be in Liverpool in three days time.'

'That's excellent' commented Billy. 'So before Halifax what were you up to?'

'We were escorting British flagged ships off the coast of North West Spain. It was pretty tedious but it did become rather lively when we were caught up in an air raid on Bilbao.

'Absolutely terrifying – I was a young shaver at Jutland but this was far, far worse. We of course could do nothing as neutrals. The City was poorly served in terms of anti-aircraft guns and the people clearly were too numerous for the shelters. It was horrific as wave after wave of bombers flew high overhead dumping high explosives and incendiaries on the civilian population.'

'Could you tell whose aircraft they were?'

'Difficult at their height but in our view almost certainly the German *Condor Legion.*'

Celia chipped in. 'I have seen the German Luftwaffe at first hand. They are very impressive.'

Mac continued, 'Impressive Celia is one word; terrifying comes to mind for the civilians. Billy, you remember the panic that the Zeppelin raids and then the Gotha bombers of the Kaiser's air-force caused in England in the Great War. There were about 2000 civilian casualties then. Just imagine what a modern air force can do to cities like London, Liverpool, Birmingham, Coventry, Portsmouth – wherever – it is unthinkable.'

Billy responded grim-faced. 'I'm afraid it is not "unthinkable" Mac. What you witnessed in Spain is Germany – and Italy to a lesser extent – limbering up. The Italians have shown the world a picture of modern warfare in Abyssinia including chemical weapons – and the World has watched and done nothing, to its shame. Now the Germans and Italians in Spain have shown the World just what to expect of them when they deem the time is right to take lands that they believe to be theirs. I apologise Mac, I must climb off my soapbox. Now, do you come from a Naval family – mine is army going way back?'

'Absolutely not. My father was a Scottish banker and also into politics… he even became Lord Provost of Edinburgh. I had done a little sailing as a boy but he was shocked to the core when I told him that when I left Fettes I wished to attend the Brittania Naval College at Dartmouth and skip University. Still, I've never regretted it – I think I would have made a lousy banker! Now we are invited to the Wardroom for dinner so I had better smarten up a little… still we have time for one more drink – same again?'

Princess Stephanie arrived in Germany the day before she was due to meet with the Fuhrer. She had arranged to stay at the Adlon where she would be joined in her suite by Fritz Wiedemann. She felt girlishly excited at the prospect.

The trip to Cliveden with Johnny had been quite fun and certainly interesting as she would be recounting to Adolf Hitler the next morning. However her feelings for Fritz were the most intense she had ever allowed herself to have for any man.

When he entered the suite he was like a force of nature, a whirlwind that seemed to sweep her up. He was undoubtedly handsome in a rugged way and his eyes were almost hypnotising. But that was not what had brought Stephanie out of the carefully constructed shell in which she had always held her emotions, the shell that made her so effective and dangerous a woman. She had tried to analyse her emotions and feelings for Fritz on so many occasions, but she just could not isolate the particular facets of the man that so attracted her.

Stephanie threw herself into his open arms and almost howled his name in pure joy. 'Fritz, my beautiful strong Fritz!'

Fritz nearly lost his balance but managed to stay upright as they fell back onto a large sofa.

Some time later as Fritz relaxed smoking a cigarette with Stephanie nuzzled against him she asked 'Is the Fuhrer in a good mood at the moment?'

'Well my love, you know as well as I do that his moods are mercurial. Today he seems almost benign but, of course I cannot vouch for tomorrow. Do you have anything interesting for him?'

'Nothing concrete really – pretty gossipy – but important I believe. I picked up some interesting things at Cliveden but more importantly, there is a whisper that moves are afoot to scupper the Windsors' visit to America.'

'I'm not surprised – the British Establishment must be furious at the prospect' responded Fritz with an ironic laugh.

'No, that may be the case, but it was suggested that it is the Americans that will block it. Charles Bedaux is seen as an impediment.'

'Now, that is interesting. Armand Gregoire is to dine with the Windsors next week and Bullitt the US Ambassador to Paris and Roosevelt's great friend will be there with his 'pretty boy'. Armand will tell us all that transpires.'

'Good' commented Stephanie. She continued, 'There is another rumour that Armand should pursue with Bullitt. You know the botched rather pathetic attempt to overthrow President Roosevelt and the elected US Government in the so called 'Business Plot' of 1933?' asked Stephanie almost rhetorically.

'Of course I do' replied Fritz 'As I recall the conspiracy involved American Veterans who had previously marched on Washington in protest at the delay in the payment of bonuses due to them. They were to be funded by Wall Street and place retired Marine Corps General Smedley Butler into the White House. Allegedly the whole exercise was to be funded by Wall Street interests violently opposed to Roosevelt's 'New Deal'.

Stephanie replied 'That's it. Nobody has ever been able to get to the bottom of it all but apparently Roosevelt has been wary of Wall Street and the vastly powerful industrial and finance men ever since. He sees them as far more of a direct threat than as a mere powerful lobby. Butler testified to the House of Representatives Special Committee on Un-American Activities and they found the conspiracy that he revealed to be credible. The essence was that whilst Butler would give support to the Veterans there were no circumstances in which he was prepared to act traitorously. In effect the nominated leader turned out to be the whistle blower. Ironically!' Stephanie allowed herself a smile before she went on.

'There were no prosecutions which says something for the power and influence of the men behind it who loathed Roosevelt. At that time they deplored his allowing America to abandon the Gold Standard and, his predecessor Hoover, who had defended it, described doing so as 'the first step towards communism – we have gold because we cannot trust Governments.' The lack of a gold backed economy was seen as undermining private and business fortunes.'

'Stephanie, this is all very interesting of course but please enlighten a mere soldier as to why it should be of interest to us in Germany today and, more particularly, the Fuhrer?'

'But you see Fritz, the very people who were implicated in the 1933 plot, its backers, are one and the same as 'The Fraternity' who are now doing so much to re finance Germany and rebuild industry here and enable re-armament. The activity of the German American Bund is seen by Roosevelt as another overt threat of revolution. He seems to think that the Rockefellers of this world would ally themselves with that organisation.

'Germany must distance itself from what is viewed as a subversive organisation if there is not to be whiplash against its friends in the USA , General Motors, Chase Bank, Standard Oil and Ford just to name a few.'

'Now I see your logic – God you are just so clever. What on earth do you see in me a simple old foot slogger, eh?'

Stephanie wriggled around, kissed him lightly and then playfully said 'Come to bed you lovely man and I will show you.'

'You only need to ask once oh Queen' laughed Fritz as he picked Stephanie up and carried her through to the bedroom.

Promptly at ten the following morning Princess Stephanie was shown into the familiar grand office of the Fuhrer.

'My dearest Princess' Hitler greeted Stephanie as the great doors were closed silently behind her. He rose from behind his huge ornate desk and met Stephanie in the middle of the room. 'Let us sit here and have some coffee and perhaps a little torte – hmm?'

'Mein Fuhrer – is that wise- surely we must both guard our waistlines?'

'Nobody else in the Reich would dare say that except perhaps Fat Hermann as I have taken to calling Goering when I want to pull his leg. Now, tell me all my dear and wise one.'

Stephanie described the conversations at Cliveden which she thought went some way towards demonstrating the dichotomy in British opinion over the question of appeasement but she then turned her attention to the situation in America and the suspicions harboured by President Roosevelt.

Hitler listened attentively then gave one of his characteristic sharp laughs – almost a bark. 'I have the answer to that one – Ribbentrop tells me that his friend the lawyer Armand Gregoire is dining with the Duke and Duchess of Windsor in a few days and William Bullitt the US Ambassador to Paris will be there. Bullitt has Roosevelt's ear. Gregoire can tell him in confidence that the German Government is distancing itself from the German American Bund and withdrawing all support both financial and political. The last thing I need now is the USA getting stirred up. That is one tap that we simply cannot afford to have turned off. As ever dear Princess, I am deeply in your debt. And now some coffee and torte?'

The Duke of Windsor turned to Wallis with a broad smile. 'Well Wallis, Charles Bedaux is off to America to make the final arrangements for our trip.'

'Yes dearest and it is very gratifying that so many people are asking us to dinners before we go to wish us well for our visit. I think that it is a really good omen. Don't you?'

'Most certainly – I feel that we shall have a triumph. Yes, a truly triumphant time in America.'

Chapter 19

Allen Dulles had deliberately lied to Celia when he said that he had already fulfilled the wishes of Secretary of State Cordell Hull expressed to him over luncheon in the Cosmos Club in Washington. He was mortified that he had confided in the beautiful English woman at all. It represented a total loss of self-control which he despised in others and now had to face in himself.

As he paced to and fro in his living room he muttered imprecations and cursed fluently. Something rare for a man who regarded himself as the master of any human situation. His anger turned to Celia. 'The bitch… that fucking bitch… she played me like a stupid fish right from the start of dinner.'

Gradually his anger, which was in reality a reflection of his disgust for his own lack of self-control, subsided. He sat for a while with his head in his hands and then, mind made up, went to his desk and picked up the telephone. His first call was brief in the extreme. It was to his brother John Foster Dulles. He arranged for them to meet that evening after he explained that he had a migraine and would not be in the office during the day.

His second call was to his long suffering wife who loyally believed everything that he told her. He apologised for being away from home for so long, explaining that he was engaged in some highly sensitive negotiations that he could not discuss. He told her that he missed both her and their young children desperately and could not wait to see them. He expressed his love fulsomely and she urged him not to work too hard and said that she was counting the minutes until he returned.

In reality Allen Dulles found his wife boring and could not bear being distracted by his young children.

He picked up the telephone and called Frances Scott, an empty headed New

York divorcee who was not interested in deep conversation but just loved going to bed… with anyone. Allen Dulles felt that an afternoon of sex uncomplicated by any emotion other than self-gratification would assuage the gnawing guilt of his indiscretion with Celia.

Feeling much more relaxed after a vigorous session with Frances Scott, Allen Dulles met his brother in a small Italian restaurant where they were most unlikely to be seen. He explained to his brother precisely what had happened and what a fool he felt.

'For Heaven's sake Allen… it will not cause a problem. Not at all' he chuckled. 'But dinner's on you and I think we should start with a fine bottle of crisp Gavi de Gavi. There will be no harm done. In fact I am sure that we can turn it to our advantage. I will tell FDR that you realised that the high born English woman almost certainly was working with British Intelligence so you decided that it was a perfect opportunity for you to unofficially tip them off that the US Government wanted to block the Windsors' visit.'

'But I did not come to the conclusion that she was some sort of spy – she's part American anyway,' Allen protested.

John sighed theatrically. 'Sometimes Allen your belief in yourself and your charm or sex appeal, call it what you will, blinds you. You surely don't believe that this beautiful young women invited you into her knickers for fun do you? You say that she is a close friend of Daisy Fellowes and almost immediately after arriving you were invited to dinner with them and then Daisy left with a lame excuse about a migraine… about as lame as yours to me earlier little brother!'

'I suppose it does look as though I was set up. The thing is, just how did they know that I had had a meeting with that old fox Cordell Hunt?'

'Wait and see. Someone at The Cosmos Club clearly put two and two together. Sooner or later we will know. In the meantime, it remains our nasty little secret that your pecker turned you into a sucker little brother.' John Foster Dulles gave his brother a light but meaningful punch on the arm that actually hurt.

Allen was inwardly seething at the apparently good natured put down by his older brother who had always taken a perverse delight in cutting him down to size. He silently vowed that one day he would have his revenge on Lady Celia. She must pay for playing him like a fool.

* * *

The American President, Theodore Roosevelt, often known as FDR, having been briefed by John Foster Dulles decided to adopt an oblique approach to the British Government. He had little confidence in Prime Minister Neville Chamberlain so he had decided to play his 'wild card' and enlist the efforts of old friend Winston Churchill whom he now telephoned.

'Winston my dear fellow… Franklin here. How are you and the lovely Clemmie?'

'Delighted to hear from you. We are absolutely fine. I trust the same goes for you and Eleanor? Oh, you know what it is like to be out of the mainstream… I cannot say that I enjoy being impotent on the side-lines.'

After a short pause, which Roosevelt naturally assumed would enable Churchill to draw on his customary cigar, Churchill continued.

'Apart from the utter frustration of watching the Government stumble blindly into the arms of conflict I am left with plenty of time to write and paint.'

'You are not building any more walls in your gardens then? I understood that you found bricklaying a therapeutic diversion?' teased Roosevelt.

'Not at the moment but I do have some plans if I am left out to grass for very much longer!' responded a chuckling Churchill. He and the President had an easy and comfortable relationship which enabled a degree of frank conversation that was a rare commodity in the heady world of international affairs.

'Well Winston I for one believe that you are absolutely right in your suspicions about the Nazis and Mussolini too. I am in an even worse position as President would you believe…

The pro-German and Italian lobbies here in America are so powerful that I dare not voice my opinions. I also fear that when the Dictators go on the offensive the Japanese may also see themselves as having an opportunity. They are flushed with their successes in Asia and I don't think that Emperor Hirohito has it in him to block the ambitions of the military.'

'I agree and, of course they will have India in their sights' muttered Churchill. 'Riches and resources beyond their dreams.'

'Quite so. Now Winston, as old friends, may I take it that this conversation is not taking place?'

'Of course.'

'Thank you. I wanted to speak to you about the planned visit to America by the Duke and Duchess of Windsor.'

Winston guffawed 'Franklin, after the stage managed circus in Germany I imagine that's the last thing you want.'

'Too darn right. I have enough trouble keeping a balance between the interests of business and the unions to have an abdicated and popular former monarch wandering around praising working systems that are generally hated. That is quite apart from his highly suspect wife. J Edgar Hoover would have her arrested if I let him. Apparently he has a huge file on her un-American activities and, between you and me, I think that he revels in some of her…well let us call them adventures.'

Churchill responded 'That is no surprise, eh?'

'Anyhow, I wanted you to know that unofficially we are scotching it. Allen Dulles, a very influential lawyer, was asked by Cordell Hunt the Secretary of State to explain the harm it could do to the business interests of his major clients. They are the likes of Rockefeller, ITT and other major players. We have also encouraged the unions to threaten action.'

'That is a relief' Winston responded. 'What would you like me to do? Y'know I once counted the Duke as a friend….but no longer.'

'Allen Dulles has deliberately told Lady Celia Ffrench-Hardy what is being done here. He believes she is working for British Intelligence' Roosevelt continued. 'For your ears only, after a botched attack on her New York house where a young woman, ostensibly her maid, was killed. Lady Celia was then spirited out of New York by the FBI. She was then flown to Halifax where a British destroyer sailed immediately with only her and a companion as passengers. Obviously a very important young lady.'

'Was she hurt?' asked Winston with concern in his voice, adding 'I know her father well.'

'She wasn't in the house at the time but intelligence points to German interests behind the attack. She is fine. When I let you know that the time is right, will you have a word with the Duke and warn him to cancel if he still has doubts?'

'Of course I will. Whether he listens may prove to be another matter I fear. I think that his head has been turned by Herr Hitler's welcome compared to the British cold shoulder.'

As if prompted by the word cold the two men ended their conversation by switching to discussing the weather but with tongues in their cheeks. Both felt huge relief in their instinctive understanding of each other and clinked glasses of whiskey over the phone before saying their goodbyes.

The first thing Celia did when she landed in Liverpool where they were to spend the night in the Adelphi Hotel was to put in a telephone call to Daisy Fellowes in New York. She and Billy had agreed that it would be prudent to do so rather than have Daisy speculating about Celia's sudden disappearance.

'Daisy, hello, it's me, Celia.'

'Where the heck are you? I began to think that Allen Dulles had done away with you. Your Butler would only say that you had gone out of town suddenly.'

'It's all rather complicated but I received an urgent message and I had to leave immediately to return to England, where I am now.'

'I hope that it wasn't anything too awful?'

'No, it's a family matter. I will explain when we next meet.'

'OK…. Now then darling girl, how did you find Allen? Was he up to snuff?' Daisy asked with a giggle.

'Frankly, not at all. He's just so self-centred. Oh he knows which buttons to push but it just feels mechanical. I almost expected him to stop and comb his hair halfway through. I certainly would not bother again.'

'Well I called him and he was very cool and when I asked him how the two of you got along he simply said 'fine' and then cut short the conversation. Did you upset him?'

'Well, I am not sure that he liked the fact that I seduced him' replied Celia in a mock alluringly sexy voice.

Daisy roared with laughter. 'By God, he would hate it. I would be surprised if he could get it up at all if he wasn't in charge.'

'Oh I had him gagging for the full works but let's say he isn't very impressive in that department is he?'

'No, but when he and I do it we play games so it is quite fun even so' Daisy said with a low and husky laugh.

'Anyhow you can go into the finer details when we get together. I shall be back in London in about a fortnight.'

After replacing the receiver Celia turned to Billy.

'Please forget what you just heard Billy. It was girls' talk and I needed to give Daisy the right amount of detail. Without that she would keep digging.'

'Rest assured Celia, my lips are sealed' Billy was doing his professional best as a spy to pretend that he hadn't been intrigued and that his emotions had not been lit up like a Christmas tree. 'But do tell me. Do you girls always exchange such intimate information?'

'Oh you men! You are so darned insecure. The answer is it depends… and that is my last word on the subject.'

'Very well. May I have the honour of taking you for a drink and then dinner? Best if we eat in the hotel… they have a fine cellar. Although best we do not partake of too much of the vino as we have an early start in the morning.'

Sir Vernon Kell had called a meeting of his senior officers. Johnny, Celia and Billy were also there. He opened the meeting formally then turned to Billy and Celia.

'It is a matter of great regret that Sarah Mountford lost her life. She was a promising young woman. Tragically she broke a golden rule and paid the consequences.'

Billy caught Sir Vernon's eye. 'Sir Vernon, if I may add that the intruders were using hollow point ammunition. That Celia was their target is in no doubt and I strongly urge that Celia should not visit New York at any time in the foreseeable future. Such ammunition is universally treated as illegal and inflicts appalling injuries. The perfect assassin's choice.'

Celia was flushed as she responded. 'I do not intend to be kept in a gilded cage Billy and that's not negotiable as I told you when we discussed this on HMS Faulknor.'

Tar Robertson intervened. 'Celia for the time being you will not travel to America. I shall be seeing Chester Harris from their Embassy later this afternoon to discuss the ongoing situation there. In the meantime, Johnny is meeting Princess Stephanie, who was due to see Herr Hitler. She was to endeavour to persuade him to give a specific order to Himmler and the Gestapo that nothing must be done to harm you in any way.'

Sir Vernon caught Celia's eye and she nodded her assent. He then spoke. 'Very well. To business. You have in your folders a copy of a New York Times editorial. I shall quote only two sections but as you will see the piece is very damning. Taken with what Celia has reported of her conversation with the lawyer Dulles it is clear that US policy is to scupper the visit.'

Sir Vernon went on to read from the newspaper.

'I shall quote just two sentences. '*His (The Duke's) gestures and remarks during the past two weeks, have demonstrated adequately that the Abdication did rob Germany of a firm friend, if not indeed a devoted admirer, on the British throne.' 'Duke is reported as declaring that the British ministers of today and their possible successors are no match for the German and Italian dictators.'*

'Putting aside one's personal feelings we have to consider what action may be most appropriate for us to take as the Secret Intelligence Service. Also in your folders there is a top secret briefing paper that Tar has been given by his friend at the American Embassy, Chester Harris.'

Sir Vernon nodded to Tar who cleared his throat then started to speak.

'The Top Secret paper that Sir Vernon has mentioned is not to leave this room. At the end of this meeting, it must be left here. Please study it but do not take notes. Much of the information is in the public domain but it is the assemblage of that information which is so revealing.

'When Johnny and Celia attended the Windsors' wedding, the host Charles Bedaux who is supposed to be organising the American visit described an organisation known as The Fraternity. You will recall that it is an international loose alliance of big business, bankers and suchlike whose members regard themselves as being supranational and aim to work towards a new World Order. Nazi Germany is their role model.

'There is another organisation based in Basel, Switzerland that was expressly created to be a supra national body – the Bank of International Settlements. It is the brainchild of Sir Montagu Norman, Governor of the Bank of England and Hjalmar Schacht Hitler's head of the Reichsbank.

At this point Sir Vernon interjected. 'And this is a really sinister development in its implications. It may sound somewhat pedestrian but the ramifications are sinister and potentially very dangerous.'

Tar then continued. 'Sir Vernon is absolutely right. The BIS, as it is known, was created to provide a mechanism for Germany to pay its War Reparations. The reparations were forgiven in 1932 but the previous loans to Germany under the Dawes and Young Plans were still outstanding. It was Schacht – who is known as 'the old fox' – who outsmarted everyone and Germany has effectively washed its hands of all obligation to repay them.'

Billy caught Celia´s eye and raised his eyebrows incredulously.

'Funding through BIS is shrouded in mystery but, it has been and remains pivotal to the German recovery and re-armament. Major American and German corporations are working hand in glove.' Tar took a sip of water before continuing. 'Also pivotal are international bankers such as J. Henry Schroder in London and Schrobanco in New York whose board Allen Dulles joined earlier this year. Kurt von Schroder is one of if not the most powerful of Germany's merchant bankers and operates through the family banks in Germany, London and New York. Kurt Schroder is also on the board of BIS.'

Sir Vernon who had been listening intently commented 'Gentlemen whilst that general information is shocking in its implications, we have more detail – do please carry on Tar.'

With a nod to Vernon Tar continued. 'Standard Oil and the German giant I G Farben are working hand in glove with technology swops – for instance the manufacture of synthetic rubber 'Buna' which is essential to Germany if it goes to war. The paper that you have goes into detail but, just to give the full flavour, other corporations involved include ITT the communications giant, Ford Motor Company and General Motors. It is also suspected that Shell is involved.'

Sir Vernon surveyed the listeners and interposed. 'I believe that you can well appreciate the magnitude of the problem. There is a grave concern within the Foreign Office that the Nazis are developing a strategy to de-stabalise other regimes by fermenting dissent amongst workers. The Duke of Windsor with his German gallivanting and ill-judged remarks and behaviour has played into their hands.'

'Remember well that the Nazis may be a bunch of unscrupulous gangsters and street fighters but they are damned clever, totally ruthless and without any spark of human decency' continued Sir Vernon. 'Sadly the Duke has become a pawn in their game. What remains to be seen is just how willing a participant he actually is.'

Tar continued. 'Charles Harvey and his wife the former Mrs Beauchamp, the Duke's housekeeper at Fort Belvedere as you will recall, are now ensconced in the Chateau at Versailles and a part of the Windsors' staff. They will be reporting on what they hear and also importantly who visits the Duke and Duchess.'

Tar paused, then continued. 'Billy. You have Vera Schalberg well placed in Society now I believe?'

'Yes, she is' Billy replied. 'And because she is young, pretty and foreign it is amazing just how much people confide in her – often unwittingly. We have to bear in mind though that she is now three months pregnant.'

'Noted' responded Tar who then turned to Johnny. 'Princess Stephanie continues to be a great asset but you have expressed concern as to for how much longer. Could you expand on that?'

'She is playing a very dangerous game with Hitler. He dotes on her but is unaware that she and his close friend and adjutant Fritz Wiedemann are lovers. In the meantime she has the confidence of the Cliveden Set. She is ultra-intelligent and I agree that she is a tremendous source of information. Let me finish by saying that I am working on an assessment of the political views and shall we say stability, of the members of that group.'

'Excellent... and now... the Duchess. What have you Tar?' asked Sir Vernon.

'Our French friends believe that she and the American Ambassador in Paris, William Bullitt, are having an affair. They watch them both and hit upon this by pure chance when their two teams met at the rear entrance to Schiaperelli the designer's salon.'

'Keep that one under your hat for now please. Do not mention it to the Americans. We may need it for a trade.'

'Now Helga dear, show me the underwear you plan to wear this afternoon. No, take your clothes off and put it on so that I can see.'

Helga, resigned to obeying Wallis, stripped everything that she was wearing and then slipped into the exquisite silk underwear that Wallis had bought for her in Paris.

'Hmmmm darling girl you look good enough to eat! But not now. Just slip out of those and get dressed again and I will show you what I want you to do this afternoon.'

Helga watched apprehensively as Wallis delved into a drawer but was relieved when she saw that Wallis was holding no more than a gold powder compact.

Seeing the look of relief on Helga's face Wallis laughed. 'You silly chump! This is the miniature camera that Joachim von Ribbentrop gave to me. I shall want you to take pictures this afternoon. Our guest must not suspect that you are doing so. You will then have the pleasure of a little trip to Germany where you will give the camera to von Ribbentrop. He will arrange for the film to be developed. I imagine that you would like to see him again?'

'Oh yes!' agreed a smiling Helga.

'Right, this is how it works… perfectly simple.'

After Helga had left her Wallis spent a few moments savouring her satisfaction at killing two birds with one stone. William Bullitt would be in her thrall with her set of pictures and von Ribbentrop would have a close confidante of the American President in his hands.

Wallis gave a low throaty chuckle… she was going to have some real fun.

Chapter 20

Alan Dulles had asked for a meeting with Kurt Von Schroeder, ostensibly on banking business but in reality to implement his part in the wrecking of plans for the Windsors' impending visit to the USA. They met in New York's exclusive Metropolitan Club. After some pleasantries Allen wasted no time in coming to the point.

'Kurt, it is absolutely in our mutual clients' interests and indeed those of your bank that the Duke of Windsor's trip to the USA is cancelled.'

'I am interested in your analysis Allen, as always… do please enlighten me.' Von Schroeder's smile did not reach his eyes nor deceive Allen, who was well aware of his companion's razor sharp mind.

'If I may, I shall start with Charles Bedaux who is on record publically as organising the whole visit. His reputation should be in tatters here in America. The Labour Unions are determined to see him destroyed and will cause whatever disruption that is necessary to that end. His clients are already feeling the lash of their anger. There are strike threats across industry generally and, the Unions are playing a very clever game. Nevertheless he is still seen to be very much at the helm.'

'Well Allen, I certainly agree on at least one point that you make… trade unions should never be underestimated, nor the intelligence of their members. But why is Bedaux so important Allen?'

'I believe he is a symbol of all that is seen as bad in this great country. The bosses have used bully boy tactics in strike breaking… bringing in hired thugs and getting away with it. They are loathed as are all their methods. Bedaux is seen as someone who is an integral part of the same oppressive and exploitative set up.'

Allan paused taking a sip of his dry martini before continuing.

'So far as the workers and the unions are concerned, rather than being the 'Speed up King' smoothing processes in order to speed up the production lines of every industry but also making conditions easier for the workers on the shop floor, his systems are now seen as a brutal tool of exploitation. He is now the 'Stretch out King' – stretch out as in the medieval torture rack. He is seen as the arch exploiter of the working man. His vast wealth is categorised as being made literally on the backs of others. To put it simply, he is hated. It has been made widely known that he is the architect of the Windsors' visit. Indeed he has made it his business to try and gain kudos by taking on that role very publically.'

Von Shroeder nodded his agreement and Dulles continued.

'I believe, Kurt, that the simplest solution is to have him publically ousted from his American company. Without that base, the business relationships and the trappings that go with it he is a man with no standing.'

Nodding again Shroeder asked 'Who is taking care of the press Allen?'

'The Unions have issued statements and it all makes for a good story so I think that Press interest will be self-generating. Also, I am given to understand that the White House has done a little subtle briefing.'

'Good. I shall make some enquiries on that front as well. When he is kicked out we want it to be a very public fall from grace. He must be discredited to the point of destruction here in America. I warn you that such will not be the inevitable consequence elsewhere.'

'I understand Kurt. The concern is stopping this infernal visit. What happens to Bedaux or what he does afterwards outside of America is not our immediate nor, indeed, direct concern.

'Nevertheless, as you will have heard eight thousand Longshoremen on the East coast covering the ports from New York and Wilmington in the North to Tampa in the South are officially on strike. It is potentially economically crippling. But the Unions have cleverly agreed a truce to enable negotiations with the shipping companies. The deadline for its expiry is fast approaching and there is every sign of the dispute being settled and the strike action diverted. Such a strike would inevitably hit many of our mutual clients very hard… no imports and no exports.'

After a short pause Kurt cleared his throat. 'Of course I am aware of this serious threat but how is it relevant to the Duke and Duchess visiting? Am I missing a trick Allen?' Kurt asked. Allen gave a mirthless laugh.

'Ha... the Baltimore Federation of Labor has warned all Unions not to be taken in by, I quote, 'slumming parties professing to help and study labour.' A direct swipe at the Windsors after their German adventure eh?' Von Shroeder laughed mirthlessly and mimed slow hand clapping as Allen continued.

'Now Baltimore is where the Duchess hails from. Their Union leader has also made a very challenging reference to the Duchess implying that she had no interest in working men's conditions and welfare when she lived in that City so why now? There is no doubt in my mind that it will turn nasty. The rumbling is that the Longshoremen will refuse to unload the SS Bremen when the Duke's party arrive and another strike will be called.'

'What an unholy mess. I am afraid that the Windsors' visit to Germany and close association with Charles Bedaux has done much harm even before the visit commences. Right, we must stop the rot.'

Allen pulled an exasperated face and gestured helplessness with his hands.

'If you will excuse me Allen I shall go straight to see Walter Teague of General Motors. He is of course in the same building as Bedaux's company and will call in the other Bedaux directors. I shall then call Sosthenes Behn the founder of ITT. I am their banker and he will heed my advice and also lean heavily on the directors of American Bedaux. You know both of them. They are very single minded when it comes to the interests of their companies.'

'Thank you Kurt. The timing is auspicious because Charles Bedaux is on the SS Europa crossing the Atlantic at this moment so he should arrive to be faced with something of a fait acompli.'

'Allen you and I both know that in business it is every man for himself. None of the people we are talking about would give a single dollar to help Bedaux once I have spelt out the danger to their corporate interests. Nor would I in their shoes. Their hard-nosed commercial opinion will be that he has served his purpose. He is as good as finished in America as we speak.'

'Chester. It is good of you to see me at such short notice.' Tar Robertson was meeting Chester Harris, Head of the United States intelligence operation, in Britain. He was based in the US Embassy in London holding the official title of Legal Attache. A convenient and traditional formal title known by all to be a fiction.

'Tar, it is always a pleasure to see you and thank you for coming to the Embassy. I am very sorry about your young agent killed in New York. That was a bad business.'

Both men nodded in sombre agreement.

'What I can tell you Tar is that we have put the squeeze on the White House to crack down on foreign agents operating in America. No, don't look concerned... we have a special relationship with you British. The real target is the German-American Bund. It is getting just too powerful.'

'I am glad to hear that Chester. Would I be right that the Bund had a hand in the raid on Lady Celia's house?'

'There is naturally no direct evidential link that would stand up in court. The interrogation of the driver was... let me say... robust. Consequently there is nothing that could be treated as admissible evidence, but undoubtedly the Bund was involved as were Himmler's agents. Chester Harris paused and then with raised eyebrows continued.

'In fact, I can go further. Our men on the ground say that Himmler's Gestapo are now embedded in the Bund. That we cannot have. Orders have been passed down from the top that they are to be identified and kicked out. At Tar Robertson's request Chester Harris then went on to describe the Bund. He explained that the Bund, formed in 1936, took over the activities of the 'Friends of New Germany' which a Committee of Congress had concluded in 1934 to have been actually a branch of Germany's Nazi Party established and active in the United States. The Bund had even established training camps in New York, New Jersey, Pennsylvania and other States. Chester opined that the Bund had been allowed far too much freedom by virtue of the perceived strength of the 'German vote' in a number of States. He concluded that it was no surprise that the Bund membership included members of the Gestapo and espionage agents. The President is very concerned about the flow of American funds to Nazi Germany. I am going to tell you something which you will find of interest and not a little surprising. It must stay between us for now as you will understand when I tell you. OK?'

'Absolutely,' responded Tar with a laugh. 'My poor head is fit to burst with never-to-be-voiced confidences.'

'It is long established that we in the intelligence world have our own 'special relationship' and agree to assist on our home territory when our respective cousins from across the Atlantic have a problem in our back yard.'

'Most certainly. The assistance that our people had from American agencies at the time of the attempt on Celia's life is a perfect case in point.'

'Agreed. I shall cut to the chase. We want the special relationship to be further developed. We are of course in the picture with what Donald MacLaren and his team of forensic accountants are doing in the USA. Unofficially they feed us information. Now we want them to act as our eyes and ears. This arrangement to be on a formal, but of course totally deniable, basis. Constitutionally our hands are tied in relation to citizen's rights in the USA but those of British agents are not. We will of course unofficially assist your people with wire taps on telephones and classified information in our possession regarding mutually identified targets. There are many ways we can work together. In return we require a full and frank disclosure to us of all salient information gathered by British intelligence services in relation to US citizens' activity which might be construed as contrary to US interests. This way we can 'hand on heart' deny any surveillance of US Citizens. Naturally we are happy to do the same with British citizens so your Government can deny illegal activity.'

'By Jove Chester that is a marvellous idea. Sir Vernon will be delighted. So effectively our Political 'Lords and Masters' can deny... let us call it... unauthorised and potentially illegal information gathering whilst we do each other's dirty work.'

Tar laughed and added 'So for once the politicians will be telling the truth.'

'I thought that would be your reaction. We would like the same facility in the UK on exactly reciprocal terms. That is a precondition.'

'I foresee no problem with that. What's the first step?'

'Assistant Secretary of State, Sumner Welles – who is virulently anti-Nazi by the way – is to visit London for discussions at the Foreign Office. Whilst in London he will see Sir Vernon so that they can formally lay down protocols. So that Sir Vernon can give the matter due consideration and consult as required I would be grateful if you would brief him in advance... in confidence of course.'

'It will be my pleasure Chester. Now, about these Nazi thugs that you are going to kick out. What if they put up a fight?'

Chester with a wolfish grin replied dangerously softly. 'Then they shall have one mother of a lesson. We would be delighted.'

'Dudley!' said the Duke in a petulant voice as he threw down a newspaper. 'Have you read Paris Soir?' Dudley shook his head rather forlornly. The Duke continued as Wallis joined them. 'These swine are really stirring things up.'

As Dudley went to pick it up the Duke snatched the newspaper and shaking it with both hands read out the banner headline on the front page, his voice breaking with fury. '*Duke and Duchess declared undesirable by American workers' Unions....*' and then, would you bloody well believe it, and I quote '*UK Comment is that 'The German visit of the Duke and Duchess was a slumming party of uninformed sentimentalists'...* would you bloody well believe it!'

Dudley had guessed that there was a real storm brewing when the Duke had not used his nickname and nervously awaited what might come next.

The Duke shook himself like a dog, threw the newspaper to the floor and spoke again in a clipped and obviously carefully controlled manner. 'Dudley I require you to contact the British Ambassador, Sir Eric Phipps, immediately. He is hosting a farewell luncheon in our honour for twenty or so friends tomorrow.'

Wallis who had sat silently listening immediately showed interest at this point. The Duke continued in the same tone.

'Please request that he be kind enough to have copies of all the American newspaper reports concerning the Duchess and me – oh, and any British or French for that matter – for me to take away when we leave. Obviously the American ones, and some of the British also, will have to be extracts by cable.'

'I shall do so immediately Sir.' A much relieved Dudley scuttled out of the room.

'Right Wallis it's time for me to be off to St Cloud for golf with Fruity, then we have our little dinner party this evening. Perhaps I shall be in a better frame of mind if the golf goes well. Do enjoy your fitting at Schiaperelli my love.'

'When will you learn, you silly man!' said a laughing Wallis, deeply relieved that the threat of a tantrum had passed. 'Fittings are no fun... really rather boring... tiresome in fact.'

'Oh my poor darling. I shall think of you guiltily as I enjoy myself this afternoon.'

After a farewell kiss Wallis permitted herself a smile at the prospect of not only a thoroughly debauched afternoon but also the money and leverage it would give her.

Before sending Helga to Joachim Von Ribbentrop with the camera for the film to be developed she would negotiate not only two extra sets of the photographs for her own use but also a substantial cash payment. The payment would be made honouring the Fuhrer's letter given to her in Cannes when the hundred thousand pounds was paid into the newly opened Swiss Bank

Account in her name. The covering letter signed by the Fuhrer referred to that payment being 'for intelligence services rendered.'

'I want to be rich and I'll darn well do it!' she chuckled to herself. 'And I don't care how.'

Always fastidious about his appearance, Ambassador Bullitt studied his face in his dressing room mirror turning this way and that. He had become bald at a young age but was nonetheless regarded as a dashing and handsome man. Apart from his sartorial elegance and almost narcissistic obsession with his looks he revelled in his intellect. At Yale had been voted *'the most brilliant'* of his year.

He had worked under Woodrow Wilson at the Paris Peace Conference of 1919 but subsequently testified before the US Senate condemning the severe terms imposed on Germany by the Treaty of Versailles.

His marriage to a left-wing firebrand authoress had left him impotent with women after she embarked upon a lesbian affair with an English sculptress. It was as a frustrated bisexual that he embarked on his long affair with fellow Philadelphian Carmel Offie, his private secretary.

With considerable satisfaction he found and clipped an almost invisible errant hair that had appeared on his left ear lobe. He then inspected his manicured nails, shot his starched cuffs, picked up his hat and left his suite. He was very excited at the prospect of another assignation with Wallis. The fact that in the evening he would be dining at her table in the company of his male lover only served to pique his sense of adventure. He had already decided not to spoil the day and evening by disclosing the news he had received from America concerning the strong adverse reaction to the Duke and Duchess' proposed visit. She would be hearing about that soon enough from others if not already.

As his official car approached the salon he tapped on the glass panel separating him from his driver who slid it back.

'Mr Ambassador Sir?'

'Drop me here please. The walk will do me good and I shall make my own way back or telephone.'

The gleaming black Cadillac with the Stars and Stripes flag fluttering on the bonnet pulled into the kerb and after discreetly checking his appearance again in a shop window Bullitt began walking slowly towards his destination.

He was a risk taker by nature having lived openly with Offie when

Ambassador to Moscow even though at that time the penalty for homosexuality in Stalin's twisted and brutal State could be beheading.

On this occasion he could have no idea where the day's little journey might lead. His intention was pleasure and self-gratification, but the outcome could be misery. That risk was all part of the thrill.

Kurt Schroeder was always ambivalent about his feelings for Hjalmar Schacht. The aura of mature and stable solidarity that Schacht had assiduously cultivated had fooled so many who had been caught in his carefully crafted snares.

Hitler believed Schacht to be bordering on a financial genius. It could be argued that in many ways he was, provided honesty was taken out of the equation. That he was a superb poker player where the stakes were the finances of a nation could be in no doubt.

Kurt lit his cigar and asked Ilse his trusted secretary of many years' standing to put in a call to Herr Schacht. Ilse was now plump and middle aged with an unflattering taste in clothes. However that was of no relevance in Kurt's eyes. She was totally devoted to him, almost obsessively. She also possessed a magnificent mind and he often gave thanks that he had chosen her out of the young people completing their Doctorates in Heidelberg when he was seeking a personal assistant of exceptional intelligence.

When the call was connected he wasted no time on pleasantries. He had an important message that affected the German refinancing operation root and branch.

'Hjalmar. Kurt here. Just to warn you that the 'speed up King' is in for a very nasty shock when he lands in New York. Our friends and colleagues are as one that he must be sacrificed in the greater interests of all.'

There was an unnaturally long pause. On the phone to anyone but Schacht Kurt would have asked if they were still there but he knew that the devious Minister would be scheming.

Schacht finally responded.

'I see. His arrogance does nothing to endear him but I believe that he still has, or has access to, much information of great value to the Reich and its business partners. One always speculates about the contents of that large document bag that never leaves his side.'

There was another long pause then Schacht continued.

'I shall ensure that he enjoys a warm welcome in Germany, although, I anticipate that he will probably have to make some substantial deposits in consideration for our continued assistance and of course as collateral.' Kurt could recognise a banker's shakedown from a mile away. 'Hjalmar don't squeeze out all the juice from the fruit. Remember his uses and the esteem in which the Fuhrer holds him.' There was no hint of humour as Schacht merely responded. 'Of course I would not consider such a thing.' With a click the line went dead. Ilse came straight into Kurt's office. She had a broad smile. 'I have a transcript just in case Schacht upsets the Fuhrer. You warned him fair and square. He will now hatch a new blackmail plan like the last one which gave him half of Bedaux's German business, plus a fortune to the Nazi Party... Oh yes, and a fortune for himself.' Ilse's amusement had stripped away the years as her eyes sparkled.

'Come on Ilse, make an old man happy. On with your glad rags and we'll have a jolly dinner speculating just what the 'Old Fox' Schacht will do this time.'

Dudley Forward, whose character rather belied his name, was not a natural thruster who would push himself to the front of the hunting field or even a crowd. He was by nature a discreet Royal Servant who looked after his charges with absolute commitment. He was the third baronet and had become the Duke's Equerry and Private Secretary by chance when the Duke was Prince of Wales. Theirs was a strange relationship and however close at times and in spite of Dudley's unswerving loyalty the Duke always expected to be treated as a Prince of the Blood by this man of gentle birth who served him with utter devotion.

Sir Eric Phipps, the British Ambassador in Paris was cut from different cloth. Smooth and suave in diplomatic salons and as deft as an Olympic fencer at avoiding potentially damaging threats he also had a mercurial temper and Dudley was now on the receiving end.

'You tell me that your Master, the Duke of Windsor, whose status here is as a private citizen of importance, no more, is giving instructions to this Embassy and through it the Embassy in Washington?'

'Sir Eric the situation is most delicate.'

'Delicate be damned. I suggest that you get onto the American and British Press and ask them to cable all relevant articles to you. That is your job Sir Dudley, not that of His Majesty's Diplomatic Service! Now, Goodnight.'

Just then the rather imposing figure of Fruity Metcalfe in his golfing clothes appeared in Dudley's small office which had been that of the housekeeper previously. With his impressive height he appeared to totally fill the room. Dudley explained his problem.

'Dudders old chap… worry thee not dear fellow. I have a chum at Reuters and another at Associated Press. The wire services will have the whole shooting match.' He rooted around in his pocketbook and produced two rather dog eared business cards. 'They look pretty ropey because I used them a lot when the Duke and I were holed up in Austria after the Abdication. If you recall I had the job of 'flannelling' the press so I had to know what the blighters were saying.'

The Duke appeared in the door looking rather agitated. 'Fruity for God's sake we'll be late. Do come along man.'

'Righto Sir … just hearing how Dudders is planning to get that stuff you wanted… good show!'

As Fruity almost jumped out of the door he gave Dudley an enormous wink. Dudley had always thought of Fruity as being like a young Labrador. You know that it will be a wonderful staid and superbly loyal dog one day but in the meantime it will be irrepressibly boisterous and impossible to discipline.

Today he had seen another thoughtful side to Fruity Metcalfe which he liked.

'Here we are. Now, the front entrance and whilst I have my fitting you can look at some designs. I want you to have some really elegant clothes… you dress well now but I think that a little more elegance will suit your position in my household my dear.'

Elsa Schiaperelli and Wallis appeared to brush cheeks but neither had any intention of making physical contact that might smudge the artful make up on which they both relied so heavily. The famous couturier then led Wallis to a fitting room where Wallis removed the elegant pale grey fitted coat dress that she was wearing. In Elsa's distinctive accent she commented. 'Ze dress… ees eett Coco Chanel?'

'It sure is Elsa – do you like it?'

'A leetel plain. Now try zees.'

Half an hour later Wallis was finished and had also approved Helga's choices.

'You have a good eye Helga' commented Wallis as Elsa Schiaperelli looked on with a benign smile as well she might, given the amount that Wallis had just committed to spend.

Helga looked concerned and almost stammered as she asked 'Ma'am… will not the Duke be angry that you have ordered five dresses and outfits for me when you told him about only one?'

'Worry not my dear he will not even notice. Now, it is performance time and remember you must capture his face on camera but not mine.'

His Excellency, the Ambassador of the United States of America, was sitting elegantly on a Louis Quinze gilt chair when Wallis and Helga made their entrance. He was still fully dressed. Wallis and Helga had dressed in an adjoining room. He gave an involuntary gasp as they stalked into the luxurious salon that Elsa had created.

Both were masked with black plumed head dresses. Each wore a boned black silk corset basque. Thigh high black patent leather boots with exceptionally high heels completed the outfits.

Wallis broke the silence after they struck matching poses. 'Bill meet my dear friend Helga. We are going to play a little for you. If you wish to join in just go behind the screen and undress then do so. Otherwise you may only watch from your chair.'

Wallis and Helga went behind a lacquered Chinese screen. They emerged and Bullitt noticed with a start that Wallis was wearing a false penis. He had heard of such but never seen a woman wearing one.

Helga went to the wall and he saw her throw some switches and he heard the unmistakeable clank and clatter of stage spotlights coming on. Helga than walked across the salon pulling open a floor to ceiling curtain that he now realised had separated one half of the actual room.

The stage lights were focused on a giant bed set on a plinth with a step running around it. The bed was covered in the palest grey, almost silver, silky satin material as were the walls and ceiling.

In front of the bed there was a single straight backed wooden chair painted black. Wallis walked out of what was now deep shadow and motioned for Bullitt to sit on the chair. He obeyed.

Helga drew the curtain again and they were now in a glimmering silver cave and the stage spotlights focused on the bed seemed even more vivid.

She and Helga then threw their masks into the shadows and slowly climbed onto the bed.

They knelt facing each other their backs straight. Wallis reached forward and her hand went between Helga's legs. Almost immediately Helga threw her head back.

Helga then leant forward and caressed the false penis as if it were real, then reached beneath it. It was now Wallis who threw her head back.

Bullitt was finding this choreographed scene intensely arousing and as the two women moved into an embrace and started kissing almost leapt from his chair and rushed behind the screen where he tore off his clothes.

When he emerged the two women were in the classic sixty nine position with Wallis on top. Bullitt climbed onto the bed and started to caress Wallis. She stretched an arm back and started to massage his still flaccid penis.

Wallis raised her head and moving aside pulled Bullitt towards her then gestured for him to kneel and she pushed his face towards Helga's sex. He needed no encouragement. Wallis then moved behind the kneeling Bullitt. Firmly she drew his legs apart then with a strong thrust forced the glistening fake penis into him. He gave a cry of pain but as she had anticipated he did not resist as she started a slow rhythmic thrusting.

Helga backed away and then climbed off the bed. She fetched the miniature camera from its hiding place and then carefully took a series of pictures from different angles clearly identifying Bullitt and what was being done to him.

After hiding the camera again she slipped back onto the bed and stroked Bullitt's head. Wallis withdrew and undoing the harness threw the apparatus into a dark corner before setting about arousing Bullitt to have sex with him as only she could.

As soon as they returned to the Chateau in Versailles Wallis took Helga into her boudoir and telephoned von Ribbentrop. Helga could only hear one side of the conversation.

'Joachim – how are you?'

'Of course it's Wallis dear silly man.'

'Why am I calling?'

'It is time that we met and added another flower to the bouquet... just like the old days in London. I am off to America in a day or two so it will have to be when I am back.'

'In the meantime I shall send my assistant and dear friend Helga... I am sure that you remember her... to you with a package. It has some interesting pictures. You remember the dinky little camera don't you? The pictures are of a very important and influential American who is a very close friend of the President.'

'Of course it's the same Helga you naughty, naughty man. Now, there are two conditions. First you give Helga two sets of the prints for me. Second, a suitable donation is made to the Swiss bank account that was kindly opened.'

'I thought that you would agree.'

'Now do look after Helga for me… I am sure that you will… and I look forward to our next meeting. Goodbye for now.'

Wallis hung up the telephone receiver and turned to Helga.

'Well, there you are my dear. Off to Berlin for you in the morning and then take a holiday. We plan to be in America for thirty seven days plus of course the crossing time. Come back in seven days' time when we should have landed and I can telephone you. We can go through the post then. Now, have fun in Germany.'

'I shall certainly do my best and thank you Wallis' replied a smiling Helga already excited at the thought of being with von Ribbentrop.

Wallis felt deeply contented as she set about preparing for the evening's dinner party.

Chapter 21

'Now is the time' thought the Fuhrer. 'Now is the time, the moment... yes... the moment for me to set out my grand plan for the creation of the Greater Germany and the destruction of its enemies.'

He took a deep breath and then rising from behind his desk in the Berlin Chancellery strode across the great room that served as his office, the steel-tipped heels of his black patent leather shoes ringing on the gleaming parquet flooring as he stepped off the huge Aubusson rug on which his desk stood.

The high double doors swung open as he approached them revealing an equally large room dominated by a long conference table at which were seated the military, civilian and foreign policy leaders of Nazi Germany.

Moving as one, these powerful men pushed back their chairs, stood and raising their right arms in the familiar salute as one bellowed 'Heil Hitler'. The Fuhrer did not break his step but raised his right arm in an almost languid acknowledgement. As he strode towards the table he thought 'This meeting is my meeting. It is I, the Fuhrer, in whom all power rests and now I will spell out a future which they must implement. It is my vision that has brought Germany so far already and it will be my inspiration and leadership that will take the Reich to ever greater glory and its true destiny.'

He paused at the head of the table and one by one stared directly into the eyes of every person present. Each felt the power of his unwavering eyes as he settled his baleful gaze on each of them one by one. More than a few shuddered involuntarily.

He sat.

The all-powerful Fuhrer was motionless and expressionless. His face a mask. The ornate clock on the mantelpiece ticked seemingly ever more loudly as breath was held. Hitler well knew the power of silence. His intention was to unnerve these powerful men. He succeeded.

Men as powerful as Reich Foreign Minister Baron Constantin von Neaurath, the Reich War Minister, Field Marshall Werner von Blomberg, the Commander of the Kriegsmarine, Admiral Raeder and the Army Commander General Werner von Fritsch were acutely discomforted and glanced at each other before tentatively resuming their seats. The only person who was not intimidated was the Luftwaffe commander, Great War flying ace, long serving Nazi and close confidante of the Fuhrer, Hermann Goering.

No aides or staff members were permitted other than Colonel Count Friedrich Hossbach, one of Hitler's Military Adjutants who was tasked with making a verbatim note of all that was to be said. He sat ramrod straight with his arms at his side as if at attention with a notepad and pen placed squarely before him.

Still the ominous silence. The tension was palpable.

'Gentlemen' the Fuhrer's voice was pitched so low that they all leant forward to hear him. 'I am going to tell you what will be accomplished by the Reich over the coming years. The plan is my vision as your Fuhrer and it is your duty and obligation to ensure that in every respect and in every detail it is fulfilled to the letter.' He then screamed 'Do I make myself clear? No failure will be tolerated at any level. If any one of you should fail me there will be no mercy.' Again he paused and looked each of them in the eye.

They were rigid in their chairs knowing that this man had the power to destroy each and every one of them, their families, their friends and even acquaintances. The Gestapo had thoroughly researched all of them and painstakingly and constantly updated their files.

Still the only man who was not intimidated by the Fuhrer's performance was Goering who whilst outwardly reacting in the same way as the others knew that he alone was immune to the unveiled threat.

The Fuhrer again spoke unnaturally quietly for a few moments then suddenly the pitch and tone of his voice changed becoming harsh, even demonic. 'The content of this meeting shall be regarded as my 'political testament' in the event that some misfortune should take my life. It is a solemn obligation which certain of my colleagues, including Hermann Goering, have pledged to fulfil.'

Again the Fuhrer theatrically paused for what seemed a long time to his audience albeit of powerful men all of whom aware that the slightest fault in obedience could mean the end of everything.

'My trusted Military Adjutant Colonel Hossbach will prepare a true memorandum as my testament but first each one of you must take a solemn oath of secrecy. Colonel Hossbach, administer the Oath.'

After each man present had formally taken the oath of secrecy Hossbach did likewise addressing his oath directly to the Fuhrer. Hitler then began to speak, carefully modulating his voice once more so that all had to strain to hear him.

He outlined Germany's increasingly weak economy and the consequent need to expand the Nation by the annexation of Austria and Czechoslovakia – such to be a priority. He declared that war with France and Britain should be avoided until at least 1941 and ideally later. In this instance he quoted Sun Tzu who in his 'Art of War' said 'The supreme art of war is to subdue the enemy without fighting'. He hinted that it may not be necessary to do battle with these two nations given their feeble leadership which he would exploit. In the meantime the aims of the Reich would be achieved by comparatively small actions of annexation which would be handled in such a manner that war would not be provoked.

Foreign Minister Von Neurath could not conceal his discomfiture at this statement. This was noted by both Hitler and Goering.

Hitler then analysed the German economy and the ability of the expanded Reich to be self-sufficient in certain essential strategic areas. He spoke without notes and in impressive detail as he continued his analysis. Gradually he allowed his voice to gain strength until he reached a powerful conclusion.

'Gentlemen. The Reich will achieve its aims by diplomacy backed by strategic force of arms. That will be your task and that of all who serve under your command. We must strike before our actual and potential enemies have re-armed. Where our Reich chooses to fight there will be absolute victory.'

At that, he stood and as the rest struggled to their feet once again pushing their heavy chairs back he gave a full Nazi salute rather than his now familiar almost casual one, turned and marched out of the room.

Nobody in the meeting wanted to catch anyone the eye of another and it was in silence that they left the room not as a group but one by one through the doors on the opposite side of the room to those through which the Fuhrer had left.

Hossbach's task was not onerous because in advance the Fuhrer had provided him with the full text of what he would be saying as drafted with Rudolf Hess. The Colonel was amazed that Hitler had delivered an almost two hour long speech without notes and without deviating from that script.

Hitler was relaxing in his office leaning back in his desk chair with an almost coy smile playing around his lips.

'Well Hermann. What did you think?'

Hermann Goering resplendent but not a little grotesque in his be-medalled sky-blue uniform adjusted his bulk in a chair which he dwarfed and chuckled before replying. 'Well my old friend, you left them in no doubt about the state of our economy and what they must accomplish if they are to have the resources that they are all squabbling for. Oh and their jobs and lives!'

Hitler gave a short laugh, almost a snort of derision. 'That was certainly the idea! The good Admiral Raeder's complaint that the prime allocations of steel and raw materials were going to your Luftwaffe and the Wermacht provided the perfect opportunity. Anyhow, I doubt whether many of them will hold their present appointments for long. Von Neurath must go first. He is too traditional a diplomat for my liking.'

'Absolutely right Adolf he does not have the spine, the nerve nor indeed the guile for what must be done. Anyhow, for all his faults von Ribbentrop is a much better man for the job. We need some more imagination… also it will be amusing to see Messrs Himmler and Goebbels spitting tacks eh?'

Goering roared with laughter then Hitler continued. 'Ribbentrop is the right man Hermann and so far as I am concerned I will not have any more of this sniping. I have told Martin Bormann to speak to them both and tell them that I shall be extremely displeased if there is any more of such behaviour.'

'Ha! You can bet that Heinrich Himmler will have his Gestapo sniffing around all the same.'

'My dear old friend, who ever said that competition was unhealthy?' laughed Hitler. 'You know my view… dogs fighting over a single bone are much fiercer than those placidly gnawing away at their own.'

'Keep them all on their toes eh Adolf?' commented a nodding Hermann Goering who then loosed another rumbling chuckle.

Wallis was well pleased with the way things had turned out with Ambassador Bullitt. She was confident that the pictures taken by Helga would be totally compromising providing her with what she saw as an insurance policy quite apart from more funds into her secret account. That she had also enjoyed the manipulation and almost ritual humiliation of so powerful a man was an added bonus. That he trusted, regarded and treated her as a good friend did not cross her mind let alone prick her conscience.

There was no doubt in her mind that von Ribbentrop and Helga would become lovers again in Berlin. She regarded that as being in her interests because it tied him to her even more. She knew that it was in her power to excite him as others could not, but in her absence she felt that Helga would hold his interest. 'Men are so weak' she thought to herself with a grim smile. 'We women hold the key to controlling them whatever else they may choose to think.'

She rang for her maid. Now it was time to prepare for the evening's dinner party. She laughed aloud at the thought of William Bullitt the suave and intellectual diplomat gracing her elegant table when only a few hours before she had had him on all fours and pleasured him in such a primitive and degrading way.

The Duke was now in an expansive mood. Although the Duke would never admit it Fruity Metcalfe had played a blindingly good game which had more than compensated for the Duke's steady but uninspired performance. The main thing was that they had won and the Duke's name would be inscribed on the Winners' Board in the grand panelled bar of the exclusive golf club. He and Fruity would be the first Englishmen to have their names there.

'Now Fruity my dear chap, how about a quick gargle before our guests arrive?'

'Nothing could be more pleasant, Sir. Let us toast our success together. After all, we have had a tremendous afternoon.'

'By Jove we have… I bet it was a damn sight more exciting than whatever our guests were doing this afternoon and poor Wallis was taking Helga for a fitting. How infernally dull, eh?'

'Certainly sounds dull to me Sir. But you know what women are like.'

'Well, bottoms up Fruity, bottoms up!'

'I have been most careful with the placement for this evening's dinner David. I have put Peggy Munster next to you and on your left Madame Armand Gregoire who I fear has a somewhat fearsome reputation.'

'Oh really? Reputation for what my dearest?'

'She is a little bohemian… for instance she believes in free love, totally equal rights for women and is utterly fearless in her political beliefs. She considers that Herr Hitler and the Nazis have found the key to success and fulfilment for all, including women.'

The Duke was smiling broadly as he lit a cigarette. 'Well dearest, she may well be right you know. 'But as I see it Wallis 'free love' is a euphemism for the old notion that 'a little bit of what you fancy does you good' responded the Duke patting Wallis' bottom.

'As long as it is only fun, maybe' replied Wallis cynically thinking of that afternoon's diversion. 'Now we must get ready… we cannot keep our illustrious guests waiting can we dearest?'

'Absolutely not. Oh, by the way, Dudders came up trumps and I have files of stuff about our American trip. I shall try to get Ambassador Bullitt on one side and sound him out.'

'Not tonight my love… far more important that you see whether Peggy Munster will bring Sybil Colefax on board and they will be our interior decorators. That, David, is tonight's priority!'

'Very well dearest, if you say so' responded the ever obedient Duke.

Chapter 22

Billy ushered Vera into the wood-panelled entrance to Sheekey's restaurant where their hats and coats were taken in the cramped vestibule. The Maitre'd appeared as if on cue and clearly recognised Billy.

'My Lord it is my great pleasure to welcome you and of course the charming mademoiselle' he intoned in a melifluous and heavily accented voice as he gave a small bow and an unctuous smile of greeting. 'May I take you to your table?' he continued and with an exaggeratedly theatrical gesture led the way into the crowded restaurant. 'Thank you Luigi' replied Billy as he and Vera were ushered forward.

Billy was pleased to note that they were taken to his and his father's favourite corner table which gave a fine view of the restaurant but was just far enough away from other tables to allow a confidential conversation. The table was laid for three.

Two waiters drew back Billy and Vera's chairs and as they were seated flicked out crisply starched napkins and laid them carefully on their laps under the watchful eye of Luigi.

'I say Luigi… a couple of glasses of your hock would be just the ticket I think. Do you agree darling?' asked Billy smiling affectionately at Vera.

'That would be lovely but a small glass for me please.' Luigi nodded and with an almost imperceptible hand gesture summoned the sommelier and whispered the order. When he was out of earshot Billy leant close to Vera and with a chuckle said 'Luigi is such an old fraud you know with his extraordinary exotic accent. He hails from Balham and inherited the position of head waiter when his father retired.' Vera glanced over at Luigi as she listened.

'His old man started with Josef Sheekey himself when this place opened as a restaurant. It was an oyster bar before that. The Cecil family own all of the property around here and wily old Lord Salisbury only permitted the change to a restaurant on condition that it would be open for after theatre dinner for himself and his cronies.'

Just then there was a slight commotion and into the restaurant bustled an extraordinary sight. A plump, bulging-eyed, exceptionally short man in an Astrakhan coat bustled across the room hotly pursued by Luigi.

The new arrival was apparently oblivious to the attention he was attracting as he threw his arms wide and cried out in a strong Russian accent. 'Billy my boy! Dearest Billy! How are you? Oh and this most beautiful consort.' He stopped dead and then raising his prominent green eyes as he did so bowed low and took Vera' s hand which he kissed saying 'Jona Baron von Ustinov at your service.' He paused theatrically. 'For life dear lady.'

Vera was dumbfounded and speechless as Luigi succeeded in taking the diminutive yet rotund Baron's coat and supervised him being seated. The Baron turned to Luigi and smiled warmly.

'Vodka Luigi… on ice as usual.' He then turned to Billy and as he drew a gold tipped black Sobranie cigarette from a gold case heavily embossed with a coat of arms asked 'Now then my young friend. Just who is this beautiful lady that you are honoured to accompany? That she is not English is plain to see.'

'But of course Klop. May I have the pleasure of introducing Vera Von Wedel…Vera, Klop Ustinov.'

Klop had risen from his chair and bowed again as smiling he sat again. Then leaning close said 'But of course dear lady. I recall that you were once married to Count Ignatieff. He was executed by the Bosheviks… hmm yes?'

'That is correct Baron' replied Vera warily. 'But do tell me, why does Billy call you 'Klop'? My recollection of Russian is that it is not a flattering name!'

Vera laughed but Billy could sense that she was very tense. He set out to diffuse the situation.

'Permit me Klop' intervened Billy. 'Klop will not be offended when I say that his nickname which as you clearly recall my dear means 'bedbug' in Russian, was given to him because some cruel boys considered that he resembled one. Since then, having been found in so many beds Klop has earned the name. Is that fair my dear friend?'

Both Klop and Billy were now laughing almost uncontrollably. Klop's laugh was so infectious that many in the restaurant smiled despite being unaware of the cause of his mirth.

Klop dried his eyes with a large purple silk handkerchief that he pulled from his sleeve theatrically and with occasional sniffs composed himself.

'Now Vera my dear… and I trust that you will call me Klop…as Billy will tell you I am 'one of the team' having been brought on board by Maxwell Knight and Tar Robertson. I assume Billy that I may treat Vera as a confidante?'

'Most certainly.'

'Good because before we talk of other matters there is something that I must tell Billy without delay. I picked up a whisper this morning that Wolfgang Goose Putlitz is under suspicion and being recalled to Berlin for 'talks'…. we all know what that might mean.'

Vera was looking a little puzzled. 'I know Wolfgang' she said. 'Is he a British intelligence asset?'

Billy nodded. 'He is a German patriot but deeply concerned about the way in which he feels Germany is being led and the consequences that he fears will befall its people. He is careful only to assist with what he sees as information which gives a true picture of the Nazi intentions and attitudes but he will do nothing to harm his beloved Fatherland. It is like a tightrope but he manages. He is a very clever man.'

'He is a very serious fellow' added Klop. 'He received a Doctorate in Berlin and has risen steadily through the ranks of the diplomatic service. He has utter contempt for the Nazis. He regards them as street fighting thugs who cloak their lust for power with pseudo ideological cant. My position is the same of course I abhor the Nazis. They are scum…. Oh my apologies dear lady I forget your gracious presence!'

Billy responded 'Well said Klop. About von Pulitz, thank you and I will warn Tar. He may well wish to take some protective measures. Now, the reason that I have introduced you is that Vera will be returning to Germany. In fact, very shortly after she gives birth to our baby.'

Klop's already bulging eyes seemed to grow even larger and then his face cracked into the broadest of smiles. 'My heartiest congratulations to you both.'

Billy raised his hand. 'You will have worked out Klop that Vera – being married to General Von Wedel – is having the child in secret and arrangements are being made for it to be brought up within my family. It is complicated but in due course we shall marry and the child, assuming that it is a boy, will inherit my titles and land.'

'I see. Presumably whilst back in Germany you Vera will disseminate the 'intelligence' that you have gathered whilst here in London.'

'That is so and I shall be employed in using that knowledge to interpret future events. Whether I shall be sent back to Britain is another matter. I think that von Wedel, who is an honourable man and one whose beliefs may not be far away from those of Goose Pulitz and yourself, may decide to engineer my return here if he fears that Germany is sliding towards disaster.' Vera paused whilst waiters handed out menus and the sommelier replenished their drinks.

Billy then commented. 'In the event that Vera is sent back to Britain and assuming that there will be a war situation, she will enter the country clandestinely. She will be captured and then taken into the custody of our service where she will conveniently disappear. You, Klop, will be in charge of her at your place in the country. Hence the introduction today.'

'And the official cover Billy?' asked Klop with a raised eyebrow.

'In depth debriefing.'

'If so beautiful a lady were to cross my path in other circumstances...'

'Do not even think it Klop' Billy snarled, then all three laughed again.

Billy had ensured that Klop Ustinov was fully briefed before meeting Vera but knew that Klop would now share the coincidences of their pasts to gain Vera's confidence. They were both multi-lingual and Billy had difficulty in following their conversation as they seemed to switch languages effortlessly as they talked more and more animatedly. A similar back ground and the fine wine ensured that Vera and Klop were soon talking like old bosom friends.

Klop paused and nodded his thanks to the waiter who had just refilled his vodka glass – a task that kept the waiter almost constantly at his side. 'Billy... I am of course being most impolite dominating the conversation with your treasure.'

'Not in the slightest. You know Klop that if anyone else referred to Vera as 'my treasure' it would sound absurd but as ever you get away with it. Now then we should order. Vera, Klop will inevitably have caviar... he claims that his forebear, Grigori, who owned vast tracts of Siberia, feasted on caviar and suckling pig daily and spent the rest of his time working up his appetite seducing young girls from his estates.'

'That is no vile calumny!' cried out Klop. 'I am immensely proud of Old Grigori. Yes Billy, caviar is a must but I shall follow with a piece of fish.'

*   *   *

'Oh my God! Don't stop... don't stop!' he cried as the statuesque blonde woman brought the riding crop down hard again on his squirming behind.

'Why not? You have been a very naughty boy and slept with other women so you must suffer... yes?'

'Yes' he gasped as the crop bit again. 'Yes... I deserve my punishment.' He was now almost sobbing and the woman decided that enough was enough. She threw the crop to the ground and quickly unfastened his wrists and ankles which had been shackled to the four corner posts of the bed.

She pushed his legs together and started to roll him over onto his back. As she did so she could see that he was fully aroused. She playfully took him in her hand very gently and leaning over him whispered in his ear 'So now that he has been chastised, what is the pleasure that His Excellency the German Foreign Minister desires?' asked Helga who then blew into his ear.

'Ha you little devil... you know perfectly well' he muttered thickly as he reached for her knowing that she would be ready.

Later as they lay relaxing with cigarettes Von Ribbentrop blew a perfect smoke ring towards the ceiling and casually asked 'So what is Wallis intending to do with her sets of prints incriminating His Excellency the Ambassador of the United States of America? I have to say that your mistress is becoming ever more imaginative.'

'I really do not know but my guess is that the pictures are some form of insurance. She is very insecure you know despite her hard shell. She is never quite sure just who her enemies are and as a result I think that she makes more enemies than she actually had in the first place... does that make sense?'

'Yes, I understand what you are saying but you are right – she does attract hostility and suspicion.'

Von Ribbentrop paused for a moment then continued almost musingly 'Yes, you know, I think that you might have hit the nail right on the head. By her own suspicions and consequent behaviour she creates much of what she fears. Interesting very interesting indeed... Now then, dinner calls but first my little hellcat...' Von Ribbentrop winced as he twisted towards Helga having stubbed out his cigarette. She whimpered and arched her back as he expertly touched her. The maestro was in control again, he thought to himself, and smiled.

Princess Stephanie von Hohenloe was with her lover Fritz Wiedemann, one of Adolf Hitler's Personal Adjutants and a trusted confidante of the Fuhrer. She knew that the subject that she had to broach was delicate in the extreme but she had been carefully briefed in London, initially by Johnny whom she numbered amongst her former lovers and then later in greater detail by Tar Robertson and Maxwell Knight.

'Fritz… I need talk to you about a very delicate matter… is now a good moment?'

'For you my love it is always a "good moment".' Fritz laughed as he stretched out in his armchair.

'You are of course aware that there are many German patriots who like yourself and Friedrich Hossbach are unswerving in your loyalty to the Fatherland and, indeed, your Fuhrer but are deeply concerned that the radical policies of Nazi Germany will pitch Europe if not the World into another catastrophic great war.'

'Of course I am but of course with Himmler and Heydrich's thugs with their ears everywhere it is not something that any of us discuss. But why do you ask?'

'Would you use your position – your official position – to assist someone who is of like mind but who has fallen foul of the Gestapo? He is not in their hands yet but the net has been thrown over him.'

'If I can I will, but you must understand that I cannot act overtly. Now, tell me more.'

Stephanie then told Fritz the well-rehearsed story that had been polished in her long sessions with Tar Robertson and Maxwell Knight, concluding 'So you see Fritz darling Goose Putlitz is one of us and at risk of being torn apart in Himmler's cellars. Not only that, it will provide Himmler with the excuse to start a witch hunt and come after all of us whom he suspects share these views.'

'Very well. I shall speak to Admiral Canaris. He loathes Himmler as you know. I shall ask him to make Goose Putlitz one of his 'assets' immediately and that should scupper any plans the Gestapo have. They hate Canaris and his Abwehr anyhow and are always plotting his downfall but so far he is streets ahead of them. I cannot say for how long but he has their measure. That sadistic pervert Heydrich served under him in the Kreigsmarin. Canaris knows the beast and loathes him too.'

'Fritz that would be excellent. Thank you.'

'It is Goose who should thank me from saving him from a grisly fate. Now then, our own affairs… or should I say affair? Actually, it is no such thing! We are only keeping it a secret because we know that Adolf will go off the deep end. When do you wish to take the plunge?'

'Soon my darling, Lord Rothermere who was paying my retainer has changed his tune and that has dried up. There is little to keep me in England now .I have the Castle that the Fuhrer 'gave' me but quite frankly I would be bored rigid stuck there without you. Also I have gleaned as much information about the so called Cliveden Set as I can. Their views are really the same as ours to the extent that they passionately wish to avoid another great war and lose another generation of young men or worse.'

Fritz paused thoughtfully.

'I fear 'worse' Stephanie. The tactics tested in Spain by our Condor Legion and by the Italians in Abyssinia have shown just how powerful a weapon 'blitzkrieg' is when brought to bear upon the civilian population. Mark my words, if there is another war it will be the soldiers, sailors and airmen who actually fight but the civilian populations will also be defenceless in the firing line.'

'Celia… we are being far too serious these days. This evening we shall dine in the Ritz and then join some chums at the Gargoyle. High time we shook a leg old thing.'

'Less of the "old thing" dear Sir – or I shall have to remind you that you are the teeniest bit older than me' laughed Celia as with her free hand she gestured for the maid to leave her after the lunch coffee had been poured. 'Will you pick me up at the usual time, seven forty five?'

'Well, actually a little earlier because a quick drink with you and a word in private before we go out would be spot on…'

'Of course. I will see you later then and have a jolly good rest this afternoon. I shall be raring to go this evening.'

'That's my girl.'

As soon as Johnny rang off Celia sent for her maid and gave instructions for her bath later in the afternoon and the dress that she would be wearing in the evening. Her butler was told that drinks would be served at seven forty five and there should be some very light canapés to hand.

The Fuhrer was in a dreadful mood. His staff were terrified. All knew that on one of his 'black mornings' when he felt groggy on arising their master's behaviour would be at best unpredictable and his rage awful.

Eva Braun recognised the tell-tale signs the moment she cast eyes on Hitler and making an excuse left the room and finding an empty office dialled the internal number for Doctor Morell.

Doctor Morell, personal physician to the Fuhrer, was a self-styled 'professor' with numerous unsubstantiated claims of having taught medicine at various prestigious universities. Many in the medical profession considered him a charlatan, a mountebank and a fraud. Nevertheless previously he had turned down the opportunity to be personal physician to the Shah of Persia.

Eva Braun had become deeply suspicious of Doctor Morell's true skills. She found his affectation of wearing a personally designed uniform as 'Physician to the Fuhrer' and carelessness with his personal hygiene to an extent that she found grossly unpleasant, nothing less than offensive. He had clashed with Doctor Karl Brandt who had been Hitler's doctor for a number of years but Hitler sided with Morell. She suspected that Morell curried favour by administering drugs that Hitler would have refused had he known what they were. Nevertheless, when the Fuhrer was in so bad a mood Eva had to admit that it was Morell with his 'magic syringe' who could lift the burden of gloom and fear.

As Eva left the office she bumped into Fritz Wiedemann who was bustling along the corridor with an armful of files.

'Ah Eva – what brings you to this neck of the woods?'

'Fritz, Adolf is in an appalling mood… he is out of control with appalling depression and anger. I slipped out to summon Doctor Morell.'

'Well done… God only knows what is in the stuff he injects… he will not say you know, I have asked him. He calls it 'Vitamultin' but none of the doctors or pharmacists that I have asked have heard of such a thing. If you can lay your hands on some I shall have it analysed.'

'I too would be happier Fritz if we knew what was being administered. I will try.'

Chapter 23

Foreign Secretary Anthony Eden was with Prime Minister Neville Chamberlain in the Prime Minister's office in 10 Downing Street. Chamberlain was as always dressed in black jacket, waistcoat, striped trousers and stiffly starched white shirt and wing collar. Eden on the other hand was, as was usual for him, immaculate in a beautifully tailored Saville Row grey worsted three piece suit with a cream silk shirt and regimental tie. Whilst both men sported military moustaches they could not have appeared more different. Whilst Chamberlain gave off an aura of nervous almost impatient and fussy irritability, Eden appeared supremely relaxed and at ease in himself. His words belied his appearance.

'Neville I really had hoped that on reflection you would have seen the great value of our having received a copy of Colonel Hossbach's notes of Herr Hitler's address to his most senior leaders, including the military ones, and then have the opportunity to put the proposition to the French that we should join together and nip the Nazi plans in the bud whilst we can.'

'And I Anthony will not be privy to underhand dealing of this sort. I find it an embarrassment to be in possession of what is essentially a document private to Herr Hitler. That it should have been furnished to us by deceit and the acts of traitors renders it even more distasteful. I have no reason to believe that Herr Hitler is anything but an honourable man. As you know – you have read his formal report of course – Lord Halifax has only recently visited Herr Hitler. I have asked him to join us for this discussion.'

Eden responded quickly but maintained his suave unruffled style.

'I would rather that you had not done so but, so be it. You realise that he and I have fallen out somewhat over that which Halifax chose to say to Hitler about Britain's intentions. I had given him the strictest most limited brief with regard to our reaction to certain actions by the Germans. He did not follow his brief, and that is by his own admission, and has given a very clear indication that we will not intervene if Germany takes steps to annexe Austria and parts of Poland and Czechoslovakia. He even went so far as to indicate that the British Government is understanding of Germany's position vis a vis such lands. In other words he gave the Nazis a green light. Frankly I am most displeased. It is likely to have the same effect in encouraging Hitler as did the importunate statement of the Prince of Wales indicating that we would not interfere if the Nazis were to re occupy the Ruhr which, of course, they then duly did.'

Chamberlain looking vexed and even more uncomfortable was quick to respond. 'But Anthony, Halifax is a fine diplomat and an elegant negotiator. Just look at the way he handled the disbanding of Gandhi's civil disobedience movement in India when he was Viceroy and Governor General. It was a masterly piece of diplomatic governance.'

As if on cue there was a discreet tap on the door and one of the Prime Minister's Private Secretaries entered and announced 'Gentlemen, Lord Halifax is here. Would you wish that I bring him to you or escort him to an ante-room, Prime Minister?'

At Chamberlain's request Halifax was shown in and took the proffered seat. Chamberlain outlined what had already been discussed, omitting Eden's criticism of Halifax and invited him to comment and give his view of German intentions in the light of his recent conversation with Hitler at Berchtesgarten.

'Thank you Prime Minister and Eden. I found the meeting with the Fuhrer to be more congenial than one might have anticipated. In my view he is a most reasonable man albeit having to reshape a nation that had plunged into despairing virtual anarchy. He railed against the vicious and punitive terms of the Versailles Treaty which had brought Germany and its people to their knees. He blames the French for the blatantly unreasonable terms and without prompting made it clear that no blame attaches to the British in this matter. In response I put it to him that we were mindful of the hardship imposed on the German people and were not without sympathy not only with regard to the swingeing level of reparations imposed but also the transfer of essentially German lands and people to other Nations such as Poland and Czechoslovakia. The separation of Austria and the terms imposed on it were also regarded as inequitable.'

Eden commented quietly 'Edward, do you not think that Herr Hitler's 'vision' for the future of his Reich goes further than attempting to restore the pre 1914 status quo? Are you not mindful of the actions of Hitler's minions, for instance the violence against the Jews not only within Germany but in Danzig?'

Halifax smiled and continued. 'Well, as I see it Anthony, Nationalism and Radicalism are a powerful force together but I cannot feel that it is either unnatural or immoral to do so. I cannot for myself doubt that these fellows are genuine haters of Communism, and I daresay that if we were in their position we might feel the same.'

At this point Chamberlain stepped into the conversation. 'It is my considered opinion that at this juncture there is no action that we as a Nation should undertake. If we were to start rearming on a full scale basis it would send a very hostile message to the Fuhrer and make our diplomatic effort to avert all risk of major conflict well-nigh impossible.'

Whilst Halifax nodded in agreement with Chamberlain's comment Eden clearly did not agree.

'With all due respect Neville, and I speak as someone who has been active in diplomacy for some considerable time our rearming would greatly strengthen our negotiating position not only with Herr Hitler but also the Italian gangster Mussolini.'

Chamberlain was becoming even more fidgety and giving a shake of his head, more like a shudder of distaste, admonished Eden. 'Anthony, you well know that I strongly dislike your manner of describing Il Duce. He is the leader of a sovereign state and as such is deserving of our respect.'

Eden responded instantly. His voice was not raised, neither was his tone sarcastic. Chamberlain totally missed the irony when Eden said, 'Being leader of a sovereign state does not of itself earn or justify respect.'

Halifax shot a startled glance at Eden but Chamberlain blundered on. 'I take it then that we shall not review any aspect of our policy in the light of Colonel Hossbach's paper?'

'I do not agree Neville' responded Eden whilst Halifax nodded vigorously earning himself a brief smile of recognition from the Prime Minister.

'In this instance Anthony, whether you agree or not, that is my decision.'

Eden had coloured slightly but that was the only outward sign of his frustration and annoyance. 'Neville, if you choose not to listen to me as the Foreign Secretary in private I shall have no option than to place the whole matter before the Cabinet. That would be my clear and certain duty.'

As Chamberlain started to interrupt Eden's equanimity slipped as in a slightly harder tone he continued. 'If we are in possession of firm evidence of the intentions of a foreign power and such include any threat to this country or its interests, I as Foreign Secretary have a duty to advise Cabinet. As Prime Minister you cannot deprive me of the right to act properly in performance of my duty.'

Chamberlain cleared his throat and with rather bad grace merely replied 'As you will Anthony. However there will be no action before the matter has been duly considered in cabinet.'

Magnanimous in this small victory Eden responded 'But of course Neville.'

After lunch Vera and Johnny returned to The Albany so that she could rest. Vera was lying on a chaise longue in the elegant drawing room.

'You know Billy underneath all that 'brou haha' your friend Klop is a very serious man.'

'Indeed he is my dear… he is an absolutely brilliant gatherer of intelligence as he potters around the clubs, restaurants, drawing rooms and boudoirs of London. Everybody but just everybody confides in him little realising that he has a mind like a razor and the memory of an elephant.' Vera smiled to herself feeling instinctively proud and appreciative of the father of her child.

Returning to The Albany after their excellent lunch at Sheekey's with Klop Ustinov Billy suggested that Vera should lie down and have a rest whilst he would go to meet Tar Robertson.

'I think that I will do just that" agreed Vera. 'You know, your friend Klop is just so amusing. I can quite see how he has so much success with the ladies. You know darling that when it comes to seduction we weak females are far more likely to succumb to a mixture of humour and undivided attention. Little Klop scores on both I can assure you. When he talks to you it is as if you are the only woman in the world. That coupled with his crazy anecdotes about himself, his father, family and friends make him utterly irresistible.'

Billy nodded, then in a mock serious tone asked. 'So, does that mean that you would allow the bed bug to hop into your bed?'

'In my present delicate condition, I think not but then dearest Billy, if things were different, who knows!' laughed Vera. 'I am something of a femme fatale, you know, so I shall keep my thoughts about Klop to myself… a mystery, yes?'

'Femme fatale eh? I think that you may be right. I do not have a specific time for my meeting with Tar so I think that I shall join you for a little rest. How about that old girl?'

'Well, you are no Klop but... oh well I do love you, so that would be agreeable. Very agreeable in fact.'

'Jolly good,' responded a beaming Billy. Vera responded by holding out her hand to Billy and laughing at the great difference between her very English lover and the Russian but now middle European aristocrat who was destined to play an important role in her future.

Anthony Eden and Winston Churchill were having a drink together in the Carlton Club, the London Gentlemens' Club that was very much a Conservative Party stronghold. They had initially met in the bar but were now sitting at a round table in the main hallway tucked in a corner almost beneath the sweeping portrait-flanked staircase. There was no point in two such well-known men making any pretence at not being seen together and as members moved around the club it was noted that the pair were in deep conversation.

Churchill's deep voice rumbled quietly as he responded to Eden's expressed concern that the policy of 'masterful inactivity' towards the rise of fascism that had been adopted by Prime Minister Stanley Baldwin was being slavishly followed by his successor Neville Chamberlain with potentially very dangerous consequences.

'Anthony I do not need to tell you that admirable fellow that Chamberlain is in many ways, he is just not cut out to be an effective Prime Minister. If I were to form a government I think he would make an ideal minister for public works – a political janitor as it were. I have tried to convince him of the dangers we face as a nation and empire but he is blinkered and has blindfolded himself to boot. So far as fascism is concerned he is the three wise monkeys rolled into one.'

Eden laughed. 'Steady on Winston – you are mixing your metaphors rather! Horses and monkeys really... but I am being driven to the same conclusion. In fact, I am considering my position. It is well-nigh impossible to be Foreign Minister working with a PM with little or no diplomatic experience under his belt but constantly interfering. He made me look a damned fool with that thug Mussolini and now he refuses to see sense with regard to Germany's intentions and plans. I have insisted on putting the matter to the full Cabinet which I shall do at the first opportunity. I anticipate that excuses will be found to try and keep it off the agenda but I shall insist. Naturally I do not wish to resign. I cherish my role.'

Churchill was wreathed in smoke from his trademark cigar as he made a sweeping gesture and said, 'Anthony you are a first-rate Minister and your experience means that you are best suited for the job. However I fear that you will find that with Chamberlain you are driving toward a dead end. Resignation may be your only course. I should know. I have resigned more times than most. However, if in the unlikely event that I ever have some influence I shall be delighted to see you as Foreign Secretary.'

After staring hard at Eden, Churchill rumbled on. 'Mark my words, if the Nazis are not checked I believe that we shall be at war with Germany within two years. Chamberlain will have no stomach for the fight and I believe that I deserve and shall have a role to play at the centre of Government. You may rest assured that I shall do my utmost to have you back in Cabinet as Foreign Secretary.'

'Thank you Winston. Your confidence is appreciated.'

Billy was delighted to find Johnny with Tar Robertson. Maxwell Knight joined them almost immediately. After the usual greetings Johnny leant forward and spoke.

'Billy, before we get down to business I want to formally record my thanks for the fine job that you did in New York looking after Celia. First rate.'

'Johnny, you would have done exactly the same. Duncan Maclaren deserves your thanks and likewise Chester Harris here in London. Harris tee'd up the FBI and American Secret Service beautifully. Their co-operation was magnificent.'

Tar broke into the conversation. 'To give you an idea of the pickle things are in America, The German Bund, presumably prompted by Himmler's people got a message through to Ambassador Joseph Kennedy here in London and Chester has had a very rough time of it. Fortunately he has full support in the States and was told to put up with Kennedy's wrath and carry on as normal. Kennedy has apparently taken up the matter with President Roosevelt.'

'What a surprise!' laughed Johnny in a mirthless mocking tone. 'Kennedy hates the British and like so many Americans of Irish descent would rather sup with the devil than do anything to support what they classify as the English oppressors.'

Tar Robertson then gave a long explanatory comment on the weird dichotomy in the Irish soul. As he put it, whilst some Irish were in open rebellion in the time of the Great War there were many fine Irish regiments. Those men fought brilliantly in their thousands alongside the soldiers of all nations in the Empire and the United Kingdom.

Tar also made a personal point that he deplored the actions and behaviour of the 'Black and Tans' in Ireland. He went on to say that in his mind they exacerbated the Troubles and that many a moderate Irishman was turned into a radical as a consequence of their excesses.

Tar nodded towards Johnny then continued. 'Right. Let me go to the nub of things. I shall summarise. Johnny, prompted by some comments made by Princess Stephanie, suggested that we look into the medication that is being prescribed by Hitler's personal physician Doctor Morrell. We have conducted two enquiries based on the information available, firstly about Morrell himself and secondly the drugs which he is believed to be administering. The former has been provided by our local agents in Berlin and the latter by our retained physicians here in London. Maxwell would you be kind enough to provide some background on Doctor Morrell first.'

'I apologise if I go over familiar ground but, if I may, I should like to give you a thumbnail sketch of Dr Morrell and then deal with the possible effects of the drugs that we understand him to be prescribing and administering to Hitler.' Tar nodded in the affirmative and Maxwell Knight then carried on to describe Doctor Morrell's background saying that Morrell came from a middle class family and studied medicine in Grenoble and Paris before specialising in obstetrics and gynaecology for which he trained in Munich. During the Great War Morrell served as a front line medical officer. After the Armistice he settled in Berlin where he had the great good fortune to marry a wealthy actress. Her wealth and status coupled with the access it gave him enabled him to develop a practice catering for the very rich. His reputation was built on his prescribing what can best be described as unconventional treatments. Knight continued explaining that there could be little doubt that Morrell was in effect 'milking' his patients. He made claims to have worked with world famous figures such as Nobel Prize winning bacteriologist Ilya Mechinov and to have taught in various prestigious seats of learning.

Apparently as well as building significant holdings in a number of drug companies he took to prescribing concoctions that he created for specific patients. His reputation was not good within the medical profession but he brushed aside criticism as being mere professional jealousy. He also took to calling himself 'Professor' despite no evidence that he ever held such an appointment.

Tar's expression was sardonic as he commented 'Well, we have quite a few of these types lurking in Harley Street, or so I believe. Sorry Maxwell, do go on.'

'Discretion is not a part of his nature and he let it be known that he had declined appointments as personal physician to various heads of state.'

'For instance?' asked Johnny.

'Well, the Shah of Persia for one' replied Maxwell who then continued with his background picture of the man on whom Hitler now relied upon without reserve explaining that Morrell clearly had seen which way the wind was blowing and had had the prescience to join the Nazi Party in 1933. Apparently he had been invited to a reception at the Berghof where he had convinced Hitler that he could cure his various ailments within a year. A potentially very dangerous ploy but it paid off. Others in the medical profession were aghast when they were told of the drug cocktail he had put together for Hitler. Nevertheless, Hitler was hooked. In fact he was hooked to the extent that he was now totally dependent on Morell.

The others listened attentively as Knight continued. 'Actually hooked is the appropriate word. The basic ingredient of the concoction that Morell uses as his standard drug for Hitler is methamphetamine. To put it simply, this is a central nervous system stimulant which initially with a low dose and pre addiction can induce elevated mood, increased alertness and concentration. On the other hand high dosage can induce psychosis and some very unpleasant side effects.'

Johnny interrupted Maxwell Knight at this point. 'Maxwell, would I be correct in assuming that Hitler's reputed mood swings are drug related?'

Maxwell immediately responded. 'Well actually, the spectrum of side effects is substantial and depending on the individual can vary tremendously. Many potential side effects are in total contrast with each other but our medics have studied recordings and film of Hitler and eyewitness accounts from people who have met and dealt with him. First I shall run through just some of the side effects and you will see what I mean. For instance they include diarrhoea or chronic constipation, loss of appetite, hyperactivity, dilated pupils, flushed skin or pale appearance, twitching and tremors and insomnia. Now, in the case of Hitler he is believed to be suffering from constipation and flatulence, irregular appetite... he is a committed vegetarian and is believed to prefer to eat alone, except of course when he is driven by the urge to wolf down his beloved torte. He famously has insomnia, suffers from bouts of hyperactivity, horrendous depressions, incandescent rages and, of course, a somewhat puzzling sexual profile. They believe that Morell will be having to administer other drugs to counter such side effects which also include the insomnia. They also believe that he is being given Pervetin to enable him to tackle his set piece speeches. The purely psychological side effects of that drug in combination with the others is likely to include, euphoria, change in libido, apprehension , anxiety, irritability, repetitive and obsessive behaviour.'

Knight then went on to explain that the consequences of the combination of all these drugs would almost certainly be fatal after a time. Not necessarily in the short term but that the British doctors who had been consulted did not think that it would be very long before Hitler started to literally fall apart both mentally and physically. Quite apart from anything else they considered that he would suffer progressive cardiac changes.'

Billy muttered an aside. 'If the bloody man were not an all-powerful dictator he would be in an asylum.' Tar ignored Billy's remark merely raising a quizzical eyebrow. 'Thank you Maxwell. Is there any more to add?' he asked.

'Yes. Whilst they have not had the opportunity to observe Hitler at first hand, carry out any tests themselves or have physical examination they do detect a tremor in his left hand. This, they believe, may be a sign of the onset of Parkinson's Disease. That is entirely separate from the drug side-effects that I have mentioned. In essence, Morell holds the key to the Fuhrer's mind and emotions. He is on call night and day and has rooms very close to Hitler in all of the Fuhrer's residences.'

Billy had listened in silence but now posed the question. 'So what if Doctor Morell met with an accident?'

Tar was quick to respond. 'Billy, put that idea out of your mind for now if, as I imagine, you are thinking that if Morell were off the scene Hitler would crack up very quickly and the Nazis would falter. I have to say that we have considered and put the idea on one side. For the moment Hitler is a relatively known element. He has obligingly set out his stall in 'Mein Kampf' and most recently in the Hossbach Note. Nevertheless we shall keep all of this in mind. Johnny. When next you see Princess Stephanie please find out how much she knows about Hitler's medical regime. Do it very discreetly. Also, perhaps Celia could gently quiz the Mitford girl. She must have noticed things when she has been with her 'Uncle Adolf'. Whilst I have poured cold water on Billy's thoughts we should not rule out the possibility that Hitler's drug dependency and consequent reliance on Morell, who sounds a total charlatan, may one day provide us with a useful weapon. Thank you for your time. Billy, before you go, please tell me just how Vera and Klop Ustinov got along.'

'Splendidly. He charmed her as you anticipated and most importantly they recognised in each other a common chord in that they are both in effect dispossessed and from strangely similar backgrounds. I am not saying that Vera's family were great landowners like the Ustinovs but it is something deeper. You could say that it is almost visceral.'

'Excellent. I hope that when the time comes for Vera to go back into Germany she will have the strength to carry things through. It will be a sore burden for a young woman and mother leaving her child behind and venturing back into the centre of the Nazi terror regime.'

'She is tough Tar. She will cope, of that I am sure. Whether I will be as strong remains to be seen.'

Chapter 24

'Your Majesty I completely understand what you are saying and indeed as you are aware I share your views with regard to your brother's attitude regarding both his finances, his wishes that the Duchess of Windsor be permitted the style of Royal Highness and that he and his wife should be free to visit Britain and indeed set up home here.'

Lord Alexander Hardinge the Private Secretary to King George, a position he had held with King Edward up to the time of the abdication, was in his daily morning meeting with the King. The King was in a foul mood and it was an uphill struggle for Hardinge to keep the meeting on an even keel. He knew that he must. If he failed to do so the King's frustrations with his brother would spill over and if, as was often the case when he became over-wraught, the King sent for the Queen the meeting could become even more taxing, with expletives flying.

The Queen would not normally allow her emotions to run free. Her upbringing, like that of her husband, had imbued in her an instinctive duty to keep all emotions on a tight rein. However Hardinge well knew from experience that when it came to her husband's frail health and the behaviour of the Duke and Duchess of Windsor neither King nor Queen could really control their feelings. Each could indulge in foul-mouthed rants.

'I d d on't think that y y you d do!' The King's voice was raised and as he lifted his cigarette to his mouth his left hand was shaking. It was more than a tremor. 'I I am paying the b b b bloody in in income t t tax on the ala ala allowance th th that I p p ppay out of m m m m my p p personal C C Civil List Allowance!'

Alexander Hardinge then went on to explain that the payments to his brother were being paid out of the King's personal funds because at the time of the decision all were well aware that this was not a matter that should be allowed to go before the Civil List Committee of Parliament let alone be debated in the House of Commons. Hardinge went on to say that it might have had very serious repercussions as there was no doubt a deal of antagonism towards his brother in the Commons and that such a debate would be hijacked by the vociferous anti Monarchists of the far left and could do lasting harm to the institution of the Crown. The King had nodded at least in assent if not actual agreement.

That point apparently having been laid to rest at least for the moment Hardinge continued. 'That we have now ascertained that the Duke deliberately misled you as to the state of his finances is regrettable. The value of his undisclosed overseas holdings is very substantially greater than he represented. Quite apart from his huge Canadian holdings he transferred cash – to be precise, eight hundred thousand pounds, abroad – or at least his solicitor George Allen did.'

'Alexander th th that is not n n n news t t to us.' responded the King tetchily.

'I appreciate that it is not Sir but it does give a reason albeit unstated for you to ensure that the status of the Duchess is not changed.' The King looked thoughtful for a moment then reached out and pressed a bell push. Almost in an instant a footman appeared and bowed. 'Your Majesty?'

The King responded without a trace of his stammer. 'Kindly ask Her Majesty the Queen whether she might spare us a few minutes.'

The footman bowed again and left the room. The King and Lord Hardinge then waited in an uncomfortable silence.

'Unity... how lovely it is to see you... gosh... it's been an absolute age!' Celia positively gushed as Unity Mitford was shown to her table in Prunier's restaurant in St James' Street.

'Oh I know Celia my dear. I have been away in Germany so much and you do gad about you lucky thing.'

Celia laughed throatily. 'Pot and kettle methinks Unity... anyhow, to business. It's my treat today by the way.' Celia waved away Unity's attempt to protest. 'I know perfectly well that your Papa keeps you girls on a short leash when it comes to your allowances. In contrast I am fortunate to have my own money.'

'True Celia, and you have your independence. Farve seems to think that by keeping us short we will try harder to make a 'catch'… you know… the right type with plenty of lolly. Hopeless for little me of course… my heart belongs to Uncle Adolf.'

Celia ordered a bottle of Muscadet from a dark blue ankle-length aproned waiter and then turning back to Unity and smiling conspiratorily asked in a hushed voice 'And just how is your dear Fuhrer?'

'Thank you for asking. Oh, you know, he is really in splendid form but he does worry and brood so. It's not good for him. The poor dear man has just got so much on his mind. Luckily he has Doctor Morrell to look after him. He is always there just around the corner so to speak.'

'So how does the 'good doctor' help?' asked Celia quizzically but ingenuously.

'Well he usually gives Adolf an injection of a special medicine that he has pioneered. It works within minutes and then Adolf is a totally different man. Sometimes he is terribly jolly and calls for me and I sit on his knee and he pets me. Other times he can be like a dynamo and he has all his staff, you know, the generals and all that lot running hither and thither… it's really just too funny when that happens… they all look terrified.' Unity giggled as she said this apparently totally unaware of the irony. 'Anyhow whichever mood he is in Adolf's eyes glitter and the twitch in his left hand gets worse.'

'You say that he "pets" you, Unity. Has he slept with you?' Unity blushed and in a strangely childlike gesture lowered her face and covering her mouth with her hand spoke in a muffled whisper 'Well, sort of.'

Celia pressed on. 'What happened… now come on, be a brave girl and tell all.'

Unity looked around the restaurant furtively then began to speak still in a low whisper. 'Well Celia, about a month ago I had arranged for some SS officers to come to the flat and see me. You remember I told you about that. But, earlier in the evening Adolf was very out of sorts and Eva… you know, Eva Braun… she and I are chums you know… we both adore Adolf… anyhow Eva sent for Doctor Morrell. She cannot stand him and says that he's nothing but an unhygienic confidence trickster, which is ridiculous. Anyway, he gave Adolf an injection. Shortly afterwards Adolf told Eva to go to her room. He told her to take Blondie his dog as well. Eva was very unhappy but off she went.'

Unity paused for a moment and Celia squeezed her hand to encourage her to continue.

'Adolf sat me on his knee then asked me to tell him what I planned to do with the SS officers. I told him that I would as always be blindfolded and this time tied to the bed so that I would be kneeling and quite in the nuddy except of course for the mask which would be one of the officer's SS armbands. Then they would play the Horst Wessel song on my gramaphone and one after the other take me. Actually the tune usually gets played a lot of times.'

'Unity that is terrible' gasped Celia. Even though she had heard this before from Unity she could sense a febrile intensity in her friend. It alarmed her even more as Unity carried on.

'No, no, no' hissed Unity. 'It is wonderful and as his faithful officers, who have all pledged to die to protect the Fuhrer, spend themselves in me I feel exulted as if it were Adolf inside me.' Celia was now even more alarmed by the expression on Unity's face which was contorted in a rictus grin as she spoke. There was spittle in the corners of her mouth and she seemed to be in the grip of a trance, almost suffering a fit. As Celia glanced around she could see that others in the restaurant were looking askance at Unity. She laid her hand on the other woman's wrist and stroking gently said soothingly as she would to a spooked horse. 'Now there, there Unity, just relax there's a good girl.' Celia could feel Unity relaxing and within moments she was talking normally albeit still in a whisper.

'Well anyhow I could feel Adolf's thingy was hard... it was sticking in my bum... so I wriggled a bit and he said that we should get more comfortable. He led me to a sort of sofa thing and told me to kneel on it face down. I felt him slide my knickers down and he made a sort of gasp. I felt his hands on me and then something was in me... I don't know whether it was his thingy or fingers but anyhow it didn't matter. He started grunting and then made a strange choking noise... I went to move my head out of the cushions to see if he was all right but he pushed my face back down. I felt him withdraw and then in a strange voice he told me to get up. When I looked at him he was no longer excited but cold and almost unfriendly. He told me that he had work to do and I should leave immediately. So I did.'

'Oh you poor, poor girl Unity. How utterly awful for you.'

'No!' exclaimed Unity loudly causing other patrons to again glance at the two young women. 'It was wonderful, don't you see silly... he, the Fuhrer, gave himself to me.'

For once Celia was lost for words. Help came from an unexpected quarter. 'Celia... my friend, how are you?' A striking and beautifully dressed young woman had approached their table unnoticed and asked in a surprisingly deep voice with a pronounced French accent. 'Hello... I hope that I am not interrupting?' Celia felt a flood of relief as she stood and they embraced. 'Simone... I was so hoping to see you!'

'Mon Dieu! I fear that I am condemned to never leave this restaurant.' They both laughed then Celia gestured towards Unity who had by now completely recovered her composure. 'Simone, may I introduce my very dear friend Unity Mitford. Unity this is Simone Prunier the daughter of the founder of the famous Restaurant Prunier in Paris and herself the founder of Prunier London.'

As the two shook hands formally Celia turned back to Simone. 'It is so long since we have had a good chinwag... could you spare the time to join us for a little lunch?'

'Enchante! I agree it is an age since we have talked.' Simone gestured to her head waiter and in moments was seated with Celia and Unity, her place laid and glass filled.

'A toast I propose to old friends' Simone raised her glass and inclined her head towards Celia 'and, of course to a new friend, Unity.' The three repeated the words 'To old and new friends.'

'I say, this is jolly. Simone, it doesn't really surprise me... Celia knows so many people but how did you meet?'

'When we were little girls and Celia's Mama and Papa used to come to my father's restaurant... oh they were so elegant... Le Grand Style Anglais... we were allowed to play together in my Papa's offices. We became good friends and later when Celia and her family were staying in their Paris house I used to be invited there to play and then later we were taken out together. Much later we were together for a year in Lausanne where a dreadful old dragon tried to teach us to be good housewives. Pff... that was a waste of time eh Celia?' The two women giggled at their memories of that time.

'Waste of our parent's money too... I was in trouble when my parents read the old dragon's report' laughed Celia. 'But Simone... do you remember the handsome brothers that we met in the cake shop and who took us boating?'

'Celia I do not think we should talk more of this now' answered a smiling Simone.

'Unity all I will say is that we had been rowed along by the boys for only five minutes when Celia suggested that we moor the boat under some trees.'

The good humour between the old friends was infectious and Unity was soon swept along a happy path of shared memories and escapades that now seemed fairly tame but none the less in their telling re affirmed a bond forged as children and young women. As the famous Gillardeau oysters from Brittany were served the conversation turned to the restaurant which Simone had opened two years previously.

'I know that I was so fortunate not only to have my father's name over the door but also on the first day that I opened an equerry of the Prince of Wales called and booked a table for eight later that day. The party included Mrs Simpson. Very, very soigne... chic...but she looked so fragile.'

'Don't believe that I can assure you' interceded Celia. 'She's a tough one make no mistake.'

'Oh, after what has happened I can believe that but, even so, she just... oh I don't know... she just didn't look like the kind of woman I would have expected to be with a handsome future King.'

'Well as it turned out you were dead right there' responded Celia almost sharply. Simone shot her a puzzled glance as Celia continued. 'Anyhow Unity, Simone is not all frivolity. Quite apart from running this busy Maison Prunier she is something of a caring philanthropist. When she heard of the desperate plight of the East Anglian herring fleet she established the Prunier Herring Trophy. It was first awarded last year to the drifter that netted the largest number of crans of herring in a night's fishing. The prize is twenty five pounds in cash, dinner here and two days sightseeing in London for the crew.'

Simone added 'My father always says that without the brave fishermen smart fish restaurants like ours could not exist. The prize is just a small thank you in recognition. They are proud independent men who would never take charity but will accept a hard won prize. It makes no difference whether they be French, English, Scottish whatever... when brave fishermen go out at night in appalling dangerous conditions to bring us the fruits of the sea which we eat in comfort.' Celia and Unity nodded in appreciation.

'Now then... my apologies for that but I do feel strongly about the fishermen. I have asked that we have the daily dish here... it is simply *Poissons du Chef* and your guess is as good as mine. He will be choosing not only what fish we have but also the manner of its preparation. He always surprises me... I can assure you that it will be good.'

*　*　*

'Afternoon Tar… spare a minute?' Billy had popped his head around Tar Robertson's office door.

'Of course dear boy – come in and take a pew. What can I do for you?'

'Well, you remember my old friend Bill Shirer – the foreign correspondent who was so helpful in Vienna?'

'Of course I do. It was he who tipped us off about US Secretary of State Cardell Hunt lunching with Allen Dulles in the Washington Cosmos Club. Doesn't he work with Ed Murrow now?'

'Yes he does, after the Hearst job folded. Actually he is more interested in writing these days but, as he puts it, the broadcasting keeps the wolf from the door. Anyhow he is a close friend of Paul Gallico. Gallico is a bit of a rum cove. He's a writer and an anglophile – now lives in Salcombe. He made his name as a sports writer when he challenged heavyweight champion Jack Dempsey to spar with him and then went on to describe just what it was like to be knocked out by the champion.'

'I vaguely remember that. Nice spot Salcombe… good sailing and pubs as I recall. Haven't been for years.'

'Well he has invited Bill Shirer and Tess, his wife, for a long weekend and Bill has fixed for me to go along with Vera. Actually it kills two birds with one stone because I can drive everybody which should be a bit of fun – that is, so long as the army isn't clogging the roads over Salisbury Plain with convoys.'

'Sounds excellent… but I am not sure just why you are telling me, except possibly to make me jealous… bloody good crabs there as I recall.'

'As it happens, that is not why I mention it although it is a bonus… no, but seriously Bill has been privy to the inside story in Central Europe for so long that he is well-nigh invisible and his sources on all sides are impeccable. He wants to talk to me face to face about the threats to peace as he sees them and to give me some inside track information. Obviously I am up for that. Are there any topics that you would like me to focus on?'

'I think that you should just let your conversations take their natural course. One assumes that he is fully aware that you are in the Secret Service, or at least intelligence?'

'Oh there is no doubt about that. He's a crafty bugger, canny, as you Scots would say and he knows that what he tells me will be reported at a suitably high level.'

'Good, but the shame of it is that the present incumbent of Number Ten will not listen, much to Sir Vernon's annoyance I might add. As he put it, what is the point of having a secret intelligence service if the Prime Minister considers it unacceptable to use the intelligence that is gathered. If we end up at war it will be as much the fault of that one man as anyone else and I include the appeasers such as the so called Cliveden Set and the bloody fascists in that.'

'Perhaps that is a little harsh Tar?'

'Billy, you had to write enough letters of condolence to bereaved parents and widows in the last show to know what the true cost of inertia and naivite could be.'

Chapter 25

As Alexander Hardinge and the King were sitting waiting for the Queen to join them the King seemed to reach a decision, and stubbing out his cigarette spoke without a trace of his stutter.

'Alexander, I have decided that I should like Alan Lascelles to be present too.'

Hardinge nodded and pressing the ornate bell push to summon a footman simply said 'Certainly Sir.' He well knew that his colleague was even more partisan than he in his disdain for the Duke and Duchess of Windsor. Lascelles regarded them as no better than grasping opportunists.

'Please ask Captain Lascelles to join us' Hardinge instructed the footman. Almost immediately the doors swung open and the Queen bustled in to the room followed closely by Alan Lascelles.

'Take a seat Alan and we shall get down to b b business.' Once again the King's stammer was much less pronounced than would usually be the case in such a meeting.

The King nodded to Hardinge who explained the discussion that he and the King had been having regarding The Duke and Duchess. The Queen had a steely glint in her eye as she interjected.

'Alexander quite apart from financial matters we must also consider the situation with regard to the Windsors' intended trip to America and her wish to be accorded the style of 'Her Royal Highness.'

'Ma'am if your Majesty is willing to broaden the discussion in this way then I suggest that we take up the suggestion. It would seem that many of the issues are interlinked in any event.' Hardinge replied with the flicker of a smile.

'Mmm most certainly they are. The bloody woman has David under a spell

I think. I never found him dishonest before she came along, at least not where money was concerned, but now he has lied to all of us. He's made a fool out of Monckton who has done more than anyone to give him wise counsel.'

The Queen's expression hardened and she flushed slightly as looking her husband in the eye. 'This proposed trip to America is a blatant attempt to upstage you as the Sovereign. It is outrageous and must be stopped. The question is how?'

Alan Lascelles then joined in the conversation. 'Your Majesties, if I may comment?' He looked first at the King who nodded and then the Queen who followed suit. 'There is a good deal of pro-Wallis feeling in America and some of the press have painted a rosy picture saying that she has done much for the Duke, for instance curbing his heavy drinking as evidenced by his having no more pouches under his eyes.'

The Queen interjected in a quiet but venomous tone. 'Yes, and just who has the lines under his eyes now?' She looked pointedly at her painfully thin husband. Lascelles carried on. 'I have it on good authority that the steps that have been taken unofficially are likely to cause the trip to be cancelled. We are all aware of the Duke's abhorrence of spending his own money except when showering gifts on his wife.' The Queen snorted. 'Come on Alan we all know damn well that he is tight to the point of meanness. I am sorry darling… I appreciate that he is your brother but let's face facts however unpalatable.'

'Qu qu quite s s so my d d d dear. So w w what action has been taken un un un off off o fficially?'

Lascelles then continued in a measured tone. 'The man Bedaux was organising the trip and funding it with assistance from the German-American Bund. However we have it on good authority that he is being ousted from his American company very publically and will face strident opposition from the trade unions and also big business… in other words his clients. He will have to step back and that will leave the whole thing wide open to ridicule.'

Lascelles paused almost theatrically, and raising his eyebrows just a little, continued.

'The New York Times has its teeth into the story as you know and others will follow. Eleanor Roosevelt is snubbing them saying that she has another engagement the day they are to go to the White House for tea. Sir Ronald Lindsay, the British Ambassador has been ordered to play down the whole visit. By the way, he has reported confidentially that the US Ambassador to London

Mr Kennedy is doing all he can to keep the visit on track.'

'And pray why would he be doing that I wonder?' asked the Queen with an impish grin that was belied by the steely glint in her eyes.

Alexander Hardinge responded to the Queen with a smile. 'Ma'am, it is no secret that Mr Joseph Kennedy is a staunch anti-monarchist and also anti-British. It is a travesty that he was foisted on the Court of St James as our greatest ally's ambassador. Sadly the President had no choice in the matter. There is something else that I believe you should know. I am afraid that it is a most indelicate matter Your Majesty. If you would prefer I shall report it only to His Majesty.'

'Don't be silly Alexander. I'm as broad minded as the next person so do carry on.'

'Our intelligence people have been tipped off by their French counterparts that The Duchess has been conducting an affair with William Bullitt the American Ambassador to France and, incidentally, a very close confidante of President Roosevelt.'

'My G G G God' spluttered the King. 'What is it with th th these A A A mericcccan am am ambassad d dors?!'

'I really cannot say Sir but the French fear a blackmail attempt. I would prefer not to go into any greater detail but Ambassador Bullitt dined with the Windsors with a lawyer who is known to be working closely with the German Nazi Government and who also represents Bullitt and the Duchess. What is even more bizarre is that the dinner party was in the evening after the Duchess and the Ambassador had spent the afternoon together.'

The Queen gave another snort. 'You see darling, your Mama and I were right all along. That woman is no more than a slut. Perverted! And to think that she wants to be styled as 'Her Royal Highness'... disgusting, totally disgusting.'

Hardinge decided to continue whilst the Queen and consequently the King were clearly in a receptive frame of mind. 'I should also mention that both the Duke and the Duchess are actively canvassing their wish to return to England. The Duke wishes to re-open Fort Belvedere and the Duchess apparently talks of taking their 'place' in London society.'

'Utter nonsense' exploded the Queen. 'He cannot come back. There cannot be two Kings.'

The King's pale face was marked by two spots of colour as he heaved on his cigarette. 'R R R R Rid d dic ul l l lous.'

'Quite so Your Majesties. If I may suggest that I should speak to Mr Churchill… I believe that he still has the Duke's ear although I am told that he is thoroughly exasperated by the German trip, or at least the way that the Duke and Duchess leant tacit support to the brutal regime of Herr Hitler. If you agree I shall ask him to counsel against the American visit. I should also wish to speak to Monckton. Although he has been treated so shabbily by the Duke he is a loyal and steady man and will counsel against both the American visit and also any prospect of the couple setting up in England.'

The King looked at the Queen.

'I I I I ag g gree . Also, tell our in t int intelligence people to k k keep t t tabs on wh wh wht t is going on in P P P Paris. I w w want t to b b b be kept in in informed. F f fully.'

Wallis and Ambassador Bullitt were enjoying a post intercourse cigarette in the luxurious salon provided by Elsa Shiaperelli.

'Bill darling. You know that David and I are having problems with our trip back to the States. Couldn't you sort things out with the President? I would be so so grateful.'

Wallis was stroking Bullitt's flaccid penis as she whispered into his ear then nibbled his earlobe.

'My dear Wallis, much as I have the President's ear I cannot influence him to become even remotely involved in a wrangle that now involves big business, the unions, the press and even pressure groups such as the German and Irish lobbies. My advice is that you should shelve your plans for now and in a year or two when the present furore has been forgotten you can have your visit.'

Wallis hid her annoyance and reaching lower started to rhythmically knead Bullitt. 'Ah c'mon Bill… you can do better than that surely. The President may be your friend but I guess he would be none too happy about what we get up to darling.'

'Now Wallis I shall not take that as a threat but you know perfectly well that it would be your word against mine and frankly my dear little minx… don't stop… whose word do you think would be believed? And, before you say anything, don't think that your lesbian Austrian acolyte Helga, would be believed.'

'Oh Bill, the last thing was that I was threatening you in any way… nothing could be further from my mind… how could I. I am just so darned upset by the whole sorry business. Now, let me make you happy...'

Bullitt did not respond immediately but Wallis was not to be thwarted. With her free hand she threw back the silk sheet and sliding down the bed started to caress his right nipple with the point of her tongue. At the same time the hand that had been kneading him rhythmically slid further between his legs and as she increased pressure with her fingers he gave an involuntary gasp.

As Wallis worked on Bullitt, bringing him back to a state of arousal, her thoughts were anything but romantic. She wanted him to be even more dependent on her, to be addicted to her skills. 'Ok you bastard,' she thought. 'Round one to you sunshine but you'll soon change your tune when Helga returns with the pictures.' At the thought of Helga Wallis felt a surge of excitement and a clutching in her groin. As her breathing changed and she started to quiver Bullitt thought that Wallis was aroused by being with him. Nothing could have been further from the truth.

Billy was driving his late father's 1932 Rolls Royce 20/25 shooting brake with Vera, Bill Shirer and his wife Tess. When he and Vera had picked up the Shirer's from their hotel, the luxurious Goring in Belgravia, the two women had rolled their eyes as the men went through their private ritual greeting both exclaiming 'Hair of the dog!' It was clear from the outset that Vera and Tess were going to get on well and it was a happy and carefree little party that set off from Knightsbridge heading west even though at Billy's insistence it was only five thirty in the morning.

'I know it's darned early but there is method in my madness.'

'I sure hope so' drawled Tess Shirer. 'I for one am not a morning girl am I Bill?'

Bill laughed. 'And that is the greatest understatement that I have ever heard! When we spent a year bumming it in Lloret del Mar on the Spanish Costa Brava in the little house that we rented, sleepy-head here sometimes only surfaced at lunchtime.'

'Aw come on darling. We were living Spanish hours and hardly ever went to bed before dawn. Anyhow Billy what is your great scheme?'

'Simple really. We shall have breakfast at The Cricketers in Bagshot. I have booked it for seven thirty. We shall then press on and I aim to reach Salcombe comfortably in time for us to freshen up then go down to one of the waterside pubs and have a drink or two watching the sunset. Bill Shirer chipped in.

'That sounds good. I'm not sure about dinner. Paul divorced wife number two, Elaine, last year. They were only married for a year. He may plan on us eating out tonight. Just so that you are forewarned he can be very moody… well, not exactly moody but he retreats into a fantasy world. It can be quite alarming particularly when you remember that he made his name as a brilliant down to earth sports writer… a newspaper man through and through and as such hard as nails.'

Billy paused for a moment as he swung the heavy car onto the A4, the main road to the West of England. 'He has a way of seeing inanimate objects as having a life and he imbues animals with human emotions. I don't know how many cats he has at the moment but I would bet on double figures. Anyhow, when he starts one of his meandering tales, just relax and hear him out. It can be magical, even mystical.'

Billy chipped in. 'That must be why he has chosen Salcombe as his home. You wait until you see it. The little town is on the hill overlooking the Kingsbridge Estuary. The harbour literally nestles at the bottom of the hill hence its popularity for boat building and as a sailing port. It is utterly beautiful with a tranquillity that's hard to describe.'

'You obviously know the place well?' asked Tess almost rhetorically.

'Well, yes I do. My family has a place on the edge of Dartmoor and we used to spend our summer holidays there or staying with my aunt who had a summer house in Salcombe. Wonderful place for boys – actually my sister too – she was a total tomboy although you wouldn't guess it now that she is a grand young matron.'

'Anyhow, you will see what I mean this evening when we go for a drink.'

'Helga my dear. I have seen the photographs. I must say they are imaginative, but then I would expect nothing less from Wallis' laughed Von Ribbentrop. 'I have arranged for you to have an extra set for yourself. Think of it as insurance my dear. You never know when they might come in handy. You are a clever girl taking the extra pictures clearly showing Wallis' face. Obviously those will not be amongst the ones which you will give her.'

'Absolutely not Joachim. Actually, will you please have the two sets for Wallis sealed in official envelopes for me?'

'Of course… it will be my pleasure. Now then, as this is your last evening in Berlin, what would you like to do?'

'That is easy, stay in my hotel and have some pleasure, yes?'

'I was hoping you would say that. Now I must return to my office for some tedious meetings then I shall come to you. Will you order a light supper for us and some champagne?'

'Most certainly darling. Now, give me a kiss and then I plan to have a massage and a long bath. Perhaps even a little sleep because I do not expect to sleep tonight.'

Fritz Wiedemann was in his office, modest in comparison with the Fuhrer's, but still impressive, in the Reichchancellery in Berlin with Baron Wolfram von Richtofen. Wolfram was the cousin of the famous 'Red Baron' who had ironically been shot down and killed on the first day that he had joined his cousin's fighter wing the Jagdeschwader l. Wolfram could not have been more different to his swashbuckling cousin who saw himself as a knight of the air engaged in chivalrous combat. He held a PhD in aeronautical engineering and on behalf of the Luftwaffe acted as liaison with the designers and manufacturers of the aircraft with which the air force was being equipped.

Wolfram had recently returned from Spain where he had been putting some of his theories to the test.

'I take it Wolfram that your resignation from supervising design and production of aircraft for the Luftwaffe resulted from your dissatisfaction with the performance of Ernst Udet when Goering appointed him to replace the capable Wilhelm Wimmer?'

'Well actually...'

'Don't be embarrassed to accept that point. I can assure you that the Fuhrer considers Udet to have been an utter disaster who has cost us at least a year in development of the Luftwaffe.'

'Then the answer is emphatically "Yes". However, as it turned out it was a great blessing in that I went to Spain as second-in-command of the Condor Legion. We were able to perfect air to ground tactics and although I was originally opposed to dive bombers as being too vulnerable to ack-ack, the Ju-87 Stuka proved itself to be formidable aerial artillery.'

Wiedemann smiled as he commented. 'I have heard that your nickname amongst the Condor Legion is The Tartar because you are considered a brilliant but utterly ruthless planner.'

'That's as may be... you know as well as me that war is war.'

'The reason that I wished to see you is that I have been instructed to prepare a report for the Fuhrer concerning the bombing of the small Basque town of Guernica in April. As you are aware it is our official policy that German forces are not active in Spain and we are apparently observing the general non-intervention policy. That is also the Italian position.'

'I understand that Fritz but the reality is very different. I have brought my diary in anticipation of this discussion. Let me show you.' Von Richtofen produced a battered tan leather soft backed book from his valise and laid it on the desk. 'Right, here we are 26 April 1937. My entry is as follows. *'The 250 kilogram bombs and EC B 1 bomb fuses worked wonderfully'* … here look.' He passed the open diary to Wiedemann who scanned the page and then turned back a page.

'This is an interesting entry' muttered Wiedemann and almost whispered as he read out a passage. *'Nationalists short of artillery. Legion…'*'that's our Condor Legion of course' commented Weidermann, who then continued, *'has batteries of 88 mm anti-aircraft guns. Deployed as ground artillery with great effect against Basque defences.'* So Wolfram you have developed a new element in our arsenal. Now, returning to Guernica. There is World outrage much stimulated by the London Times article of George Steer. He claims to have picked up bomb remnants on the ground that are clearly German.

'It is also alleged that hundreds of innocent civilians – men women and children were killed and over three quarters of the town destroyed. The other damning allegation is that the town was of no military significance and the only purpose of the attack was to intimidate the civilian population generally and demoralise the troops at the front.'

'What is alleged is true Fritz. Absolutely true in every respect. Between ourselves and the Italians we dropped thirty one tons of bombs including many phosphorous incendiaries. If you look at my diary for three days later you will see my entry when the town was captured and I was able to view for myself on the ground. Here, look. 'The town was levelled and closed to traffic for 24 hours.'

'So why Guernica?'

'The town has a special place in Basque history and mythology. The 'Tree of Guernica' symbolises the freedoms of the Basque people as a whole. The original was planted in the 14th century. There is a song celebrating the tree and the freedoms it represents. It is an unofficial Basque anthem.'

'So we are safe in saying that there was no military reason for the bombing of the town so why would we have wasted so much in doing so?' Fritz asked pointedly.

'You can certainly say that. However Guernica was the last piece in the puzzle that I was working on in relation to ground and air forces close co-operation. I am submitting a paper to the High Command, and I would ask that you submit it to the Fuhrer. I am proposing a special purpose airforce unit with the specific role of close support of ground forces. It will be able to operate from roughly prepared forward airfields and comprise Stuka dive bombers, Henschel attack planes, a reconnaissance squadron and fighter groups for protection. In all about 300 aircraft. Such a force working with fast moving battle tank groups and motorised infantry will be able to deliver a hammer blow with great speed in any future conflict. That is particularly the case with some of the old fashioned forces that we may have to tackle.'

'I think that I can guess where you are thinking of...'

'Of course you can... just imagine how effective such combined forces would be in Poland or Czechoslovakia.'

'Devastating.'

Chapter 26

'Nearly there folks... I for one could do with a hot bath and then a couple of pints at the Ferry Inn. I must be getting old – my shoulders are aching like heck.' Billy took his hand off the wheel and gave Vera's knee a squeeze. 'You must be very tired my dear.'

'Oh not too bad Billy. It's you I feel sorry for.'

'I did offer to share the driving you know' protested Bill Shirer from the back of the car. 'But then you were just too damn nervous to let me drive this precious motor.'

'Au contraire my friend! I want you and Tess to have a totally relaxed weekend and soak up the joys of the English countryside and coast. I wish that you were seeing it in summer when everything is lush and green but then the melancholy beauty of late autumn has its appeal... you know, all that "mists and mellow fruitfulness" stuff. By the way, are you warm enough in the back there?'

'We certainly are with all these rugs thanks. Do you think that we might get a little sailing in? I guess it would be darn cold. Paul has a boat?' asked Billy.

Bill Shirer replied 'Yes he does and unlike me he knows how to sail properly' Billy gave a snorting laugh. 'Did I ever tell you that I bought a sail boat off a bankrupt boxer in Berlin? Don't say it... you couldn't make it up. Anyhow he drew some diagrams of what to do if the wind was from behind, the side or in front and off we went. We haven't sunk yet but mind you we only potter around on the Wannsee... you've been there... the Berlin lakes where lots of the Nazi big wigs have grand houses. Actually the boat has two bunks so it is a great escape for us and a great way to visit friends.'

As the laughter died Billy commented. 'Sailing off the coast here is excellent but you really need to know your stuff. Once out of the sheltered harbour and in the Kingsbridge Estuary it can be darned rough. We'll just have to see but I hope that we can. Now, we are about to come off the A38 and then we shall be on Salcombe Road. The directions show Paul's house 'Landmark' to be at the head of the valley that leads down to North Sands Beach. It should have spectacular views. Right, folks, I must concentrate.'

As the headlights picked out the sign for the house Billy slowed and swung through the open gates onto a driveway which led past a garage building and then snaked up to the house itself.

Bill Shirer explained. 'Paul said that the entrance is to the front of the house and the driveway takes us to the back. So we have to park and walk round Billy.'

'Well here it is' replied Billy as the headlights picked out the high gable end of the house and to the side another garage building as he swung the large car round in a circular parking area and stopped.

Charles Bedaux was no stranger to publicity. In fact he normally craved it and with his much publicised on going African expedition he usually courted the attention of the media assiduously. He luxuriated in seeing his name in print and appearing in newsreels. Whilst the great wealth and power that he had accumulated gave him satisfaction, the close attention of the press and newsreels was his greatest stimulation and set his world alight.

Nothing gave him greater pleasure than a headline describing him as a millionaire, brilliant businessman, philanthropist, daring expedition leader or indeed any combination of these descriptions. Preferably with one of the carefully posed pictures that his office regularly released to the Press and media.

Standing at the rail of his stateroom's balcony as the SS Europa was edged into the dockside by fussy little tugs he could see that there was a larger than usual crowd on the quayside. It was nothing unusual for there to be a crowd when one of the great transatlantic liners docked, indeed it was as traditional as the military band on the quay but this crowd was abnormally large. For no particular reason Bedaux felt a nervous flutter in his stomach but put it down to the large breakfast that he had enjoyed earlier.

As the vessel slid up to the quay the great propellers threw up a flurry of water and the ship's siren sounded an ear splitting sonorously deep blast. As its echoes died the band struck up the currently popular Benny Goodman tune 'Sing Sing Sing.' Bedaux noticed that amongst the well-dressed crowd on the quay there were many men who were clearly manual workers – longshoremen from their rough dress.

'Good to be back' he muttered to himself as he went back into his stateroom and was greeted by his steward Thomas. 'Welcome back to America Mr Bedaux.'

'Well Thomas thank you for that and for all the attention you have given me throughout the crossing.' Bedaux skilfully slipped a bundle of folded notes into the steward's hand. The over generous tip disappeared without any apparent movement on the part of Thomas.

The evening before Bedaux had asked to be woken before dawn so that he could be on deck to see the dawn sun gilding the torch of the Statue of Liberty. Every time he sailed into New York he made a point of being on deck as the great symbolic statue grew closer.

Bedaux never forgot that he had first come to the City as an impoverished young man fortunate not to have been imprisoned in his native France for his pimping and petty criminal life in the notoriously lawless Pigalle area of Paris. The tough life there had prepared him for his new life in America where his quick wits served him well as did his street wise experience and ability to use his fists.

The gangs of New York and the thugs employed by employers and unions alike held no fears for him. As he was known to boast 'any man who can survive in business in competition with the vicious Union Corse in Paris can survive anywhere.'

'God bless America' he thought as that stirring anthem entered his head. It was unbidden but none the less welcome. 'It is America that has made me rich beyond counting and I walk amongst the most powerful men in the land. Now I am one of them and I am an American.'

Bedaux's reverie was broken when after a discreet cough Thomas the steward announced 'Mr Bedaux Sir there is a gentleman here to see you.' Bedaux turned away from the mirror where he had been adjusting his tie. As he did so his face broke into a broad smile and he leapt forward seizing his visitor's right hand in both of his. 'General it is so good to see you… so good… I am delighted. Do have a seat. Some coffee perhaps?'

The austere, whipcord thin, tanned and lantern jawed visitor sat down in one of the upright dining chairs. With his ramrod straight back and unsmiling face his appearance was intimidating although Bedaux did not seem to notice and was still smiling with evident delight. The General, now long retired but still accorded the title that he had earned came straight to the point. 'Charles, I am sorry to say that I am not here on a social visit. I have come to tender some advice.'

'Aw come on General, we know each other well enough that we do not want or welcome advice from 'outsiders' but between ourselves we can proffer wise counsel.'

'Quite Charles. You know me as a staunch and loyal friend and colleague. As I see it, a key element in friendship is total honesty. I am afraid that however uncomfortable or indeed disappointing you will find what I have to say, it is the lesser of evils that I tell you as a friend.'

Bedaux was still smiling but his eyes had taken on a hard glint. 'Fine and understood – please shoot.'

The General cleared his throat.

As the little group led by Bill Shirer rounded the corner of the high gabled end of the house French doors opened and for a moment their host was silhouetted in the soft glow of light from the room within.

'Welcome good people… welcome to my home, Landmark, a haven of tranquillity and beauty in an ever more frenetic and threatening world.' So did Paul Gallico greet his guests that cold but clear November evening.

'Paul my dear fellow, it is so good to see you and, indeed to be here' responded Bill Shirer. 'You are so very kind to invite us.'

'The pleasure is mine… do come in and join me in my solitary lair. It is I who will delight in your company.'

Paul stepped back through the open doors and pipe in hand gestured for his guests to follow. The large room impressed and was the essence of understated comfort and simple elegance. Cream shaded lamps on side tables glowed and next to a well-worn dark green velvet covered wing chair that was clearly Paul's stood a wooden standard lamp. Within the pool of brighter light that it cast stood a galleried side table on which there was a silver mounted glass ashtray, an old and well-worn leather tobacco pouch, a distinctive red and yellow box of Swan Vestas matches and a half full highball glass. An open book was lying face down on the chair.

Bill Shirer made the introductions after Paul had embraced Tess. Picking up the box of matches and with his pipe clenched in his teeth Paul spoke as he relit it. 'Extraordinary you know. I normally hear visitors' car engines long before the gravel crunch but I did not hear yours.'

Bill laughed and pointing at Billy responded 'Ah well, you see, we came in a Rolls Royce. Like all good children they can be seen but not heard.'

'I shall remember that. Now, how about you all join me in a drink to settle the dust. After that hot baths or showers as you wish, and then we are going down to the quayside for supper at the Ferry Inn. I hope that you all like sea food… it is really the best and we shall dine on scallops and lobster washed down with fine Devon ale for the men and perhaps a flinty Muscadet for the ladies. How does that sound?' Paul's broad smile was infectious and they all nodded smiling agreement.

Billy was sizing up their bespectacled host as he helped mix drinks on a side table. Paul was above medium height with dark thick hair slightly longer than currently fashionable, clean cut features and heavy brows. It might have been the effect of the pipe which hardly seemed to leave his mouth but he looked rather heavy lipped. It was a strong face. He was casually dressed in a zip fronted blue windcheater and what appeared to be canvas fisherman's trousers.

As if reading Billy's thoughts, as Paul started to pass round the drinks he said 'Salcombe is a sailing town. No formality here, so do please dress for comfort. I shall not be changing before we go out. Tonight we shall be in the company of sailors both amateur and professional… fishermen, boatbuilders and layabout bums like me, so you are warned.'

'Don't worry Paul we shan't embarrass you… Billy is an old Salcombe hand or should I say 'salt' and made the local rules crystal clear.'

The little group were just raising their glasses in a toast when the telephone could be heard ringing. Paul excused himself and left the drawing room. His deep voice could be heard clearly as he answered in the hall. 'Yes, that is correct, it is I. Hold please I shall just fetch him.'

He came back into the room and with a wry smile to Bill Shirer said 'Well, if I didn't know before, I sure know now why I packed in the journalist game with hungry editors always on my tail. Bill, you'll have guessed… the call is for you.'

Conversation was stilted as they could all hear Bill engaged in what sounded like a rather one sided conversation in which he listened rather than spoke except for some rather terse questions. He returned to the room and making a gesture of helplessness with both hands outstretched, laughed and said 'Well folks, after that interruption I may as well put you in the picture and you will know that you heard it here first. Charles Bedaux is for the big drop. He has been fixed well and truly, top, bottom and sideways. As we speak he is being put out to grass and from what I have just been told he will be a broken reed… almost certainly a broken man. That my friends should be the end of the Windsors' plans for their American trip.'

Paul looked puzzled as he asked 'So tell me in my capacity as a hack in exile, how, what and why?'

Bill shot a glance at Billy who nodded in the affirmative. The small exchange was not unnoticed by Paul. Bill then gave a very brief and uncomplicated summary. He outlined Bedaux's remarkable rise to great wealth and influence, his plans to broker the Windsors' visit to America after their visit to Germany, the opposition that had emerged and the steps that had apparently been taken to scupper what would have been a very embarrassing event for so many interested parties.

Paul was still enough of a newsman to see through to the way in which the whole matter would have been handled behind the many closed doors of the powerful. His response was short and to the point. 'Neat.' He raised his glass in a mock toast.

Charles Bedaux was in a state of shock. The words of the general had come as a hammer blow. He found it hard to breathe as he struggled to fully comprehend what he was being told.

'So you mean that these men whose fortunes I have made are turning against me! I cannot believe it. Without me they were nothing. Without me they will be nothing. I made them and I will break them. So help me God I will finish the disloyal bastards.' Bedaux's voice had risen almost to a scream as he ranted with spittle flying and his staring eyes darting around.

The general was apparently unaffected by the tirade and he continued to sit unmoving. His lack of any response unnerved Bedaux even more as he shouted. 'You are my friend… for Christ's sake say something instead of sitting there like a carved dummy. Well?'

In the fine chateau near Versailles where the Duke and Duchess had just sat down for breakfast in their elegant morning room at a table laid with a sparkling white, stiffly starched tablecloth and napkins, sparkling crystal tumblers for fruit juice and delicate Sevres china. The scene could not have been more different to the situation for Charles Bedaux. The couple were serene in their unawareness of the drama unfolding in New York in which they were playing so prominent if unmentioned a role.

'The Times, Your Royal Highness.'

'Ah, excellent and thank you Harvey.' The Duke of Windsor smiled contentedly as Charles Harvey handed him the neatly folded and freshly ironed copy of the newspaper. The fact that it was the previous day's edition was studiously ignored.

Senior British Secret Service officer Charles Harvey was seconded with his wife, who had previously been the Duke's housekeeper at Fort Belvedere, to work in the Duke's household. Both the Duke and Duchess were unaware of Charles Harvey's true calling or indeed that his wife, the former Mrs Beauchamp, housekeeper and confidante of King Edward was also working for the Secret Service.

As the Duke opened the newspaper carefully folding back the front page he commented with a smile 'Y'know Wallis, there is nothing finer for an Englishman than his breakfast. Well brewed Ceylon tea, grapefruit, a decent piece of toast with good salty butter and a touch of Frank Cooper's Oxford marmalade. Marry that to the best newspaper in the world. Capital, I say, capital.'

'Oh my Lord dearest, you are so darned English. Here I am in France with a delicious tasse of cafe au lait and a delicate pain au chocolat and I hear you declaiming about English breakfast… it is really just too tiresome.' That Wallis easily tired of her husband's fascination, almost obsession, with things English was well known amongst the couple's staff. Nevertheless she tempered her words with a smile, albeit on the frosty side.

The Duke laughed and almost guffawed as he riposted. 'In that case my darling I shall refrain from extolling the virtue of lambs' kidneys and black pudding… good huntin fare y'know.'

Still maintaining a strained smile the Duchess responded 'I would really rather that you did not... dearest.'

'Very well… now, to more serious matters. Charles Bedaux docks in New York today so we should soon have some news. Certainly I am greatly disappointed, almost vexed, that the President's wife will not be present when we visit.'

'It is vexing but then, she is reputed to be a somewhat annoying woman.

However perhaps a little pressure should be applied.'

'Should I make an approach dearest?' asked the Duke.

'No my dear I shall have a word with Ambassador Bullitt. After all, he has supped at our table has he not?' asked Wallis unable to resist the temptation to have a small private joke. Helga was due back later in the day having taken the overnight sleeper from Berlin so Wallis would have the incriminating photographs to hand. The only question in Wallis' mind was whether she should sleep with Bullitt before bringing up the question of the snub by the President's extremely plain wife as Wallis saw it.

Later as she dialled Ambassador Bullitt's private number she made a snap decision. She would keep Bullitt waiting for his sexual gratification. She smiled wickedly. 'I'll darn well make him beg for it' and barked an ironic laugh.

Chapter 27

Charles Bedaux slumped in a silk brocade covered armchair. He had taken a taxi to the luxurious and elegant Plaza Hotel on New York's Fifth Avenue after leaving the Chrysler Building in a daze.

For over two hours he had pleaded, cajoled, threatened and even wept as he tried to salvage his position as the founder, Chairman of the Board and Chief Executive of the eponymous Bedaux Associates America. It had been humiliating in the extreme even to someone as thick skinned as him but all to no avail. The Board's unanimous decision was final.

Now he was totally oblivious to his surroundings mired in despair and humiliation, his head in his hands as he sobbed. The butler who served his floor had brought a bottle of Wild Turkey bourbon, a bucket of ice and a jug of branch water as requested. They remained untouched on a side table.

His day of horror had started with the words of the General delivered as a friend but nonetheless harsh and uncompromising. After the initial shock of what he was being told Bedaux had marshalled his thoughts. His natural energy and exuberant optimism had begun to convince him that he could weather any storm with his American co directors. As for the major clients, he was confident that his relationships were assound as a bell. After all their chief executives, and in many cases founders, were his good friends and frequently joined him in the exclusive restaurant of the Clouds Club which occupied three floors in the Chrysler Building which also housed the offices of Bedaux Associates America.

He had telephoned Walter Teagle one of his regular lunch companions and the President of Standard Oil. Teagle was a pivotal contact and Bedaux believed him to be a good friend, indeed a close friend. Teagle was closely associated with another major client of Bedaux's business, General Aniline & Film which was the USA operating arm of the German conglomerate I G Farben. Teagle was on the board of General Aniline & Film as were Charles Mitchell, Chairman of National City Bank and Edsel Ford, son of Henry the President of Ford Motors.

John Foster Dulles, the elder brother of Allen, and also a partner in New York law firm Sullivan & Cromwell, represented General Aniline & Film and had carried out the complex legal work establishing cartels between that company, Standard Oil and the International Nickel Company of which he was a director. Each of these cartel agreements and many others negotiated by the Dulles brothers, almost cosily, between American 'big business', IG Farben and other major German businesses ensured that whilst the American companies benefitted so too did the Nazi German industrial economy and capability.

These agreements were essential to Hitler's aim that Germany should be self-sufficient in all essential materials and a raft of complex intellectual property assignments had been put in place between major American and German entitities to that end.

The tangled web of inter related legal relationships benefitted American big business in the first place and the US Government in tax revenue secondly, but in the case of Germany they benefitted the Nazi regime in the first instance and business secondly. This was a crucial difference and contrasted the essentially democratic government of America with the Dictatorship that was Germany preparing for war on a scale never before witnessed.

Bedaux was not only aware of these relationships and arrangements but had played an important, sometimes pivotal role, as a middle man and facilitator. He had thought that his position was impregnable so far as the powerful American commercial interests were concerned given his close relationship with the Nazi German Government. In the past few hours that belief had been totally shattered. He had made the mistake of assuming that he was valued as a man, a man of business with the ear of the powerful across the globe. His assumption was pitifully wrong. It transpired that he was as expendable as any individual.

Here he was marooned in the luxury of one of the World's greatest hotels having been told by his former co-directors, the same men whom he had appointed to the board of the business that he had founded and still largely drove, that he could no longer use company vehicles, that his office was being cleared by agents from the Pinkerton Detective Agency, and that he could no longer have access to the luxurious penthouse which had been his New York home since he acquired it many years earlier in the name of 'his' company on the advice of his lawyers. The realisation was sinking in that he was now homeless in this great city and, perhaps more to the point, friendless. In his despair he realised that in this city, the New York that he believed had adopted him, he might has well be a leper.

Gradually the despair turned to anger. 'The fucking bastards' he shouted to the air as he leapt to his feet. 'They have supped at my table, drunk my wine and pretended to be my friends. I made them, yes I bloody made them! Now when it suits them they have turned against me as one! Worse than the rats that I killed with my shovel when I dug out their bloody tunnels all those years ago. Fucking Americans they can rot in hell the bastards….'

He seized the whisky bottle and was about to pour a stiff drink when looking at the distinctive label of the bottle of bourbon he was overtaken by a savage urge. He drew back his arm and hurled the full bottle at the centre of the beautiful 18th Century gilt framed mirror that was hung above the sofa. The mirror shattered and the pale green silk brocade sofa was soaked in whisky as the glass showered down.

His act of wanton vandalism brought Bedaux back to his senses.

He buzzed for the Butler.

When the Butler saw the damage he may have been shocked but his face registered no surprise as Bedaux simply said 'I have had a little accident… please ensure that the bill is sent to my company Bedaux Asociates.'

After a beat he added 'Now, I shall need to leave here discretely in the morning. I imagine that the gentlemen of the press are outside the front of the Hotel?'

'Indeed they are Sir. In the past when honoured guests have wished to depart in private we have arranged for them to do so through the service stairs then into the linked staff quarters. The staff quarters have a nondescript door onto 58th Street. If you wish, I can arrange a motor to meet you there at a time of your choice.'

'Excellent… your name is?' Bedaux had produced his wallet and for the second time that fateful day handed over a very substantial gratuity.

'My name is Salmon Sir' responded the bespectacled butler who looked like an accountant or banker in his morning dress and sporting oiled but thinning grey hair. His unruffled manner would not have shamed a senior mandarin in any civil service.

'Would you wish me to brief the driver as to your destination Mr Bedaux?'

'No thank you Salmon, I have not finally decided but it will be within the City. Now, I think that a bottle of vintage champagne is called for and some smoked salmon sandwiches if you will.'

'Most certainly Sir. Would Veuve Clicquot be satisfactory?'

'Absolutely and thank you I think that a glass or two of 'the Widow' will do admirably. I shall advise you of my departure time presently.'

'Thank you Sir.'

As soon as Salmon had left Bedaux sat down at the desk and picking up the telephone handset jiggled the bar. As soon as the operator answered he asked to be connected to the Concierge. He then wasted no time. 'I wish you to secure a First Class sleeping compartment on the first train leaving New York and bound for Canada tomorrow morning. The ticket is for my friend a Mr Charles Allen. Please have it delivered to my suite as soon as possible. I shall give the bell boy two envelopes… one with the fare which he can tell me and one for you. The latter will contain a consideration for your kind offices.'

Later Bedaux savoured the champagne and settled down to draft a telegram to the Duke of Windsor. For the moment the awful sense of betrayal and despair had left him and was now replaced by self-righteous cold fury.

Once Bedaux was satisfied with the telegram that he had drafted he sent for Salmon and asked him to personally supervise its sending and then bring a copy and the hand written version back to the suite. The telegram to the Duke of Windsor was to the point.

'*Because of the mistaken attacks upon me here, I am convinced that your proposed tour will be difficult under my auspices. I respectfully implore you to relieve me of all duties in connection with it.*'

Wallis had decided that rather than meet Ambassador Bullitt at Elsa Shiaparelli's they should do so in public. After careful thought she had nominated the Cafe de la Paix. There could hardly be a more public place to meet. 'After all' she had mused 'it is said that just to sit inside the opulently decorated cafe or at one of its outside tables an encounter with a friend is inevitable.' Wallis also recalled that the Duke had been a patron when he was Prince of Wales. That was the public aspect of her plan. However the second part was rather different.

She had told the Duke not only that she was going to meet Bullitt at the cafe but that she had also booked a suite in the hotel of which it was part for the afternoon so that she could talk in private about the delicate matter in hand, namely, the apparent snub by Eleanor Roosevelt. The Duke had laughed. 'Well with Bullitt having his live in male lover there is no chance of scandal there is there my darling!'

The Duke decided to play golf that afternoon a pleasure that would be limited if not denied whilst on the American tour.

Wallis arrived at the cafe first and decided that rather than sitting outside under the green awning or one of the green and cream umbrellas she would wait inside. She had dressed carefully for the occasion, choosing a Madelaine Vionnet dress which like many of the fashionable designers' creations was cut on the bias. Wallis was satisfied that the Grecian style of the draped dress showed off her slim boyish figure at its best. That look appealed to Ambassador Bullitt as she well knew.

Her Persian lamb coat was a much more severe affair enlivened only by a diamond encrusted leopard brooch commissioned from Cartier by the Duke. In her handbag a vellum envelope contained the wonderfully clear photographs of Ambassador Bullitt's sexual humiliation. Wallis could almost feel the weight of the photographs as she moved to the table she had selected. Even in a place where celebrities were commonplace the presence of the infamous Wallis, Duchess of Windsor, was eagerly noted by the normally rather jaded afternoon clientele.

In her heavily accented French Wallis ordered a noisette. She felt that the caffeine would sharpen her reactions suitably for dealing with the delicate matters that she wished to resolve with the Ambassador.

The Ambassador's official Cadillac drew up outside the restaurant and the driver opened the door for the single elegantly dressed passenger. The Ambassador looked the part in every particular from his immaculately neat thinning hair to his mirror shined English bespoke shoes. He too attracted much attention as he approached Wallis and bowing slightly took and kissed her hand before sitting down. He glanced at the small coffee being placed before Wallis and in perfect unaccented French asked the waiter for the same.

'My word Wallis, you are as elegant as ever. What is that heady perfume you are wearing? It is delicious.' He asked with a knowing smile.

'I am sure that you remember my scent Bill don't you' responded Wallis coquettishly.

'Oh but I do… it comes to me whenever I think of you.'

'I do so hope that thoughts of me come to you often…' Wallis murmured with a mischievous glint in her eye. That the couple were flirting was obvious to many of the seasoned observers to whom people watching was an art, in a cafe that was an institution in what many regarded as the most romantic city in the world. That Bullitt was a noted homosexual was not considered in any way an obstacle to flirtation. The cafe had a reputation for good reason, and historically had been the retreat of the famous in all walks of life from the louche drinkers immortalised in the Robert Service poem *'The Absinthe Drinkers'*to intellectuals and artists such as Emile Zola, Guy de Maupassant and Sergei Diaghilev.

Wallis struck a serious note. 'Bill, I have booked a suite so that we can talk in private. David knows that I have done so and that I am seeing you this afternoon. He is off to play golf for the afternoon. Shall we go there now?' Wallis had allowed her leg to rest against his and she looked hard into his eyes as she asked.

'Er yes… that sounds like a capital idea.' Bullitt caught the eye of an attentive waiter who hurried over and was asked for the bill. It was promptly paid and the couple walked out of the restaurant and into the entrance of Le Grand Hotel as the original Hotel de la Paix was then known.

The Concierge greeted the couple and with a flick of his wrist summoned a bell boy who escorted them to the bank of elevators taking them up to the suite which looked out over the Place de l'Opera. As soon as they were alone Bill took Wallis into his arms and went to kiss her. She turned her cheek to him. 'Not yet Bill. We have a little business to conclude. Let's make ourselves comfortable. She turned in his arms and undid the front of her coat. He helped her out of it. The fabric of her dress clinging to her straight back and trim rear caused him to catch his breath. Unseen by him Wallis permitted herself a little smile. She turned back and as he removed his own coat she sat down elegantly crossing her ankles.

'Very well Wallis. What is this 'business' that you wish to discuss?'

'It should not take very long… at least I hope not.' Wallis gave another knowing look arching her pencilled eyebrows slightly. 'You are of course fully aware of the plans for our planned visit to America. Indeed, as I speak our luggage is on the quayside in Cherbourg where we shall be embarking on the Bremen.' Bullitt nodded but his diplomatic training and experience meant that he made no comment leaving Wallis to bring the conversation to its point. 'We are well aware of your close relationship with President Roosevelt. It seems that his wife Eleanor is deliberately snubbing us and will be absent when the President receives us in the White House. Will you use your good offices to persuade the President that she should be there?'

For a moment even the smooth, sharp-witted and experienced diplomat Bullitt was at a loss. Only the evening before the President had confided in him during their daily telephone conversation that his strong willed wife had not only refused to receive 'that woman' but had sabotaged the plan for the Duke and Duchess to visit Arlington Cemetery on the day of their landing, Armistice Day, on the eleventh of November to lay a wreath at the Tomb of the Unknown Warrior. The doughty Eleanor Roosevelt had apparently pulled strings to ensure that the train that was intended to take the couple to this private ceremony, a visit which she considered distasteful, would be delayed.

'I shall most certainly see what I can do Wallis. I am aware that Mrs Roosevelt will be away from Washington on a speaking tour that was arranged a long time ago. She has a very tight schedule and try as she did there is no way that she can return to Washington to see you. Steps will be taken to see whether you and the Duke can meet her on another occasion whilst you are in America. That is the best that I can offer.'

'Very well Bill but I really expect a little more than an empty promise from you. I think that you should strain a little on this one.' There was a steely glint in Wallis' eyes as she reached into her handbag and handed the envelope to Bullitt. 'Darling Bill… I thought you would appreciate little memento of the fun we had when my assistant Helga joined us at Elsa Schiaperelli's…'

'Christ Wallis these are fantastic!' exclaimed Bullitt as he flicked through the photographs.

His reaction totally nonplussed Wallis as he continued, 'May I keep this set – I am sure that you have others.'

In that moment a shocked Wallis realised that blackmail would not sway Bullitt. He had spiked her guns and she would now have to fall back on her sexual prowess.

'Of course darling Bill. You keep them.'

Wallis stood and undoing the top of her dress allowed it to slide off her and pool around her feet. She stepped out of it and in her silk shift took Bullitt by the hand and led him into the bedroom where she had piled pillows in the centre of the large bed.

'Now you just get yourself undressed Bill whilst I arrange myself.'

As he watched Wallis slipped off her shift and with only a basque, suspenders and stockings above her high heeled shoes climbed onto the bed and then knelt before the piled pillows. She then leant forward until her face was on the silk counterpane. Her voice was muffled.

Chapter 28

'You know me well enough Tar… I am not a man who lets his feelings run wild or runs with them willy-nilly. Yes, I am a believer in having a hunch about something or somebody but by nature I am analytical. I think that is why Mansfield Smith-Cumming or 'C', as he liked to be referred to, and I got along so well. We did so since before the Great War when we had the devil's own job to convince the then 'powers that be' of the urgent need to up our intelligence services as Germany prepared to go to war.'

Tar Robertson commented 'His successor Rear Admiral 'Quex' Sinclair was a different kettle of fish though, surely. I mean for some years, as I understand it, he tried to have this organisation absorbed into MI6.'

'That is true but thank the Lord common sense prevailed given that it turned out that the infernal Gestapo had infiltrated MI6. They had a complete nightmare sorting that mess out. But, we digress. The reason that I am at boiling point is down to our Prime Minister.

'I have not been this furious with utter frustration since before the Great War when we pulled in a blasted German spy. Having caught him red handed the jury rightly convicted the blighter. But then the Attorney General, Rufus Isaacs, later Viceroy of India no less, who was prosecuting, most unhelpfully pointed out to the trial judge that the then Official Secrets Act did not classify peacetime spying as a serious offence. Taking into account that the spy had spent 4 months in prison on remand the judge imposed a non-custodial sentence. That left the German free to carry on running his network of spies.

'We face the same attitude now. The PM feels that 'fair play' on our part will influence Herr Hitler. Arrant nonsense. That blasted Dictator is playing Chamberlain as a fool and laughing behind his back. Goose Von Pulitz our man in the German Embassy reports that Hitler openly refers to Chamberlain as *The Arsehole.'*

'That, I am sorry to say, is true Sir Vernon. Princess Stephanie has confirmed it to Johnny. She has heard it first-hand.'

'Well the psychologist Sinclair has been asked to prepare an in depth assessment of Herr Hitler for the PM and the Foreign Secretary. When we had dinner the other day Sinclair branded the dictator as possessing characteristics that include – and I am using his words – 'fanaticism, mysticism, ruthlessness, cunning, vanity, moods' and so on. I doubt his report will be well received by the appeasers. That unfortunately includes the PM who also refuses to believe or even consider the Hossbach Memorandum that sets out Herr Hitler's ambitions and intentions even more clearly than in Mein Kampf.'

Tar had rarely seen Sir Vernon so overwrought but could not resist adding fuel to the fire. 'You know better than I that amongst the political class there are many who deplore the use of spies. Sir George Mounsey in response to Winston Churchill advocating their use commented along the lines '*I challenge the value of 'sensational' information obtained by espionage. Spies have a secret mission and they must justify it. If nothing comes to hand for them to report these venal hired assassins must earn their pay for finding something, anything regardless of due diligence and veracity.'* You will have heard that too I believe?'

'Of course I have. It is precisely that naive attitude that will serve our nation ill. Very well my boy... I have blown off enough steam for now. I am to see Churchill later this afternoon and I am sure that he and I will share some trenchant views. Damn shame that nobody listens to us eh?'

'Darling David... did you have a good game?' Wallis had changed from her more dramatic outfit and had opted for a softer look in a pale blue cashmere twinset which toned perfectly with the diamond and aquamarine brooch that the Duke had been at great pains to obtain for her.

They had first seen it worn by Jean Harlow in the film 'Libeled Lady' which they had watched in the cinema room that had been set up in the Chateau at the Duke's insistence. Wallis had commented on the spray shaped brooch and the Duke then made it his business to find out more. He learnt that it was designed and made by the legendary jeweller Joseff. The exotic and original jewellery that Joseff produced featured in many Hollywood films.

The Duke was told that Joseff was just about to make his works available to the general public having hitherto designed and createdexclusively for the film industry. Even the by then legendary Austrian born Joseff was flattered when he learnt that the former King of England wanted to speak to him and even more so when the Duke addressed him in his perfect German. The price for the brooch was high, but, as always when it came to jewellery for Wallis, the Duke's usual parsimony went out of the window.

'I say Wallis delighted that you are wearing that brooch… it really is a beautiful thing.'

'You seem in a much better frame of mind dearest… should I guess that you played well?'

'You are right there. I may put my card in to have my handicap reviewed. Damned silly really… vanity I suppose. If the committee does pull my handicap down I shall be less competitive. I shall think on it. Now, how was your afternoon with the dashing Ambassador Bullitt?'

'Oh, you know, so so. Rather boring actually… he is a bit of a dry stick. I am not sure that he can swing anything with the President's wife. Apparently she will be off on a long planned lecture tour. I am not sure that I believed him but there we are.'

Just then Dudley Forward knocked and entered the sitting room. He looked rather pale beneath his usual ruddy complexion.

'Well Dudders, what have you?' asked the smiling Duke.

'I have a telegram Sir and I feel that you should read it immediately.' Dudley Forward handed the flimsy piece of paper to the Duke then stepped back a pace as if expecting an explosion.

The Duke's smile vanished in an instant as he read the telegram. His face twisted into a mask of fury.

'Darling what is it?' asked a visibly shocked and alarmed Wallis. The Duke made no comment but simply passed the paper to her then spun round and stalked to the French doors where he stood motionless with shoulders slumped staring sightlessly into the gardens.

'Oh my God David. Does this mean that the America trip is off?'

Dudley Forward had steeled himself for this moment. He cleared his throat and then spoke slowly. 'I am afraid that there is more.'

The Duke spun round and snapped 'Really… and what could that be I wonder eh?' His voice cracked and it was clear that he was furious and at the same time on the verge of tears.

'I have just received a telephone call from His Majesty your brother Sir. His Majesty is highly concerned with your safety if you go to America, and the American Ambassador in London advises that you should not go.'

'This is all too bloody convenient... look at the fucking timing. First the telegram and then minutes later the telephone call from my brother. What did he actually say, Forward?' spat the Duke.

'His actual words Sir were 'Tell David he's not to bloody go to America.'

'That sounds more like it. Right let's cut out the fucking flim-flam and get me our ambassador in Washington. Now if you please.

'As you wish Sir.'

Wallis knew her husband's moods well enough to say nothing as he paced back and forth.

Dudley Forward returned and with a nod to the Duke simply said 'Sir. I have Sir Ronald Lindsay on the line for you.'

The Duke did not give any acknowledgement but went to the ornate writing desk and sitting down picked up the telephone handset. There was a rasp in his voice as he spoke. 'Sir Ronald. You are a straight talker. I have just received a cable from Charles Bedaux effectively resigning from his role in our forthcoming visit to America. I am also warned that there is some risk in our going ahead and that apparently you are also of that view. Well, what do you think?'

Sir Ronald was well aware of the King and Queen's grave misgivings about the proposed American visit and that these were shared with others such as Sir Robert Vansittart. However he decided to take a soft line with the petulant Duke.

'May I first enquire Sir whether the involvement of Mr Bedaux was essential to your plans?'

'Pretty much so Lindsay. He has made all the detailed arrangements, or rather his staff have. Perhaps we could simply postpone... would that overcome any other difficulties?'

'I am afraid not Sir. In my opinion if you were to postpone you will not be able to undertake a similar tour in the future.' The Duke appeared to be deep in thought, then after a long pause asked a simple question.

'Are you alarmed?'

'Sir, I feel the tour will cast a certain discredit on the American view of the British Monarchy.'

'Sir Ronald, by using the words 'a certain' am I to understand that you to mean 'without a doubt'?'

'That Sir is my opinion. To put it another way I believe that the tour will certainly have that adverse effect.'

'Thank you for being so frank Sir Ronald. Good day to you.' The Duke turned to Dudley Forward.

'Fucking bastards the lot of them' he snarled. 'All right then cancel the bloody thing.' He turned back to Wallis. 'I am truly sorry dearest… this whole thing stinks of manipulation and I have a damned good idea just who is behind it. My pathetically weak brother and his scheming mean-minded little wife.'

The evening with Paul Gallico was enormously entertaining. He proved to be a self-deprecating raconteur who decried what he described as his own deplorable record with women including his failed marriages. At the same time he fed his friends fascinating insights into the world of the superstars about whom he had written so brilliantly.

'Thankfully all that darned stuff is behind me now and I can concentrate on writing what I want and feel that I must write for myself.'

Paul paused to relight his pipe. Bill Shirer looked around the crowded pub and with a smile commented 'Well, I'll say this for you Paul, you could hardly have found somewhere to live that is more different to New York!'

'Damn right' replied Paul. 'I just love it here. There is a sense of true peace, a timelessness. The serenity of the open skies, dawn and sunset over the estuary and the hills. Then framed in the centre of it all this beautiful little port. Tomorrow I would like to take you out in my boat and you will see a little more of the place but, more importantly, you will feel the tranquillity that I so love.'

Vera smiled. 'You sound like a man who has found his own Heaven Paul. If you have, you are a very lucky man indeed.' Paul paused for a moment then leaned forward towards Vera and fixed her with an intent gaze.

'Vera, I have only met you this evening but I sense a great sadness in you. You too can find your heaven with Billy.' Vera shot a glance at Billy.

'Yes… I have glimpsed Heaven and for the moment I believe I have it but I must return to earth and leave Heaven for some time. In fact Paul… I may glimpse Hell.' Before Paul could respond Billy cut into the conversation which he sensed was veering towards dangerous ground. 'Sailing sounds an excellent idea! What type of vessel do you have?' Paul was astute enough to see what Billy was doing and decided to play along with him.

'I have a Devon lugger. She's about twenty feet and will comfortably take seven. She is a day boat with loose-footed sails so there is no boom to worry about. I have a six horse power outboard so she is ideal for pottering around the inlets and backwaters.'

'Ah here is our food… how is everyone for drinks? More of the same OK?'

'Fine by us' laughed Billy. 'Not only do you seem to have been absorbed into the salty community of Salcombe Paul but you seem to enjoy 'absorbing' our English beer. I thought all Americans hated it in comparison with what you are used to.' Before Paul could answer Bill Shirer chipped in.

'Well Billy, at first sip it is warm and bitter… really quite unpleasant!' Then as he caught Billy's eye he burst out laughing. 'For Chrissake Billy don't look so darned offended. You are sitting here with three Americans and a German so expect a leg pull. Actually *when in Rome* and all that. I even got to quite like retsina when I was in Greece…'

'Now you really have gone too far' spluttered Billy. 'I give up! Paul help me out please!'

'With the greatest of pleasure. For the record I regard English beer as one of the finest things on this Earth and as host I declare that opinion to be the end of the matter.'

The evening was a convivial affair filled with good humour and banter. Some of the conversation was in typically quick fire American style necessitating translation of slang which in itself was amusing. By the time that the landlord rang the bell for last orders before closing time Paul and his guests were part of a boisterous group of locals. When they left they all piled into the Rolls Royce. Paul commented 'This is the ideal car for weekend parties like this. Normally I have to get old Fred Dyer with his Austin 16 to ferry us around… I only have my two-seater MG. Typical Devon I am told… Fred's the local taxi man who also doubles up as the undertaker. He's a miserable old sod but never lets you down. Right, *Home James and don't spare the horses* or something like that.'

Once they were home Vera and Bill's wife Tess opted to turn in whilst the men settled in by the fire for a nightcap. The conversation unsurprisingly turned to the situation in Europe not least because Billy wanted to hear Bill Shirer's expert analysis. To that end he had steered the conversation with a simple question.

'Bill, you are the expert here…. the spider at the middle of the web of information from across Europe. Are the appeasers like British Prime Minister Chamberlain and the so called Cliveden Set right that Hitler and Nazi Germany do not harbour territorial ambitions and are not a threat to peace… unlike the Soviets?' Bill Shirer looked pensive for a moment then spoke very slowly, clearly choosing his words with care.

'Europe is in agony. In the months and years that I have had the somewhat unusual opportunity to set down from day to day a first-hand account of just what is really happening I can say with humility but authority that Europe is sliding inexorably towards the abyss of war and self-destruction. The primary cause of this upheaval is one country. Germany, and one man, Adolf Hitler. As Bill Shirer paused Paul Gallico commented

'Surely Bill, those are harsh words?'

'Absolutely not my friend. From within the totalitarian citadel that is Berlin, indeed all Germany, I have observed how Hitler, acting with a cynicism, brutality, decisiveness and a clarity of purpose that the Continent has not seen since Napoleon has unified Germany and rearmed it, re energised its people and why? For what? That purpose is to smash and annex its neighbours until he has made the Third Reich the militant master of the Continent, and most of its unhappy peoples his slaves.'

Bill Shirer's words were received in a silence that continued after he had stopped speaking. It was Paul who broke it saying in a quiet voice.

'That is a chilling and terrifying picture Bill. But then you have seen the man and the machine first hand.'

'That is just so. Mark my words every aggressive step that Hitler takes will be supported by apparent logical argument… so called moral and legal justification. He and his advisors the likes of Doctor Goebbels may look like fools but they are anything but…. and they spin the truth. The naive who so desperately wish to believe that what Germany is doing is as peace embracing as they would hope will be blinded.' Paul stood up, stretched and yawned and topped up their glasses before signalling for Bill Shirer to continue.

'Just look at the way the German Government declared that the Locarno Pact was… and I roughly quote their diplomatic "note" that was leaked to us journalists…. 'rendered extinct by the Franco-Russian Pact'and that Germany was therefore no longer bound by it and free to march its troops into the demilitarized zone of the Rhineland and restore the full and unrestricted sovereignty of the Reich.' Billy laughed wryly thinking of the reassurance that the Duke had provided to the Nazis.

'That they then did without opposition or intervention. The naive fools could see no wrong and to this day have failed to grasp the way in which Hitler and indeed the mind of Nazi Germany works. Next to fall will be Austria and then the Sudetenland, Czechoslovakia.'

'You sound very certain Bill' Billy commented.

'My dear fellow all you have to do is read Mein Kampf and listen to Hitler's speeches. It is all spelt out for those with eyes and ears.'

'You make Europe's leaders sound like the three unwise monkeys!' quipped Paul in an attempt to lighten the mood.

'Yes Paul. Blind, deaf and mute' responded Shirer in a sombre tone.

Billy went up to bed in a reflective mood. Although Bill Shirer had not really said anything new it was the manner of his speaking and the vehemence which the normally unemotional professional foreign correspondent spoke that chilled Billy. The horror in his mind was that whilst he fully accepted Bill Shirer's view he knew that many in power in Whitehall and other positions of great influence in Britain were still blinkered.

When he climbed into bed Vera was dozing, cosily curled up with her back to him. He slipped his arms around her and drew her to him. She snuggled her bottom to him and simply murmured 'mmm' as he held her close and placed his palm on her rounding stomach. As he did so he shivered at the prospect of the risks that she would soon be facing and as his hand gently stroked her swelling belly wondered just what the future might hold for their child that she was bearing.

Indeed what might the future hold for all of them.

Chapter 29

Winston Churchill and Sir Vernon Kell were comfortably ensconced in deep leather club armchairs in a fug of cigar smoke. Churchill was nursing a brandy and soda and Sir Vernon a generous balloon of armagnac which he gently swirled and burying his nose in it inhaled and sighed.

'This is magnificent Winston. Truly memorable.'

'Glad you think so Vernon. I make a point of always asking for the '15 Nismes-Declou given that before long the Club's stock will run out. Between you and me I find this place stuffy and full of the self-righteous but I am prepared to tolerate that so long as the cellar is up to scratch.' The portly bow tied politician gave a mischievous chuckle as he said this.

Sir Vernon laughed. 'You have always been something of a maverick when it comes to clubs Winston. Your founding of 'The Other Club' with F E Smith in 1910 when you were both excluded from 'The Club' is a case in point is it not?'

'Actually Vernon we were not "excluded" as you put it... but they chose not to invite us to join – very different matter, eh? Anyhow, The Other Club is one of the few institutions from which I have failed to resign and I greatly value our fortnightly dinner in the Pinafore Room at the Savoy. After Smith's death it fell to me to be the arbiter of membership you know. I still apply the original criterion that members must be estimable and entertaining... "Men with whom it is agreeable to dine". Estimable politicians though they may be I did not consider either the socialist Clement Atlee or the conservative Lord Halifax to be entertaining. Two more enemies I expect.' The two men chuckled companionably for a moment. Sir Vernon's expression changed. He noticeably stiffened in his chair, then spoke slowly and deliberately.

'Changing the subject Winston. I am seething. You will know precisely what I mean when I tell you that the clear warnings that we in the intelligence community have been furnishing to our esteemed Prime Minister are going unheeded. I cannot say more but suffice it for me to say that whilst my direct contact with him is limited, somehow Anthony Eden has to tolerate his meddling and interference almost constantly. I am amazed that Eden has not thrown in the towel.'

'Two things Vernon. First, our Prime Minister is blinkered and naive. I may well revert to that point in a moment. Second, I think that you will find that Eden has carried on swallowing the bitter pills out of a sense of duty; he well knows that Chamberlain would wish to appoint the arch appeaser Lord Halifax in his place and regards that as not only damaging but highly dangerous. However I do not think that Eden will sit it out for very much longer.' Sir Vernon sipped his Armagnac. 'Dangerous ground this Winston. I Know that I can trust you… otherwise we could not talk like this. I suppose us old soldiers have more in common than many… although you added front line service in the Great War whilst I steered a harmless desk.'

'Your job was infinitely more important Vernon.' As Sir Vernon began to shake his head Churchill growled on. 'No don't display false modesty and disagree. I was but a single infantry officer whereas you with your chaps rolled up the whole German espionage network in the United Kingdom and did invaluable work. It is just a shame that more of the top brass did not heed what you fellows in intelligence told them. I have had plenty of time to reflect these last years and I simply cannot bring myself to believe that it was really 'The War to end all Wars'. Neither do I believe that another war would be fought in the same manner. Speed will play a much greater part as will intelligence and technology. It will not be a war where our brave men are led by the older men who have not kept up with the advance of technology and modern strategy.'

'I certainly agree about intelligence. We are working damned hard to establish our deeply embedded cadres of agents right across Europe and elsewhere. Now Winston, as an old friend, indulge me. You pick up the scraps on the wind from your political friends and network of contacts and no doubt from the actions of your opponents. How do you see things behind the false facades that are erected to shield so many real beliefs and opinions?'

'Vernon. I am cast as a scaremongering militarist who would wrongly rush our nation and Empire into rearmament. I admit that I have a deeply ingrained sense of history that exercises me greatly. I am not obsessed with the events that led up to the Great War but I cannot help but draw parallels.'

Churchill paused and inspected the growing ash on his cigar, drew on it and exhaled another cloud of smoke. He then continued after this theatrical break.

'The great gap, the gulf, between the aristocracy, the middle classes and the poor is unchanged. We have Germany re-arming at a furious pace. Unlike when with Jacky Fisher driving the Royal Navy forward we had the 'Dreadnought Malaise' with Britain and Germany building bigger and bigger capital ships, this time around we are sitting on our hands and watching as Germany races ahead. It is not only Germany that is re-arming. Nippon is doing the same and of course Italy is following suit. I maintain that history will repeat itself. Substitute Hitler for the Kaiser and you have the true picture.'

'I take your point' replied Sir Vernon. 'But, apart from the fact that both sport absurd rather music hall moustaches they have very little in common really?'

'I don't think that that is the case. Following the death of his uncle our dear old Edward Vll, the 'Uncle of Europe', as he was rightly dubbed, the Kaiser felt that he was able to indulge in his territorial claims. Up until then he had concentrated on trying to oust Britain as the 'Ruler of the Waves' which was an indirect threat. With his uncle gone he could set about achieving his territorial aims which were alarmingly similar to those of Hitler. Remember, the aim of all belligerent dominant leaders – from Alexander the Great, the Emperors of Rome, through Genghis Khan, then throughout history to Bonaparte and the Kaiser – has been to win territory and with it peoples and wealth. The excuses or causes that they give or espouse may change but the fundamentals never will. That is one element in the history of mankind that will be repeated again and again.'

Sir Vernon nodded. 'The intelligence that we have received is that Hitler is confident that he can achieve many of his aims without risk of our intervention.'

'As matters stand, is he wrong?' Churchill posed the question wryly. 'We know damn well that the now Duke of Windsor, then as our Monarch and Emperor provided Herr Hitler with the comfort that swayed the balance for him to re occupy the Ruhr – the Rhineland. Quite apart from the boost to the German national ego it is of course of immense strategic importance.

'Which brings me to another delicate matter Winston. You were long the champion of Edward VIII, especially during the dark days of the abdication crisis. Where do you stand now?'

Churchill appeared to almost bridle before replying in a formally cold tone. 'I did my utmost to support the man born to be King Emperor, and yes I believe in the Holy succession. I might not have agreed with the course of action which he followed, nevertheless so long as he was acting honourably I was his devoted servant. The moment I realised that he had turned his back on his honour my respect was destroyed. Am I clear?'

'Admirably so' responded Sir Vernon without a pause. 'It is surely tragic that the man who enjoyed everyone's unswerving and unconditional loyalty should have proved to be so shabby a betrayer. So what are we to do?'

'To the world we owe him... and yes that also means her... respect. In private, the greatest caution. I fear Vernon that the man whom I championed and supported is an utterly weak and selfish shit.'

The Princess let out a loud gasp, almost a cry as with her red hair flying she rode her lover Fritz Wiedeman to her climax. 'My God Fritz... oh my God that was wonderful' she cried in a gasping voice. 'Ha!' he also gasped. 'And not bad for me!' As the Princess raised herself and her lover slid out of her she leant forward and with her curly hair falling loose about his face kissed him on the end of his nose and muttered 'I so love you, you bastard man.' Holding her buttocks, Fitz laughed as he lifted her. 'You too, you beautiful bitch.' Princess Stephanie collapsed forward onto her lover's chest and, punctuated with paroxysms of laughter, gasped 'I do so, you utter bastard.'

As the Princess snuggled beside him, Fritz reached onto the ormolu banded bedside table and clicked open his utilitarian steal cigarette case that had been with him in the horrific trenches of the Great war when he was the Fuhrer's commanding officer. After taking out two cigarettes he put one in the mouth of the Princess and then flicked his old and battered petrol lighter and lit them.

'Oh Fritz' laughed his lover. 'You are so bloody sophisticated. I cannot smell burning petrol without thinking of being intimate with you. How crazy is that eh?'

Fritz's mood changed in an instant. In a cold voice almost alien to his normally joyously exuberant embrace of life when with her he muttered 'Sweety I'm afraid that as things are going the world is going to smell an awful lot of burning bloody petrol.' Stephanie stiffened. 'Oh come on Fritzy love, do you really mean that?'

'Oh yes, I most certainly do. What the heck do you think all the work that is going on in the Fuhrer's Chancellery and the whole bloody nation is about? Eh? Sour note I know and, sorry petal, but we, and that is Germany, are set on war and it will be a war as the world has never seen nor imagined. After the horrors of Paschendale and the whole ghastly Great War I want no part of it.' Stephanie hugged her wartime hero tight as he gave a sob in her arms. 'Shit' he mumbled. 'Sorry, so sorry but do the fucking fools have no idea of what they plan to unleash on the world? On the women and innocent children let alone the poor bloody soldiers? I am working on the plans for blitzkrieg – we tried it in Spain and it works – a terrible, fearful horror from the skies which we will unleash as our armour smashes all resistance on the ground. You have no idea just how powerful we shall be when we strike. By the time that Governments wake up they will be gone… history. I do not want to be a part of it. Will you come with me if we can escape the madness?'

'Oh my darling man, of course I will' said the beautiful woman that was Hitler's muse. 'I love you to distraction and don't forget I know just what a brave man you are… in every way. When you are ready we will have to face up to Adolf's rage… and mark my words he will go mad because in his own way he loves us both. We will do it. When do you think my darling?'

'Soon. It needs to be very soon.'

As the little red sail boat left the shelter of the Salcombe harbour walls the heavy Atlantic swell lifted the bows and the wind stiffened. The sails strained, the rigging creaked and Bill Shirer who was sitting in the stern next to Paul Gallico who had the tiller in hand as he puffed at his pipe exclaimed 'Oh Sweet Jesus… this is what it is all about!' Billy was holding the sheet for the mainsail laughed too as the boat heeled. 'Does it get any better?' The hangovers and the serious talk of the previous night were blown away as the stiff wind took hold. Vera, who was pink-cheeked in a heavily patterned Arran sweater with curling hair framing her lovely face beneath a Breton beret, screamed as a large gobbett of sea spume smacked into her face. Paul's guffaw was all that it needed for the group to settle into the sheer hedonistic delight of being all together on a fine craft in a stiff wind scudding along a beautiful coastline. It might be wild. It might have a hint of danger. But the moment held no malice.

*   *   *

The Queen was not amused. Her beloved but vulnerable husband was in an explosive expletive ridden rant. She was impervious to the stream of obscenities flowing almost seamlessly from his mouth but she was inwardly seething at the cause. Yet again her apparently uncaring and totally irresponsible brother in law the Duke of Windsor had made a stream of demands that still included his wish that the appalling Simpson woman be accorded the style and status of a Royal Princess.

Poor Alex Hardinge, the King's Private Secretary, who despite a rocky start with the Queen was now one of the Royal couple's most trusted advisers, stood to one side and patiently waited for the tirade to run its course. Inevitably it did so, but with the usual question.

'Alex. What the f f f fuck should I do?'

'Your Majesty. I would caution patience however uncomfortable that may be. The ill-starred American visit is now abandoned and there is no pressing need for any action. May I counsel a policy of masterful inactivity.' The King appeared deep in thought for a few moments but then in a rare display of gaiety turned to the Queen and with a laugh said 'Oh let the buggers stew in their own juice shall we? I've had a belly full of the whining and threats. Enough for now, eh?' The Queen was delighted to note the lack of any stammer as the King had delivered his little speech and also wholeheartedly agreed with his sentiments. Taking a gold cigarette case from her handbag she simply responded with a coquettish smile 'Drinkies then?'

Chapter 30

'David, what the heck is bothering you? You are behaving like a petulant child!' snarled an infuriated Wallis as the Duke slumped in his chintz covered armchair cradling a very large and ominously dark Scotch whisky.

'What have I done eh? What have I done to those bastards? Why are they treating me… and you my love… so badly? What is behind it all? Even my own mother is turned against me. Why? Why? Why?' Wallis could see that the Duke was close to tears and potentially one of his childish tantrums that she was beginning to loathe and would go to any lengths to avoid. On the other hand she had reached a point where, whatever logic might dictate, she felt that she had to have it out with her husband, regardless of the consequences. She knew that with the amount of whisky he had drunk there would be an argument and probably nothing achieved but she was at the end of her tether. She snapped.

'For Christ's sake David get a grip on yourself. Lay off the damned booze and stop dwelling on the past. We have a future… don't you see? Don't you get it? You are becoming paranoid and that bloody stuff…' She shouted as he looked blearily at his glass which was in danger of being spilt as his hand slowly tipped 'will only make you worse. Stop reading some Machiavellian plot into everything!'

The Duke, who had reached a point of misconceived drunken wit, responded in a ghastly mock Italian accent. 'So who is this Machiavelli? Eh? An Italian? A head waiter or perhaps a band leader or a spaghetti sauce?'

'You stupid man!' cried a now infuriated Wallis. 'For Christ's sake did they not teach you, the future King, anything?'

'Yes! Manners, oh and protocol and the order of precedence of Queen Victoria's offspring in the royal houses of Europe and our relationship with them....' He slurred. 'Not a lot else before it was off to Osborne and naval training. So who was this Italian chappy?'

'I have never read it but he wrote a famous or perhaps infamous book called 'The Prince' in which he set out the rules by which a man with no conscience or decency could exercise total power. Manipulation really. Well, that's how I understand it.' The Duke was now slumped even lower in his armchair and had slopped whisky onto his evening shirt.

'So you think that I am being manipulated.... that I am pathetic?'

'Oh David you silly man. No, no, no. You outplayed them all. They never believed that you would have the courage to do what you did. They are angry and spiteful but you are stronger... we are stronger. Now take me to bed.' As Wallis helped her clearly inebriated husband to his feet she knew full well that he would be asleep the moment his head hit the pillow. In her highly charged mood, sleep was out of the question. The Duke was snoring quietly as Wallis, who had slipped into one of her Chinese silk kimonos gently kissed his forehead, careful not to wake him, then turned off the bedside light.

Wallis smiled wolfishly as she entered her boudoir where Helga was lying on the chaise longue dressed only in a leather suspender belt, stockings and ridiculously high heeled black shoes.

'Darling Helga' Wallis purred. 'I am upset tonight and you know what that means don't you Liebchen? I will be doing to you just what you have loved doing to others.' Helga shuddered in anticipation of just what her unpredictable mistress might have in mind. It was soon clear that Helga's pleasure was not to be on the agenda on this occasion as Wallis undressed in a fury then from a bedside cupboard produced a whip and an enormous dildo attached to a harness.

Helga had been hurt before but after a comparatively light flogging could not control a scream as she realised that the agonising pressure she felt was the precursor of a savage anal assault. Wallis slapped the girl's head as she thrust mercilessly, her rictus grin a horrific mask of fury reflecting the frustration and utter despondency that consumed her at the thought of the prize that she had so nearly won but had lost. The throne.

Celia was having tea at the exclusive Phyllis Court in Henley on Thames, home of the world famous regatta, in itself a staple of the English season and evocatively immortalised in Three Men in a Boat. Her host was the urbane

Julio Gounal, a bon vivant friend, both of her father and Johnny. Julio was an art dealer and business colleague of Johnny, and by virtue of his English mother, an aristocratic opera singer, he was accepted as a member of the establishment. Whilst not conventionally handsome Julio exuded charm and with his lithe physique and Latin features was intensely attractive in an understated way.

Celia might have been in love with Johnny but at heart she could never resist a beautiful man. That was how she saw Julio. He in turn could not believe his good fortune to be sitting with the most attractive young woman he had ever met on the manicured lawns leading down to the river where his boat was moored. That she was interesting to talk to and an intelligent observer of world affairs was a delightful bonus.

Julio was a close friend and confidant of Jimmy Berwick, the Duke D'Alba, reputedly the richest man in Spain and the possessor of the greatest number of grand titles in the world. Jimmy Berwick was General Franco's representative in London living in a suite in the Dorchester Hotel. Akin to Princes Stephanie, who also kept a permanent suite in the hotel, which was the base from which he cultivated support for General Franco.

Whilst Celia naturally knew Jimmy Berwick, her purpose today and her brief from Tar Robertson was to become close to Julio and use him to infiltrate the Spanish fascists and most importantly ascertain their relationships with the German and Italian Governments. What had started out as a chore when briefed was rapidly turning into a delight as Celia gazed at Julio's chiselled profile.

'Shall we potter up the river a little Celia?' he asked, breaking her reverie.

'Oh rather! How super' she responded in what she felt to be embarrassingly gauche school-girl terms. They strolled down the immaculate lawn to the river bank where in summer months elegant couples and larger groups would have been taking tea. The men would then be almost all of a certain age in colourful blazers that in many cases no longer fitted with caps also in college colours hanging from the backs of their chairs. That these middle-aged and in some cases elderly men were happy demonstrating that they were reliving their past would not seem at all ironic in the setting. This was England and they were at its core.

'Well, there she is!' cried Julio with pride in his voice. Bobbing on her mooring lines by the landing stage was a beautiful golden varnished day boat with a bench seat running all around the hull and a fringed surrey top in soft cream canvas.

'Oh! She is lovely!' cried Celia. 'But where is the engine?'

'She's electric, silly. The noise of an engine would spoil the music and the moment. Let's cast off and then a little Mozart. Don't be depressed but I adore his Requiem and on the river as the sun goes down it is truly magnificent. There is champagne chilled in the icebox. One bottle is open. Please be pouring whilst I cast off.' As Celia settled back into the giant cushions and the boat silently and seemingly effortlessly accelerated away from the bank and headed for Henley's ancient bridge, Celia, no stranger to indulgence, thought to herself 'this is heaven'. At that moment the gramophone burst into life and Mozart's genius filled the air as the launch cleared the bridge and was flooded with soft golden evening light.

'God… perfection,' she thought as she turned back to her host who was sitting cross legged on a giant Turkey carpet covered cushion with one hand on the brass mounted oak wheel of the boat. Aloud and subconsciously aware of her true brief Celia said, 'This is not bad you know, really…'

'Well thank you Milady… you are very gracious. Now, more champagne and shall we get down to business?' As Celia's eyes widened Julio laughed, reached and stroked a strand of hair from her temple. 'No my beautiful girl. That can come later… and I sure hope that it does. No. I mean the reason that your boss Colonel Tar Robertson has told you to snuggle up with little old me… and by the way, it is such a coincidence as my boss Jimmy Berwick has told me to do the same with you. OK?'

'Shit! Oh Shit! Well then…. oh for heaven's sake change the music and we can talk about that stuff later. Look! You can moor over there under that willow and let's just enjoy ourselves. Any ideas for the music?'

'Absolutely. Brahms, the second piano concerto. It's not subtle and quite a pace… can you handle that?'

'Silly man… I've done Wagner… but not the whole ring cycle… oh for God's sake, just put it on …..'

'King Franklin my old friend, I can assure you that all is under control here in Europe. Yes, of course there is disquiet about the Germans re-arming and making highly provocative gestures, but are they that stupid? Do they really want Britain, ultimately the US and eventually Russia setting out to crush them. Utter madness. I regard Herr Hitler's posturing as being as empty a threat as the confidence of the French in the Maginot Line is misplaced.

Franklin D Roosevelt was nicknamed 'King Franklin' by some of his inner circle as a tribute to the manner in which he succeeded in disposing of so much of the business of government apparently without effort, achieving his own objectives and leaving would be opponents puzzling over just how he had done it.

'William, you are our Ambassador in Paris and a very dear friend. Of course I trust your judgement. But you seem to have fewer concerns about the European situation with the Fascists on the rise if not actually on the march again?'

'Of course I do. But at the highest level I am assured that Germany's intentions are peaceful and they seek an amicable resolution to certain matters that have rankled since 1918. Herr Hitler believes that whilst the German people must have their faith restored by being a part of an economically and militarily strong and reborn nation there is a sufficiently powerful lobby in Britain to achieve that end without force. In other words the people of peace and appeasement.'

'William, I do not assume to teach my Grandmother to suck eggs but I need more from you. Some of the Brits are in a real flap. I have had Winston bending my ear regularly and although he has called some real dumb shots over the years I am inclined to trust his judgement on this one. Justified?'

'FDR, you of all people know that "who knows?" is the key to most things British. I could try to snoop a little more informally on the German front. The French hate the idea of any further conflict… after all so much of the Great War was fought on their land and that of "brave little Belgium" I have some ideas, leave it to me.'

The following day Wallis was informed that Ambassador Bullitt was on the telephone. She took the call in the privacy of her boudoir.

'Bill dear man… what a pleasure to hear from you.'

'Wallis… can we meet in private again? Elsa's atelier as before or somewhere else equally discreet?'

'Delighted. I shall make arrangements and let you know.'

'And your young friend Helga… will she be joining us?'

'It depends Bill. She is a little indisposed today but if we were to meet tomorrow I am sure that she would be able to join in the fun. Do you have something particular in mind?'

'I shall leave that to you if I may.'

After finishing the call Wallis made arrangements for a meeting the next day at Elsa Schiaperelli's atelier. She then informed Ambassador Bullitt of the arrangements and summoned Helga. The young woman entered the boudoir in trepidation. Helga my dear… I trust that you are feeling better?'

'I am very sore Wallis… that was just too much.'

'Oh come on dear girl. That dildo was only a little bigger than von Ribbentrop and don't tell me that he hasn't gone up that path before now… I know that he loves to.'

'That is very different Wallis as you well know. A dildo is very different to a man.'

'So what shall we do with the good ambassador tomorrow afternoon? Let's put on our thinking caps.'

Helga's bottom lip was quivering but Wallis's eyes were elsewhere.

'You know Helga, I think that you must have the longest legs that I have ever seen. Take off your dress and show me. Now don't be afraid, I will give you a gentle cuddle and kiss you better.'

Helga recognised the signs and resigned herself to a session with Wallis that she could well do without as she slipped out of her dress. Wallis wasted no time and reaching forward with both hands cupped Helga's pert buttocks, then hooking her thumbs into the waistband pulled down her knickers, turned Helga around and pushed her steadily but gently towards a high backed armchair. Slightly more roughly she pushed Helga forward so that the young woman was doubled over the back of the chair, then parted her buttocks.

'There now little flower is that better?' Wallis asked, her voice muffled.

Despite herself Helga felt herself responding to Wallis' expertise as the older woman's tongue lapped her like a cat.

Julio's boat was now only moving gently in the river currents as it snagged against the mooring lines. Celia and Julio were lying on cushions on the deck of the boat, entwined as they recovered from the wild sex that they had just enjoyed. The gramophone had clicked to a stop after the lyrical beauty of the Brahms.

'My God, I must look an absolute fright' laughed Celia as she reached for her handbag and a handkerchief. Her skirt was rucked around her waist and her discarded knickers were on the deck some feet away where they had been thrown. 'Ah, here it is – now just let me clean you up a little – so much! I could really do with a bathroom you awful man. Anyway, you first.'

'Mmm… that feels very nice… just carry on a little longer and I shall be ready again…' Their eyes locked as his penis could clearly be seen to be hardening as Celia continued her ministrations that were now no longer necessary.

'Come on old girl… there's plenty more where that came from…'

Celia pushed him back on the cushions, straddled him and sank onto him giving the slightest of whimpers as he slipped inside her. The couple were much less frenzied as they moved in perfect harmony and this time there was no music playing.

The boat slipped back down the river to Henley in silence with only the whisper of the water against the hull and mooring up again at Phyllis Court the relaxed couple strolled back up the lawn towards the welcoming lights of the house. After they had bathed and changed into evening dress they studied the menu over another glass of champagne and after making their choice were ushered to a discreet corner table in the softly-lit dining room. Apart from a table of four in the far corner the dining room was deserted.

'So Celia my little vixen, just what is your brief from Tar Robertson?'

'Oh no Julio this is not a case of ladies first… and that, my dear, is a great compliment in your case… but you must tell me your brief from Jimmy Berwick. After all he could just as easily have approached me directly.'

'Very well. It is simple really. It is an open secret that Germany has its Condor Legion flying in support of Generalissimo Franco's campaign. Jimmy's concern is simply that since such is in direct and flagrant breach of the Non Intervention Agreement, will Britain be taking the matter up at the League of Nations or even intervening physically in some form?'

Julio outlined General Franco's position with regard to Great Britain and Celia did likewise outlining the British position as she had been briefed.

Celia smiled as she replied. 'Kind of 'snap' I would say. My brief is to find out whether the German and Italian support for General Franco will now be scaled down in the light of world condemnation of what is seen as the fascist governments trying out their concept of 'blitzkrieg' on innocent and unprotected civilians.'

Julio leant back in his chair and after a moment's thought smiled. 'Celia my dear. I think that we can both regard our tasks as complete and report back accordingly. We should respectively report that the German and Italian involvement in the Spanish civil war will now be scaled down and Britain will not intervene. It must now be for the diplomats to take matters to the next stage. Let us enjoy our dinner and I repeat my offer of hospitality here if you wish it?'

'It is so very kind of you Julio but I must return to London tonight. Another time perhaps.'

They both knew that there would never be another time.

Chapter 31

Following his conversation with the President Ambassador Bullitt was hatching a plan. One that could backfire on him badly with even worse implications diplomatically. Whilst President Roosevelt was in a sense complicit in what Bullitt had in mind, he harboured no doubt that notwithstanding their long and close friendship, if there were to be problems arising from his initiative there would be total denial from the White House. The phrase 'hung out to dry' sprang to mind.

Bullitt knew that Wallis had enjoyed an intense physical relationship with von Ribbentrop in London and the secret intelligence reports that he had received from the FBI in Washington indicated that Wallis' personal aide, Helga, also enjoyed a relationship with the German minister. That the FBI reports were undoubtedly edited at the instigation of the sexually repressed Director J. Edgar Hoover did not escape him.

Bullitt was well aware that Hoover always wanted something held back; a 'ransom piece' which he might be able to play on another occasion to his personal ends. He hated Hoover whom he ironically saw as a pervert, and who quite apart from anything else he knew had a substantial personal file on him. That was a score to settle another day.

The big question in his mind was just how he could convince Wallis, and via her Helga, to arrange for him to meet von Ribbentrop in private. His mind was spinning as he ran through the different scenarios that he could conjure up but every time he came to an impasse; Wallis was simply too damn shrewd to be fooled. In the end he decided that a straightforward approach was the best bet. Risky yes but utterly deniable. After all, the adventuress turned Duchess had a sullied reputation and in intelligence circles was regarded as highly suspect. If she decided to discredit him, his credentials were impeccable in comparison.

In Berlin, Heydrich, who was nominally Himmler's deputy, and who revelled in the common joke that 'Himmler's brain is called Heydrich' was signing off a highly confidential memorandum. This was confirmation of an instruction that he had given by telephone the previous day to a 'sleeper cell' of German operatives in England authorising an act of sabotage which if successful would result in the murder of a German National, her English lover and an American foreign correspondent whose insightful reporting was becoming more than an irritant to the Third Reich which Heydrich served so assiduously.

After dinner with Julio in Phyllis Court, Celia had telephoned Tar Robertson on his private home number and had arranged to meet her at his office immediately on her return to London.

She had returned to London cocooned in a warm post coital glow of intense sexual gratification. She knew that she could trust Julio's discretion absolutely. Not least, she was well aware of his wife's reputation as a firebrand with a terrifying temper matched only by her vast wealth on which her husband relied. Celia smiled at the thought that Julio would not only be cast out penniless if his wife had even a sniff of infidelity but he would also be singing falsetto.

She instructed her driver to take her straight to the office of Tar Robertson so that she could report her conversation in full whilst fresh in her mind. As the Lagonda growled back to London Celia rehearsed her report. She also decided that she would not mention the physical side of her time with Julio; Tar was a great keeper of secrets but he was also an intelligence man down to his boots and she had quickly learned that friend or foe, sensitive information was at the heart of so much of the intelligence 'great game'.

Tar with his customary Player's Navy Cut cigarette in hand rose from behind his remarkably tidy partners' desk and gestured for Celia to take a seat.

'Well my dear girl. Good fishing trip?'

Celia blushed to the roots of her hair as her mind scrambled to work out whether Tar actually knew what had gone on in the boat. *Surely not*, she thought... at this time of year there was no one else on the river and the boat trip had been a spur of the moment idea. 'Or was it...? After all Julio's beautiful and very distinctive boat had been moored directly in front of Phyllis Court. Oh, what the hell. Best to ignore it.'

'Yes Tar it was very interesting, hence my rushing back to see you tonight. Shall I give you a quick resume? I can write it up tomorrow if you wish?'

'No, I will not need a written report… best not perhaps… so do please carry on.'

'Firstly he knew I worked for you and at the same time he told me that Jimmy Berwick the Duke d'Alba, his friend and boss, had instructed him to get close to me! I was rather shocked by that at first.'

Tar laughed lightly. 'Celia my dear that is precisely what I had hoped for. Anyhow tell me the essence of what he said.'

'It was actually quite simple. General Franco sees Britain's strict adherence to the non-intervention agreement in a very favourable light. He is also mindful that it was an unacknowledged British effort that took him to his army in North Africa. The General's intention is that if Britain and the Axis powers of Italy and Germany go to war Spain will remain sympathetic to the fascist cause but will not become embroiled. Spain will not become a route to the Mediterranean neither will it agree to airfields or harbour facilities for either side on Spanish soil.'

'Well done! That is truly excellent. My dear young lady that is the most excellent news. If we do end up in a war Spain could hold the balance when it comes to the Med, and of course the vital Suez Canal thence the whole Middle East and India. This is excellent. Jimmy Alba can be trusted but we have yet to have a chance to judge the mettle of this Franco chappie. Ruthless devil and his North African troops are truly terrifying. You know the old joke that 'Africa begins at the Pyrenees'? Well, now with those savages, one could say it really does. Anything else?'

'No, that was really it. Shall I go now?'

'Well, stay for a cup of tea… Johnny has flown in from Paris and is on his way.'

'Thank you Tar but I am a little tired and I think that I shall go home and have a lie down.'

'As you wish, but once again, very well done.'

'Well actually I really had to do very little.'

With a smile and a twinkle in his piercing blue eyes Tar responded 'Ah yes, but it is how you do it that matters.'

As previously, Ambassador Bullitt instructed his driver to drop him near to Elsa

Schiaperrelli's atelier. Out of habit as much as vanity he checked his appearance in the window of Fauchon, a shop that was the pinnacle of French good taste and haute cuisine. The window display in front of which he stood was simple in the extreme. A Magnum of Armagnac next to a bottle with a row of miniatures. Bullitt chuckled at the thought that the window dresser had clearly envisaged a duck and its offspring. His good humour did not diminish as he set off to walk to his assignation with Wallis and Helga.

When he was shown into a salon with Wallis and Helga elegantly perched on a French Empire chaise longue he was shocked. They were both wearing stylish but severely cut suits with hats and gloves in their laps, legs demurely crossed at the ankles and formal court shoes.

His expression amused Wallis who asked with raised eyebrows. 'Did you not think that we are ladies?'

For once the ever urbane Bullitt was speechless. 'I am enchanted' he muttered. Wallis stood and at her nod so did Helga. In her high heels Helga towered over the almost birdlike Wallis who gestured to Bullitt to follow as the two women turned and walked to a door at the back of the salon.

'Don't be nervous Bill… we are intimate friends after all, n'est pas?' Bullitt's pulse quickened as they entered a darkened room with a large bed in the middle. Above it the ceiling was mirrored and from each corner chains were laid out with leather lined handcuffs on the bed. The theatrical scene excited Bullitt and thoughts about his mission of the day that had brought him here vanished as Wallis and Helga started to undress him.

He did not resist when he was pushed back onto the bed and his wrists and ankles were locked into the cuffs. He strained for a moment then realised that all he could achieve was an inch or two on each chain.

Wallis and Helga disappeared for what seemed like an eternity but then returned in masks and leather basques. Neither was wearing knickers and Bullitt eagerly eyed the sex of each woman.

It was only when he felt a searing pain that he realised that Helga was dripping molten wax onto his genitals.

'Christ!' he screamed. 'What the fuck's that for?'

'Don't worry dearest' purred Wallis. 'You will get to rather like it.'

Bullitt's face was in a rictus of pain as Helga continued to pour molten wax and his breathing was becoming uneven. Wallis raised her hand and touching Helga's arm to attract her attention then shook her head. Helga stopped pouring.

Bullitt whose groin area was now covered in the rapidly setting wax groaned and looking pleadingly at Wallis asked again 'Why Wallis, why?'

Wallis smiled wolfishly. 'Because you are a naughty boy. Now tell me why you asked to see us?'

As Bullitt noted that Helga had returned with a fresh jug which he assumed also contained hot wax he made an instant snap decision. 'I need to see von Ribbentrop and you ladies are the key. The German Ambassador here in Paris must not know, nor must anyone else. Do you agree?'

'Oh dearest Bill. You only had to ask. Of course. Now, shall we see about shifting all this wax? I don't think that Opie would be impressed with it… there might be some awkward questions for you.'

Helga started to peel away the wax as Wallis climbed onto the bed and turning her back on Bullitt lowered her sex onto his face.

'Eat me you bastard' she growled as Helga ripped away a handful of solidified wax taking a large clump of pubic hair with it. 'Sweet revenge!' she thought as she seized some more wax and ripped out another clump of hair. Bullitt was now between heaven and hell as Wallis ground into his face and Helga continued to rip off the wax and hair. When Wallis came with a gush he gulped with relief as her writhing stopped and Helga changed from aggressor to comforter gently cupping him, in one hand and gripping him with the other. He was not hard… that would take Wallis. But, after the wax agony, Helga's gentle hands gave him exquisite sensations.

'So sorry it's back to London for us Paul.' Bill Shirer was the last to climb into Billy's venerable Rolls Royce shooting brake as winter dawn sun lit the house in golden light. 'Some of us have desks waiting I'm afraid… so jealous of you my friend. Thank you so much again… it's been a wonderful break.'

Paul Gallico in a heavy roll neck sweater, pipe in hand as usual, waved away the thanks. 'It's been a grand time for me. I get lonesome but that's the fate of a writer. You have a good drive back to London. I am taking my dogs for an early walk.'

As Billy drove down the driveway Vera squeezed his knee and in a soft voice, almost a whisper said 'What a lovely man but so troubled, yes?'

'I think so my dearest.' He reached up and twisted the centre driving mirror. 'I thought as much, the other two are asleep. Perhaps Paul is a tortured genius… I don't know. Lovely chap but he cannot keep a woman; his last marriage only lasted months… and somehow his life seems rather false. Why would a successful New York journalist… actually a journalist known throughout the whole of America… end up in a sleepy Devon coastal town?'

Vera punched Billy lightly on the arm. 'Oh silly man! You English have no soul. I think that he is a slav at heart and will always be searching for his true love.'

'Really my dear. You are a slav… or do you now see yourself as a pure Aryan German? And you have yet to find happiness ah?'

'No Billy, my love, my search is over. I have you, the most wonderful man I could ever have met. But I am very sad that I have to go back to Germany. And I am frightened.'

'Sshh… not now my sweet.'

Wallis decided that it was too risky to communicate Ambassador Bullitt's request to meet von Ribbentrop other than in a face to face conversation. Much as she would have enjoyed seeing him it was clearly out of the question, so Helga would have to be the messenger.

'Helga my girl, you are in luck. I am giving you a week's additional holiday to go to Berlin and see von Ribbentrop. I am sure that he will be as delighted as you!'

Sir Vernon was yet again experiencing the acute frustration of dealing with Prime Minister Chamberlain. As usual they were in the Prime Minister's rather depressing private study and, at Sir Vernon's insistence, alone.

'Yet again Prime Minister I must insist that it is recognised that our intelligence with regard to Spain's intentions in the event of a war with Germany and probably Italy is sound.'

'And I tell you again Sir Vernon that I do not deal in second hand information leaked through the back door. If and when the time comes I shall ascertain Spain's intentions through established diplomatic channels. Until then I have instructed the Chiefs of Staff to assume that they will actively throw in their lot with Germany and Italy. And that of course depends upon this General Franco fellow succeeding which is far from certain.'

'But Prime Minister on the assumption that our intelligence is correct – and I have every faith in its veracity – our intelligence points to General Franco succeeding as the other forces squabble amongst themselves and seem intent on fighting each other rather than their common enemy, and some of our vital resources and forces can be released from the Western Mediterranean.'

'That's as may be but I have made my position clear. Now good day to you as you return to your office.'

Sir Vernon recognised that he would get no further with the obdurate Prime Minister whom he was beginning to detest ever more daily. As his anonymous Government Humber whisked him away he decided that another chat with Winston Churchill might be worthwhile. He made a mental note to arrange it.

The King and Queen had just seen their daughters and the nanny had taken the girls off for a high tea before the run up to bed. It was one of the rare moments when the royal couple could relax and be themselves without the constant round of courtiers and duties.

'Darling' asked the Queen as she relished her gin and Dubonnet. 'Do you not think that there is any problem with your relatives in Germany being so involved with the dreadful Hitler?'

'Well, to b b b be pr pr precise, there are v v v very few of them. I have had r r rep reports from our intelligence b b b boys who who who say that those who are committed to the Nazi cause are very visible. But I I I sh sh should also tell you that our intelligence people suspect the Windsors of being Nazi camp followers.'

'Hah' snorted the Queen. 'Much as we thought. Nothing would surprise me when it comes to that woman or, I have to say it, your weak brother.'

'Well I cannot believe that my b b b brother would f f follow s some someone like this H Hitler f f fellow.'

'Oh darling…I know it hurts but look at the way they behaved in Germany and remember that the conniving bitch has him eating out of her hand. He is putty in her hands. You mark my words, along the way they will be trouble.'

'What, more than brother George with his rackety friends?' snarled the King without the slightest hint of a stammer.

'Oh darling, George has a good heart but he is rather lost don't you think? After all, as the youngest son he will always be something of a lost cause won't he?'

'Well he must start p p p pull pull pulling his ww weight. He has a beautiful wife – at least that has scotched some of the rumours about him… and he h has his children. He is v v very keen on f f flying and the RAF so I I I am asking that h he be lined u u up for a j j j ob w w with them.'

'That's a wonderful idea. Also my dear he is well placed to keep in touch with your family around Europe, including those in Germany. He can do that on an informal basis, something that you cannot do. It's important you know.'

Chapter 32

Von Ribbentrop had been delighted to receive a message from Wallis informing him that Helga was to have a brief holiday in Berlin. He sent for Herr Strack who whilst officially Head of the Protocol Section within the German Foreign Ministry also acted as a 'fixer' at the highest diplomatic level.

At first sight Strack was an austere looking individual but his eyes sparkled with an almost mischievous twinkle that gave a hint of the great charm of which he was capable.

'Minister, you sent for me?' Strack did not offer the customary 'Heil Hitler' as normally given by a subordinate but then he was no Nazi and made no attempt to disguise the fact that he regarded himself as a servant of the German people, a true civil servant, and not a man whose loyalty would ever be to any particular political party or individual, however powerful. His consummate skills ensured that his repeated breaches of what had become mainstays of Hitler's rule were ignored.

'I have a delicate question to put to you. Through an intermediary I have been asked to meet the American Ambassador to Paris, William Bullitt, on a clandestine basis… even without the knowledge of our Ambassador to France. I am uncertain as to whether I should comply with such a request. How would you play it Strack?'

'Minister, I assume that the request was relayed through the good offices of the Duchess of Windsor?'

'How the hell did you fathom that out?' blurted an obviously annoyed Ribbentrop whose urbane facade had slipped.

'Minister I would not wish to venture further on that aspect of the matter but I must advise that you should not agree to such a meeting. Although one must consider the Americans... let me put it delicately... rather naive and inexperienced when it comes to matters diplomatic... after all they have so little historical experience to draw upon... they are at times cunning as individuals and Bullitt most certainly is. I fear a trap and respectfully suggest that you agree to there being a meeting with a 'go between'. Obviously someone highly placed but also someone who does not have a specified brief or position in the German government.'

'Hmm. You could be right... anyone in mind?'

After a pause Strack's face broke into a broad smile. 'Why yes Minister I believe that I do, may I suggest Charles Edward the Duke of Saxe-Coburg and Gotha. He is well placed being a descendant of Queen Victoria holding the title Duke of Albany until he was stripped of his British titles and honours in 1919. He was a first cousin to the late King George the Fifth and, indeed closely related to most of the crowned heads of Europe.'

Herr Strack then went on to explain in a rather pedantic manner that as so far as the British dimension was concerned, quite apart from being a close relative of the King the Duke was actually a member of the Royal family and his sister was Princess Alice who had worked hard to 'bring him back into the Royal fold.' The Duke had been at Eton with Sir Neville Henderson (the British Ambassador to Germany) and had maintained the most impeccable international links that only someone of his Royal birth could have achieved. He was President of the German Red Cross, which was in fact by then an element of the German Government and the Fuhrer had appointed him president of the Anglo-German Friendship Society. He was perfectly placed to monitor international activities of all persuasions and his connections and status ensured that he had access at the very highest level. And, of course he had entertained the Duke and Duchess of Windsor when they were visitors.

'Ambassador Bullitt will see the worth of meeting with him... of that I am sure.'

'Well done Strack... perfect... Bullitt should not feel short changed and the Duke can express privately held views. I wish to brief him personally. Please make arrangements for him to attend me as a matter of urgency.'

'Of course Minister. Now, if you will excuse me I shall contact him and make the appropriate arrangements. May I assume that you will inform Ambassador Bullitt that unfortunately you will not be able to see him but that the Duke shall do so?'

'Correct, Herr Strack, and thank you.'

When Strack had left the room Ribbentrop pondered for a moment as to just how it was that Strack was always so well informed. That Strack was a confidante of Admiral Canaris the head of the Abwehr, Military Intelligence, might be a clue. After all Canaris – like Strack – was no Nazi but a true servant of Germany and its people. His thoughts were dashed when a telephone on his desk began to ring loudly.

When Ribbentrop saw the flashing light on the black telephone he felt the familiar clenching of his stomach muscles that he always experienced when his beloved but dangerous Master, the Fuhrer, called him.

In a tricolour-garlanded viewing box overlooking the Champs Elysee the Duke and Duchess of Windsor were honoured guests watching as the massed bands of the French Legion Etrangere played the traditional march 'Le Boudin' to which the Legion marched at only 88 paces to the minute rather than the 120 of all other French regiments.

After the band came the spade bearded Pioneers in their leather aprons with axes on their shoulders. The slow march of the Legion only served to emphasise their power and strength.

The one eyed old General Claude de la Blois who had the profile of a bird of prey was the couple's nominal host for the occasion. He had served in the Legion for many years and quietly explained that the song to which the Legion marched gained its name from the kit traditionally rolled in a red blanket that was strapped over the top of the Legionaires' backpacks and was said to resemble the blood sausage of that name.

As the old general quietly sang the words the Duke translated for the benefit of the Duchess.

'We are crafty.
We are rogues.
We are no ordinary guys.
We've got our black moods.
For we are legionnaires.'

Then came the chorus which offered blood sausage to the Alsations, the Swiss and the Lorrains but none for the Belgians, explained the Duke.

'But why not the Belgians?' asked a puzzled Duchess. The Duke turned to the General, who broke his singing to say 'After the Franco Prussian war when

Alsace- Lorraine was annexed by Germany many of its men joined the Legion. They were influenced by the fact that in maintaining Belgian neutrality in that conflict the King of the Belgians had requested that Belgian members of the Legion should not fight the Prussian invaders and they stayed in their barracks. The Belgians were forever tainted in the eyes of other Legionnaires.

The old General wiped a tear from his eye as the sun browned faces of the men in his beloved Legion were turned in rigid salute as they marched past the saluting base below the stand. 'Magnifique.' he muttered to himself again and again.

Wallis shivered as the marching men's eyes appeared to be unblinking and terrifyingly bright. The Duke felt her move and placing a gloved hand over hers said 'These are the eyes of men who live in the midst of death. Their song is symbolic but acknowledges that they are willing to die and may be called upon to do so at any time. The last time that I saw that expression was when we visited the SS training unit on our German visit. The men you are now watching are known also as the 'Legion of Missing Men'. That my love is why they are so feared.'

The Duke paused in thought and then added 'The difference is that these men are battle hardened and owe their loyalty to the Legion and their comrades. The young SS men we saw in training owe their allegiance to one man and one man only... their Fuhrer.'

Wallis hesitated and then commented. 'So my love, does that make Herr Hitler something of a Messiah?'

'To many Germans, I think that it does.'

Chapter 33

Ambassador Bullitt was becoming impatient and was finding it a challenge not to contact Wallis to find out just why he had not had a response to his request to meet Ribbentrop. He summoned his personal aide and lover. 'Offie my sweet, please keep my diary as free as possible for the next two weeks. Discreetly mind you… it must not be obvious.'

'It is my pleasure Billy… do you wish to dine in the official residence this evening or would you prefer to eat out and then maybe venture into the Pigalle… incognito of course?'

Ambassador Bullitt appeared to give the matter some thought but then after a deprecating shrug shook his head with a rueful expression 'I am sorry sweety but I am up to my neck in stuff I must read up on before my meeting with Von Ribbentrop and then reporting to the President. I shall have a sandwich in my study… do not wait up for me, I may be very late.'

Bullitt was furious at having to effectively rebuff Offie but after the painful session with Wallis he was in no shape to indulge in love-making even in the passive role. Neither could he face having to tell Offie the manner in which he had lost so much of his body hair. The thought flashed through his mind that friend and lover as she might be on one level he would one day revel in vengeance on the Duchess and her sadistic handmaiden.

Ambassador Bullitt's mood lifted as only half an hour later he was told that the German Foreign Minister wished to speak to him. It fell to Offie to make the connection and he listened in to the call as was his custom.

'Joachim my good friend, how good it is to speak to you.'

'Indeed Ambassador, it is my pleasure also.' Bullitt immediately recognised the snub in Ribbentrop not returning the Christian name greeting but chose to ignore it. Ribbentrop continued.

'I am so very sorry but pressing international matters which I can assure you do not affect American interests prevent me from meeting you personally. However, the Duke of Saxe-Coburg and Gotha will stand in for me. He is admirably placed to do so, as I am sure you will agree?'

Whilst Bulllitt smarted at the perceived rebuff he knew that there was no way around Ribbentrop's suggestion and, in any event, he was well aware of the Duke's activities which were carefully monitored by the American Government agencies whose reports crossed his desk.

'Delighted Von Ribbentrop. When and where shall we meet?'

'That Ambassador I shall leave to Herr Strack to arrange, our Head of Protocol... you have of course met him?'

'Yes, of course... I shall await his call and in the meantime, thank you.'

'Not at all. Good day to you Ambassador.'

Bullitt tried to comfort himself with the thought that he was deemed important enough to warrant a meeting with one of if not the most important of Nazi Germany's 'go betweens' the sub rosa unofficial diplomats who were doing so much to not only gauge opinion and international intentions towards the regime but also influence attitudes and even policy. Nevertheless he felt cheated.

Tar Robertson was studying a file when Johnny was shown into his office – he was clearly deep into its content and merely acknowledged Johnny's presence by waving him to sit down. After a couple of minutes he looked up and reaching for the silver cigarette box on his desk offered it to Johnny before taking one himself. He had a twinkle in his eye as he chuckled.

'Well Johnny... we have a juicy one here! Young Vera has managed to forward a report to us which we were clearly meant to receive if you get my drift? Let me put it another way our friends in the Abwehr have picked up rather a juicy plum. In essence, their men in Paris have reported that the American Ambassador there and chum of President Roosevelt, one William Bullitt – the American version of a renaissance man who openly lives with his male lover, has been enjoying sessions with none other than the Windsor woman and her Austrian accomplice in the Atelier of Elsa Schiaperalli. It was she who confided in fellow coutourier Coco Chanel who in turn is an Abwehr source.'

Johnny shook his head in disbelief.

'It gets better! Bullitt has tried to set up an off the record meeting with Von Ribbentropp who has ducked it and on the advice of Strack appointed our old friend the Duke of Saxe-Coburg and Gotha to the task. That must come to us almost directly from Canaris.'

'Christ Tar, that's quite something. So what is our stance or course of action?'

'I have discussed the situation with Sir Vernon and he is of the opinion that Bullitt wants the meeting to try and gauge the German intentions but also their perception of just how other European Non Axis nations would or will react to Germany pursuing its broader aims. Saxe-Coburg is a highly dangerous animal. Because of his status he moves in exalted circles all over Europe... effectively without boundaries... I am afraid that there is nothing we can do except wait and see whether Canaris and co give us any more information after the meeting.'

'Does Billy know that Vera has been involved in this way and that effectively her cover such as it was is probably blown... surely she must now be in grave danger?'

'No, he does not and he must not be told; he will be wild with worry for her and of course the child that she is carrying. Whatever suspicions there may be about her true loyalties, I believe that given her previous Abwehr official brief to infiltrate British society they will see her as an ideal conduit. Canaris the old fox will harbour doubts but keep them to himself. He greatly values having lines of communication to us. Anyhow she is now safe with Billy having a break in the West country.'

Johnny protested 'But Tar how can we be sure? Shouldn't we get some urgent local protection in place?'

'Johnny you know as well as anyone that the world of espionage is brutal and nasty. I cannot risk another one of our "assets" to ascertain whether Vera's "protection" by virtue of her husband's position is compromised to the extent that the Gestapo led by Himmler and of course Heydrich will now feel empowered to show their muscle and attack Vera, notwithstanding her Abwehr "protection". I am sure they would see doing so as striking a blow against Canaris who they detest.'

Johnny looked shocked as he started to speak. 'But Tar, by all that's Holy...'

Tar stopped him with a raised hand and spoke very slowly and carefully. 'Johnny you will see that the hardest and most soul searching times in this profession are when one has to sit here in safety having had to make a decision which leaves an operative at risk. Do you understand?'

Johnny shook his head slowly and then with a wry expression nodded that he understood the older man's position.

'That leads me to another one of our stars and closer to home for you Johnny... namely Princess Stephanie. Has she even hinted to you that she and Fritz Wiedemann are planning to leave Germany?'

'Not at all but I would not be in the least surprised Tar. The files which we have now assembled regarding her past make extraordinary reading. Thank you for letting me have sight of them. I feel that I was a fly caught in the web of an extremely voracious spider... lucky to escape with my skin I reckon.'

'She is certainly a brilliant player at whatever game she chooses but from our point of view I think that you will be relieved to hear that she is no longer to be cultivated as a source. If she summons you, by all means go. If only for old times' sake.' The hint of a smile played around Tar's mouth as he made this last remark.

'More than that Tar... from my point of view we have a relationship of convenience and I no longer suffer any pangs of conscience. Nevertheless, Like Saxe-Coburg she manages to move in exalted circles and I will keep my eyes and ears open. That leads me to Celia. Frankly Tar, having tasted the excitement of the world of espionage she is well and truly hooked. She is at her wits' end with boredom and when not focussed on a project for the Secret Service she is desperate to do something with her time.'

'Very well. I think that a little visit to France is called for... I shall suggest the Windsors' place in the South... it sounds magnificent. If you are invited as well, all to the good. Can she engineer an invitation?'

'I am sure that she can... she's a very resourceful young lady as you well know... how soon?'

'Perhaps in a week or two?'

'Righto Tar, leave it to me.'

'Celia my dear girl, how just lovely to hear from you... we were only talking about you the other day.' The Duchess of Windsor was almost purring with pleasure at receiving the call from Celia the next day. 'It seems an age since we saw you. Tell all... how are you... and the handsome Johnny?'

'Oh, so, so Wallis... mustn't grumble but you know what it's like here as winter looms. Really rather depressing and I fear that the sun has taken a holiday.'

'You poor chicken. David and I have decamped to our villa here and although the weather is not high summer it is warm, actually hot in the sun… and of that we have plenty. I say, why don't you come down here for a break? You and I can gossip away and the men can play their golf and mess about on the water?'

'Oh Wallis, that would be lovely… just to escape for a few days would be bliss.'

'Very well I shall send you an invitation by telegram and you can persuade Johnny… I am sure that you will succeed!'

'Dearest Wallis you are so, so kind…a big kiss and I shall look forward to hearing from you… then I can I will work on Johnny and let you have confirmation that we are accepting!'

'That's my girl' laughed Wallis, turning as the Duke came into the room, gesturing to him that she was on the telephone. 'Now goodbye for now… I must go.'

'Bye bye Wallis and love to David.'

As Celia replaced the receiver she gave Johnny a broad smile and theatrically lowering her gaze and fluttering her eyelids simply said 'See silly? Easy peasy!'

Tar Robertson was leaning back in his chair with hands behind his head and feet on the desk when Johnny entered his office again.

'If you want a progress report Tar you can have it right now. Celia...........'

Tar had almost sprung forward from his previously totally relaxed position and as he did so he violently signalled for Johnny to stop.

'Johnny. We now know where the meeting is to take place… Brantridge Park, the Earl of Athlone's place.'

'I know it. Went there with my parents. Decent enough house but all slightly… oh, I don't know quite how to put it… almost schizoid. Here you have what is essentially a German family living in England with English titles and manners and a curious mixture of styles. Really quite odd.'

'Quite Johnny. Could you and if possible, you and Celia, wangle an invitation to stay there whilst Ambassador Bullitt is meeting Coburg?'

'Well Tar, I can but try. Something of a tall order I fear. Which comes first, Brantridge Park or the South of France?'

Before Tar could answer his telephone rang. He picked it up and almost instantly shock registered on his normally implacable face. His cigarette case clattered to the floor as he raised his right hand to his forehead.

'Keep me fully informed by the minute' he barked and slammed the receiver down.

'First report received. Car answering description of Billy's has crashed on a steep Devon cliff road. Apparent devastation. Local police and ambulance in attendance with fire brigade and lifeboat on way. No news on casualties. Police cordoning the area. I must contact our Special Branch people in Devon. Excuse me Johnny.'

Johnny was white with shock as he shook his head slowly and really to himself muttered 'After Celia in New York… is this the beginning of something very unpleasant…Christ I hope they are OK…'

The cold hand of fear gripped his heart.

'Are we being taken for suckers Offie? The Duke wants the meeting at his sister's house in England… why? I ask myself… Why?'

'I venture to suggest Bill that all parties seek total discretion following your original request that a meeting with von Ribbentrop be without the knowledge of his colleagues… I don't think you can complain if the other side do likewise… I have done some research. Do you want to hear it?'

'Oh very well then!' The elegant Bullitt, who was in an extravagant full-length silk dressing gown, cravat and monogrammed slippers, flung himself into a sumptuously upholstered armchair. He adopted a theatrical, Noël Coward-like pose, with an arm along the chair back and a leg casually over an armrest. 'OK Offie… shoot!'

'Here goes. Brantridge House is where the Earl and Countess of Athlone live. In fact she is Princess Alice; a granddaughter of Queen Victoria and a member of the British Royal family.'

'So pardon my ignorance, but how come the Duke of Coburg a senior Nazi is her brother?'

'Perfectly simple really he had the good fortune – or perhaps the bad luck – to be the sovereign of two duchies in Germany until its defeat in 1918. These European Royal families are all intertwined as you know and he is no exception. His English title was the Duke of Albany and until he was stripped of his British titles in 1919 he was a British Royal Prince. Whilst he might no longer be His

Royal Highness for the Brits, he was still by tradition a Highness as head of the Ducal Houses in Germany although legally all such titles were abolished.'

Bullitt gave a regal flourish of his hand for Offie to continue.

'Anyhow, he has spent the past few years as a very willing tool in the hands of dear old Adolf.'

'How did he end up in the Nazi Party… it seems a very strange place for a man who was a prince, eh? A bunch of street fighting thugs?'

'It's not so odd really. Apparently, or so I have been told by a pal from the German Embassy here… before you ask, I met him by chance at the reception we both attended in the Hungarian Embassy. And yes, he is quite a dish but sadly, spoken for.' Offie teased his lover.

Bullitt chuckled as he riposted 'You promiscuous little monkey… if I had the time I would put you across my knee and give you a darn good spanking… anyway, go on.' Offie simpered and then carried on in a deliberately camp style 'Oh, but that would be ever so nice…now… where was I?'

Offie then continued to explain that the Duke of Saxe-Coburg and Gotha had become an outcast in Britain as even though some of his own family had understood the situation high society had not. Their view was that he had been a general in the hated German army and this branded him a traitor, despite the fact that he had never had an active command. Offie went on to explain that just after the Armistice the Workers'and Soldier's Council of Gotha had deposed him and he had been forced to formally relinquish his rights as Duke.

'It was then that he became attracted to Hitler and the politics of the far right. Remember that the Tsar and his family were cousins and the great fear amongst the royal families, aristocracy and even many of the middle class in Europe was bolshevism.' Offie finished.

'So that was the road that lead to him becoming an SS Gruppenfuhrer was it?'

'In essence, yes. As I said, he now moves seamlessly from one royal house to another and is entertained at the highest level wherever he goes in Europe… apart from the communist countries of course. I must warn you that he looks much older than his years, but do not be deceived, he is a very clever chap.'

'Right. I have made a decision. I am going to formally appraise State of the intended meeting and I shall refer them to the President if it sticks in their craw… as it probably will. I must speak to the President first. Please check his availability.'

Chapter 34

In the golden light of a wonderful dawn Billy had been extolling the exceptional view that would soon be revealed to his friends. He joked that if Vera suffered from vertigo she should overcome it and simply enjoy the views.

Suddenly in a bellow that had not been heard since he was fighting on the Western Front Billy shouted 'Get on the floor now and hang on to the front seat frames – the brakes have gone!'

Momentarily he cursed the decision to drive down the steep and winding scenic road with the edge of the high cliffs on his right and the rocky shore far below. To the left flanked by a stone retaining wall was the heavily wooded steep hillside out of which the road had been carved.

He began to wrestle with the steering wheel as the heavy car gained its own momentum on the vertiginous hill. He risked taking a hand off the wheel for a moment to switch off the ignition in the hope that the engine would provide some braking, and slammed the gears into second.

He realised that the only hope of avoiding crashing over the cliff edge to certain death on the rocks far below was to try and scrub off speed by deliberately scraping the car along the rough stone wall on his left.

At his first attempt the car lurched alarmingly and the large steering wheel nearly bucked out of his grip.

For a terrifying moment the car was veering towards the cliff edge.

Frantically heaving on the wheel he managed to regain control in time to negotiate the next sharp bend.

Straining every muscle and sinew he once again managed to scrape the car along the rough stone wall. There was a loud bang and then a crashing sound from behind him and as the car gave another great lurch he it became evident that parts of the wooden shooting brake body were being torn from the chassis.

The headlong helter-skelter was temporarily slowed and after the next tight bend Billy managed a much longer contact with the stone wall which made a noticeable difference.

Even so the partially wrecked car was still building momentum.

Billy knew that he was rapidly tiring and could not hold the almost three ton vehicle on the road for very much longer.

He had cycled down this road with his friends as a boy and remembered that approximately half way down there was a turning to the left into a path used by ramblers. His only hope was to try and swerve the car into that opening in the wall if he could hold out until then.

Another tyre screaming bend and then more scraping the car along the stone wall and more ear shattering noise of the car's body being torn apart.

One more bend and there was the entrance on the left.

With his last reserves of strength Billy threw all his weight onto the steering wheel and what was now virtually a bare chassis with four desperate people hanging on as best they could swerved off the road.

The remains of the car smashed into a tree and the passengers were thrown out by the force of the impact.

Billy crashed against the steering column as the wheel buckled in his hands and his head hit the windscreen.

After the massive noise of the crash there was a sudden unnatural quiet except for the ticking of the cooling engine and the whispering sound of one of the front wheels still rotating as the remains of car lay on its side.

There was silence, broken only by the distant cries of seagulls and the splashing of the waves on the rocks far below the cliff edge.

The crumpled shapes on the ground and the bloodied Billy did not stir.

Finally the eery silence was broken by a human groan.

The telephone rang stridently in the drawing room of Winston Churchill's Kent home. He pushed himself out of his armchair and dressed in a magenta velour version of his signature 'boiler suits' crossed to the side table and picking up the receiver barked 'Churchill here!'

'Winston – Anthony Eden – I should be grateful for an urgent talk with you face to face. May I come down to Chartwell and see you? There is a deal of urgency.'

'Anthony my dear fellow I shall be delighted to see you – you are welcome at any time but, then, there is no time like the present so, are you able to come this evening?'

Churchill paused for a moment waving a hand to attract the attention of his beloved wife Clemmie for her to listen to the conversation. She put down her needlework frame with the intricate embroidery in which she had been immersed and nodded to indicate that she was now listening.

'How will you be coming Anthony?'

'By train to Westerham and then taxi – I do not want the visit logged by my official driver.'

'Righto then, let me know which train you will be catching – Grace Hamblin, my secretary, would normally pick you up from the station but she will already have left so I shall send my valet Blair in the Austin. Of course you will join us for dinner, informal in the circumstances, we shall not dress, and spend the night eh?'

'That's very kind of you Winston and do please thank Clementine.'

'No trouble my dear fellow – I shall await your call.'

Eden's urgent visit to Churchill was prompted by a telephone call that he had received early in the afternoon from Sir George Ogilvie-Forbes the Counsellor and Charge d'Affaires in the Berlin Embassy – in other words, the deputy to the British Ambassador to Germany.

Sir George had served with great distinction in Spain during the savage civil war which still continued and had run the British Embassy in Madrid with considerable bravery. In the midst of the brutal fighting he and his staff had helped the evacuation of some 17,000 refugees. He was an experienced diplomat and did not allow himself to be drawn to either side but believed that the conflict represented private suffering on an immense scale which he sought to mitigate.

He considered that the order to move the embassy from Madrid to Valencia to lessen the risk within the reign of terror that gripped Madrid was both cowardly and dishonourable. He had made his views known very forcefully. It was then that he was appointed to the Berlin Embassy and his services in Spain were recognised by the award of KCMG.

He was close to Sir Robert 'Van' Vansittart the Permanent Secretary to the Foreign Office and its most senior Civil Servant, who kept in touch with

Sir George and on being informed about Ambassador Henderson reporting directly to the Prime Minister had immediately appraised Eden.

Sir Neville Henderson had been appointed as Ambassador to Berlin shortly after Sir George, an appointment that Eden was later to deeply regret and others to regard as a serious error of judgement. Henderson and Forbes held strongly entrenched differing views of Hitler and the Nazi regime and from the outset their relationship was strained.

Henderson was a member of the so called 'Cliveden Set' of recognised people of influence who favoured appeasement of Hitler rather than confrontation. He was a vain 'ladies man' who never married and when he learnt of his appointment to Berlin, one of the 'great embassies' in the eyes of the Foreign Office said that he believed that 'I have been specially selected by Providence for the definite mission of helping to preserve the peace of the World.'

He had read Mein Kampf in its entirety and so was fully aware of the ideology behind Naziism and Hitler's aspirations. Nevertheless he was determined to see the good side of the Nazi regime as well as the bad.

Henderson had met Chamberlain in London shortly before Chamberlain took over as Prime Minister from Stanley Baldwin and found that their views corresponded closely. He was with Chamberlain after lunch in the Carlton Club when Chamberlain posed a question.

'If I were to ask you to keep me appraised of developments in Germany directly on a regular and totally confidential basis would that offend your sense of duty?'

'It is certainly outwith Foreign Office protocol that all my reports should be directed to Vansittart and it is then for him to report to you accordingly when you are Prime Minister.' Chamberlain gave a rapid small shake of his head and responded 'Yes, yes, of course I am aware of the protocols but I feel that our stance on the future relationship with Germany so resonates that you will provide me with a more accurate picture than might be the case in the formal Foreign Office briefs that I shall receive, don't you see?'

'I shall be more than pleased to do so and, in turn, if you feel that there are matters under discussion which might be relevant to my mission will you agree to a reciprocal arrangement?

'Most certainly' replied Chamberlain with one of his rare smiles.

Sir George Ogilvie-Forbes was boiling with anger after he was accidentally provided with a copy of a letter from Henderson to The Prime Minister in which Henderson expressed his views as to just how the British Government could best control Adolf Hitler and push him in the direction of peace.

Ogilvie-Forbes was annoyed by the conclusions expressed in the letter but even angrier that Henderson as Ambassador was bypassing his superior, Vansittart, and defying all the long established rules of the Foreign Office. He entered Henderson's immaculate office in the Embassy and placing the offending letter on the desk asked in a controlled tone that failed to disguise his fury.

'Neville why are you reporting directly to the PM and not to Vansittart as we are required to do?'

'George, it is none of your business in the first place – no, do not interrupt please – and secondly I share certain views with the Prime Minister and he seeks my comment without any third party editing.'

Sir George responded in a cutting tone. 'With respect it is for Vansittart to absorb your brief with those of others and then appraise the Foreign Secretary. If there were to be any bypassing and variation from the established protocol you should be reporting to Eden as Foreign Secretary. It is he who will be briefing the Prime Minister and Cabinet.'

In a more conciliatory tone Sir George continued. 'Neville, although I share your view that the Versailles Treaty was unduly harsh on Germany and should be varied in some respects, if not too late, that point should be shared in our joint report.'

Sir Neville stuck to his guns. 'That's as may be but I am reporting to the Prime Minister as I have arranged with him directly. I am also keeping Lord Halifax appraised of my conclusions.'

Sir George did not respond immediately but then in a measured tone said 'I am sorry Neville but I must register my opposition to your doing so.'

'As you wish. I trust we may now end this discussion because I have a large volume of paperwork to deal with.'

'Of course but I shall record our meeting and the matter in hand in my daily log. Further I shall appraise Vansittart and the Foreign Secretary.'

Henderson merely nodded as he turned his attention to a document that he had now placed on the desk blotter.

Sir George returned to his office and started to make notes for an urgent message he would send to Anthony Eden and Vansittart requesting an early meeting.

Having completed his notes and written up a near verbatim account of what he regarded as a most unsatisfactory conversation he reflected that In the comparatively short time that the two men had worked together in Berlin he had become increasingly concerned about aspects of Henderson's behavior and actions which he found surprisingly unprofessional and ill-judged in so experienced a diplomat.

On his arrival at Chequers, Eden was as always immediately comforted by the tranquility of the beautiful house that in some ways was so much at odds with its mercurial and at times brilliant owner. He noted that Churchill's velvet boiler suit really did not suit his rather corpulent frame and was incongruous to the extent that it was partially unzipped at the neck, revealing a crisp white shirt and a white spotted navy bow tie. He was wearing monogrammed velvet slippers.

The butler had taken Eden's overcoat and his usual homburg hat and Churchill greeted him in the hallway. Churchill, then planting his hallmark cigar in his mouth, shook hands vigorously and with his other hand steered Eden into the spacious drawing room where Winston's wife Clementine stood and welcomed him with open arms. 'I imagine that you would like a wash n brush up before dinner?'

'That would be capital Clementine but I see that Winston is preparing drinks so I shall do so later. Thank you.'

Churchill ambled over and passed a glass to his wife saying 'Now then, Anthony has scuttled down here post haste with something on his mind so he and I will flit off to my study and then he can spruce up after that.'

'Very well darling' responded Clementine with a smile towards Eden and a slight shrug of her shoulders acknowledged that this evening Winston was in control.

Churchill's study was in fact a rather grand room with a vaulted ceiling. As well as his large Georgian writing table there was a sofa and armchairs. The writing table was big enough for an array of family photographs in an eclectic mixture of frames and a miniature painted bust of Admiral Lord Nelson. A large cigar box was rather distressed in appearance but clearly of a size to accommodate the cigars that were a Churchill hallmark.

Churchill's desk chair was surprisingly austere being a simple upholstered wooden framed tub chair and for his guest, on the other side of the table, a chintz covered upright wing chair.

When they had settled with their drinks and Winston had balanced his cigar on the silver framed crystal ash tray he smiled and said 'Very well Anthony, what has you in a lather?'

Eden smiled, inclined his head slightly and then started.

'As you know I appointed Neville Henderson to Berlin having been given a short list of three possible candidates by Vansittart all of whom handled autocratic leaders well. I chose Henderson because he spoke perfect German and I felt that he had a well balanced approach to the extreme behavior of such leaders and those around them. He is a fine shot and I correctly predicted that he would hit it off with Goering. I now believe that I made a terrible mistake. He is in favour of appeasement – I knew that, of course, he is a member of the so-called Cliveden Set. What I had not bargained for is that he is bypassing Vansittart, and hence me, and reporting directly to the Prime Minister and also it seems Lord Halifax – another appeaser member of the Cliveden Set.'

'Outrageous' muttered Churchill, signalling with his cigar that Eden should carry on.

'He is encouraging Chamberlain's appeasement views and convincing him that Hitler is a reasonable man who can be cajoled into peaceful solutions notwithstanding that Germany is racing towards becoming the most well equipped military state in Europe.'

Churchill who was shrouded in aromatic cigar smoke did not interrupt as Eden went on to describe Hendersen's unhealthily close relationship with Hermann Goering the powerful head of the Luftwaffe and one of the Fuhrer's most intimate confidantes. The relationship was founded on their joint skill and love of hunting but also now appeared to embrace a common thread of political philosophy. In other words, Henderson had lost his objectivity and consequently had become that person whom an ambassador should never be. He explained that Ogilvie-Forbes had found out about the improper reporting and alerted Vansittart and himself.

Eden had requested that the Cabinet Secretary would where possible provide copies of Henderson's reports.

Nevertheless Lord Halifax, a fellow member of the Cliveden Set, and a very senior member of the Cabinet was also in receipt of Henderson's reports. He had of course recently visited Hitler and clearly indicated that Britain was likely to take a bystander position in relation to Hitler's aims. Halifax had indicated that he found Hitler to be a most strange character but had been greatly impressed by Herman Goering when entertained at his home. It appeared that Goering had smoothed over any concerns that Halifax might have harboured concerning Hitler.

Eden continued 'The sheer naivety Winston and its great danger is that these men – and I include our Prime Minister – believe that they are dealing with a leader who will respond well to reasonable argument and despite putting his nation on a war footing happily follow a peaceful path.'

Churchill now responded 'I hear all that you say Anthony and it is of great concern because in addition, as I understand it, the Prime Minister is ignoring hard intelligence gleaned by the Secret Service as to Herr Hitler's intentions and further that, despite appearances, the German armed forces are presently not strong enough to stand up to a military intervention by Britain and France. That situation will not obtain for very long given the energy with which the Germans are rearming and training.'

As always, Eden was surprised at Churchill's range of knowledge but then reminded himself that a lifetime in and out of high office had resulted in the controversial politician having as many friends with influence as he had detractors.

Churchill continued. 'Anthony, I fear that there is little overt action that can be taken at present and, indeed, it would be wrong for any of you to show your hand. You are forewarned and you know who and what to brief against. I shall remain a pariah, a warmongering lone voice calling for our rapid full re-armament to counter the threat that fascism poses but we must bide our time. In reality, Chamberlain holds the upper ground both practically and constitutionally.'

Eden nodded agreement then continued. 'I really do not think that I can tolerate being treated as I am for very much longer in all honesty.'

Churchill smiled. 'Please stick it out if you can stomach it. You are a very senior and experienced cabinet minister and politician. That is of great value in curbing the Prime Minister.'

'I really hope so' responded Eden with a wry smile.

'Right, let's finish our drinks with Clemmie… then dinner Anthony.'

Tar Robertson was in Sir Vernon Kell's office when he received the call that they had all been waiting for. Tar listened intently then finished the call. 'Thank you very much Superintendent – please keep me fully informed at all times as a matter of urgency. It is necessary for the forensic examination of the motor car to be carried out immediately. Thank you again, good bye.'

He put the telephone down and reported. 'Right. The situation is that all four are alive and in hospital. Vera and the other two passengers are seriously ill but now out of danger. Vera has lost the baby she was carrying. Billy I am afraid is very seriously injured and causing great concern. They are operating as I speak and we will be informed the moment there is any fresh information.'

Sir Vernon was visibly moved as he heard about Billy Brownlow. 'We can but pray. I smell a rat here you know.'

Tar Robertson nodded his agreement.

Epilogue

The following afternoon Anthony Eden was alone with the Prime Minister in Downing Street.

'Neville I implore you to reconsider our position with regard to Germany and also Italy. Both are rearming at an alarming rate and as we have seen in Spain they cannot give a fig for international agreements given their brazen disregard for the International Non Intervention Agreement. Just look at it, they have sent in massive amounts of equipment, weapons and even troops on the ground. Take the horrific bombing of Guernica and massacre of innocents by German aircraft.'

The Prime Minister looked irritated in the extreme. He shook his head peevishly and in an angry almost petulant tone responded. 'Anthony, for the last time, I will not act on information obtained through so-called intelligence… it is the dishonorable product of spying. Not only that but I have every reason to believe that we are dealing with a responsible duly elected government.'

Chamberlain paused, then continued. 'I believe that Herr Hitler is a reasonable man in whom I, and we as a nation, can place our confidence.'

About the author

Hugh Robertson practised as a commercial lawyer for many years in the City of London. He now lives in Spain, where he is currently working on his fourth novel in The Fools' Crowns series.

Lightning Source UK Ltd.
Milton Keynes UK
UKHW021927100522
402797UK00010B/525/J